AWAKENINGS

New Pantheon: Book 1

Edward Swing

Enjoy the Adventure
Edward S

Cover Art: Larry Wilson - http://larrywilsonart.com
Editor: Josiah Davis - http://jdbookservices.com

ISBN: 1709737158
ISBN-13: 978-1709737152

To my children Sabrina, Valerie and Gareth:
My own New Pantheon

CHAPTER ONE
A New School

As his mother's car pulled into the parking lot, Mike Rhee's entry into the adventure known as high school began. "Are you ready for your first day of high school?" she asked.

He gave her a hug, stepped out of the car, and retrieved his backpack and trombone case from the back seat. "Yeah—not like I haven't been here before." He had practiced with the marching band during the summer and familiarized himself with the school's layout.

Mike walked through the front doors and into the throng of students. *Of course, it wasn't nearly so crowded during band rehearsals.* Proceeding first to the band room, he awkwardly wove through the various knots and cliques of students crowding the halls. Mike waved to Mr. Bridges, the elderly band teacher, as he stowed his trombone in the instrument storage area.

"Good morning, Mike. Welcome to ninth grade. Excited?"

"Morning, Mr. Bridges! I'll see you in sixth period!" Mike liked the elderly teacher. Mr. Bridges looked frail, but when he conducted the band, Mike could see the fire in his eyes.

Heading out the door, Mike navigated toward his homeroom

with Mr. Oxinos—or Mr. O as some of the older band members called him. He'd met his homeroom advisor during band practice over the summer. Mr. O had occasionally visited the band room to listen to the students or chat with Mr. Bridges about their music.

Mike stepped into room 203 and glanced around his homeroom. Mr. Oxinos was a tanned man with dark curly hair who Mike guessed was about thirty years old. Mr. Oxinos taught art and helped out with physical education at school. His classroom clearly showed he preferred art: art posters decorated the walls, and a plethora of art supplies peeked out from different containers around the room. Mike thought the room was fascinating, and looking at all the pictures inspired him. He wasn't sure if the other ninth graders had similar homerooms, but he doubted it. Though the other classrooms had their own decorations, most lacked the spirit of the art room.

The electronic whiteboard displayed a seating chart, so Mike found his desk. He searched the chart for band members or students from his previous school, and located a few other band members. Bored, he checked his supplies, then arranged his pencils into different patterns.

While he fiddled with his impromptu artwork, Mr. Oxinos walked by his desk. Startled, Mike dropped one of his pencils. His teacher paused, picked up the pencil, and looked at Mike's desktop design. He carefully placed the pencil into Mike's design, perfectly adding it to the pattern before he wordlessly moved on to circulate among the other students.

I'm lucky to have such a cool homeroom teacher, he thought.

2

Mike had scheduled band, his favorite class, at the end of the day so he could continue right into the after-school marching band practice. After Mr. O's art class—his other elective—he was in a good mood. On the way to the band room, he noticed a dark-haired girl carrying a flute case. Despite her bewildered expression, she looked familiar.

"Looking for the band room?" Mike asked.

"Oh, yes. I'm so confused. This school is so big," the girl mumbled.

Big? Mike thought. After weeks of marching band practice the school no longer intimidated him, but the girl seemed overwhelmed. "I'm going there too. It's this way." He pointed down the hall. "We're all getting used to the new school. Don't let it bother you. I'm Mike. We're in the same homeroom."

She relaxed and mumbled, "I'm Aliki." She walked with him, but said nothing more.

Not one for walking quietly, Mike filled the silence. "Jefferson Hill High School is shaped like a big cross, so it's pretty easy to figure out after a bit. We're in the south wing where all the offices are. The library and computer rooms are here too, up on the second floor. The band room is in the west wing, past the cafeteria and auditorium. Most of the classrooms are in the east wing. That's where our homeroom is. The athletic stuff is in the north wing. They all connect around the central courtyard. See?" He gestured toward the window overlooking the courtyard.

They arrived at the band room, and Mike went to retrieve his trombone from the instrument storage area. Mr. Bridges introduced himself to the newer students and passed out folders of music for each of them. Mike scanned the music, trying to get the motions right with his trombone's slide.

At the end of the period, Aliki left the band room. Mike shrugged and prepared to practice with the rest of the marching band. All in all, it had been a reasonable first day.

After marching band practice, Mike waited for his mother to arrive. He spotted Mr. Oxinos walking toward the faculty parking lot from the school building. Most teachers drove only modest cars, even at an upscale school like Jefferson Hill. But Mike saw Mr. Oxinos get into a fancy gold-colored luxury sedan. Mike didn't recognize the model, but it was the most beautiful car he'd seen in a while. It stood out from the other faculty cars, shining like the sun on a cloudy day.

The car piqued his curiosity. *How can an art teacher afford such a luxurious car? Is he independently wealthy, teaching school for fun? Could it be a loaner from a dealer?*

As the golden sedan pulled out of the parking lot, Mike thought quickly and snapped a few pictures with his cell phone. After a few minutes, his mother arrived, and Mike sat in the front seat. He ignored his younger brother and sister in the back and examined the pictures he'd taken instead.

The vanity license plate began with CHA, but he couldn't make out the rest from his photos. He couldn't see a make or model name either.

The next morning before school, Mike looked for the car in

the faculty lot, but instead of the golden luxury sedan, there was a small white compact car in Mr. Oxinos' reserved space.

Like most ninth graders, Jason King felt apprehensive about high school even on the second day. Despite his athletic prowess, Jason worried about the upcoming academic challenges. He navigated through the school halls that had become familiar during football practices over the summer. A talented middle linebacker on the junior varsity squad, he hoped to make the varsity team in his sophomore year.

Jason looked again at his schedule and eased through the crowded hallways toward homeroom. Other students' chatter filled his ears, but Jason wanted to get settled early. *I hope Mr. Oxinos is a cool guy*, he thought to himself. He had been late yesterday, and he hoped Mr. Oxinos wouldn't hold it against him. But today he had arrived early.

As Jason entered room 203, he saw a few other students already there. None stood out. Three obvious band members were pretending to play different air-instruments as a cell phone played songs. A couple of girls were talking about boys, he guessed; they fell silent when they saw him looking at them, then giggled behind closed hands. Jason's eyes turned to his homeroom teacher, Paul Oxinos.

"Mr. Jason King, welcome to my classroom," Mr. Oxinos greeted him with a smile. He stood near the electronic whiteboard, adjusting a seating chart on the screen. Jason glanced at the display and found his seat. Once settled, he gazed around the room, noticing the various art displays.

"Sorry I was late yesterday, sir. My kid sister messed with the clocks in the house and made us all late. She doesn't like school."

Mr. Oxinos gave Jason a piercing gaze. "And do you like school, Jason?"

"Yes, sir. I set an extra alarm this morning, just in case Helen did it again"—he held up his phone—"and hid it under my pillow!" He heard more giggles, but ignored them. He really wanted to make a good impression. He'd heard Mr. Oxinos helped out in the gym, so his teacher's favor could improve his chances for making the varsity squad.

"Very well. Hopefully you can inspire your little sister. Go ahead and take your seat."

Jason settled into his seat, took out his notebooks, and doodled until the bell rang.

After his third period biology class, Jason hurried towards the gym. Jason was a natural athlete and enjoyed his time in gym class, even though Coach Brown had them playing soccer this week. As he approached the entrance to the courtyard, he spotted Carson and Pete, two of his fellow junior varsity football players, hassling an Asian boy. Around them, several books and notebooks lay scattered on the floor.

"I guess you chinks don't know how to walk straight either!" Pete sneered.

"Please pardon me. I need to get to class," the boy replied, bending down to gather the books on the floor.

Pete's face curled into a nasty grin. "So, Mr. China wants to

6

get to class. That's too bad. Right, Carson? I think he should bow down like they do in China."

Jason remembered the other boy from his homeroom. He had been playing air-trombone that morning with the other band members. As Jason assessed the situation, the Asian boy shifted his weight slightly, his eyes fixed on Pete and his mouth turned up in a wry smirk.

Uncertain of the other boy's intent, Jason jumped forward to intervene. "Carson, Pete. You're not being cool. He's already apologized. So chill!"

Though Carson immediately backed down, Pete's nasty grin remained on his face.

"Pete! You don't want to be kicked off the team, do you?" Jason warned.

"C'mon, Pete. Let's get to gym," Carson added.

Pete turned away from the Asian boy, still glowering. The two walked towards the gymnasium. "Coming, Jason?" Carson called.

"In a minute," Jason replied. He stooped to help the other boy gather his books. "I'm Jason. I'm sorry about Pete and Carson. They're usually all right, but they sometimes get carried away with their whole macho image."

"Many thanks for helping me. My name is Mike Rhee." Mike offered his hand, and Jason shook it. Mike was shorter than Jason, but Jason felt the tension in Mike's grip. He wondered what would have happened between Mike and the others had he not intervened.

"So you're Chinese?" Jason asked, trying to figure out what to say.

"Half Korean," Mike answered. "Thanks again. But I expect neither of us wants to be late to class."

"Right. I'll see you later." Jason hurried toward his next class.

Long ago, Jason had discovered his passion for making things with his hands. As a magnet school, Jefferson Hill offered a variety of special electives unavailable at most schools, including metalworking, industrial design, culinary arts, and a wealth of technology courses. Jason had already developed good skills with carpentry and looked forward to learning metalwork from Mr. Johnson. The metalworking room even opened onto a covered patio where advanced students could learn how to work with molten metal—under strict supervision, of course.

Mr. Johnson was demonstrating the proper safety techniques with some of the metal tools. Jason already had a reasonable grasp of most tools, so he scanned around the room in desperate boredom.

He spotted a locked display cabinet with different pieces of metalwork. Some were mostly complete, while others looked half-formed. He noticed what looked like a short sword without a hilt, slightly curved, sitting on the middle shelf. Delicate etchings were traced along its center. Even half-finished, the beautiful blade distracted him.

"Jason?" Mr. Johnson's voice yanked him back to the class. "Are you paying attention?"

"Yes, sir. Are those student projects, sir?" Jason asked, pointing to the cabinet.

"Some are. Some are my projects too," Mr. Johnson replied with pride.

"Your blade there is really pretty." Jason guessed Mr. Johnson would never let a student craft a weapon.

Mr. Johnson chuckled. "That's not my work. Coach Brown made it."

Jason sat up in surprise. "The football coach?" He stared at the blade. The coach clearly had some interesting talents.

By Wednesday, Aliki Papadaki had accustomed herself to her class schedule. She had gotten lost again on the way to her science class yesterday; Kyle Coleman had tried to help her find her way. They'd gotten even more lost, and Kyle had become worried. Aliki giggled at the memory—they'd wandered into the Chinese language room by accident.

Her homeroom routine settled into familiar patterns too. Mike, who'd helped her find the band room on the first day of school, would play air-trombone along with fellow band members Joe, Dave B. and Praveen. Kyle would read a library book at his desk, ignoring the rest of the students. The cheerleader, Tiffany, would giggle with her friends. There were some jocks and jockettes too—Carson, Jason, Pete, Julisha, and Kate.

Two goths, Sarah and Jen, always sat together in the corner. Sarah had approached her on the first day of school, mistaking her shyness and dark clothes for a goth attitude. Aliki didn't care for the goth lifestyle, so she had intentionally picked brightly colored blouses for the past two days. Sarah sulked when Aliki had come to school wearing a bright orange blouse yesterday.

There were twenty-seven students in the homeroom, and most of Aliki's classes had a similar number. She had no disreputable people in her classes—no druggies or gang members —at least that she could tell. Only her programming class had fewer students. Aliki enjoyed working with computers, and she'd qualified to be in the programming class normally reserved for sophomores.

Aliki gazed around the homeroom as she prepared for her first period English class. Artistic decorations covered Mr. Oxinos' walls, from prints of the works of Renaissance masters to abstract artworks that hinted at some deeper meaning. She tucked her literature book into her backpack and decided study Mr. Oxinos' art collection more carefully.

In addition to the art prints, the classroom had many other decorations. In one corner near Mr. Oxinos' desk, a marble bust wearing a laurel wreath sat on a small table. A framed copy of a page from an illuminated manuscript hung near the door. Mr. Oxinos' teaching certifications hung behind the desk. A wooden shelf containing art supplies stood near the back of the room, creating an alcove where more supplies were stored. Near this alcove, Aliki discovered a framed scroll with writing in ancient Greek.

Aliki realized the scroll wasn't made of paper, but something else. It looked ancient, and she doubted anyone else could read it. Aliki's parents had emigrated from Greece though, and they still used Greek at home. The scroll was an award for a sculpture competition. No date appeared on the scroll, but the seal bore the name Michael VIII Palaiologos. Because it used older language, Aliki had some trouble reading the entire scroll.

"Do you read Greek?" came Mr. Oxinos' melodic voice from behind her.

Aliki turned and answered yes before even realizing that he had spoken in Greek, and she'd automatically answered in it as well.

Switching to English, Mr. Oxinos continued. "It's a beautiful scroll I had the fortune of coming across a few years back. The owner had no idea of its age or historical significance."

Aliki felt like she should explain. "My parents immigrated to the United States before I was born. They still keep in touch with relatives and try to keep some of their traditions alive. They're still a little wary of most Americans though."

"I was born in Greece too and came here years ago. Perhaps I can help your parents get used to life in this country."

"That would be nice," Aliki murmured. She continued to stare at the scroll, finding the delicate whorls of the floral border fascinating. She wondered if she could ever create something so beautiful. She tore her gaze away from it, only to lose herself staring at an art print nearby.

The bell sounded, interrupting their talk. Aliki shook her head to clear it, glanced at Mr. Oxinos and the scroll again, grabbed her books from her desk, and left for her first class of the day.

Thursday... Tiffany Gardner thought as she wandered into homeroom and tucked her books under her desk. She checked her makeup in her compact and glanced down at her cheerleader uniform. The opening Junior Varsity game was tonight, and Tiff wanted to look her best. She had worked hard to get on the cheerleading squad and was one of only two freshmen to make it. Once she was satisfied with her appearance, she turned to chat with her friends Mara and Shelly.

Though she was enrolled in honors classes, Tiff normally affected a carefree cheerleader persona to fit in with the others on her squad. She'd always feared being shunned for being too smart. She enrolled in the most advanced classes, but took electives to be with her fellows rather than to enhance her academics.

She'd also developed a natural grace, and felt comfortable with physical activity. School didn't challenge her, so she spent a lot of time daydreaming—about boys, about fashion, about her future. She even imagined dating different boys in her class.

Jason was handsome, in a jock sort of way. Burly and tanned with sandy brown hair, he had a good nature about him. Carson was dark, and maybe a little dangerous—possibly exciting. Mike seemed to be earnest, but she couldn't figure what they might have in common. Pete—well, his voice got on her nerves.

Her gaze rested on Mr. Oxinos. He was handsome, with Mediterranean features and a bright smile. His curly dark hair had a strange golden sheen. Something about him captivated her attention. Tiff knew some of the other girls in class were already fantasizing about him. She tried to clear her mind, but found herself watching him again.

As she, Mara, and Shelly whispered and giggled about some of the boys in the class, Tiff saw Mr. Oxinos glance their way. Tiff pretended not to notice and kept chatting gaily, but Shelly blushed. *So much for subtlety*, Tiff thought.

The cheerleaders had agreed to do a mini-pep rally immediately after lunch. While the squad would hold a real pep rally the next day for the varsity team, they wanted to remind everyone that the younger players played for their school too. Even though it wasn't an official pep rally, the students gathered anyway. They had about fifteen minutes before the next class started, so Tiff and her fellow cheerleaders began their routines of cheers and acrobatics.

In the transition between the second and third cheer sequence, Tiff was doing a handspring toward Rachel and Kennedy. But Rachel had turned to start the wrong cheer instead of helping to catch her. When Tiff realized the danger, her reflexes took over. Halfway through her handspring, she twisted enough to avoid clobbering either Kennedy or Rachel, but she couldn't prevent herself from sprawling onto the dirt.

"Ow!" Tiff yelped. Aside from the minor pain of the fall, Tiff felt a sharper sensation in her calf. Though the grounds were supposed to be clear of rocks, Tiff had the misfortune of landing on a small stone.

"I'msorry I'msosorry!" blurted Rachel while she and Danielle helped Tiff up. But Rachel looked so ashamed, Tiff couldn't be angry with her.

"I'm okay," Tiff replied, dusting herself off.

Kennedy and Danielle noticed the cut on her leg at the same time. "You're bleeding! We should take you to the nurse's office!" Danielle exclaimed.

Mrs. Finney, her gym teacher, arrived. "Danielle's right—let me take you to the infirmary," she said in a tone that invited no disagreement. She pulled a small notepad from her pocket and jotted down a note. "You have Mrs. Wells for history next period, correct?" Not even pausing to see her nod, Mrs. Finney turned to Danielle. "Danielle, see that Mrs. Wells gets this note. Hopefully Tiff will be in class shortly."

Tiff followed Mrs. Finney to the infirmary. She'd never visited a school infirmary before, so she was a little scared. Mrs. Finney guided her to one of two comfortable chairs near a cot.

"Ida! We have a minor accident here."

The school nurse came out of the small washroom, wiping her hands on a paper towel. "What happened? Is it serious?"

"An accident in the courtyard. Fortunately, Miss Tiffany Gardner here is both resilient and thinks quickly." She paused and turned to Tiff. "This is Miss Ida Olsen, the school nurse. She'll take care of you and make sure you're okay."

Tiff winced as Miss Olsen turned her leg to examine the cut. "A bit of antiseptic should clean this right up. This isn't so deep that it would need stitches." Tiff winced again at the thought.

"I need to get to my next class. Tiffany's next class is with Mrs. Wells." Mrs. Finney left the infirmary, waving to Tiff on the way out.

Miss Olsen rinsed the cut and dabbed antiseptic on it. "Mrs. Finney was right. This isn't serious at all. It will heal in a few days. Why don't you tell me how this happened?"

"We were doing our cheer routine, and Rachel got the

routine wrong and forgot to catch me."

As Tiff told her about the accident, Miss Olsen dabbed her wound with more ointment. Then she rose and moved to her desk. Several folders lay scattered across the desk, and pictures of Miss Olsen skiing in the mountains and working in a garden sat near a small rectangular basket of apples. Miss Olsen pulled a piece of paper from one of the folders and frowned.

Seeing her reaction, Tiff blurted out, "It was an accident! Please don't blame Rachel! She's a freshman like me, and we both worked so hard to get on the squad."

"Don't worry. I'm not planning on punishing anyone. But this is my least favorite part of my job—filling out the paperwork."

Tiff waited patiently for Miss Olsen to finish writing the accident report. She felt a little odd, so she stared vacantly toward the nurse. Miss Olsen was about average size, blonde like Tiff, but she wore her hair in a braid. She looked young for a nurse—had Tiff met her at the mall, she would have guessed her to be about nineteen. But Tiff knew a nursing degree took several years, so she had to be older.

Friday finally arrived. Kyle Coleman slipped into his homeroom desk this morning, just like he had every day for the past week. He'd stopped by the library to check out some history books. Kyle loved history of all types, but the history of Africa fascinated him. When he read about the Yoruba peoples, Great Zimbabwe, and other ancient African cultures, he had to know more. He wanted to learn about his African heritage and history, but he also enjoyed reading about the rise and fall of all nations, their cultures, and their technology. He'd read a lot of information on the internet, but the weight and smell of a physical book made him feel like a real historian.

Kyle had searched through the school library, but found little he hadn't already explored. He did borrow one book that had a thorough description of ancient Nordic culture. He had a few minutes before class began, so Kyle opened the book and started to read.

More students filtered into the classroom. Tiff, Mara, and Shelly arrived, chatting about the football game last night. Even though the team had lost, Jason was bragging about intercepting a pass. The band clique started their usual air-instrument antics. Kyle frowned. He wasn't much for socializing, but he gave up on reading his book.

Once the bell sounded for the first period, Kyle headed toward the gymnasium. He wasn't fond of physical activity, but his parents insisted he keep in shape. Kyle's father worked as a foreman for a construction company, and he'd played many sports during his school years, but Kyle had inherited his mother's much smaller build.

He knew his bookishness frustrated his father. David, his oldest brother, played football in college, while John captained the swim team as a senior at the high school. Kyle was the baby of the family, and his mother coddled him. But now that Kyle was attending high school, his father insisted on some physical activity.

Kyle changed into his gym uniform. The first period gym class included freshmen and sophomores who weren't particularly physically adept. The school had done a good job separating the students into different groups based on their physical abilities. No jocks would bully the unskilled, and there was no stigma for being the last chosen for a team—so far, at least.

The gym teachers watched the students as they played soccer on the field. Jorge kicked the ball at the goal, and Sarah jumped to block it. Only Sarah got herself tangled in the net, and some of the old, worn strings tore apart.

Coach Brown inspected the net with a frown on his face. "I'll need to fetch another net from the storeroom. I need someone to help me carry it. The rest of you can pull the old net off the frame and haul it off the field."

Kyle craved a respite from the warm morning sun, so he promptly raised his hand. "I'll go with you, coach!"

The coach nodded, and started walking toward the gym. Kyle trotted beside the large man, trying to keep up. They stopped at his office to retrieve his keys, and Kyle peered into the coach's office from the doorway. Then he saw the sword.

In a display case high on the wall was a hunga-munga—an African throwing sword, which Kyle recognized by its distinctive multiple blades and asymmetric design. The weapon was framed, with a tribal pattern as a backing. Kyle recognized that too.

"Is that a hunga-munga sword? Wow! I've never seen a real one! Is it an original or a replica? Where did you get it?" Kyle could hardly contain his excitement.

"It's an heirloom. My father gave it to me," the coach replied as he closed the door. "I'm not sure where he got it. But don't go blabbing about it to the other students. I don't want someone trying to use it. So you know about African history?"

That was all the invitation Kyle needed. "Oh yes! I've read about the Yorubas, Bandas, Zulus…" He kept talking about his favorite subject the entire time they were retrieving the net, oblivious to the coach's apparent lack of interest.

For the rest of the day, Kyle could hardly contain his excitement. He drew pictures of the sword and the tribal pattern he'd seen in the margins of his notebooks and fantasized about the civilization he'd glimpsed in the artifact. He was particularly distracted in algebra class. Jason had to kick his desk twice to snap him out of his daydreaming.

Jason… he's a jock. Maybe he could find out more.

After class, Kyle followed Jason to his locker. "Jason? What do you know about Coach Brown?"

Jason paused to think about the coach. "He played football at college, but I don't know where he went to school. He was a running back, so he focuses on the offense right now. Believe it or not, he's also talented with metalworking. Mr. Johnson showed me a blade that the coach made. Why?"

Kyle ignored Jason's question. "But what about his background? His family?"

"He's never mentioned them. He's my football coach and gym teacher. But it's not like we're buddy-buddy."

As Kyle waited for the bus after school, he called his brother

David, who was away at college.

"Hi, David. It's Kyle."

"Kyle? What's up, little bro? Already having problems at school?" David's voice sounded amused. "Or is it girl trouble?"

"None of that. Who were your coaches when you went here?"

"You mean for football or for classes or what? There were several of them."

"Did you have a Coach Brown?"

"No. There wasn't a Coach Brown when I went there. He must have started in the past few years. Hey—is he giving you a hard time?"

"No, nothing like that. I was curious."

The conversation went on for a while. After David answered Kyle's questions, he asked about the first week of school, adding a lot of good-natured teasing.

That night, Kyle dreamed of African warriors at the height of their civilization.

CHAPTER TWO
A Fateful Day

By the third week of school, Kyle and the other students had settled into their routines. They spent their days with classes and homework, mixed with teenaged socializing. The teachers also had settled into their routines and began assigning longer and more challenging homework.

Kyle waited impatiently with the other students in his gym class while Coach Brown chatted with Mr. Oxinos. Kyle didn't think he'd done anything wrong, but he didn't want to be in trouble. He hadn't seen Mr. Oxinos in the athletic area before.

Kyle remembered homeroom that morning, when Mr. Oxinos had received a phone call. Like most other teachers, he avoided answering his phone during class, but this call seemed to be important. He had answered it immediately, going into his storeroom for privacy. Now, he seemed to be discussing something with the coach in his office.

Kyle approached the door, trying to look nonchalant. He fidgeted with his water bottle as he listened at the door.

"Are you sure they said *five*? I've never heard a day for five since... well, since the Bronze Age! And today? What's so special about today?" Coach Brown asked.

Mr. Oxinos chuckled. "That's what they said. They like to play mind games, but they never lie. So keep your eyes open for anything unusual."

Kyle heard them approaching the door. He quickly backed away, but his fidgeting had loosened the strap on his water bottle. The bottle popped out of the strap, dropped to the floor, and rolled behind some folded floor mats and out of his sight. Kyle went behind the mats to retrieve his bottle, only to find that it had bumped into another one. Unfortunately, both were identical school water bottles.

Kyle picked up both of them. Both bottles had liquid in them. Just then, the door opened, so he put one back, and ran to join his classmates. Mr. Oxinos headed back towards his classroom, and Coach Brown called to the students to begin their warm-up exercises.

Kyle groaned, but he knew the worst was to come. They were running laps today, something Kyle hated. The class went pretty much as Kyle expected. He had never been particularly athletic, so running laps was torture for him.

Running laps... gasping for breath... legs and lungs burning...

Finally they'd run the mile, and all the kids grabbed their water bottles and drank deeply. Kyle started to drink, but what he gulped down was not water. *I must have switched the bottles*, he thought.

The liquid had a mildly sweet taste with an underlying bitterness. *Some sort of tea, or energy drink?* he wondered. But he was too thirsty to stop drinking until he'd drained the bottle.

Then he noticed the coach was eyeing his own bottle curiously. *Was it the coach's bottle?*

The coach seemed too distracted by his conversation with Mr. Oxinos, so Kyle decided he would tell him about the bottle tomorrow.

It was a stupid stunt, Jason had to admit to himself, as he rubbed his aching back. He had been trying to show off at lunch to impress the cheerleaders. They'd cleared some space in the cafeteria, and Jason had posed with Tiff and Rachel each sitting on one of his shoulders. He could handle that. But when Carson called to him and feinted a charge, Jason's instincts had asserted themselves and he'd started a dodge to the right. But with the extra weight, all he'd managed to do was wrench his back.

Tiff had volunteered to help him to the nurse's office. She was waiting patiently near the door while Jason talked with Miss Olsen.

Fortunately, Miss Olsen wasn't too surprised by Jason's accident. She laughed at him a bit and chided him about his exploits. "So our young warrior met his nemesis! And on such a battlefield! I'm sure they will sing songs about this day!"

Jason blushed.

She continued with a twinkle in her eyes. "Oh, think nothing of it. Even the wisest among us make foolish mistakes, and there are always those who ridicule them. Many young men made fools of themselves around me in my younger days." Her face calmed. "I'll write you a note to excuse you from football practice this afternoon. But don't go playing the fool for at least a day or so."

Younger? Jason puzzled. *She doesn't look that old to me.*

Glancing at Tiff, Miss Olsen smiled. "Even Miss Gardner here has paid me a visit after a strange loss of wisdom." She stood and walked over to her closet for some painkillers.

Jason looked quizzically at Tiff. She looked a little embarrassed. Jason also noticed she glanced a few times at the basket of apples on the table. He remembered Tiff hadn't eaten lunch before helping him, so he guessed she was hungry.

"Miss Olsen? Do you mind if I grab a couple apples for Tiff? She didn't get any lunch."

He heard her call from the closet, "Go ahead, but don't…" Then some boxes fell over, and he didn't hear the rest. He heard something that sounded like a German curse-word. But all German sounded like curses to him. Tiff giggled.

Jason quickly scanned the basket of apples. Underneath the top layer of typical red or red-green apples, he spotted three that looked almost golden. He grabbed two and tossed one of them to Tiff. He wrapped his hand around his apple, imagining it was an exercise ball for hand strengthening.

Miss Olsen came back out of the closet and gave him two pills and a cup of water. He gulped them down and thanked her, and the two returned to their classes, munching on apples.

Aliki had become familiar enough with the school that she no longer got lost. She had also relaxed a bit as she got to know some of the other students. She also felt happy and invigorated whenever she came to school. She particularly loved her computer class—the first programming assignments were easy enough for novices to understand, but the teacher included extra challenges for more advanced students.

That afternoon, Aliki returned to Mr. Oxinos' classroom to meet Jen and Hitomi for a shopping expedition after school. She arrived promptly and double-checked that she had all the books she needed for homework. Thankfully, she only had a few assignments, and her mother would allow her to go to the mall with her friends. Jen, one of the goths from her homeroom, and Hitomi, who she knew from her computer class, had decided to hang out at the mall and do a bit of shopping. Aliki didn't need anything, but she wanted to look at some jewelry and accessories.

Mr. Oxinos had stepped out—he sometimes helped with after-school activities—and she was curious about him. She looked at some papers on his desk, but saw nothing unusual. She gazed at the scroll again, but didn't find it so fascinating. *Could Mr. Oxinos have something to do with that feeling?*

She decided to sneak a peek in his desk. Mr. Oxinos had left a portion of a snack in a plastic container inside the top drawer. He hadn't sealed it properly, and the lid slid off. "I'll just seal it for him," she told herself. She picked up the container and lid, but stopped. The food looked a bit like hash, but had a fragrant, sweet smell.

The next thing she knew, she had eaten half of the stuff. She didn't know what it was, but it tasted like a combination of honey, fruit, and several savory flavors she couldn't identify. Only Jen's arrival prevented her from devouring all of it. Fortunately, Jen didn't figure out where the container had come from.

"We could get something at the mall, you know," Jen groused, a look of disgust in her eyes. "You don't need to wolf down your snack. I'm sure the food court has something tastier."

Not likely, thought Aliki. *I've never tasted anything so wonderful.* "Can you see if Hitomi is lost? She hasn't been to this room before."

"Sure." Jen stepped back into the hallway.

While Jen stepped outside, Aliki quickly sealed the container and returned it to Mr. Oxinos' desk. *What is that stuff?* she wondered, remembering its exquisite taste.

After school, Mike's family went to the town mall. They ate an early dinner at the food court, and Mike had some time while his mother took his siblings shopping.

Mike wandered out of the music store at the mall. He saw Aliki, Jen, and a Japanese girl wander by and waved at them. They were chatting about accessorizing their wardrobes. Mike ran his hand through his hair and turned toward the sporting goods store where he would meet his family.

As he wandered toward the store, he heard a bit of a commotion. Two little boys, maybe six or seven years old, ran out of the toy store with their mother hustling after them. The kids ran headfirst into another young woman, knocking her purse from her hands and scattering the contents. The kids ran off without stopping; their mother gave the young woman an apologetic look and continued her chase.

Mike bent down to help the young lady with her belongings.

He began to gather the various items, and noticed a strange cylindrical object, apparently made out of wood. But it had some odd glowing symbols on it that looked like some sort of electronic display. *Some sort of weird electronic pad?*

He handed the items. Including the strange cylindrical object, to the young lady. To his surprise, the woman was Ida Olsen, his school nurse. "Umm... here's your... whatever this is..."

Ida quickly took the object and collected the rest of her belongings. "Thank you. Kids these days..." They both smiled.

"I'm here with my little brother and sister, but they're not that bad. Are you okay?"

"Fit as a fiddle. I've suffered worse," she replied with a smile.

Afterwards, Mike found his siblings and mother in the sporting goods store. They purchased some gear for their after-school activities—his sister needed some soccer shoes and his brother needed a new field-hockey stick after using the last one as a battle-axe. They started to leave the mall, but Mike saw the gold car again.

It has to be the same car. There couldn't be two such fancy golden cars in this area. Was Mr. Oxinos at the mall too? What is it like inside?

Mike stepped into the parking lot and took a few steps towards the golden car, almost mesmerized by it. Unfortunately, he didn't see the blue minivan as he stepped out. His mother screamed. Brakes squealed. He felt disorientation and a brief pain, then his body went numb.

Fighting to stay awake, he heard voices, as if in a dream. His siblings cried. His mother did too. Another familiar voice—*Miss Olsen?*—tried to reassure them.

"I've called 911. They're sending an ambulance." Miss Olsen didn't sound confident though.

Am I going to die? I don't feel any pain.

He tried opening his eyes. Vague images appeared before him. His mother looked worried and frightened. He didn't see his siblings, though he could hear them. Miss Olsen was also there.

"You're the nurse, right? Can't you save him?" his mother pleaded.

"I'm not a doctor, not a miracle worker. I'm just a nurse…" She sounded distracted, as if she were wrestling with a dilemma.

The ambulance arrived. Unfortunately so did the pain. His back and ribs hurt like nothing he could have imagined, and he had trouble breathing. As the paramedics lifted him onto the gurney, his head swam.

"I'm a nurse. I'll come with you," Miss Olsen told them. "Mrs. Rhee? I'll ride with Mike, and you meet me at the hospital." She glanced at Mike's brother and sister. "You may want to have someone watch your other children."

His mother hesitated, so Miss Olsen continued. "Mrs. Rhee, I promise he will be fine."

But on the way to the hospital, the ambulance became snarled in rush hour traffic. Ida Olsen looked at her patient while the drivers tried to get through the gridlock. Even with the sirens blaring, other drivers could only get out of the way so fast.

Mike's face grew even paler now. His breathing became ragged.

"How much longer to the hospital? I think we're losing him!" she cried to the drivers.

"Sorry miss. We're at least fifteen minutes away if the traffic doesn't clear. We hate this as much as you do."

Ida swore in a language no one nearby could understand. She retrieved the cylindrical object from her purse.

"You're a good young man. You don't deserve this. I promised you'd be fine." She deftly moved her fingers over the device, and the symbols changed. Several short needles protruded from one end. Ida held the cylinder firmly and jabbed the needles into Mike's chest, near his heart. A few more symbols changed, and she pulled the device from his chest.

A few minutes later, Mike's breathing eased, and color returned to his face.

CHAPTER THREE
Emergence

Aliki couldn't sleep. She had seen the commotion in the mall parking lot and watched the ambulance crew lift Mike into the ambulance. She and Jen had told their friends about the accident, and the school social network spread the news quickly. By the time she'd finished her homework earlier that evening, at least half of the school knew about the accident.

Of course, the school gossip chain exaggerated the events. Aliki sighed. He seemed like a nice guy. She turned over and tried to sleep, but sleep wouldn't come that night.

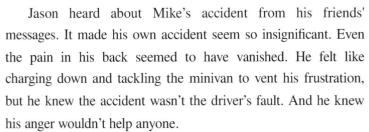

Jason heard about Mike's accident from his friends' messages. It made his own accident seem so insignificant. Even the pain in his back seemed to have vanished. He felt like charging down and tackling the minivan to vent his frustration, but he knew the accident wasn't the driver's fault. And he knew his anger wouldn't help anyone.

Jason couldn't settle his mind, so Jason tried to find things to occupy himself. He double-checked his homework and repacked his books in his backpack. He set out clothes for the next day, and rechecked his alarm clock. Fortunately, Helen hadn't messed with his clock since the first day of school.

He started doing push-ups to distract himself. Only when he'd finished his fifty push-ups did he realize the pain in his back had vanished.

"I'm reading, Mom!" Kyle called down. He frequently read in bed, and his mother didn't mind at all. Compared to his older brothers, who'd always been a handful to get to bed, Kyle preferred to settle himself by reading several chapters of a good historical novel.

He finished one book and started another. A few hours later, he finished that one. As he picked up the third book, he looked out his window and noticed the pre-dawn light filtering in.

Tiff's mind whirled and she couldn't sleep. She guessed it was either the strange apple or the news about Mike—possibly both. She browsed the internet on her computer, looking for information about golden apples. Aside from a lot of game references and some myths, the few golden apples she read about were usually yellowish. None of the pictures had the right rich golden hue she'd seen.

Its taste, rich with sweetness and intense flavor, lingered in her mind. She resolved to ask Miss Olsen about them in the morning.

Mike woke in the hospital. He didn't know what time it was, but he did feel better. The pain in his back and ribs had mostly disappeared, though he still felt sore. His mind seemed clear. "Powerful painkillers," he thought. "I'm sure I'll feel it when they wear off."

His mother slept in the chair beside his hospital bed. He guessed she had waited there for a while. He glanced at the clock —2:30 in the morning.

"Mom?"

She stirred. "Mike? Honey, how are you feeling?"

"I'm still a little sore. But I think I'm okay. The car must not have been going too fast."

His mother wept again. But this time, they were tears of relief. "Oh, Mike! I thought I was going to lose you!" She came over to his bed and gently gave him a hug—without squeezing, of course. Mike hugged her gently too.

"Whatever the docs gave me must be pretty good. I'm not looking forward to the drugs wearing off. But they're covering the pain really well." He smiled at her, trying to be reassuring.

But don't such powerful painkillers make your head all funny? he thought to himself.

The next day, Mike was absent from school. No one expected him to return for at least a week. But Mr. Oxinos was also missing, and a substitute sat in his desk.

It seemed like the classroom's vibrant energy had evaporated. The specter of Mike's accident hung over the class. Aliki had placed a collection jar on Mike's desk to buy flowers, and a few students had contributed. The students went about their morning routine without the usual antics. Even the air-band performances in the homeroom were gone today.

But it was more than Mike's tragedy. Mr. Oxinos radiated a powerful charismatic energy, and all the students benefitted. Without him, the class became too dull.

Kyle was surprised Coach Brown was absent today too. The substitute coach mentioned that Coach Brown had some family business to take care of, but Kyle guessed there was more to the story.

He remembered the discussion Coach Brown and Mr. Oxinos had. It seemed to be serious. Maybe their conversation had something to do with both of them being gone at the same time.

Kyle thought of the drink he'd inadvertently switched. Did the drink have some sort of medicine in it? Maybe the coach was sick?

He resolved to ask the school nurse about it. But when he stopped by the nurse's office between classes, he found she was absent today too.

Three individuals, quite different in their appearance, sat around a table in a fancy restaurant during lunchtime. The first was an imposing African-American man, with the powerful build and mannerisms of an athlete—or a warrior. Coach Greg Brown spoke to the others.

"So, Mike Rhee is one of the five, thanks to your first aid."

The young blonde woman, tall and fair with her hair tied in a long braid, replied, "I couldn't let him die. He helped me at the mall, and I promised his family he would be fine. They need him —his father's gone, and his younger siblings look up to him. And he's a good young man." Ida Olsen stared at the two men, a defiant look in her beautiful eyes.

"And he hopefully will be for a long while," the third added. He was a handsome man with Mediterranean features. His dark hair had an odd golden sheen and he had a dazzling smile, but he ignored the fascinated glances from their waitress. Nearby, other patrons stared at restaurant decorations or folded their napkins into animal shapes. Paul Oxinos asked, "Do we have any clues about the other four?"

Ida spoke again. "Jason King and Tiffany Gardner may be two of them. I think they took two of my golden apples."

"Jason's a good kid. Earnest and eager to please," Greg said. "He should be fine, once he knows the rules of the game. I'm not so sure about the cheerleader. As for the fourth, one of the students in my first period class drank my soma yesterday. I'll see if I can find out who."

Paul grinned. "As for the last, I think I have an idea too. I'll set some bait."

Ida thought for a few minutes while finishing her lunch. "With five new immortals, we'll have our hands full. Training so many will challenge us."

"I've had some premonitions about that," Paul replied. "I'm sending a few inquiries to our fellow immortals to see who could help."

They left the restaurant in a beautiful golden sedan. Had anyone been watching, they would have thought they were looking into the sun itself.

33

That afternoon, Jason went to football practice, even though the school nurse had told him to take it easy at least until Wednesday. He felt full of energy. During his normal gym class, he felt like he couldn't slow down. He'd drunk plenty of coffee and caffeinated soda before, but even they didn't give him the rush of energy he still felt.

He wondered if someone had slipped him some sort of drug. But Jason felt clear-headed and threw himself into football practice with a vengeance. He blitzed. He tackled rushers. He knocked over practice dummies.

"Jason, take it easy! I know you want to move up to the varsity squad, but you don't have to push yourself so hard!" Carson protested. Carson's ribs were feeling the effect of Jason's energetic tackles too.

"Sorry, Carson. I'm not sure what's gotten into me today."

"You're not... *taking*... anything, are you?" Carson asked, giving voice to what Jason feared.

Jason tried to sound jovial. "Not unless someone slipped me something. I had a great breakfast today and a good steak dinner last night. Maybe it was the apple I got from the nurse yesterday!"

The next day, Coach Brown returned to school. Despite feeling intimidated by the coach and his powerful physique, Kyle wanted to make sure he wasn't responsible for the coach's absence. He struggled through his warm-ups as quickly as he could, though he found them easier for some reason. He marshaled his courage and approached Coach Brown.

"Kyle? What can I help you with?"

"Um… sir…. I hope you're feeling better, sir… Were you sick yesterday, sir?" Kyle mumbled.

"No. I had some family matters to deal with. Why?" The coach had a strange look in his eyes.

Kyle gulped. "Umm… no reason…" he mumbled.

"*Kyle…?*" the coach asked, with the same tone Kyle's father used when he knew he wasn't telling the whole truth.

Seeing he couldn't avoid admitting his mistake, Kyle continued. "Well… um… I think I got our water bottles switched the day before yesterday. Yours tasted funny, and I think it might have had medicine in it…"

The coach's face seemed to soften, and Kyle thought he saw an amused look flash across the coach's face. He replied, "It wasn't medicine, Kyle. Just some special tea."

"I'm sorry, sir! I'll buy you some more! Tell me where to get it!"

"I'm afraid you cannot simply buy this tea. But I think I'll have a way for you to repay me. Trust me."

Kyle couldn't be sure, but he thought the coach's eyes had that amused look again.

The dish had sat on Mr. Oxinos' desk all day, under a glass cover. There, underneath the cover, was the mysterious hash-like food Aliki had tasted on Monday. She tried to ignore the strong temptation during homeroom. Fortunately, the bell rang before she could do anything rash.

During the day, she found herself wandering by Mr. Oxinos' room between classes, taking longer paths just to stare at the mysterious food. It beckoned to her.

Finally, after a tasteless lunch, she found herself at Mr. Oxinos' door again. With Mr. Oxinos' class still in the cafeteria, the room stood vacant. Aliki quietly crept into the room.

She looked around. *Still no one there. He wouldn't miss it if I had just a little bit...* Aliki lifted the cover.

A voice from behind startled her as Mr. Oxinos emerged from his storeroom. "And so you make five, Miss Aliki Papadaki."

CHAPTER FOUR
An Unexpected Gift

Mike returned to school the following Monday, feeling like his accident never happened. His rapid healing had mystified both him and his doctors. He'd been bored at home over the weekend, and pestered his mother until she'd agreed to let him return to school.

His mother had mentioned Miss Olsen had ridden in the ambulance with him to the hospital. For some reason, she had also checked on him every day while he recovered. That seemed strange—wasn't he just another student?

That morning, the students in homeroom all welcomed him back, even some he barely knew. Normally, Mike loved being the center of attention, but he couldn't explain his rapid recovery. He covered his confusion with jokes and thanked everyone for the flowers.

Mr. Oxinos didn't show any signs of surprise when he returned to school. Instead, he asked Mike to attend a special meeting in his room during third period. Mike stopped by his geometry class to get notes so he could catch up on his schoolwork, then walked to Mr. Oxinos' classroom for the meeting.

When he entered the art room, he saw four other students already seated in a half-circle. He recognized all of them from his homeroom. Kyle sat next to Aliki, his nose in a book. Tiff moved her backpack from the empty chair beside her to give Mike a place to sit. Jason seemed relaxed, doodling in a notebook. Coach Brown sat in a chair next to Mr. Oxinos' desk; another chair sat empty beside him.

Seeing him, Jason smiled. "Hey, Mike! How are you feeling?"

"Ready to take on a semi next!" Mike quipped, taking his seat. "What's this meeting about? Were any of you hurt too?"

"Well, I wrenched my back last week, but it wasn't as bad as I thought. I played in the game last week."

"Played? You dominated the game," Tiff added. "It was a rout. The other team didn't even score a point. How many sacks did you have?"

"Four, and two interceptions," Jason answered, but without his usual braggadocio. "I might have been able to get a few more, but the coach benched me in the fourth quarter. It was too easy. Did anything weird happen to you, Tiff?"

"I've had trouble sleeping." Tiff nibbled at her pencil. "And when I did sleep, I had some wild dreams."

"Me too." Aliki joined in the conversation. "Did you eat anything strange?"

"Just the hospital food," Mike joked. "How about you, Kyle? Anything weird?"

Pulled out of his reading, Kyle looked annoyed for a moment. He placed a bookmark in his book and closed it. "Well,

I've read twelve books in the past week. I was feeling a bit hyper on Saturday, so I went swimming with my brother. I could almost keep up with him in the pool."

Miss Olsen stepped into the classroom and closed the door. Mike wasn't surprised when she joined the circle. But he still couldn't guess the connection all of them shared.

Tiff watched as Coach Brown blocked the door with a heavy wooden box. Paul Oxinos addressed the gathered students. "We've asked you here because each of you has been exposed to something extraordinary. Each of you—by your own action or ours—have ingested, or been injected with"—he paused, looking at Mike—"substances that have changed you. You've probably noticed some of the changes: increased energy, vivid dreams, enhanced healing, or maybe other things."

He paused to let the students soak in his words. "First, we want to set your minds at ease. These changes are not dangerous —just the reverse. And they are usually permanent. The three of us have been similarly blessed, and we went through the same changes."

Mr. Oxinos let the revelation sink in for a moment before he continued. "For reasons we cannot share yet, we need you to keep this information between the eight of us. We will let you know who you can tell about the changes, or anything else we'll be doing together. I'm sure you'll understand soon enough."

Coach Brown spoke. "We also will need some time to teach you about the changes, and what they mean. This means we will be contacting your parents to arrange a time for us to get together for training. It will be tough, but fun too. And I guarantee it will be unique."

He chuckled and continued, "This won't be a formal training like a class. You could almost consider it more like an apprenticeship. Our role is to help you develop your new talents and grow into your role. It should be a natural growth into areas you never expected."

Coach Brown nodded to Ida, who took over. "As far as the changes you've already gone through, they include an enhanced metabolism that lets you recover from injuries or disease. You also won't get fatigued as easily and can push your body to higher levels of performance. Your reflexes and mental acuity are also higher. Essentially, your body and mind have improved to their peak levels and beyond."

Mr. Oxinos' phone rang, so she paused. Oddly, Mr. Oxinos didn't go into his back room as he answered. "Yes... I told you we'd bring them together. We're discussing just the essentials for now. You know, the things they noticed first. They're all young, and a little scared... Yes, I'll send pictures later. So why did you arrange for five anyway?" Evidently the phone call ended before Mr. Oxinos got his answer, because he had an annoyed expression on his face.

"Typical," he scowled. "Sometimes I think it's all a game to them. They never provide useful information."

Miss Olsen replied, "Maybe it's because they can't." She turned back to the students. "Anyway... my apples, Coach Brown's tea, and Mr. Oxinos' food all contained something that caused this change. As for Mike... when the van hit him, his injuries were life-threatening; I happened to be there, and I accompanied him in the ambulance to the hospital while his mother calmed his siblings. Unfortunately, his condition worsened in the ambulance, so I injected him with a dose of a curative we use among ourselves. Only that curative could have saved his life."

Mr. Oxinos took over again. "We have a lot more to tell you, and you will learn a lot on your own. This will be an exciting and confusing time for you. Though we can't answer everything now, I'm sure you have some questions we can answer."

Tiff considered Mr. Oxinos' words and looked at her fellows. Mike looked thoughtful. When he'd heard the revelation about his miraculous healing, he looked both confused and relieved. Kyle stopped playing with the bookmark in his book and was the first to raise his hand.

"Coach Brown? Does this have anything to do with the hunga-munga in your office?"

Coach Brown smiled. "Yes, it does. But let's stay focused."

Tiff quickly whispered to Kyle, "What's a hunga-munga?"

He whispered back, "A multi-bladed African tribal throwing sword that—"

Jason raised his hand next, so Tiff waved him off. Jason asked, "So does this mean we have, like, superpowers? Can you do other things?"

Mr. Oxinos replied. "If you want to think about it as superpowers, you can. But we're not in the business of wearing capes and fighting supervillains. It's a little more complicated. And yes, we can do other things too."

Tiff spoke up. "There's obviously a society of you. It's not like random people have this thing—whoever was on that phone call is some sort of coordinator, right? So what does this society —what are we and you—supposed to do?"

"Good question, Tiff," Mr. Oxinos replied. "The full range of what we do is best left until later. But we could say that we make sure things work the way they should."

Miss Olsen chimed in. "We each have different roles or specialties. For instance, I help with the health of our fellows."

Jason blurted, "Can you show us some other things you can do?"

Tiff smiled. He seemed far too interested in superpowers.

The teachers looked at each other. Finally, Mr. Oxinos held up his hand. It began to glow with a warm light. Jason stared with a fascinated expression, and even Aliki seemed to come out of her shell of shyness. She leaned forward, staring at Mr. Oxinos.

Mike seemed to be wrestling with something in his mind. Finally, he raised his hand, looking at Miss Olsen. "So, I'm sure you consider this a blessing, and that you were doing the right thing when you saved me. But why did you save me? Why not someone else? What makes me so special to receive this gift? The others had a choice. I didn't."

Miss Olsen looked at Mike, a kind smile on her face. "Mike, you've suffered a tremendous trauma. But you're a young man with a good heart. I believed you should have a chance at life. It was not an easy decision, but I still believe I made the right choice. Your family would have been devastated if you'd died. I saw how much they all cared about you. Please don't doubt yourself."

Jason raised a hand. "Coach Brown? So how will this affect

me playing on the team? I mean, if I'm a superhero, it wouldn't exactly be fair."

Coach Brown smiled. "You're right, it won't. I planned to speak to you privately, but since you mentioned it… I know you enjoy playing football, but we'll need to figure a way to either moderate you, or you'll have to learn to hold back. But I can also promise you this gift will grant you interesting challenges you never dreamed of. And no, there are no super-villains involved."

Finally, Aliki asked, "So we don't get sick? How does that work? How long does this last? The rest of our lives?"

Miss Olsen replied. "Yes, this will last the rest of your lives. When a normal body heals a wound, it tries to restore itself to a healthy state without the wound. When a normal person fights off a disease, their body creates antibodies to fight germs. The process in our bodies works in a much stronger fashion. We can be killed, but otherwise we recover quickly, as Mike already discovered."

Tiff remembered her first impression of Miss Olsen was that the nurse was older than she looked. She also recalled Aliki talking to Mr. Oxinos about Greek culture and history and Kyle's question about the hunga-munga. "So our bodies fight off diseases, right? But isn't aging a function of cells not copying themselves correctly or something like that? Isn't that like a disease? How old are you? How long has this been going on?"

Miss Olsen quietly replied, "Mr. Oxinos was right. You do ask good questions, Tiffany. The aging process is indeed stopped in us, and in you. You will grow to maturity, but never age beyond that. We are different ages, but each of us is over a thousand years old. And to your implied question… Yes, you are all now immortal."

CHAPTER FIVE
New Challenges

The rest of the week flew by in Jason's mind. *Immortal? Super-powers? Too strong for the team?* He had a lot to think about.

On Tuesday, Coach Brown trained him and the other defensive players on some "special techniques," but Jason knew the coach had implemented these techniques for his benefit. Some of the drills involved the players trying to get past the coach himself—he'd donned pads and worked with them as an offensive linesman.

He, Mitch, and Rodney worked on their blitzes, with Coach Brown playing as part of the offensive line. Coach Brown told the other students that he wanted to show them how to handle the blitz, and each of the school's middle linebackers led the defense in turn.

Jason noted that when Rodney or Mitch played in the formation, Coach Brown restrained himself, playing at normal human levels. He was an incredible player, able to stop every blitz attempt. When Jason played, Coach Brown's speed and strength rose to meet his, and the older man easily blocked him too.

Jason tried going faster and harder, and each time the coach still handled him easily. The coach simply grunted, "Wrong way."

Jason understood. As long as the coach opposed him, he could prevent Jason from dominating the game. But instead of trying to power through, Jason needed to learn to restrain his physical ability. So he tried to hold back enough to look good but not go too much faster or stronger than his fellows.

The coach noticed it and nodded. The next day, Jason worked again with Coach Brown, and spent extra time on the drills. He succeeded in restraining his abilities just in time for Thursday's game. He still led the defense in tackles, but he and the coach made sure he didn't dominate the game like before.

But the victory that night still seemed hollow.

Kyle could barely contain himself from pestering Coach Brown with questions throughout the week. There was so much he yearned to know—if the coach was a thousand or more years old, he'd *lived* through a lot of the history Kyle had read about. But the coach simply told him they'd have a lot of time to talk about it. And when he meant a lot of time... immortality? That *was* pretty long.

Kyle realized the coach's original name could not be Greg Brown. That had to be an American name he adopted when he came to America. Was he brought over as a slave? Did he come over later? What part of Africa was he originally from? Kyle had so many questions.

But he had a lot of time to learn the answers. He grew even more excited. He thought forward to Saturday morning, when they would have their first training session. Mr. Oxinos had told them all to wear something comfortable and lightweight, but rugged enough to survive some outdoor activity. He didn't reveal what kind of activity they planned, either to them or his parents.

The five of them were supposed to meet at the school, so Kyle could walk there. His mother had asked if she should go with him, and his brother John had asked if he wanted company. Kyle appreciated the attention, but he also recalled Mr. Oxinos wanted them to keep their abilities a secret for now.

On Tuesday, Aliki's parents begrudgingly agreed to let Aliki come to Saturday's outing. It helped that Mr. Oxinos was Greek. Her immigrant parents still clung to their traditions, so they visibly relaxed when he told them he would chaperone the students.

But she had no idea what to plan for. Mr. Oxinos had free time during third period, so she rushed to his room at the end of her third period science class. She paused as she came to the door, hearing Coach Brown's rich voice as well as Mr. Oxinos' almost musical one.

"So you think animals would be a good start?" Mr. Oxinos was saying.

"Certainly. It's one of the most familiar concepts. And I think it will reinforce what they're involved in. Ida agrees too," Coach Brown answered.

"I expected her to recommend something else. She doesn't

have a particular affinity there. But you're right. I'll tell them what to bring."

Aliki heard the doorknob turn, so she quickly moved on. She considered what she'd heard. *Animals? Are we going to the zoo? Or a veterinarian?*

The week also flew by for Mike. He'd caught up on his schoolwork—thanks to his "gift," he could work quickly through his backlog of homework. He also had to field a lot of questions about the accident, and thank everyone for the flowers and gifts. But Mike tried to return to a normal routine as quickly as possible.

Or as quickly as possible for someone who isn't normal, he thought to himself. *So what is normal for me now?*

He also found his musical technique had sharpened. Rather than sounding like he'd missed a week of practice, his playing sounded almost perfect. He adjusted and corrected his mistakes quickly. He spent a little time trying some new jazz songs and thoroughly enjoyed himself.

Mike had heard about Jason's dominance of the football game last week, so he avoided his taekwondo class—not that anyone expected him to attend. *After all, I should be dead*, he thought.

Miss Olsen had called his mother on Monday to arrange a weekly time for them to get together. She'd asked for them all to meet this Saturday, and had evidently told his mother they'd been selected for a special all-skills competitive team, which needed a weekly practice. *I guess that's as close an explanation as they could come up with,* he thought.

It was their regular after-school cheerleading practice, and Tiff's routines were off. She'd been too lost in trying to figure out the implications of what Mr. Oxinos had said—and more importantly, what he hadn't said. Immortality and super-health were nice, but they obviously had been recruited into something big. But she didn't have enough information to figure it out yet.

"Tiff! Pay attention!" Kennedy yelled.

Tiff's mind had wandered off in the middle of a routine, but Kennedy's shout snapped her from her daydream. Rachel was halfway through a handspring toward her, and she and Kennedy were supposed to catch her and hoist her to their shoulders.

Reacting without thought, Tiff pivoted into position and hoisted Rachel in perfect time for the routine. As Rachel steadied herself, Tiff and Kennedy braced her.

Kennedy gasped, "Wow! I've never seen you move that fast." She looked straight ahead toward their imaginary audience, but Tiff knew Kennedy had spoken to her.

Tiff thought to herself, *Maybe Jason's idea about super-heroics isn't so far-fetched. I have to pay more attention.*

On Saturday morning, Jason was the first student to arrive, followed by Kyle. Coach Brown and Miss Olsen had already arrived, several duffel bags at their feet. Mike and Tiff arrived shortly afterwards. Mr. Oxinos had given Aliki a ride, so they arrived together.

Once they'd assembled, Coach Brown led them to the gym.

It wasn't in use, so they had total privacy. The students filed inside. Strangely, Coach Brown didn't turn on the lights.

"So what kind of training are we doing today? Should we change into our gym clothes?" Mike asked. There was nothing out of place in the bare gym.

"No. We're going on a little trip," Mr. Oxinos replied. "Go to the center of the court, and stand in a circle." He paused and addressed the other teachers. "Should I do the honors?"

"Feel free." Miss Olsen smiled. Coach Brown had an amused expression on his face, as if he expected something funny to happen.

"A trip? I didn't see a van or bus." Aliki joined the others in the center of the court. "Shouldn't we be going to your cars instead of the middle of the gym?"

Jason felt anxious. He liked to prepare for his activities, but he had no idea what to expect. So he joined the other students in the center.

The three teachers had arranged themselves in a triangle surrounding the students, who faced out towards them. "We're not traveling by vehicle," Miss Olsen quipped. Then the world changed.

Jason felt his senses blur, and the gym faded from view. He felt hungry, even though he'd eaten breakfast an hour ago, and smelled something he couldn't identify. He saw images of swirling leaves mixed with high-pitched noises and the smell of the ocean. An exhilarating feeling of freedom overcame him, and clouds exploded into his vision. He sensed fear, and saw images of rapidly moving fur, followed by darkness.

The strange sensations stopped, but as his senses cleared, he found himself in a wilderness. The other students stood near him, but he gazed around at his surroundings. They stood in a small clearing, and tall trees surrounded them. A family of rabbits scattered in surprise, and the song of birds filled the air. A pair of deer strolled nearby, unafraid of their presence. Squirrels ran up and down the trees. Jason thought he saw a large dog stalking in the trees, but realized it was a wolf. He picked up a rock to throw, but Coach Brown shook his head.

Jason kept his eye on the predator, but the wolf moved away. Two of the squirrels paused to look at the group. They scampered up a nearby tree when Miss Olsen waved at them.

"What happened to the school?" Tiff blurted.

Mr. Oxinos laughed. "It's here, all around us. Look carefully. We're still in the gym... sort of."

Jason looked again. The clearing had a vaguely rectangular shape, roughly the same size as the gym and the school's central courtyard combined. Beyond some trees he could see open, grassy meadows, and their size and shape coincided with the fields around the school's gym. In the other two directions, the trees grew denser, and the structure of their canopies vaguely resembled the multiple stories of the classroom wing and the administrative wing of the school. Roughly where the band room and shop would be, a low stone cliff rose from the ground.

"It IS our school—made out of trees and nature!" Jason exclaimed. "Where are we?"

Coach Brown laughed. "You may want to look at yourselves first."

The students turned to look at each other. Tiff and Aliki shrieked, Mike gasped. "What the...?" sputtered Jason. Kyle examined his arms, lifted his shirt, and finally took off his shoes, revealing a pair of hooves.

Each of them had changed as well. They were still unmistakably themselves, but bits of animal parts replaced their normal features. Fur and fine downy feathers had sprung up across Tiff's face, and her hands had shortened to feline paws. Jason's own broad frame seemed to be composed of a patchwork of different fur patterns and colors—gray, tawny, white, brown. Aliki's skin was mostly smooth, but had some scales and fur in places, and a black shell-like structure had replaced her black hair. Mike had the muzzle of a dog, and his black hair stood straight up, looking coarser than usual. The rest of his skin was a similar mottled mixture of textures. Black fur covered Kyle's face, and he'd grown a set of boar-like tusks. His forearms and head were covered with leathery armor like a rhino.

The teachers looked the same as they always had. Even Miss Olsen and Mr. Oxinos smiled, trying to hold back laughter.

"What happened to us? What's going on?" Mike asked.

Mr. Oxinos laughed. "Welcome to what we call the Animal Realm. As you see, you've each taken on bits and pieces of different animals. Don't worry, this is perfectly normal."

CHAPTER SIX
The Animal Realm

"Normal? We're freaks!" Jason blurted.

Mike recognized Jason's false bravado was only concealing his anxiety. He also saw that Tiff looked like she might cry. He whispered to her, "I'm sure the teachers have a good reason for this."

Meanwhile, Kyle seemed to adapt without any problems. He was jumping and running through the clearing.

Aliki stood, gazing around. She murmured, "I can't see colors, but I can see things far away."

Kyle finally spoke, a low growling sound underscoring his voice. "This is cool! I can smell lots of different things. Can you?"

Mike shook his head, but noticed he could hear much better than normal. He turned to address the teachers. "So our bodies and senses have changed into weird animal hybrids. But what are we here for? And why didn't you change?"

"Good questions, Mike," Mr. Oxinos replied. "We didn't change because we have control over the transformations. And *that's* what you are here for. Care to demonstrate, Greg?"

Coach Brown nodded. Within seconds, he dropped to the ground as his hands and feet became paws. His dark skin grew golden fur, and his eyes became larger and yellower. His clothes disappeared, spots appeared on his fur, and a tail emerged. In less than a minute, he had transformed into a leopard.

"Incredible! We can learn to do that?" Aliki asked. "We can turn into animals?"

"Indeed you can," Coach Brown purred, "once you learn how."

Mr. Oxinos continued, "The laws of nature work differently here. In our normal world, your body is composed of different types of cells—blood cells, muscles, nerves, and so forth. In the Animal Realm, the animal itself is the basic element, so your body is a combination of different animals. You need to learn to control the composition of your body. Your first task is to focus on a particular animal and imagine yourself changing into it. Don't pick anything too exotic—you don't want to have to learn how to move eight spider legs."

Miss Olsen added, "Whatever animal you first fully transform into will become a special animal for you. It will be more natural for you to transform into that animal than any other. Some of you may only learn to transform into that animal, but you might master several animal forms. It all depends on your hidden talents."

Tiff looked a little embarrassed. "What about our clothes? Coach Brown's clothes kind of faded into his fur. Will ours?

Miss Olsen responded, "No, that requires something else you'll learn about. So we brought you these." She pulled some tan clothes from one of the duffel bags, and handed three sets to

Mr. Oxinos. She led Tiff and Aliki to a dense thicket, and Mr. Oxinos did the same for the boys. They all changed into the garments, which were loose tunics, coupled with pairs of shorts.

"These thickets are the locker rooms!" Jason exclaimed.

"Yeah, they seem like it," Kyle responded, glancing around.

Jason insisted. "No—you don't understand. The big clearing where we arrived is about the same size and shape as the gym. These thickets are exactly where the gym locker rooms are in our world. It seems like this world and ours are sort of a weird parallel."

"So this is some sort of parallel world?" Mike asked. The three boys looked at each other, totally bewildered.

Mike considered his appearance, and that of the others. Everyone looked like they were thinking of animals. *Maybe a fox*, Mike thought, looking at his current canine nose.

After several minutes, he felt something change, and he felt a pain in his backside. He glanced behind him and saw a fox's tail poking out of his shorts. He loosened his belt to relieve the pain and experimented with wagging his new tail. Aliki, Tiff, and Kyle burst out laughing.

Once the moment passed, Mike gazed at the others. Tiff had chosen a bird of some type. He noticed she grew a few more feathers, and her feline paws seemed to be elongating a bit. Aliki seemed to be losing her hair slowly, and her skin turned gray. He couldn't figure what she was trying to change into. Mike didn't notice any change in Jason's appearance despite the jock's obvious efforts. Then he heard a growl.

They all turned to look. Where Kyle had been standing now stood a black bear. His tunic and shorts had fallen off, and lay on the grass. Miss Olsen stood beside him, speaking quietly.

"Seems we have a natural," she remarked. She stepped closer to Kyle and placed a hand on his large ursine head. "I'll walk with you for a while. I want you to explore your surroundings and adjust to moving and sensing like a bear."

Mr. Oxinos nodded, and the two of them walked slowly out of the clearing. Miss Olsen continued to talk to Kyle in a low voice, but Mike had managed to turn his ears into those of a fox, and his hearing sharpened further.

He overheard her tell Kyle, "While you are a bear, or any other animal, you need to resist the natural instincts of your form. Do not succumb to intense emotions, and always keep your identity in your mind. You could forget you were originally human." They wandered off into the wood together.

Kyle returned shortly before lunchtime. Jason felt jealous— Kyle had turned into a bear with so little effort, but he couldn't even grow fur or a tail. Tiff had turned herself into a weird half-bird, half girl, though she couldn't fly yet. Aliki hadn't managed any complete form, but had changed partially into both a dolphin and a rhino. Mike was still mastering his transformation into a fox, but hadn't progressed much farther than his ears, tail, fur, and a fox muzzle.

Jason sat, irritated at himself. He hated feeling like a failure. Mr. Oxinos had been coaching the others, and Miss Olsen and Kyle joined them.

"Everyone has strengths and weaknesses, Jason," a low voice purred beside him. He turned to see Coach Brown, still in leopard form, sitting next to him.

"It's just that... well, I expected to get this. Everyone else has made progress. I'm stuck." He tried to keep his voice level, but failed. He'd been presented with a bold new adventure, and he had failed to make any change in his weird patchwork hybrid form.

"It may come in time, but then again, it may not. Give it some time. Keep trying. Not all of us can attune to each particular realm, Jason. The Animal Realm may be denied to you, but you could be a natural in another realm. I'm sure it's frustrating, but you're old enough to handle hard truths."

Jason pondered his coach's words. He didn't like feeling inadequate. He was a naturally gifted athlete, but this new world baffled and frustrated him.

"Why don't you help get lunch out?" the coach asked. It seemed like he was almost holding back a laugh. "I'm a little short on opposable thumbs right now." He rose and softly stalked over to the packed lunches.

Jason followed the leopard-coach toward the camping supplies. *At least I can help with this*, he thought to himself.

The alternative senses of the animal forms intrigued Aliki. During lunch, she experimented by focusing on her eyes, nose, and ears. She noticed a dramatic change in her hearing, and her sense of smell sharpened. She couldn't figure how to change her senses without changing her features, but the novelty of it fascinated her.

After they finished their lunches and cleaned up, she joined the other students in a circle. Mr. Oxinos and Coach Brown, still in leopard form, stood in the center.

"Now, imagine your own form, and try to change back into it," Mr. Oxinos said to the students. "Keep in mind who you are —a strong sense of identity is important here. Greg?"

Coach Brown's leopard form became stockier, and his fur thinned. Paws elongated into hands and feet and his tail shrank. His eyes darkened to their normal brown, and his ears shifted to the side of his head. His clothes reappeared as he transformed back into human shape. Within a minute, Coach Brown had resumed his original form.

"Now try to return to your human form," Mr. Oxinos instructed.

Aliki seemed to catch on first, followed by Mike. Both returned to their basic human shapes within minutes, though each retained some animal features. Before changing back, Mike had taken the time to wriggle under his tunic and poke his fox-head out, eliciting a fresh round of giggles.

Tiff struggled a bit, gradually shedding her plumage. Jason's body still stubbornly refused to change. Kyle remained in bear form.

"Kyle? It's time to be Kyle again…" Miss Olsen's voice sounded kind, but insistent. Aliki thought she heard concern and a bit of fear in her voice.

"Mr. Oxinos? Will he be stuck that way forever?" Aliki asked.

Coach Brown replied instead. "No, he should be able to

return to his normal form—unless he doesn't want to." He walked directly to Kyle the bear. "But he could never learn about the civilizations of Africa—and the time I lived among them."

Kyle the bear looked up at the coach. Aliki thought she saw a spark in the bear's eyes. Evidently, the coach did too, and he draped Kyle's tunic over the bear's head. Slowly, Kyle began to change back, until he returned to a near-human form like the others.

"That was so strange," Kyle whispered.

CHAPTER SEVEN
Monster

It was their third Saturday in the Animal Realm. Mike had stuck with a fox and had finally managed to shift completely into a fox shape on their second week. He enjoyed showing off with different partial transformations, and the girls giggled as he slowly added different fox features. He showed off by wiggling his fox-ears, then transformed fully into fox shape and chased his tail.

Over the last two weeks, Kyle had developed more control over his bear transformation and could shift back and forth quickly. Mike watched as Coach Brown coached Kyle. He decided to have some fun and slinked off in fox form.

Aliki still had not succeeded in fully transforming. Miss Olsen accompanied her to a nearby lake, which coincided with the school swimming pool. Mike watched from the underbrush as she slipped into the water and tried another transformation. Her skin became grayish, and sleek, and Mike watched her partially transform into a dolphin. When Aliki submerged, she stayed underwater for almost five minutes.

Mike grew bored and crept over to where Jason sat beside

the coach, who had resumed his leopard form. Jason's shoulders slumped, and Mike could almost feel his frustration.

"Still no luck?" Coach Brown prodded Jason.

"Not at all. I keep trying to transform. I even hung pictures of lions in my room, and read about them in the library. But nothing."

"Perhaps the lion isn't the right form for you. Why did you choose it?"

"Well, lions are strong, fast, powerful. I thought it would be cool to be stronger and faster."

"Before you gained immortality, you were already the strongest and fastest among the group. A lion would add to what you already have. Consider Kyle—he isn't strong. But as a bear, he is. Tiffany is trying to transform into an eagle, gaining flight and superior vision."

Jason pondered the coach's words. "So I should think of something other than lions?"

"Don't worry about being the strongest or fastest. An animal form offers gifts beyond your natural skills. Your animal affinity can complement your natural gifts, so worry about being yourself. That is where you'll succeed."

Once Aliki returned from the lake, Mike resumed his near-human form and joined the other students. He watched as Mr. Oxinos coached Tiff on her own transformation. Tiff was getting closer to transforming into an eagle. She could elongate her arms into full-sized wings. Her legs had similarly shortened into strong talons, and a feathered tail splayed behind her.

"You look like a harpy!" Aliki teased, drying her hair.

"Of course," Mr. Oxinos replied. "Where do you think the

original harpy myth came from?"

"So harpies were people like us who could change into birds?" Mike blurted.

"Exactly. But they wanted to be able to speak, so they kept the hybrid form rather than transforming fully into birds—vultures in their case."

Mike was dumbfounded. *If some mythical creatures were based on beings like us, what else might be true? Furthermore, Mr. Oxinos spoke about it like he was there. How old is he?*

Tiff felt proud of herself. The practice had gone well for most of them. With Miss Olsen's coaching, Kyle had managed to transform his hands into paws. She had also vainly tried to suppress her giggles as she watched Mike's antics.

As the students gathered the trash from lunch, they began to hear a crashing noise, like the sound of wood cracking and trees falling, mixed with a bellowing roar. It seemed to be getting louder.

Nervous, Tiff turned to Miss Olsen. "Miss Olsen? Is that a bear or something?"

Miss Olsen replied, "Too loud. Too big. Bears aren't particularly stealthy, but they don't make that kind of crashing."

The noise grew louder and more ominous. The students gathered in the central clearing, and Tiff noticed that even Coach Brown looked concerned. And then the monster broke into the clearing.

The creature stood around twenty feet tall. It was vaguely humanoid, but had a patchwork animal appearance, like the students when they'd first arrived. But while the students had random animal parts, the monster looked like it had assembled animalistic elements with a desire to inflict as much pain as possible.

Thick, rhino-like hide covered its chest. A long alligator's snout dominated its face, and the horns of a bull crowned its head. Its claws resembled a tiger's, while its legs ended in hooves. A tail, with spikes like a stegosaurus, grew from its backside. It wore a primitive loincloth and sash, both made of some type of animal hide. The monster spotted the assembled group and roared.

"Nothing like a party crasher," Coach Brown muttered. As Tiff watched, a pair of multi-bladed weapons—hunga-mungas, she guessed—appeared in the coach's hands as if by magic. Armor, composed of leather and metal and decorated with bits of fur, suddenly covered most of his body. Tiff ran to the opposite side of the clearing, but watched as Coach Brown hurled one of the hunga-mungas at the creature.

The multiple blades of the weapon caught in the creature's chest, but it only seemed to anger the beast. A shaft of light struck the creature, followed by a second. Tiff turned and saw that Mr. Oxinos glowed brightly, almost fiercely. He too wore armor of some sort, though his armor looked like decorated golden leather. He held a glowing bow in his hand, and fired the light shafts like arrows.

"Hurry!" Miss Olsen called. Like the others, she now held a weapon and wore armor. Hers looked like leather as well, though it seemed sturdier than Mr. Oxinos'. She carried a stout staff, and a small round shield covered her left forearm. As she waved for the students to join her, the plants around her grew thicker, forming a protective barrier.

Kyle and Aliki had already reached the opposite edge of the clearing, diving behind Miss Olsen's thick hedge. Jason, still in the same patchwork animal form he'd had since he arrived, brandished a large stick as he backed slowly toward the edge of the clearing. Mike had already moved into the underbrush. But the sight of the monster froze Tiff with bewilderment.

As Mr. Oxinos continued to fire shafts of light, Coach Brown used the barrage as cover and cautiously approached the creature. The hunga-mungas disappeared from his hands to be replaced by a large, slightly curved sword. He carefully dodged the creature's horrid claws and struck. His sword bit deep into the creature's leg.

Mike watched the battle from the edge of the clearing. Coach Brown and Mr. Oxinos harried the beast, but it fought with tenacious fury. Mike wasn't sure if they were trying to kill it or drive it off. Coach Brown fought defensively, trying to keep the creature focused on him. Already, the creature's claw had struck his left arm, and it hung limply at his side. A trickle of blood stained his ornate armor.

Aliki, Jason, and Kyle hid behind the thick hedge Miss Olsen had created. She stood before them, holding her thick staff protectively in front of the hedge. Mike saw Tiff staring at the creature, not bothering to hide or even retreat. The coach hadn't noticed Tiff standing dumbstruck.

Before Mike realized he was moving, he'd charged into the

clearing. "Tiff! Snap out of it! You'll be killed!" As he did so, he felt his feet change into fox paws; his shoes fell off somewhere along the way.

At the same time, Kyle lumbered forward in bear form. He stood on his hind legs and growled a challenge to the creature. Jason also emerged from behind the thicket, ready to pull Tiff to safety.

Either Kyle's growl or Mike's warning startled her out of her daze. Tiff noticed her predicament, and in the blink of an eye, she transformed fully into an eagle and soared into the sky.

"They're not going to stay hidden. We need to take him down fast!" Miss Olsen shouted. Her face hardened in concentration, and she silently mouthed some words. As the teens watched, the trees around the creature grew. Thicker branches emerged, entangling the beast. Smaller growths entwined around its feet.

"Thanks, Ida," called the coach.

With the creature's movement hampered, Coach Brown shifted to stronger attacks. One sword strike hamstrung the monster, and another severed its left arm at the elbow.

But the coach focused on defeating the monster and didn't notice Kyle had joined the fray. Kyle clawed at the creature's right side, while Coach Brown methodically slashed the creature on its wounded left side.

The monster feinted at Kyle with the sharp claws of its right hand, then twisted the attack into a roundhouse slash at the coach. At the same time, it swung its spiked tail directly into Kyle's side.

Kyle had never experienced actual combat. The blow caught

him off-guard, and he tumbled across the clearing. Blood gushed from several deep punctures, and Kyle slumped, whimpering in pain.

Mr. Oxinos intensified his barrage as he slowly moved toward Kyle's body. In response, the creature roared with fury and wrenched a thick branch from a tree. It hurled the stout branch at Mr. Oxinos, forcing him to jump out of the way.

Then a rhino charged the creature, and struck its good leg. Well, it was mostly rhino, Mike noted, but a patch of curly black hair and a human-colored flank revealed its true identity. "Go, Aliki!" Jason cheered.

As the creature doubled over, the coach leapt onto a low branch, and struck at the creature's throat. His sword bit deeply into its neck, and blood sprayed over the coach and Aliki.

The monster clutched at its neck, and fell to the ground. Its tail struck Aliki, but the blow lacked the force it had earlier. The coach's sword struck again, slicing deeply into the monster's side. It made one last flailing attempt with its remaining claw, pitched forward, and crashed to the ground.

CHAPTER EIGHT
Revelations Around the Campfire

Aliki studied the fallen creature. She could see its back rising and falling, but its breath came in bloody gasps. She expected it would die soon, and she felt emotionally confused.

She turned to look at Coach Brown. His armor had vanished, but he was drenched in blood. The crimson gore splattered over his face gave him an almost demonic appearance, contrasting with his usual jovial nature. He carefully wiped the long, curved sword he still held with a cloth. Despite herself, she shuddered.

So she turned toward the monster again and shifted back into her near-human form. "What is that thing?" Aliki asked, trying to put the memory of the coach's bloodstained visage out of her head.

But Mike gaped at her, a strange expression on his face. She noticed Jason awkwardly backing toward her, holding clothes and trying to avoid looking at her. He blushed furiously.

Suddenly, Aliki realized her loose garments had flown off during her charge, and she now stood naked in the clearing. She gave a little squeal, grabbed the tunic from Jason's hand, and dashed behind a tree. After the harrowing life-or-death fight and danger, it was too much. She could hear Mike and Jason laughing.

She wondered if she could face them when she re-emerged, but when she finished dressing and peeked out, she noticed they were simply laughing in relief, glad to be alive.

"Coach Brown went to the pond to wash off." Mr. Oxinos stood near the body of the creature. He still held his light-bow, ready to fire again if necessary.

"Is Kyle okay?" Aliki asked Miss Olsen.

Miss Olsen bent over Kyle's body, tending his wounds. She covered each with some sort of leaf, then carefully wrapped the wounds with bandages. Once she finished, she pulled a strange cylindrical object from her purse. Small runes glowed on its surface. Miss Olsen watched the runes as she passed it over Kyle's body. She tapped one of the runes, and small needles sprang from one end. She carefully, but firmly, pushed the needles into Kyle's side.

She looked toward the other students. "He'll be fine, but he needs to remain still. I think Kyle and I will have to remain here overnight while his body recovers."

"So what is that creature?" Aliki asked again. Jason and Mike had gathered around it.

"Titan. Giant. Formorian. Rakshasa—they've been called all those names and more," Mr. Oxinos scowled, a hard edge to his voice.

"You mean there's more of them?" Mike asked, suddenly alert.

"Not nearby, otherwise we'd have attracted them with our fight. But yes, there are more. They aren't native to this realm, or to our Earth, fortunately. But we should decide what to do with this one." Mr. Oxinos paused. "Ida? What do you think?"

"He raised his weapons against us and threatened our innocent charges. For that, I say we should let him expire here." Miss Olsen spat. She had a strange, hard edge to her voice too, Aliki noted.

"Personally, I'd prefer to throw it into a deep, dark pit, but Greg would agree with you," Mr. Oxinos sighed. "Still, they normally don't rampage mindlessly like this."

Suddenly, Jason spoke. "Umm, does anyone know where Tiff is?"

Tiff's fear had vanished to be replaced by joy. The battle site seemed so small and distant. She could see for miles and utterly embraced the joy of flying. She savored the air currents with her feathers and peered down to see animals scampering in the trees below.

After a while, she needed to rest her wings. She spotted a tall, stout tree and alighted on one of the upper branches. As she gazed about, deciding what to do next, she spied a red-tailed hawk approaching. It landed on a nearby branch and regarded her curiously.

"Not from around here, are you?" it asked.

Tiff gasped. "You speak English?"

"No, I speak bird. And so do you," it replied. "What is English?"

Tiff paused, confused. She stared at the hawk, and replied, "It's the language I speak, at least usually. I'm a human girl."

"Human? What's that?"

Tiff briefly considered turning back into her normal form, but thought better of it. She doubted that the tree branch would be able to support her weight. So she improvised and tried changing just her wings back into arms.

As the transformation began, the hawk fluttered curiously. "Ah, a shape-changer. I've met a few other lycanthropes, but I've never learned the technique. I'd like to be able to change into other animals. Perhaps a shark, to get those tasty fish that are too deep in the ocean to reach."

"Well, I'm not from here. I guess I'm from..." Tiff paused. *Do the animals of this realm know of other realms?* "Far away," she continued.

"Well, I... Rabbit!" It dove out of the tree towards its new prey.

Tiff watched the hawk swoop in for the kill and decided to take off again. It was then she realized her mistake. She hadn't mastered her transformation yet, and panic had spurred her shift into a full eagle form. She'd transformed her wings into hands, but couldn't transform them fully back into wings.

Stuck high in the tree as a bizarre eagle with human arms instead of wings, Tiff felt like crying. But she fought her despair, and instead she peered in the direction of the clearing where they'd arrived. It was still visible to her sharp vision, so she tried to fix its direction in her mind. She hopped down the tree, alternately grabbing the branches with her hands and talons during her clumsy descent.

By the time she reached the ground, her hands ached and stung from numerous cuts and scrapes. *It's going to be a long walk*, she thought.

After he dispatched the monster, Coach Brown took Jason, Mike and Aliki into the woods in search of Tiff. He paired Jason and Mike together, while he and Aliki searched elsewhere. Mr. Oxinos remained behind, ready to signal everyone if Tiff returned.

As Mike and Jason split off from Aliki and the coach, Mike asked, "So these woods are pretty thick. Are you afraid we'll get lost ourselves?"

Jason had selected a walking stick, with which he moved brush and low branches aside. "I've camped with the scouts for years, so I can handle the wilderness. Sometimes we explore for an hour or so, then work our way back to our camp."

Mike laughed. "I guess I'm too much of a city boy. Give me a game console and a controller, and I'm fine."

Jason chuckled along with him.

As they called for Tiff, they looked both in the tree branches above as well as through the low brush. That slowed their search, but they saw many animals as they traveled. Deer and rabbits didn't flee from them, but looked on curiously. At one point, a squirrel jumped on Jason's back, startling both of them.

They also saw a trio of wolves stalking through the trees. When the leader gazed in their direction, Jason raised his walking stick threateningly, and they moved on. But the snake gave them the biggest surprise.

Jason moved some brush out of the way while he entertained Mike with a story from one of his camping excursions. "...so

71

Pete and I found this cave in the hills. Pete didn't want to go in, but we had some daylight left. I figured we could at least look in the—"

"Jason! Look out!" Mike yelled.

The snake struck at Jason from the underbrush, but Mike's hand snapped out, knocking it aside. The snake turned to regard the two of them.

"Wow! How'd you do that?" Jason gaped.

"I'm a black belt in taekwondo, but I never could block so fast before. I can block a snake strike?"

"Mike, it doesn't look like the snake is going away."

Indeed, the snake had coiled itself up again, and regarded the two of them. Suddenly, its head began to change, shortening as the snake's eyes shifted forward. Within seconds, its head had morphed into the shape of a human head with serpentine features. It spoke in a hissing voice. "Huumannnssss. Not from here. Why disssturb my home?"

The snake also grew larger. Mike and Jason looked at each other. Mike spoke. "Uhhh... We're terribly sorry we bothered you. We're not used to being in this realm. Did we hurt you or damage your home?"

"Had you sssstepped further, you could have crussshhed my eggssss with your carelesssssnesssss."

"We're terribly sorry, ma'am. We're looking for a friend who is lost. Have you seen her? She is human like us, but may have taken the form of an eagle," Mike apologized.

"I have not ssseeen her. If ssshhee is flying asss an eagle, ssshhe may be in the treesssss. Look there, and do not disssturb me."

"Excuse me," Jason interjected, "but how are you able to transform yourself? The snakes of our world cannot change shape at all."

"Jussst as your friend can take the ssshape of an eagle, ssso can sssome of the denizensss of thisss realm take the form of another. It issss a rare talent," the snake proclaimed.

"Thank you, ma'am. We'll be more careful." Mike bowed his head and gestured to Jason to continue.

Coach Brown had shifted into his leopard form, and was stalking through the trees. Aliki walked slowly nearby. Her side still hurt, but the minor punctures had already healed, and only some painful bruises remained. "As long as you don't make me laugh, I'll be fine," she told the coach.

The coach stuck out his tongue a little in response. Aliki laughed despite her warning, then winced. "Oww! Don't do that!"

The leopard-coach nodded his head, then moved onward without a sound. Aliki found herself admiring the coach's uncanny mastery of his transformation. Nothing about the way he looked or moved suggested he was anything other than a normal leopard.

After a few minutes of walking, Aliki felt the need to break the silence. "You can speak when in leopard form, right?"

The leopard coughed and spoke with the coach's voice, though a purr still permeated his words. "Not normally. To speak, I transform part of my throat back to human form. It takes practice, but you'll learn the technique eventually."

73

The coach's mastery of shapechanging impressed her, but she realized he'd had a great deal of experience over centuries of life.

"So... Kyle says you're from an African tribe? When did you come to America?"

"I arrived in the New World in the late 1780's. A rival tribe captured several friends of mine and sold them into slavery. By the time I realized what had happened, they were already stuck in the hold of a ship bound for Haiti. So I used my talents and smuggled myself aboard. But I made a mistake—I couldn't free anyone without revealing my abilities or endangering the lives of everyone on the ship. I ended up with the rest of them, as a slave."

Seeing her puzzled expression, the coach continued. "After the Haitian Revolution freed the slaves, I spent more time there before immigrating to the United States in the 1840s. I worked as a smith in Philadelphia, and even helped to arm Union soldiers before and during the American Civil War."

"But... a slave? You could have escaped, right?" Aliki asked, still baffled.

"Yes, but Haiti was already a powder keg when I arrived. So I spent a few years sneaking in and out of captivity, bringing food to those who needed it. I also helped arm the slaves, creating hidden caches of weapons for their use. I'd learned from my mistakes, so I was cautious," the coach responded.

"Mistakes? But you already know so much."

"We all make mistakes—a long lifetime doesn't prevent that. I rushed onto the slave ship out of anger, thinking I could leave easily. I was careless. I've learned to plan better, particularly when other lives are at stake." To lighten the mood, the leopard-coach quipped, "I also learned that I don't like being on boats."

She smiled. But with so much to think about, Aliki didn't talk again until they saw the flare.

As Tiff walked, she experimented with turning her hands back into wings. By the time she approached the clearing, she had succeeded in transforming into a full eagle again and glided into the clearing on wings elegantly rather than waddling awkwardly on her talons.

She saw Kyle's bear body lying in the middle of the clearing, breathing heavily. Miss Olsen and Mr. Oxinos stood near the corpse of the monster, inspecting it and searching for clues, but Tiff didn't see the other students or the coach. When he spotted her, Mr. Oxinos drew his bow-like weapon and fired straight up into the air.

A brilliant light like a miniature sun shone from the arrow tip, and floated in the air. Unlike a normal burning arrow, which flared and disappeared, Mr. Oxinos' signal lasted for about an hour. During that time, both Aliki and the coach returned, followed by Jason and Mike.

Once they had gathered, Tiff related her experiences to the other students while the teachers started a thorough search of the monster's body. After a while, Coach Brown and Mr. Oxinos flipped the body onto its back and continued to inspect its body.

Meanwhile, Miss Olsen searched through a pillowcase-sized pouch from its belt. Tiff stood beside her, watching as she pulled primitive-looking possessions from the pack—bone jewelry, trinkets made of hardened clay, an animal hide of some type.

"No clan tattoos," Coach Brown called from atop the giant's chest. "Our friend must have only awakened recently."

"Nothing noteworthy in the pouch either. Perhaps following its trail to where he arrived might yield a clue." Miss Olsen tossed the pouch and its contents aside.

"Wouldn't the monster turn into his natural form when it died?" Tiff pondered aloud, gazing at the colossal corpse.

Miss Olsen answered, "If he died in his own realm or on Earth, he would revert. But here, animal elements form the natural state of things."

Mr. Oxinos surveyed the area, glancing from the monster to Kyle's prone body. "With Kyle hurt and unable to be moved, should we take the others back, or all remain here?"

"All remain here," the coach immediately replied. "If our departed monster friend has allies, we may need to fight, and defending a wounded ally would hamper us."

Miss Olsen nodded. "I agree. We did tell their parents that some of these trips might be overnight expeditions. And I'm sure you can apply your usual charm to help persuade the parents it's necessary, Paul."

Mr. Oxinos smiled. "I agree. It might also benefit us to find out more about what may have caused the titan to go berserk like that."

"You mean aside from sensing us?" Miss Olsen retorted. "They don't always need something to provoke them."

"If we're going to stay, I can go hunt some dinner," Coach Brown volunteered, shifting back into leopard form.

"Wait for a bit. I'll step over to Earth to phone the parents.

Once I get back, I'll join you on the hunt. We'll need a large catch for all of us." Mr. Oxinos stood and faded into a warm glowing light.

Mike suddenly blurted. "But the animals here are intelligent, aren't they? I don't know if I feel right about hunting another sentient being."

Miss Olsen replied, "Here, the hunt is part of the cycle of life. Better to kill the weak so the strong can survive. It's harsh, but it's the way things are here. Do you think the predators here think about how killing deprives another creature of its life?"

Tiff remembered the hawk. It had been hunting too. Predators had as much a right to life as herbivores.

"We hunt our prey with respect. Besides, they will simply reincarnate," Miss Olsen continued.

"Reincarnate?" Jason gaped. "You mean they will become another animal?"

Miss Olsen elaborated. "Usually they will become the same animal, as it is suited to their soul. But sometimes they will be reborn as a higher or lower animal. They might even be reborn on Earth as a human, or something else. But we should set up a camp first. Tiff? Jason? Can you gather materials for a lean-to? Mike, if you can help dig a fire pit, that would be helpful. Aliki, you're on firewood detail. There should be plenty nearby. Once Paul returns, I'll find some edible plants to go along with whatever the hunters bring back."

An hour later, when Mr. Oxinos and Coach Brown returned with a deer, Mike and Miss Olsen had finished preparing the fire pit. After building shelters, Jason helped Mr. Oxinos skin and dress the deer, but Aliki still felt uneasy about eating the animal. Both Mike and Tiff looked like they shared her hesitation. To distract herself, Aliki took the antlers of the buck and borrowed a knife from Jason to whittle them.

Coach Brown separated the venison into large portions, and then Miss Olsen spent several minutes smearing various herbs and spices over the flesh. Once she finished, Coach Brown spitted it and began cooking the venison. Meanwhile, Miss Olsen boiled some vegetables in a pot. Despite Aliki's reticence, the aroma of the cooking meat made her mouth water.

After several hours, the coach pronounced the meat ready. Mike unpacked the supplies, and passed out plates, utensils, and napkins. Coach Brown carved portions for each of them, and they gathered around the fire to eat.

Aliki still felt confused about how they could eat the deer. To her, meat was something her parents purchased in a store.

Then Miss Olsen spoke, a touch of reverence in her voice. "We thank you for giving your flesh to us so we may eat. May you find tranquility in your next life as well."

Jason had already started eating, and both Mike and Tiff tried a bite. Finally, hunger overcame her reluctance, and she tried her portion of the venison. The delightful flavor surprised her, and her unease vanished.

As they ate their fill of the deer and vegetables, they told stories of their adventures while separated. Eventually, Tiff asked the questions all the students had on their minds. "So you mentioned the animals reincarnate. And that there are different realms, like this one and our own. And then there are these monster-titan-giant thingies. So how do they all fit together? Why are the giants so hostile? And how do we fit in?"

The coach and Miss Olsen looked to Mr. Oxinos. "You're by far the best tale-teller of us, Paul," Miss Olsen suggested, smiling.

"Very well." Mr. Oxinos rose to his feet. "First, our native world, Earth, isn't considered a realm like the Animal Realm is. It is far more important. Clustered around Earth are eight realms, each of a different nature. I like to conceptualize them as the corners of a cube, floating around the center which is our own world."

"This sounds a bit like Buddhism," Mike interrupted. "Buddhists teach that there are six realms: the Human Realm, Animal Realm, Heaven Realm—"

"And they are partially right. Most religions have shards of the truth. The Buddhist Realm of the Hungry Ghosts resembles the Greek realm of Hades, the Norse realm of Niflheim, and so forth," Miss Olsen answered.

"So what are the other realms?" Jason asked.

"Well, there's what many might call the Heaven Realm. There is also a Demon Realm, which you might consider Hell, though most of it doesn't resemble fire and brimstone. There is also a Spirit Realm, an Elemental Realm, a Ghost Realm—"

"So will we be going to each of them?" Mike interrupted again.

"Yes, eventually," Coach Brown replied.

"'So how do you travel to the other realms?" Jason asked.

"That's really not something I want to teach you yet. If I taught that to you, you might enter the Demon Realm by

79

accident. So let's avoid that for now."

"You were telling us about the giants and why they're so hostile." Aliki prodded, hoping to hear more.

Mr. Oxinos continued. "Right. Well, our world is special. When a person on Earth dies, their soul usually migrates to the realm that is most appropriate for them. A thoroughly evil person might be drawn into the Demon Realm, while one who lives with animals, or like an animal, might be drawn here. Once the soul enters the realm, it reincarnates as a denizen of that realm. So the truly evil person may reincarnate as a demon."

"In most cases, the denizens of a realm will reincarnate within their realm when they die. But the Earth is at the center of the realms and holds the Fountain of Souls. Souls only come into existence on Earth. Thus, it plays a crucial role."

Mr. Oxinos paused, took a drink of water and continued. "But Earth is not the only world that could serve as the Fountain of Souls. The titans, or giants, or whatever you want to call them, come from a different world called Yothrun. Yothrun is also surrounded by various realms. Some of the realms surrounding Yothrun are the same as Earth—for instance, the Animal Realm is shared by both, which is why this fellow could be here," he said, pointing to the fallen monster. "But there are other realms that are not shared."

Mr. Oxinos looked over the students and resumed his tale. "One of our roles, since you asked earlier, is to preserve the balance of the realms and protect the Fountain of Souls. The titans would love to have the Fountain of Souls back on their own world. It used to be there, before the dawn of our civilization. Because they lost the Fountain of Souls to humanity, many of the titans still hold a great deal of resentment towards us."

While the students contemplated their teacher's words, Kyle groaned and slowly regained consciousness. He changed back into a near-human form.

"Careful, son. We're glad you're awake, but you need to rest and give your body a chance to heal," Mr. Oxinos said.

"Is it gone?" Kyle whispered. "Is everyone okay?"

"We're fine, Kyle," Mike said. "You did a heck of a job on the monster, and Coach Brown finished it off."

"Smells good..." Kyle said weakly.

Miss Olsen carved a small portion from the deer and added some vegetables to the plate. Jason helped Kyle to sit up. "Go slowly," Miss Olsen advised. "Your body has been through a lot."

Kyle ate slowly, but devoured the food with increasing vigor. As he helped himself to a second slice of venison, the other students filled him in on the rest of the day's events.

Miss Olsen couldn't resist teasing him about his appetite. "I'm not sure whether to credit that to the bear or the teenage boy."

Kyle smiled weakly. "So we're camping here tonight?"

"We should try to find out about why the titan attacked us— aside from general animosity." Mr. Oxinos replied.

The cool night air, exhaustion, and pleasantly full bellies sapped the students' strength. They all lay down and soon fell fast asleep. "I'll watch first," Coach Brown volunteered.

Miss Olsen nodded. "Wake me for second watch. Paul prefers the sunrise shift."

"Of course."

The next morning, after packing their camping supplies and gear, they followed the monster's trail. The trail ended abruptly in a small clearing littered with shattered trees and a few animal corpses. The teachers and Jason searched through the wreckage, and Aliki and Mike poked around a bit, but the animal bodies made Tiff feel squeamish.

Coach Brown crouched down, inspecting the end of the giant-sized trail. "He must have transferred from his home realm. I see nothing that might suggest otherwise."

"But the giants have largely remained quiet in recent centuries. That type of rampage reminds me of the great battles of ages ago," Miss Olsen remarked. "There are much fewer of them now, so they've become much more cautious. This kind of recklessness suggests something else was at work. Something drove him berserk like that."

"Can all titans shift realms? Or assume such scary forms?" Aliki asked.

"No. They have a larger fraction of gifted individuals than Earth because their population has declined. Titans also naturally live longer than humans," Mr. Oxinos replied.

Miss Olsen beckoned the students toward the center of the clearing. "We should return and let others know what happened here."

"Agreed. Care to lead the way home?" Coach Brown replied.

CHAPTER NINE
Recovery

Most of the students spent Sunday resting from their physical efforts and reflecting on what they had learned. Fortunately, their bodies returned to normal when they returned to Earth.

Jason still felt depressed about his inability to transform while in the Animal Realm. He went jogging that evening to clear his mind. His path took him near Kyle's townhouse. Jason remembered Kyle was still a little weak when Coach Brown had dropped him off that morning, so Jason knocked on the door.

When one of Kyle's brothers answered the door, Jason introduced himself. "Hi! I'm Jason. Kyle and I have been training together. I wanted to check on him and chat about something we learned last night."

"I'm John," the other young man responded. "Kyle's downstairs in the basement, reading." Jason noticed John's emphasis on the word "reading." John evidently didn't share his brother's habits or interests. "Come on in. Want something to drink?"

Jason was thirsty after his jogging. "Some water would be great. Thanks."

John scooped some ice into a cup and filled it with water from the faucet. "This way," he said, and led Jason into the basement. Kyle was reading on a couch in the basement, a small pile of books beside him.

"Hey, Kyle. How are you feeling?" Jason asked.

"Better. A good rest and good books are exactly what I needed... after my fall out of the tree," Kyle said.

John still lingered in the doorway, so Jason got the hint. "Uh... yeah. I'm glad to hear it. You did get pretty banged up, but you made it pretty high first. So what are you reading?"

Kyle smiled. "Oh, a little of this, a little of that. The stories we heard around the campfire made me interested in some of the histories of the Greeks and Norse and how they connect with myths. I'm searching online for information too."

Jason picked up one of the books. "Find anything interesting?"

"A bit. Some of the Greek myths tie into historical events, like the fall of Troy. And some historical figures are supposed to be descended from gods. But who knows—it all may be a type of ancient propaganda."

Jason laughed, "I'm glad you're on our team. I've never been too strong in academics. Well, I just thought I'd see how you're doing." He turned to leave. "Nice meeting you, John."

Jason felt John's eyes on his back as he left. *Is John curious, suspicious, or merely protective?*

Aliki went for a swim in the indoor community pool. She'd cajoled her younger brother Leander into joining her, and he played with his friends in the shallow end. Aliki split her time relaxing and casually swimming.

She had always been a good swimmer and was proud she could swim the length of the pool underwater with only a single deep breath. Occasionally, she had to navigate around the youngsters playing, but that made it more challenging. Only today, it didn't seem as challenging. So she decided to see how far she could really go underwater. Aliki swam to the deep end, took a deep breath, and pushed off underwater.

The first length was easy, so she did a flip-turn in the shallow end and swam back to the deep end. As she touched the point where she'd started, she felt she could still keep going. Another trip to the shallow end, another flip turn. And still she felt she could continue.

Aliki realized she was drawing upon her abilities. She popped to the surface in the shallow area, glancing around to see if anyone had noticed.

"Hey, sis! You were down so long you're turning blue!" her brother called out.

Aliki looked at her arms and belly. Sure enough, her skin had started to turn not blue, but gray—the gray of dolphin skin. Embarrassed and frightened, she willed the transformation to reverse while keeping herself mostly submerged. Once she was confident the changes were reversed, she climbed out of the pool.

"But I thought that only worked in the Animal Realm," she whispered.

That afternoon, Mike played his favorite jazz pieces on his

trombone in his room. But he grew bored and was dwelling on what had happened in the Animal Realm. Kyle had almost been killed, Tiff had gotten lost, and of course there were the transformations and the talking animals. He felt overwhelmed.

So Mike did what he usually did to lighten his mood—he goofed around. First, he practiced blowing raspberries with his trombone, but it got old. He slid under his bed, hiding from invisible demons. But that seemed juvenile.

Finally, Mike decided to have a little fun with his transformations. He concentrated and—*Yes!*—there were the fox ears. He hadn't been able to watch himself transform in the Animal Realm, so he found a lot of amusement watching himself in his mirror. He tried adding the fox muzzle to his features. He experimented with other partial transformations, replacing his hair with red fur or adding a long vulpine tongue.

That kept him amused for a little while. He loosened his belt and grew out a fox tail. He practiced swishing it back and forth until he'd perfected a few debonair tail moves.

His mother knocked on the door. "Mike! Time for dinner!"

Panicking, Mike reverted his face to its normal appearance. "Coming, Mom! Give me a few minutes!"

"Is everything all right? Can I come in?" She opened the door before getting Mike's answer.

Mike hadn't had time to revert his fox tail yet, and he couldn't hide it from her. His mother stared. "What... is that?"

Mike thought quickly. "Oh, it's a funny fox tail Tiff lent me on our camping trip. She thought I'd appreciate it. It's supposed to move when you attach it, but I haven't figured it out yet."

"Well, it certainly looks realistic. How does it work?"

"I'm not sure. Tiff had the directions messed up, but she thought I could figure it out. Umm... if you wouldn't mind, putting it on and taking it off can be a little embarrassing."

"Oh... of course. I'll give you some privacy." His mother closed the door. Mike couldn't tell if she were amused or suspicious—or both.

The next morning, Tiff arrived early at school. She wanted to talk to one of the teachers, but she knew students would surround Mr. Oxinos once he arrived in his homeroom. So she waited near the nurse's office.

Ida Olsen arrived and unlocked her office. Tiff saw her turn, realizing she wasn't alone. Tiff stepped towards her, unsure of what to say.

"Miss Olsen? Can we talk? Inside?"

"Of course. Come in." Ida put down her purse and satchel. She began her normal morning routine, brewing coffee and logging into her computer. "What can I help you with?"

Tiff wrestled with some of the many questions on her mind.

Seeing her uncertainty, Miss Olsen prompted her. "Are your questions about this weekend? Things we talked about around the campfire?"

"Well, sort of." Tiff wandered over to Ida's basket of apples. She looked at them, trying to find something to say, then took a deep breath. "So when you said the titans lost the Fountain—was that the reason the myths talk about the gods fighting the titans? Is that the basis of the myths?"

"In part, yes. When the Fountain moved to this world, the

giants fought the earliest immortals to regain it. Some of those conflicts formed the basis of the early tales of conflict between the Greek gods and the titans, between the Aesir and the giants, the Tuatha and the Fomorians..."

"So does that mean the gods... Zeus, Thor, and the rest... were immortals like us?"

Ida Olsen smiled. "We do wield abilities the ancient peoples thought to be divine. Now people might think them superpowers, like Jason does."

Tiff chuckled, imagining herself and the others in capes. "Well, I need to get to class." As she headed towards the door, Tiff paused. "Miss Olsen... the Fountain... did it move here on its own, or did we steal it?"

Ida replied solemnly. "No one knows for sure. The giants claim we stole it. But those times predate most of us. What really happened... we don't know."

CHAPTER TEN
Building Bonds

Their teachers gave them the next weekend off, so Aliki found herself shopping for clothes at the mall. As she wandered through the stores, she saw Tiff with some of her cheerleader friends, also shopping. Tiff had already purchased a few accessories and was waiting for her friends to check out.

Aliki turned toward the food court. She wandered down the length of the mall, peering at the different stores and the people. Aliki had never been particularly social, so she was surprised when she heard someone call her name.

"Aliki! I thought it was you!" Tiff and her friends had caught up to her. "Aliki, this is Kennedy and Rachel. Girls, this is my friend Aliki. She's doing the same special training as me."

"You don't look like a cheerleader, or a gymnast." Kennedy's eyes narrowed.

"You're not being tutored, are you, Tiff?" Rachel blurted. "I thought you were in honors courses." While the words weren't hostile, Rachel's tone was clearly judgmental.

Aliki felt small and worthless. The other girls clearly didn't consider her a worthwhile friend for Tiff. Aliki felt like they were already sharpening their claws, preparing to shred her—either physically or by reputation.

All three cheerleaders exuded such charm and confidence. Aliki felt like she didn't belong anywhere near them. She glanced around for an excuse to leave.

Tiff finally chimed in. "Our families are part of the same country club, and they're looking for talent for a show. So Mr. Oxinos is working with both of us."

It sounded far-fetched to Aliki, and Kennedy apparently didn't believe it either. "A talent show? C'mon, Tiff. You've got talent, but what kind of skills does she have?"

"I play the flute," Aliki replied, eyes downcast.

"Yes, and she's pretty good," Tiff added, trying to continue the charade. Aliki remembered Tiff had never heard her play.

"So what talents is Jason showing off?" Rachel asked. She had an obvious crush on Jason—even Aliki could tell that.

"He's... uhh... helping with the stuff on stage. You know— moving stuff on and off," Tiff babbled. The rest of the cheerleader clique didn't look convinced, and Tiff looked like she'd run out of ideas.

Aliki realized she was making things awkward between Tiff and her fellow cheerleaders, so she replied, "Well, I need to grab something and find my mom, so I'm going to run."

As Aliki left the cheerleaders behind, she wondered whether she and Tiff could really be friends, or were only joined to each other by weird coincidence.

Questions filled Mike's head, so he tried calling Kyle. But

Kyle's brother answered and told him Kyle had stepped out. So he phoned Jason, and the two of them met at Jason's favorite sporting goods store. Mike felt he had to talk to someone.

He wandered through the unfamiliar store, getting lost among the jerseys and sports gear. He picked up a football helmet and considered trying it on when he heard Jason's voice. "Hey, Mike! What's up?"

Mike returned the helmet to the shelf and turned towards Jason. Jason looked like a lion surveying his domain, fully in command of his surroundings.

"Sorry I called you. Things are confusing me and I need to work through some of this stuff."

"You should have talked to Kyle or Tiff. I'm probably the dumbest one of us. I doubt I can really help you figure things out." Jason sighed. "There's a burger place down the street, and I'm hungry."

Mike's stomach growled when Jason mentioned food. He'd been eating more, but he wasn't sure if it was due to his new status or adolescence. "Sounds good to me."

A short walk and a few burgers later, the two chatted over a basket of fries. "So, what's going on, Mike?" Jason asked between mouthfuls.

Mike gazed at the tabletop. "All of this stuff is really making me think. One day we're ordinary kids at school, and the next, we're immortals with powers and part of a group protecting the whole world. It's a lot to take in. And I still haven't figured out why they selected us."

"Hah! That's easy for me. I snagged a couple of golden apples out of Miss Olsen's basket. I ate one, and Tiff had the other. So there we are." Jason paused thoughtfully. "But maybe the apples are like the apples in the Garden of Eden—now we know about the sins of the world."

"Do you think the apples are from the Tree of Knowledge? I never really thought about the religious implications of all of this."

"Well, I guess they could be. I don't know enough myths. I don't think Miss Olsen is ready to tell us about them, though. She seemed pretty defensive. For all we know, they're Johnny Appleseed's apples!" The two laughed at the joke, and both gobbled a few more fries.

After the moment passed, Mike continued, "You and Tiff, even Aliki and Kyle... you all happened on this by luck, or curiosity. But from what I know, Miss Olsen gave me something after I got hit by the van in the mall parking lot. So she picked me. I guess I'm grateful I'm not dead, but kids get killed by stupid accidents every day. So why me? Why not some other, more worthy victim? I'm not that special, or at least I wasn't. I'm not sure I deserve this."

"That's bull, Mike," Jason responded. "You're always there to help, and who knows? You may have hidden depths and skills. Me? I can't even master the animal shapes like you can. I've been feeling like I'm the dumb jock, and who needs human muscle when we have a bear or a rhino? We have to wait and assume better things are going to happen."

Mike pondered Jason's words for a moment. "Maybe. But worse things may happen too."

Jason wolfed down the last of the fries. "Maybe they will. But that's something we'll tackle together, right?"

Kyle went to the park in the early morning. He'd asked Miss Olsen to meet him there to help him master his transformation, but she hadn't arrived yet. There were a few joggers, and several people walking dogs. Clouds hid the early morning sun, so the day seemed gray, and a chill pervaded the morning air.

The cold didn't bother him, but Kyle shivered anyway. He took off his jacket and noticed that his arms had grown a thick fur. He touched his hands to his face, but both hands and face were human. He quickly pulled his jacket back on, and looked for a place where he could remain unnoticed.

As he walked around the park, a golden retriever pulled away from its master and ran towards him playfully. *Great*, Kyle thought. *That dog will smell the bear on me and freak out.* He braced himself for the encounter.

But instead, the dog rolled over on its back right in front of him. The dog put its paws in the air playfully. Kyle stared, as did the dog's owner. "I've never seen her so friendly towards a stranger," he said. "She's a rescue dog, so she's normally not comfortable with strangers. You must have a natural touch. Her name is Aurora." He rubbed the dog's belly and invited Kyle to pet her too.

Kyle gingerly stroked the dog's chest. He noticed scars along her side. *Maybe they're from a former owner?* Kyle murmured, "Good girl, Aurora," not knowing what else to say. He'd never had pets of his own. Aurora wagged her tail as she licked him and playfully lunged to reach his face.

Aurora's owner stared at him. "She likes you. Your noises

there sounded like she does sometimes." He glanced at his watch and continued, "I'm afraid I have to get back to my house. But if you're in the park again, I'm sure she'd love to play."

"Okay. It was nice meeting you," Kyle said. "See you later, Aurora!"

Aurora gave a playful yip and trotted after her master as he jogged away.

Kyle puzzled over the man's words. He was still reflecting on the encounter when Miss Olsen arrived. She wore a light shirt and comfortable jogging pants. The cool air evidently didn't bother her.

"Good morning, Kyle. How are you doing this morning?"

"All right, I guess." Kyle quickly filled her in on the unusual dog encounter.

"Well, you seem strongly attached to the Animal Realm. Perhaps the dog sensed that."

"But I thought she would smell the bear on me and be afraid!" Kyle exclaimed. "Look!" He rolled up the sleeve of his jacket, showing the fur on his arm.

"Not necessarily. Perhaps you weren't as frightening because she could relate to you. Tell me—did she respond when you talked to her?"

Kyle recalled the encounter. "Yeah, she really loved it," he admitted.

"It's possible you spoke in an animal tongue."

"I can speak DOG?" Kyle said, shocked.

"Maybe. But we'll have to find a less public place to test that. In the meantime, let's find somewhere to focus on your challenges with transformation." She led him into a small copse of trees with ample underbrush. She pushed a few branches aside, and Kyle noticed the branches stayed where she guided them rather than snapping back.

Once hidden from potential observers, she guided the underbrush to obscure them even further, and formed a small clearing. She sat on a low branch, leaving him in the center of the clearing.

"You'll want to take off your jacket, at least. Your loose pants should be okay unless you change completely into a bear."

He obediently removed his jacket and loosened the drawstring of his sweatpants. He removed his shirt and shoes as well, and noticed fur also covered his chest.

She looked him over and said, "First, I think we should work on that fur."

CHAPTER ELEVEN
New Teachers

On the following Tuesday morning, Mike entered the homeroom, expecting to see Mr. Oxinos there. But a substitute teacher sat at Mr. Oxinos' desk. She was an older woman, with short dark hair. Her name, Mrs. Florence, was written on the whiteboard.

So he introduced himself. "I'm Mike Rhee. Is Mr. Oxinos sick?" He doubted immortals would get sick. But he'd occasionally used the excuse himself.

"No. He will be in later today. He had a couple of guests arriving in town. He's meeting them at the airport, but should be here around lunchtime."

Mike thought to himself, *Must be immortal business. Perhaps they've come to help figure out this thing with the giant.* He glanced at Kyle, Jason, and Aliki. Tiff hadn't arrived yet, but the others' questioning glances suggested they assumed the same thing.

Once the bell rang to start first period, he whispered to Jason, "Miss Olsen is on the way to my next class. I'll drop by and let her know." Jason nodded and casually walked next to

Aliki. Mike could hear him passing his message to her. Aliki glanced at him and nodded.

He entered the nurse's office and found Miss Olsen sipping her coffee. Mike waved and said, "Mr. Oxinos is picking up some friends from the airport."

"They're already here. Paul is filling them in. We'll talk later."

Mike nodded and turned towards his first period Biology class.

Mike wasn't too fond of biology, so he daydreamed through class. He remembered Kyle chattering about his dog encounter over the weekend. Suddenly the teacher's voice snapped him out of his reverie. "Mike Rhee? Please answer the question."

"Uh..." he stammered, looking around quickly. Tanya, the girl sitting next to him, was pointing to a picture of a turtle; he remembered they were discussing reptiles. "Turtles, sir," he answered. Tanya rolled her eyes, and some of the other students chuckled.

"Yes, Mike. We were discussing turtles. Once again—can you tell us what order turtles belong to?"

Mike had no idea, so he thought quickly. "I think Tanya's family has a turtle." The classroom chuckles grew louder.

The teacher rolled his eyes. "Perhaps Tanya can answer the question."

Tanya glanced at Mike and smirked. "Turtles are of the order Testudines."

Mike thought to himself, *Maybe I'll ask a turtle myself, next time I see one.*

As Aliki walked to the English Literature class she shared with Jason, she wondered about the visitors. She guessed they were here because of the titan. But another thing occupied her mind. Mike's efforts to pass them information during homeroom made her realize they needed some way to communicate with each other discreetly.

She noticed Jason striding towards class ahead of her, so she sped up and tapped him on the shoulder. In a soft voice, she suggested, "We need some signals, Jason."

"Huh? Yeah you're right. The teachers don't want us texting each other in class, and I'm not sure everyone has a smartphone. Besides, I can't carry a phone when I'm at practice."

His remark gave her an idea. "Don't you use signals and stuff in football?"

"Some, but it's mostly audibles, and usually only on offense. The quarterback uses a bunch of codes to tell the offense how the play should go based on where the defense lines up against them. But what we might need is something that's both audible and visual, so we could pass info without making sounds. Baseball uses hand signals to pass info from the catcher to the pitcher."

Aliki nodded. "Perhaps you can work on some mix between code words and hand signals. But it should be easy to remember and work into conversation too."

"Okay. I'll think about it."

As Kyle left the lunchroom, he noticed Mr. Oxinos entering

the school with two strangers, a man and a woman. The tall man looked vaguely Arabic and wore a button-down shirt and slacks. The woman was of medium height, but much fairer, with auburn hair. She wore a t-shirt with a logo from some tavern. They went into the office, presumably so Mr. Oxinos could sign them in.

A few minutes later, they came out of the office. He must have been staring, because Mr. Oxinos waved him over.

"And here is one of our bright students, Kyle Coleman. Kyle, this is Mrs. MacKenzie Morgan and Dr. Tom Fathy."

Dr. Fathy extended a hand. "It is a pleasure to meet such a promising student. Paul has been telling us about your aptitudes. We are both quite impressed."

"Brave. That's good. Foolish, though. That's bad." Mrs. Morgan said. Kyle noted that she spoke with a bit of an Irish brogue.

But Kyle didn't know what to make of her comment, and the woman's intimidated him. Fortunately, Mr. Oxinos came to his rescue. "I'm sure we'll have a lot more to discuss on Saturday at our next get-together."

"Are we going on another trip?" Kyle asked.

"No. We have everything we need right here at the school," Mr. Oxinos replied. "I'll let everyone know."

The next morning, Jason suggested they gather at lunchtime. At lunch, he presented a combination of simple hand signals and keywords they could use to pass information to each other.

"We'll use colors to indicate who we're talking about, and hand motions or positions to convey the message. Only we use the two together does it mean anything," he explained.

"Show us," Aliki urged.

"Okay, the hand signal for 'want to meet' is hands steepled together, like this," Jason demonstrated. "And the signal for danger is your fist touching your face. 'Investigate' is rubbing your forehead."

"You said we'll use color codes for each of us?" Mike asked.

"Yeah. You're red, Mike, like a fox. I'm blue, Tiff is yellow or gold and Aliki is black because of their hair, and Kyle is brown, for the bear. We can use white, green and silver for the teachers."

Tiff nibbled at some fries. "What if we need to get a message to everyone?" Tiff asked.

Jason paused. He'd overlooked that possibility. "How about gray?"

He showed off a few remaining hand signals, and the others experimented with them. Mike suggested a few new signals for silly messages like "throw a paper ball at him," and the lunch devolved into goofing off.

That evening, Paul Oxinos consulted with his visitors in his home. He'd already filled them in about the titan attack, but the conversation inevitably turned to the students.

"Five of them? You expect me to be training five of them? Are ye codding me?" MacKenzie protested.

Paul thought a moment before answering her. "We've managed it so far, but we could use help. It's been centuries since we've had more than one or two new immortals at the same time. And I have a hunch more titan problems are on the way."

"From what I hear, your hunches are usually spot on," MacKenzie sighed. "How many of them have any physical talent at all?"

"Well, Jason King is a football player, and pretty talented. I think I heard Mike Rhee practices martial arts, but I'm not sure of the type. Tiffany Gardner is a cheerleader, which requires more physical coordination than most people realize."

"Oh, I know all about cheerleaders' coordination, Paul. After all, I dabbled myself a while back."

"Times were different sixty years ago, MacKenzie," Tom Fathy countered. "But I'm more interested in what led the beast to attack you. From what you've said, it sounds like he wasn't in his right mind."

"Unfortunately, we didn't have the luxury of trying to calm him down. The safety of the students was paramount," Paul replied. "He wasn't a titan of any significant rank, and I'm not sure which clan he belonged to. He had no identifying insignia at all."

"That's unusual. No clan trinkets at all?" Tom asked.

"Not one. I checked again while the other students were searching for Tiffany. The titan either was an outcast, or had lost his clan emblem. Or perhaps he came from a clanless group. Could his rampage be linked to the disappearances, Tom?"

"Perhaps. I haven't discovered any significant leads," Tom answered. "Do you think it might be a good idea to send a group to their world to look for clues?"

Paul thought only for a few seconds before answering. "With

no identification, I doubt we could discover where the titan came from. And I'm not sure that exposing any of us to danger when we've already suffered some disappearances is such a good idea."

CHAPTER TWELVE
Lessons in Warfare

Jason arrived early at the school gym on Saturday for their training session. As he entered, he noticed the girls' volleyball team using the main gym room. He spotted Coach Brown standing to one side, so he sauntered over to the coach.

The coach smiled at him as he wandered over. "We'll need to use the side gym. I've already started setting it up, but I could use some help."

Jason followed the coach to the side gym—a half-court sized gym room used for weight training and other intense exercise. As he entered, he noticed the coach had shoved most of the equipment into one corner. Floor pads covered most of the floor.

The coach inspected a rack filled with wooden swords, padded maces, paintball guns, and other similar non-lethal weapons. He had the amused expression on his face again. Two punching bags flanked the weapons rack. As Jason helped the coach move the remaining exercise equipment into the corner, the other students and teachers arrived. Two new people entered with Mr. Oxinos, and Miss Olsen carried a large first aid kit.

Mr. Oxinos introduced each of the newcomers. "This is Dr.

Tom Fathy, a scientist and investigator from Egypt who will be helping to research the titan issue. Miss MacKenzie Morgan is a combat instructor, originally from Ireland. She is here to teach you how to handle yourself in a real fight. In our long lives, we eventually run into challenging situations we can't talk our way out of. And yes, they are both gifted like the rest of us."

Jason regarded the two with curiosity, and a bit of wariness. Dr. Fathy was tall and lightly built, and moved with grace and precision. He inspected the exercise machines, but avoided getting too close to them. Jason guessed he might be more of an academic.

MacKenzie was different. She had a fierceness in her eyes, her muscles were toned, and her movements reminded him of a wild animal. Jason realized that she was as physical as the coach despite her smaller stature. She made him think of an army drill sergeant, even though he'd never met one.

Dr. Fathy extended a hand to each of them in turn. "It is a pleasure to meet such promising students. Paul has been telling us about your aptitudes. We are both impressed."

MacKenzie proclaimed, "All right, students. First, I'll be hearing about your physical talents an' aptitudes. If you have any experience in physical combat, let me know. If you're involved in sports, or any type of regular physical activity, I want to know that too." Jason noted she spoke with a bit of an Irish brogue.

Jason stood. "Ma'am. I play football and work out regularly. I also hike, do some rock climbing, and other similar stuff with the scouts."

MacKenzie turned to face him. "Okay, first order of business. Call me MacKenzie. Now, what position do you play,

Jason?"

Jason met her gaze and felt a moment of sheer terror. He tried to suppress the chills running down his back. "Middle Linebacker, ma'am," he replied, trying to keep his voice even.

Coach Brown informed her, "Jason was one of the more talented young players, before—"

MacKenzie interrupted him. "So you're used to breakthrough assaults, and usin' both physical power and speed. Fair play to you. Next?"

Mike stood next. "Black belt taekwondo. Other sports at a recreational level only."

"Deadly, Mike. Are you still practicing?" MacKenzie regarded him with curiosity.

"I stopped after the accident. When I got out of the hospital, I needed some recovery time, and time to reflect on what happened."

"The time for quiet reflection has passed, boyo. But I'll be teachin' you from now on," MacKenzie snapped.

Noting his confusion, Paul spoke. "MacKenzie has black belts in most forms of martial arts. She could probably teach your instructor a thing or two."

"My taekwondo is a little rusty," MacKenzie admitted. "It's been a few years, so I'll re-familiarize myself with it." She looked toward Tiff. "And how about you?"

"Umm.... I'm a cheerleader, ma'am."

Jason could tell from the tremor in her voice that Tiff felt intimidated too. There was something scary about MacKenzie— as if she might erupt into bloody violence at a moment's notice.

"Anything else?"

"Uhh... gymnastics, I guess, and dance. Does that count?"

MacKenzie nodded. "Of course. Some of your best combat styles are as intricate as a good dance. Kyle? What about you?"

"Well, I swim with my brother sometimes. He's on the swim team, and my older brother played football when he was here. But I'm not as good as they are."

Mike quipped, "He's a bookworm and BEAR-ly exercises. Right, Kyle?" Kyle grinned sheepishly while Aliki giggled.

"Well, it's something, I guess. And you?" MacKenzie turned her gaze to Aliki.

Overwhelmed by MacKenzie's presence, Aliki stammered, "N-Nothing at all. I don't have any skills at all."

"You may have done nothing until now, but whether you have innate skills is for to me to decide. Now, let's see how you handle some weapons."

MacKenzie challenged them to lay a blow on her with any weapon they picked, and Coach Brown let them handle the different weapons.

Mike pulled on a pair of padded gloves. He'd used similar things for sparring before. The weapons rack didn't have any padding for his feet or shins though. As he stretched, he watched MacKenzie test Tiff's aptitude with several different weapons. Tiff first tried using a padded quarterstaff, then a shorter, baton-length weapon. Each time, MacKenzie gave her a chance to become familiar with the weapon, then waited for Tiff to attack. In both cases, MacKenzie expertly disarmed her in less than fifteen seconds, even though she fought with no weapons.

He watched Tiff wielding a wooden sword shaped like a Japanese katana—a boken, he remembered—and doing reasonably well with it. But MacKenzie seemed to anticipate every move Tiff made. She dodged Tiff's amateur swings, measuring her skill, and knocked Tiff's right arm with her palm. The boken went flying.

"Owww..." Tiff grimaced, holding her forearm.

"Ye'll be fine. I only gave it a tap, not enough to break it. Go have Ida look at it. Mike? Ye're next." Mike noticed her brogue became thicker when she grew excited.

Mike stepped onto the sparring mat and bowed to her.

MacKenzie bowed in return. "Well, since I'll not be disarming you, I'll settle for forcing you off the mat. And ye must strike me with hand or foot. Fair?" Mike nodded. "Whenever you are ready."

Mike fared better than Tiff, lasting a full minute in the ring. Whenever he punched or kicked at MacKenzie, she effortlessly blocked as if she could read his mind. Mike even tried fighting without thought, in case she really could read his mind. But he still ended up falling off the mat with his legs swept out from under him.

Mike stood and bowed. MacKenzie bowed in return, then turned to Jason, who had chosen a large two-handed axe-like weapon.

Dr. Fathy and Mr. Oxinos had retired to the coach's office, where they could talk without being overheard. Coach Brown kept an eye on the combatants, acting as a referee when needed.

Tiff sat with Miss Olsen as she checked her arm. Meanwhile, Kyle fumbled with a padded sword, accidentally tossing it into a weight machine while trying to mimic MacKenzie's swing. Jason had stuck with the padded greataxe, and seemed fairly adept at it, but Aliki had been as hopeless as she claimed, and Kyle didn't seem much better.

Tiff confided in Ida, "MacKenzie is amazing. I've never seen anyone as ferocious as her, even on TV."

"She's had centuries of experience. She's also focused on the arts of war. Each of us has our own areas of expertise."

Tiff considered Miss Olsen's words. "So I assume we will each develop our own areas of expertise."

"Most certainly," Ida replied. "Kyle already seems to have an affinity for animals, particularly bears. You mastered the form of an eagle and flew. How did it feel?"

"Amazing," Tiff replied without a thought.

"Remember that feeling. It will guide you as you grow into your talents."

Suddenly, Aliki interrupted. "We may have a problem." Outside the door, members of the girls' volleyball team had gathered, and were watching their sparring with wide-eyed amazement.

CHAPTER THIRTEEN
Gossip Chain

The next Monday, in homeroom, Aliki noticed Julisha and Kate whispering and glancing in her direction—and toward Kyle and Mike too. Both of them were on the volleyball team, so they'd seen the sparring with MacKenzie. Both Coach Brown and Mr. Oxinos had suggested they simply avoid discussing it, but Aliki didn't believe their unusual activity would be easily forgotten.

Julisha and Kate kept glancing at her as they talked. Fortunately, Aliki had her geometry book and a piece of paper out, and was pretending to do some schoolwork. They didn't seem to think she'd overheard them. She had a hunch they'd be gossiping about the weapons training, so she tried to listen without being obvious about it.

"... and did you see that red-headed woman? She even kicked Jason's butt..." Julisha said.

Kate responded, "Yeah, but what were Mike and Kyle doing fighting with someone like that? And Tiff and Aliki?"

When Mike arrived, she used the hand signals they'd devised. She signaled "Need to talk" and "Danger." She continued listening to the jockettes. They'd moved on to talking about their next game.

Aliki breathed a sigh of relief. But she still noticed them watching Tiff and Jason as they entered the classroom together.

Mike met Aliki and Jason after the first period Literature class they shared. Mike and Jason both had history during second period, so the three of them could chat for a few minutes as they walked.

"So some of the other students are talking about us. Big deal," Jason said.

"But we need to keep our talents hidden. That means we shouldn't stand out too much, particularly as a group," Aliki responded.

"Let me think of what to do about the rumors we started," Mike proposed. "We've already told our parents we're on some sort of all-skills competitive team, so let's run with that. One lie is easier than two."

"Hey, Julisha's in our history class, right? We could start with her," Jason suggested.

Mike agreed. "Sounds good. Follow my lead."

Aliki headed off to her class, so Mike thought about how to convince Julisha that their weapon sparring wasn't suspicious— or at least less weird.

As he and Jason entered class together, he noticed Julisha's eyes on them. So he grabbed onto an idea.

"Miss MacKenzie sure taught us a thing or two about weapons and stuff, right Jason?"

"Uh... yeah! Man, that was a good workout!" Jason responded, obviously improvising.

"Using the weapons is a great way to learn about how they were used in history too. That greataxe you were using could smash through enemy shield lines. I read they even could take out a horse's legs in mid-charge."

Julisha had her pencil in her mouth, and as Mike glanced toward her, Julisha's gaze abruptly shifted from him and Jason to a nearby map on the wall. Mike immediately realized she was trying not be seen eavesdropping.

"It's a big help for our all-skills team," Mike continued. "The special teachers are a huge bonus too." He hoped the bit about the all-skills team would dissuade Julisha from trying to investigate further.

As Jason ate lunch with his friends Carson and Pete, he noticed Julisha making her way toward his table. They'd finished their lunch and had started their normal lunchtime bantering. He felt nervous and worried that Mike's hasty ploy hadn't satisfied her curiosity.

"Got a moment, Jason?" Julisha asked.

"Woah, Jason! Don't let Tiff know you're flirting with her!" Carson jibed.

"We're not a couple, dude," Jason retorted. "Uh... sure, Julisha." He shrugged and gathered his lunch tray. "Catch you later, guys."

As he threw away his trash, he followed Julisha into the courtyard. "What's up, Julisha?"

"I saw you, Mike, and the others on Saturday fighting with all those weapons. So what's this about an all-skills team? I heard you and Mike talking about it."

"Oh... uh... we were randomly chosen by Mr. Oxinos for a special team. Nothing big, but it means we have to learn a lot of different things and work together." Jason thought he sounded unconvincing. Unfortunately, Julisha's reaction confirmed it too.

"What kind of all-skills team? Do they have any more openings?" Julisha blurted. "That weapons stuff looked fun. I'd love to try out."

"Clearly you didn't see the bruises I had on Sunday," Jason joked. He wished he had Mike's silver tongue. "I think the team is full. I'm the token jock."

"So Mike is your band geek, Kyle is your history nerd, and Tiff the cheerleader. What talents does Aliki add?"

"Computer skills, and deductive thinking," Mr. Oxinos' voice came from behind them. "Kyle needs me to review his report on the weapons practice. And you have to start yours." He gave Julisha a dismissive glance.

Jason followed Mr. Oxinos as he left the courtyard. "Thanks, sir," he said.

"Aliki warned me about Julisha and Kate. I overheard you and thought you could use an assist." He smiled for a moment and continued. "Unfortunately, I'm sure others in school will talk about the practice. Rumors can spread like wildfire."

"Ye want me ta spar with the whole school?" MacKenzie sputtered.

Paul Oxinos gathered the other immortal teachers at his house that evening to discuss their latest challenge. He'd predicted their activities would eventually attract attention, but hoped they'd have more time to prepare. He felt the burden of training five new immortals at once, but tried to present his plans to the others in a positive light.

"It may be the only way to quell the rumors. We can make it a spectacle, and even hopefully scare off some of the school snoops," Paul replied. "With a bit of finesse, I think we can scare off anyone else who wants to insert themselves into our merry band."

"Do you really think an exhibition is such a good idea? You've always liked grand performances, but it could attract students instead." Ida cautioned.

"I'm sure we could handle another dozen," Greg Brown joked. Ida and MacKenzie rolled their eyes in unison.

Paul considered Ida's words. "I'd rather distract the students with a plausible lie than risk students snooping."

MacKenzie wrestled with the idea, but eventually gave in. "Fine. Set up a sparring exhibition. But let's be trainin' our students so they're deadly skilled. I think Jason works well with the greataxe, and Tiff handles the boken just fine. Mike's martial arts are solid. Kyle and Aliki are more of a challenge. I saw Kyle get a little furry during our bout. I had to end it quickly, or that volleyball team would have had a lot more to gab about. Aliki didn't seem to have any combat skill whatsoever, though."

Ida spoke again. "Intentionally inflicting harm—even if it is with padded weapons—can be challenging for some. I remember how learning to fight bothered me. And I grew up in a fierce culture, just as MacKenzie did."

"Maybe she could handle herself in other ways. After all, Ida fought effectively against the giant even without an offensive weapon," Greg suggested.

"So let's see what MacKenzie can come up with for Aliki," Paul responded. "Now, I'm going to need Kyle and Tiffany to help prepare for this exhibition."

Coach Brown convinced the principal that the sparring exhibition would be good for the students. So on a Friday, almost two weeks after the volleyball team had seen the training session, the "World Renowned Combat Expert" MacKenzie Morgan would demonstrate her skills to the school.

MacKenzie found time to spar with the immortal students several more times after school during the next two weeks. She added padded martial arts armor to the weapons rack, and Kyle was growing accustomed to wearing it. Jason's skill with the greataxe grew, and Coach Brown added a padded spike at the base of the haft. By the end of the first week, he could keep his weapon for two minutes against MacKenzie. Similarly, Mike and Tiff also improved. Tiff's skill with the boken had grown quickly; she and Jason sparred against each other at times.

Coach Brown provided Mike with a pair of tonfas—police-style billy clubs—and he and MacKenzie helped him adapt the weapons to his martial arts techniques. Mike's speed also rose to the point where he could hold his own against Jason's superior strength and reach with the greataxe.

Kyle hadn't found a weapon that he had any aptitude for.

However, with Coach Brown's instruction, he could prevent himself from transforming when he got excited. Most recently, he had tried a padded mace, thinking he might be able to use the weapon while partially transformed into a bear. But he fared little better than he had on the first day.

MacKenzie helped him up from the ground following a leg sweep from her padded glaive. "Yer showin' some improvement, Kyle. You'll learn to fight, but you won't learn it in a week. Don't get discouraged, okay?"

"Yes, Miss MacKenzie. Thanks." Kyle glanced around to find his mace, then stepped off the mat.

"Aliki? You're next," MacKenzie called. "Let's try to find somethin' ye can wield effectively. Remember—pick anything on the stand." She glanced at Tiff and Mike, sparring on the other mat while Coach Brown watched.

Kyle heard her reply, "Yes, ma'am." Then MacKenzie yelped in surprise and pain. With an astonished expression on her face, MacKenzie looked down at the large green stain on her shirt, then at Aliki, still standing by the weapons stand with a paint-gun rifle cradled in her hand.

MacKenzie grinned, and raised her arms in defeat. Everyone broke out in laughter.

"I think we found her talent," Coach Brown snickered. "We're old-fashioned enough that we didn't think much about modern weapons. But I suppose the team could use a sniper."

Aliki carefully returned the rifle back in its place. But she smiled and joined in the laughter.

CHAPTER FOURTEEN
The Sparring Exhibition

The day of the exhibition arrived, and the students gathered in a special assembly in the gym. Coach Brown had fashioned more padded weapons. He had also removed the paint-rifles for safety reasons. Tiff, Jason, and Mike stood beside Coach Brown as part of the demonstration, wearing their padded armor. Aliki and Kyle sat in the front row, next to Miss Olsen.

Paul Oxinos introduced MacKenzie, lauding her talents with weapons. She and Coach Brown stepped onto the mat and sparred against each other in a fierce series of matches. First, Coach Brown used a pair of short wooden swords against MacKenzie's longer one, then MacKenzie employed a short-spear and shield against a long curved wooden sword wielded by the coach. The matches were close, but MacKenzie prevailed both times.

Tiff noted both MacKenzie and Coach Brown had held back the full extent of their talents. She wondered what would happen if both went at full power. "Who knows... they might wreck the gym if they did," she muttered.

Mike and Jason looked at her with puzzled looks.

"I mean if they really both fought with everything they had."
They all chuckled at the thought.

Paul stepped onto the mat. "Now, I want to show you what some of your fellows have learned from Miss Morgan. Jason King, Mike Rhee, and Tiffany Gardner were among several students who we randomly selected to receive special training as part of a new program. They have trained for several weeks, so let's see what they've learned. Many of you know Jason King as an exceptional football linebacker. But he has learned more than how to sack a quarterback."

The collective students gasped as Jason stepped onto the mat, whirling his padded greataxe. He waved at the crowd, and some of his teammates chanted, "Jason... JASON... JASON!"

"All right, Jason. Ye'll be using your full speed and power. Let's really give the students a show."

"Seriously, MacKenzie? Full speed and power?" Jason replied.

"I'll be matchin' you. It's part of Paul's plan." MacKenzie picked a pair of padded wooden short swords from the rack.

Coach Brown shouted, "Begin!" and Jason quickly closed the gap. Tiff wondered if any of the students would notice his unnatural quickness, but the distance was too short for Jason to reach his full speed.

Jason feinted with his axe, then whirled it around to jab with the spike. MacKenzie dodged both the feint and the spike-thrust, but didn't close in where her shortswords would be effective. Jason jumped back to steady himself.

He tried a thrust-feint followed by a powerful swing, but MacKenzie parried the thrust, which fouled his follow-through.

He still managed a strong swing, but it was slower than he expected. She closed in on him, but he brought the axe haft up to block her right sword, then her left.

The bout continued for over three minutes. Finally, after one of Jason's strong swings, MacKenzie whirled to catch the axe-head with one of her swords and used its momentum to yank it out of Jason's hands. The second sword struck Jason in the chest with a smack that echoed throughout the gymnasium. Had he been normal, the blow might have cracked his ribs, despite his padded armor. But he was now tough enough that the blow might only leave a large bruise.

The students gasped and applauded as he and MacKenzie shook hands.

Mike's bout was similar. MacKenzie opted for a mace and buckler against Mike's pair of tonfas. Using the buckler, she parried Mike's attacks until she walloped him with her padded mace. The bout lasted longer than Jason's, though it failed to impress the gathered students.

When it came to Tiff's turn, MacKenzie fought without a weapon. As Tiff stepped onto the mat, Coach Brown whispered to her, "Remember, moderate yourself. Not full speed. You're the con-girl here."

Tiff nodded, remembering their plan. She and MacKenzie sparred as they had in practice, and MacKenzie swept her feet from her and sent her sword flying right after the two-minute mark. As MacKenzie helped her up, she gave Tiff a quick wink.

Tiff retrieved her boken. A few of her fellow cheerleaders cheered for her, and most of the rest of the students gave her polite applause.

Tiff gulped down water from her water bottle as Mr. Oxinos stepped into the center again. "Now, many of you have volunteered to try out for the sparring. But as you can see, MacKenzie is a fierce opponent. So in order to gauge your skill, you'll have to best one of the students here in a sparring match with your choice of weapon. Remember, only students with signed permission slips are allowed to try out."

Carson, Julisha, and several other students quickly formed a line. Carson had been itching to jump into the ring, and Julisha was obviously still curious. Aliki and Kyle joined the others on the mat to help the students into padded armor.

Carson moved around, trying to get the feel of the armor. He called out, "Hey! Is it okay if I fight Tiff? Would that be fair?"

"Are ye judging her to be weaker 'cause she's a girl? Have ye mistaken me for a man?" MacKenzie replied. Many of the students laughed. "Of course you're welcome to choose Tiff."

"Okay! Sounds good to me!" Carson said, stepping onto the mat. He'd selected a padded greataxe similar to Jason's. He gave it a few test swings and announced confidently, "I think I can take her."

Coach Brown whispered to her again, "Full speed, but don't break him. A light bruise is fine."

As soon as the coach shouted "Begin," Carson launched into an attack with his axe. But with Tiff's enhanced reactions, she anticipated his attack. Carson managed a few swings, but Tiff evaded them all. Stepping inside the swing of his axe, Tiff swung her boken directly into his abdomen, knocking his breath out. The entire match took twenty-six seconds.

As Carson wheezed, trying to catch his breath, Tiff smiled

wryly, please that the sound thrashing she'd given him had effectively demonstrated that the match was not as easy as they thought.

Julisha also tried sparring against her, with similar results. After Tiff trounced Julisha, most of the other students chose not to participate. Tiff prevailed over few remaining foolhardy students.

Mr. Oxinos stepped onto the mat again. "This combat demonstration is only part of MacKenzie's instruction. Another part is academic enrichment. These students have spent considerable time researching their chosen weapon and documenting its history, its use in combat, and so forth." He flourished several reports, each apparently from one of the five students. "If you choose to join us, you'll be expected to do the same."

Kyle had written all of the reports himself, since he enjoyed researching and writing articles on historical topics. But most students loathed writing history papers. By linking the research paper with a physical challenge, Mr. Oxinos dissuaded any casual students from trying to join. Most students who took an interest in the physical combat wouldn't be willing to write extra reports.

Mr. Oxinos explained their plan when he visited Kyle earlier that week. Kyle had jumped at the chance to contribute. He'd worked through the night twice, counting on his enhanced stamina to finish the papers. Coach Brown provided a lot of useful information, particularly on weapons manufacturing and the necessary metalworking skills.

Now, at the end of the demonstration, he watched Tiff join her fellow cheerleaders, who seemed even more in awe of her. Mike helped Coach Brown pack away the padded weapons.

Kyle overheard Jason teasing Carson about being beaten so soundly. "So how's it feel to have a cheerleader beat you up?"

Carson glanced away. "Embarrassing, I guess. Hey, do you guys really write a lot of reports and stuff? The weapons stuff seems fun, but writing papers on it? Yuck."

Jason nodded his head vigorously. "Oh, yeah. That's one of the things keeping me busy these days."

Kyle weaved through the crowd toward MacKenzie. The fierce woman had become an instant celebrity. Many students— and even a few teachers—gathered around her, trying to get her attention. Kyle could see the discomfort on her face. Her gaze shifted from person to person, and her forced smile and tense posture revealed that the crowd of admirers bothered her.

He paid attention to which students crowded near MacKenzie though. Julisha was particularly interested in MacKenzie, and Kyle remembered that Julisha fancied herself an author. She wouldn't be so easily dissuaded.

As the crowd dispersed, Kyle summoned his courage and approached Julisha. "You looked pretty good out there," he said.

Julisha looked surprised at his directness. Kyle had never been particularly bold. "Umm... thanks, I guess. But Tiff really gave me a good thumping." She rubbed her stomach where Tiff's blow had landed. "So could Miss Morgan teach me to fight like that?"

"I'm sure she could. But there is a lot more to what we do than sparring and writing reports," Kyle responded. "We also have to camp, learn about animal handling, and even some metaphysical stuff. It's a lot to do, and—"

"That sounds really cool! I'd love to try out!" Julisha gushed. "Where do I sign up?"

Neither his words nor the threat of additional work would deter Julisha, so Kyle decided to let the teachers handle it. "Mr. Oxinos is kind of in charge of everything. But I think all the spots are full."

"I'm sure I can convince him to let me try it!"

Sure enough, Julisha pestered Mr. Oxinos in homeroom on Monday morning about joining the all-skills team. Even though he told her that all the positions were filled, she suggested that she could be an alternate. She continued on Tuesday with the fierce persistence of a child used to getting her way. Finally, on Wednesday, he agreed to let her go camping on their next outing.

Of course, Mr. Oxinos had to hastily schedule a nearby campsite, but he already had a plan.

CHAPTER FIFTEEN
Camping with Julisha

Paul Oxinos arranged for a camping trip ten days later. On that Saturday, the students gathered in the parking lot and helped Coach Brown load tents and other gear into a large van. Julisha's mother dropped her off, along with her new camping backpack and a spare blanket. The other students packed lightly, knowing what they might expect.

"Ready for the war, Julisha?" Mike teased.

"I hope you all are," Ida Olsen answered from her car. She pulled a first aid kit, a cooler full of food, and several containers of water from her car. Jason and Mike hustled to help her with the load. "Dr. Fathy won't be joining us. He's not much for roughing it."

MacKenzie and Coach Brown had already loaded the padded weapons into the van and were discussing the directions to the campsite.

Mr. Oxinos had picked up Kyle and arrived late. By then, everyone else had their gear in either the van or MacKenzie's SUV. MacKenzie had already decided that the girls would ride with her, while the boys would ride in the van. "A good chance for us girls to gossip," she teased.

Paul Oxinos had arranged for a fairly rustic campsite with a few amenities about an hour's drive away. As the students and Coach Brown prepared the camp, MacKenzie pulled Julisha aside and tested her sparring skills while Mr. Oxinos and Ida Olsen explored the wooded areas nearby.

After watching her try several weapons, MacKenzie selected a wooden sword for Julisha, judging that it would be a fairly easy weapon for her to use. During the late morning, MacKenzie worked with all the students, even Julisha. Ida led them on a nature walk, pointing out various plants. Later, Mike brought out a frisbee, and everyone enjoyed a game of Ultimate.

By mid-afternoon, the students and teachers finished unpacking and assembling the tents. Once they finished setting up the campsite, Greg Brown built a campfire and brought out a spit. The late fall weather grew cool, so the students gathered around the fire to keep warm. Paul Oxinos went for a walk in the woods, carrying a hunting bow.

After a bit, he returned, carrying a deer carcass. Ida Olsen had gathered several herbs to use for seasoning while on their nature walk, and the two of them skinned and dressed the deer. Paul told stories about his sister's hunting exploits as they worked.

"Do you do this every time you go camping?" Julisha asked. She tried to maintain a good front despite her obvious discomfort.

"Oh, no," Paul Oxinos responded. "We're fortunate it's deer

season."

"I never pictured you as a hunter, Mr. Oxinos," Julisha said.

"It's been a while, but I keep in practice. My sister is a much better hunter than I am."

Aliki and the other immortal students savored the delicious venison, but Julisha looked uncertain until Kyle urged her to try a taste. Between Miss Olsen's seasoning and Coach Brown's expert care with the cooking, the meat was cooked perfectly. Some fresh vegetables and pumpkin pies from the grocery completed their meal.

After cleaning up the dinner, the teachers organized a capture-the-flag game in the evening light. Kyle, Mike, and Tiff formed one side, while Julisha joined Jason and Aliki on the other. Coach Brown explained the rules and told them he'd be checking on their progress. As he sent them off toward their respective home bases, Aliki thought she saw him give Kyle a wink. Then Aliki noticed Miss Olsen and MacKenzie also entering the game area.

Aliki, Julisha, and Jason quickly decided on a strategy. Jason and Julisha would raid the other team's base, while Aliki served as lookout to intercept any raiders of their base. Julisha challenged Jason to see who could reach the enemy base first. Aliki smiled. To win, a team had to have both their flag and the other team's flag, so defense would be as important as offense.

As the game progressed, Aliki intercepted a clumsy attempt from Mike to capture their flag, but Tiff took advantage of the distraction to snatch the flag and run toward their base. Aliki noticed a similar ruckus near the other team's base, so she assumed Jason or Julisha had succeeded in grabbing the enemy's flag.

As she chased Tiff, she noticed the trees moving about in an unnatural fashion. Ida Olsen was clearly making things more challenging for all of them. *So it's going to be this type of game...*

She whistled a warning, hoping Jason or Julisha could intercept the faster Tiff. She saw Jason sprinting toward their base, the enemy pennant in hand. "Julisha's after our flag," he called. "Go help her!"

Jason returned to their base to secure the enemy pennant. Aliki tried to navigate toward the enemy base, expecting Tiff to reach it soon. Julisha might be able to intercept, but Aliki knew Tiff was faster.

She spotted movement in the trees—a spotted feline shape. Suddenly, she guessed what Coach Brown really had planned. She turned towards him, taking a deep breath, and met his gaze.

"Do you mind a minor bit of mauling? Nothing too serious," Coach Brown asked in his purring feline voice.

Aliki shuddered. "I guess if it could help solve the Julisha problem. Go easy on me."

"As long as you do the same," he purred, amusement evident in his voice.

Aliki wandered away from the coach, hoping to remember her way. She caught up to Julisha, who looked frightened. "There's a bear near the enemy base. How are we supposed to get the flag?" Julisha gasped.

Inwardly, Aliki smiled. Kyle had been busy too. "Let's drop back a bit. Maybe we can go around it. Did Tiff get our flag back to her base?"

"I'm not sure. The bear kind of freaked me out when it saw me and roared."

"Okay... Let's see what other path might lead to the base," Aliki responded, trying to lead Julisha back toward where Coach Brown was waiting.

She didn't even have to pretend to scream as Coach Brown, still in leopard form, pounced. She flailed at the feline body, and felt his claws rake her skin—nowhere vital, and he mercifully didn't try to bite her with any force. But Julisha's screams were even louder.

As Coach Brown continued his attack, Aliki realized his attacks were playful, not menacing. Her family had cats, so she knew how cats played and wrestled. Of course, playing with a house cat was not as intimidating as wrestling with a full-size leopard. But the realization calmed her enough, so she could focus on defending herself.

Then MacKenzie arrived.

"Miss MacKenzie! Help!" Julisha gasped.

MacKenzie apparently ignored Julisha's plea and swore something in Gaelic. "C'mon, lass! That's no way to handle the beast! Have ye forgotten the lessons I taught you?" MacKenzie called.

Julisha looked on in amazement.

MacKenzie continued to shout encouragement, punctuated by Gaelic swearing. Finally, she strode forward and whacked the leopard on the flank with a large stick. He sprang away, growling, and fled into the brush.

"Cop on, girl. I taught you better than that. Let's get you

back to camp." She pulled out a whistle and gave three short blasts on it, signaling the end of the game.

Shortly afterwards, Coach Brown arrived in human form. He carried Aliki back toward camp. Julisha followed, her eyes wide as saucers. She glanced around nervously the entire way back.

Once everyone returned to camp, Ida went to work on Aliki, applying ointment and bandaging the cuts. Jason assisted her, while Tiff and Kyle gathered more firewood. Paul Oxinos played a guitar near the campfire, entertaining the students and trying to calm Julisha's nerves.

Julisha held her legs to her chest and stared at the fire. Mike sat down beside her.

"Are you okay? That must have been scary," he asked. She had been crying.

"Is... is she going to be okay?" Julisha stammered through her tears.

Mike nodded. "We've had much worse. Miss Olsen is a wonder at patching us up. Once Kyle got mauled by a...." He paused, remembering the titan. "I think it was a grizzly or something. But he's fine now."

"And it doesn't scare you?"

"A van hit me at the mall, remember? I almost died." Mike's voice trailed off as he remembered the events of that fateful day. He still sometimes felt like he should have died.

He took a deep breath and continued. "But I'm sure you can find a way to manage."

On Sunday morning, the teachers divided the students. Coach Brown led Tiff and Kyle into a separate clearing, and MacKenzie took Mike and Jason to a nearby field where they practiced sparring. Ida Olsen remained with Julisha and Aliki near the campsite.

Julisha watched as Miss Olsen helped Aliki into her tent to change her bandages. With no one else nearby, she worried about wild animal attacks. She thought she heard a bear growling again and spotted an eagle in the trees gazing at her.

After about an hour, the other students returned, only to switch teachers. Mike accompanied Coach Brown, while Mr. Oxinos led Jason and Kyle into the woods. MacKenzie asked her to join a sparring session with Tiff, and she gladly tried to lose herself in the fierce woman's instruction.

After a lunch of sandwiches and leftover venison, Mr. Oxinos asked Julisha and Tiff to join him while the others began to strike camp. He led them to a small clearing and sat down. Julisha followed, though she felt terrified. She felt Tiff's reassuring hand on her shoulder.

Julisha sat beside him, but kept glancing into the woods. "Mr. Oxinos? What happens if the cougar, or whatever it was, attacks again?" She could feel the eyes of animals on her, but tried not to shake in front of Mr. Oxinos.

"I don't think we have to worry about that. We gave it as much of a scare as it gave us," he replied.

"But..."

"If you want to continue with this, you must conquer your fear. That's the first step. All of them," he said, gesturing toward Tiff, then vaguely across the clearing towards the other students, "have had to face some severe challenges. Facing danger is a part of this team."

Julisha tried to focus on his words and not her uneasiness. "Are there similar programs at other schools? I've never heard of this before."

"This concept is relatively new, and the only one of its kind. We don't want to advertise it yet, in case it doesn't succeed. We do have a fairly ambitious program."

"But won't Aliki's parents freak when they see all those scars? How will you explain them?"

"You'll see. When Kyle got injured, we told his parents he fell out of a tree."

Julisha became more suspicious. "Wait! You mean when he got attacked by the grizzly? His parents thought those wounds were from falling out of a tree? They must be the most gullible people in the world!"

Mr. Oxinos looked amused. "A grizzly... now that's ironic. Who told you about that?"

"Mike did." Julisha suddenly became convinced something more was going on. "It wasn't a grizzly, was it? Wait a minute— is this some sort of survival combat competition between schools? Did he get hurt fighting against another school team?"

"No. Nothing of the sort. You've been reading too many fantasy books. We're not sure what Kyle ran into, but I think it might have been a badger, or maybe a small bear. Anyway, part of what we're teaching is self-reliance and survival skills, true. But we're also teaching some other things, considerably beyond a normal school curriculum."

He paused, as if considering his words carefully. Suddenly,

Julisha saw something reddish moving in the underbrush. She guessed it might be a fox. She held her breath, unsure what to do.

Mr. Oxinos noticed her reaction and followed her gaze. He tossed a small stick toward the fox, and it dashed away. A smirk passed over his face.

"What kinds of things are they learning?" Julisha asked.

"Combat, obviously, and how to avoid injury. Hunting and similar skills. Self-control and discipline and the necessary mental fortitude. You'll get hurt—possibly seriously—if you continue. Beyond that, they're learning some truths about the world that you would normally learn much later in life. It isn't an easy set of tasks we've set before them. You have to seriously consider if you're willing to endure the hardships. Could you handle the type of mauling you saw Aliki suffer?"

Julisha pulled her legs to her chest again. "I don't know."

Monday morning came, and a normal mix of chatter about weekend activities filled Mr. Oxinos' classroom. Kyle read some obscure book he had borrowed from Coach Brown, while Jason listened to Pete brag about a high score on an online game. Tiff sat with the other cheerleaders, planning a shopping expedition and speculating on who would ask each of them out for the homecoming dance.

Mike watched Julisha carefully. She sat with Kate, but was unusually quiet.

"How was the camping trip?" Kate asked her friend.

"Okay, I guess," Julisha responded with no excitement in her voice.

"Did anything interesting happen?" Kate's face showed she was hoping for a more engaging answer.

But Julisha gazed toward Aliki's empty seat. "No. Nothing really happened."

Kate continued her questions. "Are you going to camp with them again?"

Julisha glanced toward Jason, then Kyle. "I don't know," she answered.

With no satisfying answers from Julisha, Kate finally gave up.

When Aliki entered the classroom a few minutes later, Mike noticed Julisha's eyes widen in surprise. He guessed she expected Aliki to be absent for a few days because of her injuries. Aliki took off her jacket, revealing the short sleeve blouse she wore underneath.

Julisha slowly walked over to Aliki's desk, staring at her as she approached. She looked up and down Aliki's arms.

"Hi, Julisha. How are you doing this morning?" Aliki asked, an innocent smile on her face.

"B-but your wounds..." Julisha stuttered, incredulously.

"Wounds?" Aliki responded.

Julisha walked back to her desk slowly, a shell-shocked look on her face. Mike stood and intercepted her. "Are you okay, Julisha? You look like you saw a space alien."

"B-but the claw marks... H-how?" she stammered again.

"Is there something wrong, Julisha?" Mr. Oxinos called from his desk.

Julisha looked at him, then Aliki. "No, sir," she said with a small voice, and returned to her seat.

Jason sat eating lunch with his buddies when Julisha tapped him on the shoulder. "Can we talk? I need to figure some things out."

"Sure," Jason replied. "Hold on a minute." He stuffed the last of his burger into his mouth, wrapped some fries in a napkin, and put the rest in the trash. Jason ignored the snickers from Pete and Carson.

He followed Julisha to a bench outside. "Is this about the weekend?"

"Yeah," she said in a subdued voice. "I'm not sure I'm cut out for it. I mean, attacks by wild animals, wounds disappearing overnight, mysterious teachers. What's it all about, Jason?"

Jason ate a few of his fries while he tried to think of a good response. "Well, the teachers know best. But yeah, it gets intense."

"Have you ever been hurt yet? I mean like Aliki or Kyle."

"Not yet, but I wouldn't be surprised if it did happen. So why did you want to join this group anyway?"

"Well, the weapons fighting seemed fun—and it was. I could even get used to the camping. But things like Mr. Oxinos suddenly becoming a bow hunter seem weird. And getting hurt like Aliki did—that scares me. She could have died."

"From what I hear, MacKenzie and Coach Brown had things under control. They turned the attack into an impromptu think-on-your-feet training. They do that a lot."

"Coach Brown wasn't there," Julisha countered, looking at

him curiously.

"Oh, right," Jason said, realizing his mistake. "But anyway, I'm sure there's lots of other fun things you could do instead. No need for you to get yourself hurt."

"So why do you do it? You have plenty of excitement playing football."

"I made the commitment, and I stand by it. And I'm learning a lot. Even if I play football in college, there's only a small chance I could go pro. I'm not the greatest at academics, so I need to learn other skills. What about you? Is this really something you'd want?"

Jason waited for an answer, but Julisha sat, lost in thought. He stood and spoke with a gentle voice. "You might be happier forgetting all of this. I've had to face some harsh failures. Before I started this, I excelled at sports and physical activity." He paused, remembering the frustration he felt in the Animal Realm when he couldn't master any forms. "But I failed at our last real task, and that still hurts."

Julisha turned to look at him again. He couldn't read her expression. Sadness, maybe. "Thanks, Jason."

The next day, Julisha told Mr. Oxinos she wouldn't continue. He could tell she hadn't slept much last night. He guessed she'd been wrestling with her decision.

"I understand," he said as kindly as he could. "Perhaps there is some way you could still help out occasionally. I've already talked to MacKenzie about having a student workshop for weapon sparring. Other students have also asked about it, so she's agreed to schedule a regular workshop after school after the winter holidays."

She brightened a bit. "Thank you, sir."

"You're welcome. Now, spend some time checking over your homework."

CHAPTER SIXTEEN
Homecoming

The next week was homecoming week, and the students all found themselves busy with both schoolwork and preparations for the games and the dance. Jason's junior varsity game was on Thursday night, with the varsity game on Friday and the dance on Saturday. Jason spent long afternoons practicing with the team and the coaches to prepare. Likewise, Tiff and the rest of the cheerleaders drilled their jumps, dance moves, and cheers. Mike found himself busy with band preparations as well—the marching band was planning a half-time spectacle for Friday night's game.

On Monday morning during homeroom, the selections for Homecoming King and Queen were announced. Two seniors were chosen to be King and Queen. But Jason and Tiff were shocked to discover that they had been selected to be the Prince and Princess.

Mr. Oxinos' entire homeroom class applauded for them. Jason looked embarrassed, while Tiff simply smiled.

Julisha teased, "And she'll knock anyone who disagrees on their butt!" That got a good round of laughter. Even Mr. Oxinos chuckled.

The Thursday night junior varsity game began with homecoming festivities. As Prince and Princess of Homecoming, Jason and Tiff entered in a convertible, waving at the crowd. Tiff wore a beautiful rose-colored dress, and Jason wore a blue tux which matched the school colors. Tiff thanked everyone and said some encouraging words to the football team and the student body. Jason simply stood and looked slightly uncomfortable.

After the convertible drove them off the field, they both dashed to their respective locker rooms to change. Jason hurried back to the field in his football gear. Tiff carefully hung her dress and put on her cheerleading uniform. Then the Jefferson Hill Javelineers faced the Wilson City Wildcats on the football field.

Midway through the third quarter, the brawl started. Jefferson Hill led 21-10, and some of the Wildcat players had grown frustrated at their inability to stop the Javelineer blitz. Jason had restrained his full skills as much as he could, but Pete, who played safety, had just sacked the quarterback in a safety blitz. On the next play, two of the Wildcats linemen jabbed Felipe, one of the defensive linemen, in the ribs during the play. The referee didn't see it, but the Javelineer defense did.

As Felipe held his bruised side, several of the Javelineer players retaliated, and soon the linemen on both sides were engaged in a melee. The referee tried to stop the brawl, but the tensions had gotten too high.

Jason had seen the cheap shots from the opposing team, but as captain of the defense, he knew he should set a good example.

So he grabbed the first Javelineer brawler he could reach, and forcefully yanked him out of the fight. He moved to the second one, fending off several punches from Wildcat players in the meantime.

He continued to push or hurl his own teammates out of the fight. "This is a football game! Not a street brawl! We're not going to sink to their level, so sit on your butts until you cool off!" he yelled at them.

Finally, he turned to the Wildcat players with a fierce glare. He growled, "If any of you still want to fight, I dare any of you to throw another punch at me. I can take any or all of you on. But this ends now!"

Fortunately, none of the Wildcats accepted his challenge.

Jason turned to the referee to discuss the fight. "Sir, I apologize for my team's conduct. But two of the Wildcats linemen hurt Felipe Torres with illegal rib punches." He pointed to where a replacement player and the defensive coach talked with Felipe, who had removed his helmet and held his side.

Nearby, he noticed the Wildcat quarterback and one of the running backs talking. The two of them approached the referee and joined their discussion. The quarterback glowered, but as the referee watched, he offered his hand to Jason. "You're nuts, but fair. Robbie told me he saw what happened." He confirmed Jason's statements, and the referee ejected the two Wildcat linemen from the game.

The Javelineer coaches lambasted the players involved in the brawl for several minutes, then benched them until the fourth quarter. Felipe also sat out for several plays nursing his ribs, then returned to the game amid cheers from the crowd.

After the game, Jason shook hands with the members of the opposing team and tried to ignore the sullen and angry looks from some Wildcats players. When he shook hands with the Wildcat quarterback, he gave a genuine smile and tried to project a friendly air. He hoped that despite the brawl and hurt feelings, they could eventually be friends.

No brawl spoiled the Friday night varsity homecoming game. A clear, cool night provided the perfect weather for the game. Both Aliki and Kyle watched the game and the performance with their respective families. MacKenzie also watched from the stands, occasionally yelling either cheers or the occasional insult when the team made a bad play.

Mike performed with the rest of the marching band, and they dazzled the audience with their spectacular performance at halftime. Tiff and Jason attended in their role of Homecoming Prince and Princess.

Ultimately, Jefferson Hill's team fell to their rivals, the Sanderburg Stallions. But the mood remained festive.

The homecoming dance on Saturday was an elaborate affair. The school cafeteria had been transformed into a festive dance hall, complete with streamers and helium-filled balloons. Most of the students who attended wore formal clothes; the girls looked beautiful in their dresses, and the boys fidgeted in suits or tuxedos.

Aliki didn't have a date for the dance, but came anyway. Though she felt self-conscious, she wanted the experience. To put her parents' mind at ease, she told them that Mike had asked her to the dance. But Mike hung out with a group of his friends from band, who seemed to be goofing off more than dancing. Kyle didn't attend the dance, feeling too shy and awkward.

So Aliki watched the other students. She watched as the Homecoming King and Queen led the first dance of the evening, and saw Jason awkwardly dance with Tiff during the next song. She chuckled a bit inside—he was so graceful on the football field, or even when he sparred against MacKenzie. But the dance floor seemed to be his nemesis.

The dance ended, and the next song started. Jason sought the company of his fellow jocks, taking comfort in their shared discomfort. Most had cooled off and forgiven him after the brawl, but Aliki noticed that a few of them still glared at him when he wasn't looking.

Coach Brown helped to chaperone the dance and looked splendid in his tux. She wandered over towards him. During the next break in the music, she told him, "I think some of the football players are still angry at Jason. I saw them giving him some angry looks behind his back."

Coach Brown nodded. "I'm sure Jason can handle it. But it may be good to let him know some other time."

She danced with Mike for a few dances. Unlike Jason, he was clearly comfortable on the dance floor. After he rejoined his friends, she chatted with a few acquaintances, but mostly just watched.

Jason, seeing her standing alone, crossed the dance floor towards her. "Um... want to dance?" he asked.

"I thought you didn't like dancing," she answered.

"I'm not good at it. Tiff had to tell me what to do while we were out there."

"You looked fine. But I don't really know how to dance either."

"I was faking it." He held out his hand. "Come on. Let's fake it together."

She grinned and took his hand.

She enjoyed letting loose during the first peppy dance. The energetic music was too loud for her to talk, so she matched Jason's smile with her own. Then the next song started—a slow ballad. Aliki held his hand for a moment. Jason got the hint and tried leading them both through the dance.

As awkward as it was, Aliki felt wonderful.

CHAPTER SEVENTEEN
Holidays

With homecoming behind them, the junior varsity football team only had one more game after the Thanksgiving holiday. Jason sat on the bench during Monday afternoon's football practice, pondering uncharacteristically. The coaches planned to play the second-string in the last game. Jason's presence there was largely to support his teammates.

Coach Brown had mentioned to him that some of the players still held a grudge after he'd stopped the fight. But that wasn't what bothered him. Even before becoming immortal, he'd had superior physical skill and ability, and he'd led a Javelineer defense that had dominated most of the games they played.

But with his immortal prowess, he found no challenge in the game. He could easily break through the opposing line and sack the quarterback on every play. He wanted to be part of a team, not the superstar.

After practice, his mother picked him up. His younger sister Helen moped in the back seat. She was ten, in the fifth grade, and used to having her mother's undivided attention after school.

"Hey, squirt! How was your day?" he said, getting into the

front seat.

"MOM! He called me squirt!" Helen whined.

His mother admonished him. "Jason... Don't tease your sister."

Jason smiled. He welcomed the normal family banter—a refreshing change from school, football, and the challenges of immortality. "Hey, Mom? What are we having for dinner tonight?" he asked.

"Steaks. Do you want to help me cook them?" his mother responded.

"I DO!" Helen yelled from the back seat.

"You'll burn them, squirt!" Jason teased.

"MOM!"

Jason had to laugh.

Kyle visited the county library after school. He'd already exhausted the school library's world history section. But he found that, like the school library, most of the world history books in the public library focused on European history, with some recounting Asian history. He selected a few on various topics, including a copy of *Romance of the Three Kingdoms*, but he found little on African history outside of ancient Egypt.

Kyle wandered over toward the library computers to search the other libraries in the county system. He spotted Dr. Fathy at one of the computers, alternately writing on a notepad and typing on the keyboard. So he decided his search for history books could wait.

"Hello, Dr. Fathy," he said. "Are you finding anything

interesting?"

Dr. Fathy looked at him and replied in a soft voice. "I'm using the computers for another investigation I'm pursuing. I'm also taking notes about the history of this area. I thought that might give a clue about why our large friend arrived here of all places."

"But he didn't arrive here..." Kyle began, confused.

Dr. Fathy lowered his voice even further. "The realms reflect this reality, remember?"

"Oh... of course, sir." Kyle felt embarrassed. He should have remembered how features in the Animal Realm resembled the school. "Any luck?"

"Not yet. So what brings you to the library?"

"I like to read about history. I've read most of the history books in our school library. I've read all about European history and colonization and a lot about the Roman Empire and that era. I've read about Egypt, but it's hard to find books about some of the sub-Saharan cultures and kingdoms. I hoped the county libraries might have some good books to read," Kyle explained.

Dr. Fathy gestured for Kyle to sit beside him. "So what languages do you know? What can you read?"

"Just English," Kyle admitted. "And a little French, but I couldn't read a book in French."

"If you're going to be a historian, you'll want to learn to read many of the ancient languages. But perhaps I can help. I do have some books of my own. I could loan them to you, if you promise to be careful with them."

Kyle grew excited. "Yes, sir!"

"Look for them in a few days. Now, if you don't mind..."

"Thank you, sir!" Kyle answered, leaving Dr. Fathy to his work.

Two days later, a small package arrived at Kyle's house. Inside were three books and a return envelope. One was a modern book on African tribes during the colonial era. Another was a diary from the previous century, translated from Egyptian, describing the author's travels through sub-Saharan Africa. The last looked ancient, but when Kyle opened the book, the pages looked strange. They weren't made of paper, but of some sort of plastic sheet. Furthermore, the text wasn't in English, but some strange language.

Kyle sighed and muttered, "I guess he gave me the wrong book. I said I only could read English." But as he watched, the characters rearranged themselves into English text.

Kyle looked at the pages with amazement. He spent the next several hours reading the mysterious book.

Thanksgiving Day at Aliki's house was typically busy. Aliki and her two older sisters Malva and Giada helped their mother prepare the Thanksgiving dinner in the kitchen. The family had decided to have a traditional Greek feast, rather than a turkey. So the sisters occasionally bickered as they each tried to add their own touch to the dishes.

Aliki's younger brother Leander watched the parades on television while Aliki's father and Malva's husband chatted in the family room.

The doorbell rang. Simultaneously, Aliki and Giada shouted, "I'll get it!" and raced toward the door.

"Giada! He's Aliki's guest!" their mother admonished. Chastised, Giada stopped and let Aliki open the door.

Mr. Oxinos stood in the doorway. "Thank you for the invitation, Aliki."

"Please come in. I'm so glad you could come." Aliki led him into the house. "Mom? Dad? Mr. Oxinos is here." She introduced each of her siblings.

Mr. Oxinos offered a bottle of wine and a covered pan filled with pastries to Aliki's mother. "I made *kantaifi*," he said. "Thank you so much for the invitation, Mrs. Papadaki. Mr. Papadakis, it is good to see you again," he said, shaking her father's hand.

Her father smiled warmly. "Please join us in the family room while they finish making dinner. It can get pretty scary in there while they work, so it's best to stay clear."

So Paul Oxinos and her father spent time reminiscing about Greece, talking about the many historic sites, beautiful beaches, and favorite restaurants. Once the dinner was ready, they all gathered at the table for a scrumptious feast.

As they dined, Aliki's mother engaged Mr. Oxinos in conversation. "So do you have family in the area?"

Mr. Oxinos sipped some wine. "I have a sister, but she's out of the country right now. No other family."

"Living alone as a bachelor. My my..." Her mother had an odd look in her eye. "Malva's already married such a nice young man." Malva's husband, engrossed with her father in a discussion about soccer, didn't notice.

Her mother continued. "Aliki has told us so much about you. She loves it there. My other daughter Giada is a first-year medical student. She's doing well in her classes and will be a fine doctor some day."

Giada smiled at Mr. Oxinos as her mother continued to brag about Giada's education and many fine qualities. Aliki noticed Giada eying Mr. Oxinos and realized her mother was trying to play matchmaker. She felt a little confused about it, but reassured herself that Giada had little chance of enticing Mr. Oxinos.

The students took a break from their training during the month of December so they could study for tests, prepare for holiday events, and enjoy the holidays.

The school held its annual Winter Concert, featuring the band, chorus, and smaller musical numbers. Mike and Aliki played as part of the full band, performing numerous holiday songs. Mike also performed a few lively holiday tunes as part of a jazz brass ensemble. Both Mr. Oxinos and MacKenzie watched the performance, chatting with each other.

After the performance, the band students returned to the band room to pack their instruments. When Mike returned to the auditorium, he noticed Mr. Oxinos having a conversation with his mother, as well as Aliki's parents. A mob of other students surrounded MacKenzie; Mike guessed they were pestering her with questions about the sparring exhibition, Ireland, or personal details.

Turning his attention back to his mother, Mike worried that she and Aliki's parents might start probing Mr. Oxinos about the details of their training. He thought about trying to eavesdrop, but with all of the parents, children and teachers chatting with each other, the noise was deafening. He even considered using his fox ears, but quickly decided he wouldn't be able to pinpoint their conversation, even with sharpened hearing.

Mike glanced around, looking for his siblings. Sure enough, his brother and sister were chasing each other around the crowded auditorium. Worried that they might hurt themselves or trip someone, he walked towards his mother and Mr. Oxinos. He put on his best smile as he entered the circle of adults.

"Hello, Mr. O. Hi, mom. Carol and James are chasing each other around. We might want to leave soon."

"It's okay, Mike," his mother responded. "They're not hurting anyone. You remember Mr. and Mrs. Papadakis. We met them when they dropped Aliki off for one of those training trips, remember?"

"Um... yeah. We've been doing a lot of training together," Mike mumbled.

"Yes. We were discussing that," his mother replied. "Has anything strange happened on these outings?"

"Well, Kyle fell out of a tree and got hurt on one of the trips, but other than that, nothing really," Mike lied.

"What's this we've heard about combat training?" Aliki's father asked.

"Oh, yeah. We had a special combat trainer too. I think it was to help build self-confidence or something," Mike answered. He looked over at MacKenzie. "She's right over there," he said, pointing her out.

MacKenzie looked back at them and smiled. It was obviously forced; Mike imagined that a trapped wolverine would have looked calmer. She really didn't enjoy being in crowds.

Mr. Oxinos reassured the parents. "She takes special care to make sure the students aren't hurt. Mike mentioned that he's gotten less bruises from her than from taekwondo." He paused, smiled, and suggested, "Mike? Perhaps you should rescue MacKenzie before she forgets where she is."

Mike nodded and headed toward the cluster of students around MacKenzie. As he left, Mr. Oxinos smiled broadly and said, "Let me tell you about some of the growth that we've seen in each of your children over the course of this program."

CHAPTER EIGHTEEN
The Primal Realm

January arrived along with cold temperatures, more schoolwork, and, for the immortal students, more training. With school in session again, Mr. Oxinos planned for more excursions for the immortal students. So on the following weekend, Aliki and the others gathered once again in the gym, along with all five of the senior immortals. MacKenzie looked bored, but Dr. Fathy chatted with Ida Olsen. Coach Brown checked the doors to ensure they were locked and prevent any accidental witnesses.

Mr. Oxinos addressed the students. "It's time for you to venture to another realm. This one is more dynamic and a bit more dangerous than the Animal Realm, but it's also one of the more useful realms to master. We're traveling to the Primal Realm, also sometimes known as the Elemental Realm."

Jason asked, "You mean like iron, gold, that sort of stuff?" Aliki had wondered the same thing.

Mr. Oxinos shook his head. "No. Think more of the classic elements—earth, air, fire, water. But other cultures had other primal elements too—lightning, wood, and metal for instance. The Primal Realm is where these concepts come from. Matter there is formed of those more pure substances."

Dr. Fathy added, "Believe it or not, we've even noticed the emergence of plastic as an elemental material over the past century. The Primal Realm and the Animal Realm are the most common realms for immortals to attune to. That is why your teachers initiated you with the Animal Realm. And now we will be visiting the Primal Realm."

"So we're going to try to find our primal element there, right?" Tiff asked. "So, out of curiosity, which elements are each of you attuned to?"

"Metal and fire for me," Coach Brown answered. "Paul is attuned to light, as you've already seen, and wood for Ida."

"So you can attune to more than one?" Aliki asked.

"Yes. You may be able to attune to more than one form in any of the realms. It all depends on your aptitudes. We have not determined how or why some of us can attune to multiple forms in one realm, but fail to attune to any in another," Dr. Fathy responded.

"Let's get this show on the road," MacKenzie muttered.

Coach Brown whispered to Jason, in a stage-whisper clearly meant to be heard, "She's grumpy because she never managed to attune to the Primal Realm." MacKenzie turned to glare at him, but he gave her a smile in return.

Dr. Fathy tried to soothe her. "Remember, I am not strongly attuned to any element either, MacKenzie. Just slightly attuned to all of them."

"What does it mean to be slightly attuned?" Mike asked.

"I can manipulate them to a small degree, but cannot transform into any particular element. Nor can I create the element, as Paul can with light," Dr. Fathy responded. "We have found that each person who attunes to the Primal Realm does so in different ways. Some are able to transform fully into the element. Others create the element, producing small jets of flame or gusts of wind, for instance. The variance is truly fascinating."

"First, the students need these," Mr. Oxinos interrupted. He held some clothing for the students to change into. Rather than the loose tunics and shorts they used for the Animal Realm, he held sleeveless shirts and shorts that looked like they were made of a thick plastic. "Fireproof and impermeable to water. We don't want you burning your clothes off or splashing out of them," Mr. Oxinos said with a smile.

The students went into their respective locker rooms to change and returned a few minutes later. The clothes weren't particularly comfortable. But the students gathered around the teachers, anxious to see what this new realm was like.

The world changed. Aliki felt wet, then hot, and images of stone and glass filled her mind. Winds drifted through her hair. Finally, the sensations stopped, and Aliki opened her eyes.

"And here we are," Dr. Fathy announced.

Jason looked around the transformed gymnasium and at the other students. Just as with the Animal Realm, each of the students' bodies had taken the form of a mishmash of primal elements in the Primal realm. He noticed that, unlike the Animal Realm, the transformation wasn't stable—different parts of their bodies were changing from one element to another at random. The teachers, including MacKenzie, all looked normal.

He looked at himself. Currently, one of his shins was fire, changing to metal above the knee. Earth made up his other leg, and a mix of plastic and glass comprised his torso. He looked at his watery left arm, then at his right arm... *Where's my arm? Oh, it's made of air.* As he watched, the wind-arm slowly transformed into light.

The elemental version of the school itself was also composed of different primal elements, but they didn't change over time. The gym room was roughly the same size, but made from a combination of stone, metal, and electricity in most areas, plus water and air roughly where the plumbing lines and air conditioning ducts ran in the walls and floors of the real school. He saw no doors, only openings, and the roof was apparently made of air or not present at all, giving the room the feel of a large arena. Jason noticed some markings on the ground and tried to imagine elementals playing some type of sport.

Beyond the open doors, only a few smaller buildings clustered around the primal version of the gym. Jason wondered about it, but assumed that not everything matched in each realm.

Once he and the others had surveyed themselves and their surroundings, each teacher paired off with one of the students, and led them into different areas of the elemental school. Jason stayed with Coach Brown in the gym-arena, and listened to him describe attuning.

"Each element within the Primal Realm has its own distinct characteristics. Focus on those, and how they relate to you. For instance, if you focus on stone, imagine becoming more solid, harder, denser. If you focus on winds, think of yourself as a drifting breeze or fierce gale."

Jason first concentrated on fire. Like most young men, fire captivated him. He had spent many nights as a Boy Scout building campfires. He imagined himself catching fire, being very hot, even exploding. But he had little luck attuning. "So how does the fire work for you, Coach Brown?" Jason asked, trying to puzzle it out.

"Like this," he replied, and his hands and forearms ignited. Fascinated, Jason examined the coach's arms. Though still flesh and blood, Coach Brown's forearms were surrounded by an aura of flame. "I'm more talented with metal, but the fire comes to me. I can use the two together in my forgework."

"So you really made that fancy sword I saw in the metalworking room?" Jason asked.

"Of course. Metalwork is one of my real passions. Football coaching is... Well, it's kept me busy for a few decades and provides a good workout," the coach responded. "I try to keep my hand in at the forge whenever I can."

"So why don't you take over as the metalwork teacher? I'm sure you could teach Mr. Johnson a thing or two."

"Yes, I could. But a specialist teacher only instructs a small fraction of the students. An athletic coach has more influence within the school. Furthermore, you've learned to hold back when playing football. I've had to do the same with metalworking."

Jason looked expectantly at the coach. Reading his expression, Coach Brown manifested some of his metal ability. His brown skin turned to steel or some other metal, and the coach created a bar of metal from between his hands. He handed the bar to Jason. "That's pure iron. Good for forging. See if you can do anything with it."

But the metal bar did not respond to Jason's efforts. He tried feeling the metal with his mind. Then he tried tensing his muscles, trying to mimic the iron's hardness. But after fifteen minutes, the iron bar was just a bar to him. "No luck, sir."

"Don't give up. There are several other elements you can try."

MacKenzie looked on as Mike experimented with different elements, trying to make any of them manifest. "Try fire again," she suggested. "Foxes and fire go hand in hand."

Despite her encouragement, Mike could hear her frustration in her few comments. He guessed that without an elemental affinity or a foe to fight, she felt useless. But he followed her instruction and continued experimenting.

"Think about what ye like, lad. From what I understand, ye're naturally drawn to things that you could attune to," MacKenzie advised, hoping something would help.

"Well, I like music and art. Is there an element of music?"

"Not in this realm, lad. But ye're a creative type. This realm should appeal to you. There's much to create with."

Mike thought about the different elements and spent an hour trying to attune his body to one of them. He imagined transforming into each of the primal elements, but nothing worked. Remembering Mr. Oxinos' command over light, he visualized himself radiating light, fire and wind. Trying a different tactic, he traced symbols and doodled in the ground with his finger. When that failed, he let his mind wander to elemental-themed game characters and superheroes. Finally, he needed a break.

"You're from Ireland, right?" he asked. He was curious about the fierce woman.

"Yes, originally. I spent my earliest years in Ulster. Once I became immortal, I mostly traveled between modern Scotland, Wales, and Ireland. I'm a Celt, but I traveled a lot. Wherever a troublesome warlord or noble caused a ruckus, I would visit them and deal with the problem. Me and my sisters."

"You had sisters?"

"Two." Her eyes grew distant. "We haven't seen each other for a few years."

"Wait, your sisters are immortal too?"

"Yes. We're so similar, we're sometimes confused with each other. We even have similar aptitudes and talents. Last I checked, one was travelin' through the Middle East, the other wanderin' through Europe."

Mike thought for a bit. "I never thought about my family growing old without me. I have a little brother and sister."

"It's hard. But ye'll be able to look after their children, and their children's children."

"Can we have children, MacKenzie?"

She burst into laughter. "Comin' on ta me, lad, are ye? I think ye're still a bit young."

Mike thought for a moment, then blushed. "I mean... um..."

"I know what ye meant, lad. And yes, sometimes we do have children. But most of us don't want the pain of watching our own child die. Though the immortality sometimes passes to a child, it usually doesn't."

Mike decided to change the subject. "Well, I think I'll try to experiment with more elements for a bit. I haven't heard the coach's whistle to call us for lunch yet."

She smiled and continued to watch.

"MacKenzie? Do you have any idea why you can't attune to this realm?"

She thought for a moment. "Nothing for certain. But remember that I mentioned this realm should appeal to you because you're a creative person?"

"Of course."

MacKenzie's voice was distant and had a strange tone. "I'm not a creative person. Far from it."

Ida Olsen took Kyle outside, and they wandered toward a group of trees. Kyle noticed that the trees seemed to be made entirely of wood, though the wooden leaves were still green. The ground was pure dirt or rock, and he drank from a refreshingly pure water spring. Even the sun looked like an actual ball of flame.

Miss Olsen sat near the trees and relaxed. Kyle looked down at her blonde hair, which was in its usual braid. They were from different cultures, and even different centuries, but he felt like he could relax around her.

"Calm yourself and try to reach for the elements. Focus on one at a time. See if you can intuitively grasp the reality of that element," she said with a calming voice.

But after a few hours, he'd tried to attune to each element, with no success. He tried to maintain his composure, but found it difficult. "The bear was so easy. Why is this so hard?"

Seeing his frustration, Ida replied gently, "Perhaps because the bear was so easy. You didn't have to even try to attune to the Animal Realm. Here, it's different. You seem to have an aptitude for animals beyond the bear. Remember your conversation with the dog?"

"Yes, but—"

"So you're strongly attuned to the Animal Realm. But that could make attuning to other realms more challenging," Ida said.

Kyle paused, remembering his efforts. "I thought I felt something a few minutes ago, but I'm not sure."

"What did it feel like, Kyle? And which element were you attempting to attune to?" she asked eagerly.

"Either earth or wood. I forget which. It felt like I could feel something beyond my senses. It was a little like sensing as the bear, but different."

"You're likely attuning to one of the elements and using it as a sensor." She walked over near a tree and put her hand on one of the tree branches, gripping it tightly. She drove the point of her opposite foot into the ground. "Now try and sense me, either through the ground or through the wood."

Kyle tried attuning with each. After a few minutes, he felt something poking him in the... no, it wasn't his ribs... or his leg... or.... He answered, "I think I can feel your foot poking into me, or the ground, or something."

"So it seems you have an earth sense. Very useful, especially to a bear." She smiled. "Good job."

Kyle had always wondered what a big sister would be like. He imagined that she might be a lot like Ida. "I'm glad you're helping me, Miss Olsen."

Aliki sat on the floor of the elemental gym, gazing at Mr. Oxinos. She hadn't discovered any element she could attune to yet, so she asked Mr. Oxinos for some demonstrations. At first, he caused his hand to glow, as she'd seen before. Then he increased his glow throughout his body, becoming so bright she had to turn away. Finally, he dimmed his light and glowed only faintly, giving his body a godlike aura.

Aliki watched him carefully. She tried to imagine radiating fire, water, or any other element instead of light. Of course, Mr. Oxinos was handsome enough that she didn't mind having an excuse to gaze at him—particularly when his glow made him look like an ancient Greek god.

"... and by varying the intensity, you can produce different effects. Aliki?"

She had let her mind wander, but refocused herself. "Yes, sir," she stammered. "Let me try again."

She had already tried water several times, as well as earth, fire, and air. She'd tried to change her body into wood or metal. Lightning scared her a little, but she tried to generate electricity. She even tried rubbing her hands on some plastic to generate static, but that didn't seem to work here. She'd tried plastic, glass, and even a few other things she thought she'd seen here. No luck yet.

What am I missing? she thought to herself. She called to Mr. Oxinos. "Are there any other elements I haven't tried? I've tried everything I can think of here."

"Give it some time. I'm sure something will work," he answered. But he didn't sound completely confident.

"Is there some other element? Like soul or radiation?" she asked.

"Did you try cold?" he suggested.

"Isn't cold the absence of heat?"

"It is in our world. But here, cold is a separate element. You overlooked it because you thought of it as not-heat. Give it a try."

She obediently did, thinking of snowflakes, ice skating, and shivering in the snow. But that failed to feel anything different.

She flopped onto her back. "Aargh. It's no use."

"Relax for a moment. You've been trying for a while. A little mental relaxation goes a long way. You just need something to inspire you, and inspiration usually comes when you're more relaxed."

She turned her head to look at him. She grinned, thinking the other girls in her class would be jealous of her if they knew she was spending time with their handsome teacher. He still glowed too. Evidently, he didn't need to concentrate to keep the glow active.

She remembered him talking about cold. If cold wasn't the absence of heat, but a separate element, perhaps... She sat up suddenly and thought of shadows and night. It seemed right.

Mr. Oxinos stared at her.

"What?" she asked.

"Darkness," he said. "You're dimming the light around you." He stopped glowing. "Wait a moment." He pulled a satchel from somewhere and opened it. He looked through it and found a

160

small mirror. Holding it carefully, he turned it so Aliki could see herself in the mirror.

Almost like a dark smoke, a wispy, insubstantial aura of darkness surrounded her. She felt elated and exhausted.

Tiff walked with Dr. Fathy to the place corresponding to the school courtyard. Instead of the picnic tables where some students ate lunch on Earth, she saw short squat bushes, a roughly rectangular rock, and two plastic shapes that resembled tables.

She had so many questions, and Dr. Fathy seemed to enjoy providing answers. She guessed he taught at a college.

"Is there any correspondence between the forms we attune to in different realms? I mean, if we attune to a bird in the Animal Realm, would we attune to air in this one?" she asked.

"Sometimes. Those who transform into aquatic forms frequently attune to water here, and there is a higher correspondence of air-users among those attuning to birds. But it is not exclusive. For instance, I've attuned to two different animal forms, one of which is a bird. But as I mentioned before, I have not strongly attuned to any of the elements."

"Can you change into an animal form while in this realm?" she continued, while trying to focus on winds.

"We can try that later. Let's focus on the elements first."

She focused, but failed to either create winds or turn her arm into air. But she still had many questions

"So if MacKenzie hasn't attuned to this realm at all, why does she still look normal, but we look like a mishmash again?"

"We have stronger control over our forms, but you are still learning. MacKenzie has a stronger sense of self because of her age and experience." He paused, then suggested, "Try something other than wind."

Tiff obediently tried changing her arm to fire. She thought she saw a little glow, but she wasn't certain. She tried water and earth, with no luck at all.

"Remember, there are more than the classic four elements here. Try metal, or wood, or even lightning," Dr. Fathy suggested.

She tried both metal and wood without success. When she focused on lightning, she thought she felt something.

"Good. You seem to have some capabilities with both fire and lightning. That's a pretty potent combination. Focus on those two, and see what you can do."

Tiff continued to focus on each, and after several minutes, her hard work was rewarded—her arm transformed first into lightning, then fire. She tried transforming one arm into fire and the other into lightning. After a few minutes, both arms obediently transformed. "Wow," she muttered, staring at her glowing hands.

"Excellent. You seem to be a natural," Dr. Fathy said.

"Dr. Fathy? You mentioned MacKenzie had a strong sense of self because of her years of experience, and that's why she retained her normal form. So... if you don't mind... um... how old are each of you?"

"Paul and Greg are around three thousand years old. MacKenzie and Ida are younger, about two thousand years old, maybe more." He paused. "I am by far the oldest among us, over five thousand years old. I was born in what you know as ancient Egypt."

Tiff's jaw dropped.

After the students spent the morning trying to attune to different elements, Coach Brown and Miss Olsen provided a picnic lunch. They gathered everyone in the Primal Realm's version of the school courtyard, and the students hungrily gobbled down sandwiches and sodas. Though he hadn't been physically active, Mike felt famished.

Between mouthfuls Tiff asked, "So why doesn't the food take on elemental forms? I'd think if we brought something here, it would take on an elemental form too."

"You have it backwards, Tiffany," Paul Oxinos responded. "All of you assumed the elemental mishmash forms because immortals have the ability to attune to the realm. Something mundane, like this sandwich, doesn't have the ability to attune, and thus retains its normal form. If we had brought Julisha along with us, she wouldn't change into an elemental form either."

After lunch, the students chatted about their successes or failures, and even showed off a little. Tiff demonstrated her breakthrough with fire and lightning, and Aliki showed the small control she had over darkness. Mike felt a little envious, but was glad some of them had succeeded.

Suddenly, MacKenzie stiffened and her eyes glanced into the distance. "We have company," she warned.

Both she and Coach Brown immediately stood to face whoever approached. "Another giant?" the coach asked.

163

"Nay. Three locals, I think. It's hard for me to tell here."

"What should we do?" Mike asked. "Do we need to fight?"

"With what?" MacKenzie responded. "Calm yourself and let us handle any problems."

After a few minutes, four elemental beings entered the courtyard area. One looked like a short older man made of earth, with rock covering parts of him, standing about three feet tall. The next was a young-looking woman, about four feet tall, composed of wind. Her form was mostly translucent, but Mike thought the winds swirling around her vaguely resembled wings. Glass apparently made up the third human-like being, and the fourth looked like a dog made of lightning. A cord made of plastic ran from the lightning dog's neck to the arm of the glass man.

"More visitors, Aleara," the short earth man said to the wind girl. His voice sounded like grinding stone, and his posture suggested that he was on his guard.

"At least these are smaller," Aleara responded. Her voice reminded Mike of a flute—light and airy, and pleasant to listen to.

The glass man handed the leash to the earth man and stepped forward cautiously. "I am Tarskax. This is Dornum and Aleara," he said, indicating the earth man and wind girl respectively. "And this is Zinniz," he said, pointing to the lightning dog. "What brings you visitors to the Primal Realm?"

Paul Oxinos stood and introduced everyone. He explained, "We are visiting here to train our students about the different realms and their place in them. We mean no harm and ask for your forgiveness if we intruded."

The elemental beings appeared to relax a bit. "Thank the stones," said Dornum.

"You mentioned other visitors... larger than us?" Miss Olsen asked. "Are they much larger than us? And are they hostile?"

"Yes to both. Two are about three times your height, one even bigger. As far as their hostility... two days ago, they seized control over the Artisan Exchange about five miles in that direction." Tarskax pointed toward the southwest.

"They wrecked everything. They even captured a few of our friends," Aleara lamented. Mike thought she sounded like she might cry. He wondered if elemental creatures could really cry.

"It sounds like more giant problems, Paul. If these three are as hostile as the last one, we need to act," Coach Brown insisted.

Dr. Fathy suggested, "Perhaps a bit of reconnaissance might give us more information. It would let us plan for an assault, or we could discern whether they might respond to intelligent conversation. Not all of them are mindless brutes, Greg."

"Agreed. But you and MacKenzie are the only ones of us with avian forms, and I want MacKenzie here to help guard the students. It might be dangerous to go alone," Mr. Oxinos said.

Mike finally asked, "What about Tiff? Eagles have great eyesight."

The adults looked at each other. "She hasn't mastered an element in this realm yet, nor does she have the control to revert to flesh. An eagle made of different elements wouldn't be able to fly. So that's not feasible," Coach Brown replied.

Tiff glanced over the elemental patchwork of her body, watching her arms slowly transform from darkness and wood to plastic and water. She felt her earthen torso slowly crystalized into glass and wondered how her face looked. "But if I could fully transform, would that work?"

Dr. Fathy answered, "Yes. If you were fully fire or lightning, you'd be able to maintain cohesion and balance, and therefore flight. Your form would be stable and unlikely to change. Without either a flesh form or a pure element form, you might unexpectedly shift elements while in the air, which could throw off your flight. But an eagle's eyes would be helpful, and you could fly much faster than I could."

Aleara chimed in with a hopeful tone, "I can fly fast, and I'm a lot harder to see. I'll come too."

Mr. Oxinos looked at Dr. Fathy and Tiff. "If you're willing, spend the next few hours trying to achieve a full elemental form. Tom, you work with her. You've obviously made good progress already."

He turned to the others. "Kyle? Do you have any idea how far your earth sense extends?"

"No, sir," Kyle responded.

Ida answered, "Let's find out. I'll work with him. Dornum? You might be able to help him too. He seems to have an affinity for earth."

"Umm... okay." Dornum replied, looking at his fellow elementals.

"How can I help?" asked Tarskax, taking Zinniz's leash back from Dornum.

Dr. Fathy responded, "Tell Paul and MacKenzie anything you might have noticed about the giants. Elemental compositions, social dynamics, anything that might motivate them to be destructive."

Dr. Fathy sat with Tiff as she struggled to control her transformation. Aleara floated above, watching. But after an hour, Tiff had only managed to change her arms and legs into fire. She could transform her head, shoulders and arms into electricity.

Tiff sat on a bench, frustrated. Aleara hovered beside her, while Dr. Fathy withdrew to let the two of them talk. He busied himself with an electronic pad that had appeared in his hand.

"So what is your world like?" Aleara suddenly asked.

Tiff paused and thought for a moment. She'd never thought about how her world might seem to a resident of one of the Realms. "Everything is made from a lot of different materials, kind of blended together. Here, everything is pure. And, well, we don't normally look like this," she said, indicating the jumbled elements making up her own body. "We normally look more like him," she said, pointing to Dr. Fathy.

"He is larger than you. Are you mature?" Aleara asked

"Almost. I have a few years before I'm an adult," Tiff answered honestly.

"Only a few years? I still have three decades," Aleara said.

"Three decades? How long do your kind live?" Tiff asked.

"Well, I'm not sure. Dornum has lived for over five hundred years, but he's growing old. I've only lived seventy-four years."

Tiff did some quick math in her head. "If you mature at around a hundred years, and Dornum is old at five hundred, it seems like five or six of your years are about the same as one of ours. So that would make you a little younger than me. I think."

She noticed Aleara's confusion. "Humans like us normally live to about eighty or ninety years of age. But I think there's a lot more of us. It's a lot more crowded where I come from."

"There are more of us than you might think. I live up there with my family," she said, pointing to a nearby cloud, "and Dornum lives underground. We were at the Artisan Exchange when the creatures attacked. They killed a lot of us, and captured some too. It was horrible."

"What is the Artisan Exchange?" Tiff asked, curious. She also wanted to keep Aleara from dwelling on the attack.

"It's where our artisans—the crafters—create goods and exchange them with others. My family crafts artistic winds for decoration. We even sometimes mix in other elements. I was talking to Tarskax about using glass to make chimes when they attacked. Then everything went crazy."

"Your family... so you have a mother and father like us?" Tiff asked. "Do you have siblings?"

Aleara looked confused. "We have elders, who teach us, and we form small family groups."

"But you look like a girl. Are there boy... umm... what do I call your race anyway?"

"I'm a sylph. What are boys?"

Dr. Fathy interjected, overhearing. "All sylphs are apparently female, but they are a one-gender race. Aleara, humans like Tiffany and I have two genders, boys and girls, or men and women. We need both to have children."

"Oh," the two of them said simultaneously, and started giggling.

CHAPTER NINETEEN
Freeing the Artisan Exchange

As they waited for Dr. Fathy to return with Tiff and Aleara, Kyle listened attentively as the elementals described both their adversaries and the building itself. According to Tarskax, the three giants were composed of a mixture of elements, just like the monstrous one in the Animal Realm. The largest one had legs composed of water, arms of ice, and his body was metal. He wore a thick helmet which obscured most of his face, but Tarskax thought his head radiated darkness. The first of the smaller ones had legs of earth, fiery arms, a torso of wood, and a head of water. The giant's shoulders, where the fire and wood met, continually billowed smoke. The last had legs of lightning, a plastic torso, a metal head, and glass arms. Coach Brown dubbed them Blue, Smoky, and Zapfoot respectively. The giants had killed anyone who resisted them and trapped many elementals inside the Exchange.

After another hour, Dr. Fathy, Tiff and Aleara returned. "Tiffany has succeeded. She can maintain a lightning form, and even learned to transform into an eagle while retaining her electrical composition. Aleara helped Tiffany relax while they talked about the Primal Realm."

Tiff stepped forward to demonstrate. Her body shimmered and began to glow, and sparks jumped between her limbs. After a moment, her entire body transformed into electricity, though it kept its human shape. Then her arms broadened into powerful wings, and her legs shortened into talons. Her body and head completed the transformation into the shape of an eagle. She flapped her wings, rising from the ground.

"Wow," Jason gasped. "You're a real thunderbird."

"That's probably where the myth came from, Jason," Mr. Oxinos remarked. "Great work, Tiffany."

After Tiff reversed her transformation and rested for a few minutes, the group set off on foot and eventually arrived at the Artisan Exchange. The sprawling building reached high enough for the giants to shelter in. According to both Tarskax and Dornum, the interior had two levels, but the upper one had a lot of balconies, bridges, and open areas. However, the giants had collapsed a few of the balconies and bridges.

When they finally arrived, Tiff murmured, "I thought so. That's our town mall, or the elemental equivalent of it."

Kyle recognized the mall's approximate shape, despite the different materials used in its construction. Part of the roof gaped open to the skies though. Kyle's gaze traveled to Aleara; he guessed that the air elementals would want to enter and leave through the roof.

Tiff transformed into her thunderbird form, and Dr. Fathy transformed into some sort of wading water bird, though Kyle couldn't identify it.

As they prepared, Dornum said, "Aleara, please be careful.

Let these visitors remove the other ones." His manner reminded Kyle of a doting uncle.

"I'll be careful. We all will be," she assured him. They took flight and soared over the building to spy into the roof opening from above.

While they were gone, Kyle grew curious about Zinniz. "What kind of creature is Zinniz?"

"Zinniz is a shock hound, a lower form of elemental life." Tarskax replied. "Do you not have pets in your world?"

"Sure, but I never expected to see a dog made of lightning," Kyle answered. Zinniz seemed like any other canine companion. "Are all lightning elementals like Zinniz?"

"No, there are sentient lightning elementals too, like the boltlings. Most elements have more than one sentient race, and many different lower forms of life. One of my best friends is a boltling." Tarskax responded.

"Sorry. This is all new to me." Kyle hoped he hadn't offended Tarskax.

"You're all visitors to our realm. The differences with your own world may bewilder you, so please don't hesitate to ask me anything. Ignorance is an enemy we can always confront."

Kyle relaxed and smiled. Tarskax seemed friendly and earnest. Perhaps the elementals weren't so different.

The scouts returned some time later and described the situation. According to Dr. Fathy, Blue was inside sitting in a pile of rubble. Strangely, he sat fairly still, not doing anything. The other two guarded the captives at either end of the Exchange.

Jason saw MacKenzie and Coach Brown withdraw from the group to discuss tactics. After a few moments, she glanced at Jason and waved him over.

Jason was astonished.

MacKenzie grinned. "Ye might have some good ideas in that head of yours, with your experiences on the field. So we'll be includin' you in our strategy."

"Let's get back to the plans. Jason, please share any ideas you might have. If we assume that Blue is the leader, we should eliminate him first. But we'll need to prevent Zapfoot and Smoky from joining the fight," Coach Brown said.

MacKenzie sketched out a diagram of the Artisan Exchange in the dirt. "Greg, you and I will take down Blue. Paul is a good shot with his bow. Ida can handle herself in a fight too. So we'll have each of them take one of the smaller ones. Tom isn't really a warrior though. Keep him airborne to coordinate."

"Good idea. What about the students? It might be useful to at least have Tiffany, Jason, and Mike armed and ready. I'd arm Aliki, but since she hasn't completely stabilized her elemental form, I'd be afraid that she might accidentally set off a rifle," Coach Brown responded.

MacKenzie thought a moment. "Jason should assist Paul, and Mike and Tiff should follow Ida. Have Aliki and Kyle, along with Tarskax and Dornum, help to get the captives to safety. Aleara should stay airborne with Tom."

"Do we want Tiffany in the air or on the ground? She doesn't have a Pocket yet, so either she's airborne or wielding her sword," Coach Brown asked.

MacKenzie responded, "I'd prefer to keep her on the ground

172

and ready to fight, just in case. She can drop the sword and transform if she needs to flee."

Coach Brown had a pained expression on his face. "And ye can always make her another if it gets damaged," MacKenzie added, trying to soothe his pride.

Jason summoned the courage to speak up. "We should decide who strikes first. The giants will react as soon as one is attacked. Blue is the biggest, and in the center. The others might pull away from their captives to come to his aid."

"Good idea, Jason. Let's go with that. Any other thoughts, Jason?" Coach Brown smiled.

Jason thought for a moment and added, "Put Miss Olsen against Zapfoot, not Smoky. From what Tiff said, there's a stand of trees near his position she could use. Wouldn't she be less effective against Smoky's burning arms too?"

After they talked a little more, they presented their plan to the others. With only a few suggestions and questions, the group agreed to the plan.

Coach Brown spoke to the gathered students. "Each of you should avoid combat unless absolutely necessary. Don't be reckless—even though you've learned a lot, you're far from ready to fight giants. You may be ageless, but you aren't unkillable." He looked at Aleara and added, "That applies to you as well. I don't want to have to explain a tragedy to any parent."

"Now, I have something for Mike, Jason, and Tiffany." The coach stood. He held out both arms, and a real katana in a scabbard appeared in his hands as if by magic. "Ladies first. Tiffany?" He handed her the katana.

Tiff reverently drew the blade, her mouth hanging open in

amazement. "This is... for me?"

"Did ye expect to fight with wooden swords forever, girl?" MacKenzie teased. "Greg made that for you after we determined which weapon would work best for you."

"Careful. It is razor sharp," Coach Brown said, obviously proud of his work. Tiff sheathed it, and attached it to her belt. The coach produced a double-headed greataxe for Jason, obviously modeled after the wooden practice weapon he used. It had a piece of wood covering each blade, and another covering the end of the haft where it ended in a dangerous spike.

"No sheath for this one, so keep those covers on unless you really need to use it," Coach Brown said. Finally to Mike, he provided a set of tonfas, but these were considerably higher quality than the ones he'd used in practice. They also incorporated some metal reinforcement into the wood. With the tonfas, the coach also provided a sling-loop to attach them to a belt.

Mike threaded the sling-loop through his belt, and twirled the tonfas around to get the feel of them. "Thanks. These are beautiful."

Indeed, each of the weapons was also a work of art. The katana looked as elegant as any blade Jason had seen in museums, with blue cord wrapping around the gold-colored handle. On his greataxe, etchings of graceful curves and knots decorated the side of the blade and the upper part of the shaft. Mike's tonfas incorporated burnished metal and lacquered wood seamlessly, and a Chinese dragon design twisted around them.

"I built a special rifle for you, Aliki, but it would be too dangerous in the elemental realm—at least until you can stabilize yourself," the coach said.

"I'm sure I'll master it sometime soon," Aliki said quietly.

The group split into their respective teams. Aliki followed Jason, Dornum, and Mr. Oxinos as they all crept into the south entrance of the Artisan Exchange to face Smoky. Mr. Oxinos found a vantage point that offered some cover. The four of them stayed hidden; Aliki even tried projecting some darkness to help conceal them all.

She looked at the surrounding structure, realizing it really did resemble the town mall. The stores and stands themselves seemed larger on average, but there were fewer of them. She could almost imagine wandering down to the food court.

Smoky had cornered a number of the elemental beings in two of the storefronts. A large metal vendor cart partially blocked one entrance. Smoky sat facing the entrances, but seemed to be looking at some crafted goods from the stores, which sat in a pile nearby. From Smoky's shape and proportions, Aliki determined the giant was female.

Kyle, Tarskax, Mike, Tiff, and Miss Olsen would enter the north entrance in the same way to handle Zapfoot. Coach Brown and MacKenzie would engage Blue, who Tarskax had described as both the biggest and most hostile of them.

Out of the corner of her eye, Aliki saw movement in the center courtyard, followed by a loud bellow. She heard MacKenzie utter some sort of Celtic battle cry in response. She turned her head toward the central plaza and could see Blue's massive form rise out of his rubble throne.

Mr. Oxinos rose to his feet, with his glowing bow in hand, and fired shafts of light at Smoky. Aliki could see more of his weapon. She guessed her gentle aura of darkness acted like sunglasses, so the glow from his bow didn't seem as strong.

It did look like a bow, but there she saw no string. Instead, the "arrow" emerged from the central part of the bow, right above his grip. As he pulled the shaft back, it glowed brightly. Whether he charged it with his own power or the glow was a function of the weapon, she couldn't tell.

The first glowing shafts struck Smoky in her fiery arms. Aliki guessed that he wasn't trying to kill her or his first shot would have struck in her chest or head. For some reason, she was grateful.

While Mr. Oxinos fired, Jason and Dornum crept forward, trying to reach the captives and avoiding Smoky's attention. Aliki hung back, trying to keep a line of sight on each of the others.

Mr. Oxinos' shots seemed to pin something—perhaps solid bone?—within the fiery arms, but Smoky yanked her arm free. Aliki tried not to think about how the fire could be pinned at all. Smoky kicked some rubble towards them with her earthen legs.

"Duck, everyone!" Aliki cried, hiding behind a bench made of wood.

As the dust from the rubble settled, Smoky lifted the metal vendor cart in her flaming arms, and held it in front of her to protect herself from Mr. Oxinos' arrows. As the giantess shielded herself against the glowing light shafts, the metal of the cart heated until it had become red-hot.

Mr. Oxinos tried to fire shots at her legs, but she ignored

them, even though she twitched in pain as the light-arrows sank into her. Grunting, she heaved the cart towards Mr. Oxinos.

Fortunately, he had taken cover behind something resembling a plastic panel, and it protected him from most of the damage. Aliki vaguely remembered a mall directory sign at the same spot in the real mall. But the impact shattered the panel, knocking Mr. Oxinos flying.

She saw Smoky reach into the store where the captives cowered. The giantess snared a metal elemental and threw it toward Dornum. As Smoky reached for another of the hapless captives, Aliki heard Jason shout.

Kyle followed Miss Olsen and Mike into the northern entrance of the Artisan Exchange. Tarskax, Tiff, and Zinniz followed, carefully sneaking forward. Zapfoot had corralled a group of captives in something resembling an arena. Kyle remembered that Tarskax described this area as an amphitheatre used by entertainers. Zapfoot had fashioned a wall by piling up the seats, trapping the elementals.

Tiff said something about movies to Mike, so Kyle guessed the amphitheater corresponded to the movie theaters in the real mall. He didn't visit the mall too much, but he knew Tiff loved to hang out there. She seemed to take offense that the giants were ruining it, even in the Primal Realm.

As they watched, Zapfoot grabbed a plastic elemental with his glass hands, and began to carve shapes on the elemental's torso with his sharp fingers. The plastic figure squirmed, but couldn't free itself.

Tarskax grimly pointed out several piles on the floor—stone, plastic, wood, and metal. When Kyle noticed they were vaguely person-shaped, he gasped, horrified. "He's torturing and killing them? Why?"

Tarskax grimly shook his head.

The group heard Blue's bellow and MacKenzie's war chant. The battle had started.

Zapfoot quickly dropped the plastic figure, who landed among the other captives with a thud. He grabbed a large metal mallet and moved toward the sound of battle.

Ida's team had selected the north entrance because it included a stand of ornamental wooden trees. As Zapfoot moved through the stand of trees, Miss Olsen caused them to bend around Zapfoot. She couldn't make the trees move fast enough to hurt the giant, but the hindrance confused him and prevented him from helping Blue.

Tarskax loosed Zinniz and gave the lightning dog a quick command. Zinniz raced forward to harry Zapfoot. Oddly, his electrical attacks seemed to cause Zapfoot pain. Zapfoot tried to swing his mallet at Zinniz, but the trees hampered his arms, and Zinniz was agile enough to avoid the clumsy blows.

As Zapfoot slowly broke free of the trees, Kyle, Mike, Tiff, and Tarskax hurried to free the captives. They started pulling down the wall and helping the captives to the exit of the Artisan Exchange. Then they heard the sound of cracking wood.

Kyle heard Tiff yell, "He's free!"

The three students looked over at Miss Olsen. She had her war-staff in her hand, and a wooden shield on her arm. "Get them to safety, children! I'll try to—"

A crash of Zapfoot's metal mallet landed on her shield. Though she'd used her superior speed to sidestep away from a direct hit, the impact still hurled her back into the nearby wall. A grunt escaped her lips, and she staggered to her feet.

"I've faced worse, monster." She glared up at the giant.

But Zapfoot quickly closed the distance, and kicked at her with his electric legs. She screamed in both anger and pain, then fell silent. Zapfoot turned to look at the captives.

As one, Mike and Tiff drew their weapons.

With Mr. Oxinos dazed, Jason decided he'd have to be ready to fight. Aliki had no effective combat skills, and he had no idea of Dornum's abilities. He quickly removed the edge-guards from his axe-heads and from the spike at the end of the shaft. He moved into a better position and watched.

Jason saw Smoky peer into one of the stores where she'd held her captives. She reached in with her burning hands and grabbed a metal elemental. The figure struggled, but she hurled the hapless victim at Dornum.

Fortunately, the elemental's wriggling hampered her aim, and her impromptu ammunition landed a few feet away from Dornum. The little earth elemental quickly helped the metal man to his feet and found shelter behind a ramp to the upper level of the Exchange.

Unfortunately, the next elemental Smoky grabbed was made of wood. The poor creature immediately began to smolder and burn. It screamed in terror and pain.

"NO!!!" Jason yelled. He charged forward. *I have to MOVE!*

Smoky saw him and flung the burning wood elemental toward him. It crashed into the ground in front of him, so he leaped over the burning figure. He saw Smoky reach for another elemental to throw. A family of plastic folk screamed in fear.

Jason ran faster than he ever had, closing the gap quickly. Smoky abandoned trying to throw the captives at him and tried to kick at him with her earthen legs instead. Jason dodged as easily as when he blitzed a quarterback.

He dashed between her legs, swinging the axe at one of her earthen shins as he passed through. The blade bit deep into the rock, then came free. Smoky grunted in pain.

Jason turned quickly to face her, standing between her and the captives. She kicked at him again, but the wound from his axe seemed to throw her balance off. He dodged easily and moved in to swing the axe at her midsection. She tried to block with one of her fiery arms, but the blade bit deeply into her forearm.

Smoky screamed in pain. She retreated and tried hurling some rubble at him. One chunk knocked into him, but didn't have as much power as he expected.

Jason approached again, threatening the giantess with his axe. He tried a trick MacKenzie had demonstrated. He swung the axe in a great arc at her abdomen again. In response, Smoky took a step back, exactly as he'd anticipated. With the axe head past her body, she raised a blazing arm to counterattack.

Then he drove the spike into her abdomen with all his strength.

Smoky cried out and fell on her back. She struggled to rise, but clutched her wound. She started to make a strange sound.

With Smoky defeated, Jason quickly glanced around. Mr. Oxinos had regained his feet and held his bow ready. Aliki was tending to the wood elemental, who no longer burned.

Reassured, Jason carefully moved over to see Smoky's face, holding his axe ready. But what he saw shocked him.

She trembled, and the expression on her face mixed both pain and fear. She was terrified—of them.

Zapfoot swung his mallet wildly at Mike. Mike jumped upward and back, avoiding the blow. In response, Tiff darted in and slashed upward at his plastic torso.

Unfortunately, Zapfoot was quick on his feet and jumped to the side, and Tiff's swing missed. He kicked at her and connected with a glancing blow.

Tiff staggered but kept her balance. She grinned and assumed her electrical form. "Two can play at that game," she said, flourishing her sword.

Mike took advantage of Zapfoot's distraction and slammed one of his tonfas into the back of the giant's knee—or at least where he thought the knee should be. Zapfoot slashed down with his sharp glass hands, stabbing into Mike's shoulder. Mike cried out in pain and twisted away.

With his wound, Mike knew he'd become a liability, so he dropped back. He hoped Tiff could hold Zapfoot off a little longer. As he watched, Tiff, in full electrical form, slashed Zapfoot's plastic torso with her katana.

Mike noticed Miss Olsen stirring, so he worked his way over to her. She had several bruises, and blood dripped from her mouth. He helped her stand and noticed she favored one leg.

She grimaced. "Mike! Stay out of it and tell Tiffany to bait him toward the trees. I have one more thing to try. But first, help me into the stand of trees."

"Yes, ma'am." He bent over slightly and said, "Climb on my back. It'll be faster."

Miss Olsen grunted and climbed onto his back. Mike ignored the pain in his injured shoulder and hustled toward the trees as quickly as he could. With his increased strength, he could carry her easily, but he worried about attracting Zapfoot's attention.

Unfortunately, Zapfoot landed another blow with his mallet, and Tiff slumped to the ground. Zinniz continued to torment his legs, but the giant slammed the hammer first to one side of the shock hound, then the other. Zinniz backed off, scared.

Zapfoot had numerous cuts on his plastic abdomen, but he turned toward the captives. He brandished his mallet and yelled something. Though Mike couldn't understand the giant, Zapfoot's voice had grown louder, and he seemed to be getting frustrated, almost as if he were throwing a tantrum. The giant savagely smashed his mallet at any available target, with little strategy or skill.

As Mike carried Miss Olsen into the stand of trees, he glanced toward the central plaza where MacKenzie and Coach Brown were pressing their attack on Blue. He couldn't see them well, but the two of them seemed to have Blue at a disadvantage. Mike could hear Blue's bellowing shouts and MacKenzie's Celtic war cries clearly.

Mike set Miss Olsen down and turned his attention back to

his own battle. The captives had mostly escaped, but Kyle and Tarskax were still helping some of the slower ones. Zapfoot closed in on them, still yelling something they couldn't understand. Kyle tried shifting into bear form, but failed. Like most of the students, he couldn't stabilize his form in the elemental realm. As Zapfoot approached, both Kyle and Tarskax backed away, looking for something to hide behind.

Ida Olsen coaxed life and animation into the trees. At her command, the trees grew. Roots erupted from the ground near Zapfoot, far from the stand of trees. Mike guessed she'd been growing the root system to extend her range. The roots lashed out at Zapfoot and wrapped around his torso.

Zapfoot kicked at the roots with his electric legs, charring some of them. He tried to pull the roots, and staggered forward a few more feet. But he had lost his momentum and could no longer move. Frustrated, Zapfoot hurled his hammer at Kyle and Tarskax.

With his enhanced reflexes, Kyle evaded the hammer. Unfortunately, Tarskax wasn't so lucky. The mallet struck with the force of a truck, and Tarskax shattered.

Ida's face grew dark, and a thick root wrapped around Zapfoot's neck. A second one sharpened into a point and stabbed into the small of his back. Zapfoot struggled weakly, but couldn't move. He bellowed and tried to pull the root from his neck. But the root poking into his back jabbed him again, and he stopped resisting. His fight was over.

The only sounds left came from the center courtyard. Coach

Brown fought with discipline and precision, striking and defending as if he'd been born with a weapon in his hand. MacKenzie, on the other hand, reveled in the combat with a terrifying glee. She dashed in, struck with her greatsword, then danced away. While Coach Brown seemed to regard the combat as a necessary challenge to overcome, MacKenzie basked in the carnage.

They hadn't escaped unscathed. One of the coach's arms moved stiffly, and the armor on that arm was bent and cracked. MacKenzie bled from many wounds, but none of them seemed to hamper her. All three combatants panted with exertion.

MacKenzie feinted an attack to Blue's leg, prompting the giant to step back. In response, Coach Brown charged in and struck Blue in the chest with a powerful blow. The coach's blade sliced deeply into Blue's metal chest. The giant reacted to the unexpected damage by swinging a fist at Coach Brown. But before the blow landed, MacKenzie nimbly jumped onto his arm, ran up to his shoulder, and with a swift motion, sliced Blue's head off.

Blue's body crashed to the ground. Then there was silence.

CHAPTER TWENTY
Aftermath

With Blue dead, the fight was over. Smoky sat in the rubble, her eyes darting between Jason and the central courtyard. She pulled her knees to her chest, rubbing her arm where his axe had cut into it. The giantess sniffled, but watched both Mr. Oxinos and Jason as if they were monsters.

Mr. Oxinos congratulated him. "Excellent work, Jason."

"It seemed natural. I guess my instincts took over, and I felt like I was on the football field again. Of course, the quarterback here was a lot bigger."

"Your instincts also let you tap into something else, Jason. Have you looked at yourself?" Mr. Oxinos asked.

Jason looked down, and nearly fell over with surprise. His entire body had transformed to water. Around his legs, water swirled in crashing waves.

"The water form helped you move in combat. It enhanced your speed and mobility while giving you some protection, particularly against her fiery arms," Mr. Oxinos explained. "It also had the beneficial side effect of extinguishing the fires on that poor woodling."

185

"Wow... I knew I was moving fast, but I assumed it was adrenaline and our immortal physique. But... wow...."

Jason felt elated. After failing to attune to anything in the Animal Realm, and seeing Tiff's ease of transforming here in the Primal Realm, he'd worried that something was wrong with him. But now, he felt like a hero.

"Great job, Jason," Aliki said. "Now what about her?"

"She has a lot to answer for," Dornum said angrily.

Mr. Oxinos turned to Smoky and spoke in a strange language. The giantess nodded, responded in the same language, and slowly got to her feet.

"She understands that trying to escape would only cause her more pain at this point. I think we can guard her without too much trouble," Mr. Oxinos replied. "But we will have to decide what to do with her."

The group, along with Smoky, walked to the central plaza. When Smoky saw the body of Blue, she broke into tears, muttering in her language.

Kyle watched as Ida Olsen steadied herself and walked around to the front of Zapfoot. Fury raced across her face, and she turned that fury upon the captive giant. Kyle also felt rage at the young giant, but it was coupled with guilt.

Miss Olsen spoke harshly to Zapfoot in a strange language, emphasizing her points by tightening the root around his neck. Kyle wondered if she would kill Zapfoot. However, his captivity and Blue's death seemed to have taken all of the fight from him. Miss Olsen bent some wood into makeshift manacles.

Kyle turned toward the shattered glass shards littering the floor and wept. He gathered some of Tarskax's pieces, hoping that the elemental could somehow still be alive. He heard a soft voice near him, and looked up to see Aleara.

The young sylph held her hands over her mouth in alarm. "Tarskax... is that..."

"The giant hit him with his mallet, and he shattered. I couldn't do anything. It happened so fast." Kyle sobbed. "He's gone, isn't he?"

Aleara sighed. "Tarskax is gone. But he will eventually return. We will mourn his passing, but we also celebrate each awakening. When a soul joins with a primal element to form new life, it is a joy."

Kyle found a larger glass chunk about the size of his hand. "Would it be okay if I took this?"

"His essence has already moved on. Once the soul has fled, what's left is just matter. There is nothing wrong with using it for something," she answered.

"I'd like to keep it to remember him. We sometimes like to keep things to help us remember."

"That sounds like a nice idea. I think I will do the same."

Mike steadied Miss Olsen as they led the captive Zapfoot to the central plaza area. Tiff, still groggy from the fight, leaned on Kyle for support. Aleara floated above, but none of them said much. Kyle cradled a large chunk of glass in one hand.

The rest of the teachers and students were standing in the rubble-filled central plaza already. A few elementals gathered, watching them with a mix of awe, curiosity, and fear. Mike spotted Dornum among them, looking apprehensive.

Meanwhile, Aleara and Tiff, still in her lightning form, searched the various storefronts, looking for any other elementals who might need help.

Miss Olsen gestured and spoke a command in the giant's language. Zapfoot obediently sat down. Then she limped over to Dornum and told him of Tarskax's death.

Mr. Oxinos continued to talk to Smoky in the giants' language. Dr. Fathy and Coach Brown searched the body of Blue and the nearby area for clues. MacKenzie muttered that she needed a bath and wandered off to find a large source of pure water.

Mike picked his way through the wreckage of the plaza to Dornum and sat beside the small stone man. "I am truly sorry for the loss of your friend," he said.

Dornum's rough voice belied his sorrow. "Tarskax and I have been friends for over a century, and we've shared many experiences. I look forward to the day he rejoins us, but it will be hard without him."

Tiff and Aleara returned from their search, followed by Zinniz. "We found him wandering in an empty shop, so I tried to comfort him," Tiff explained.

"C'mere, Zinniz. I guess I'll be taking care of you now." Dornum stroked the lightning hound sadly. He and Zinniz were about the same height, so he had to reach to pet Zinniz.

"Does it hurt when you pet him?" Mike asked.

"A little. Earth feels lightning more than glass. But I'll gladly tolerate it. Tarskax would have wanted him to have a good home," Dornum replied.

"Does Tarskax have a family?" Mike asked, trying to imagine a family of glass people.

"A small one, though he lived alone. I'll let them know he died helping others. To us, that is a noble thing," the small earth elemental responded.

"It is for us too," Mike said solemnly.

Aliki stood by Mr. Oxinos as he talked to Smoky and Zapfoot. Zapfoot crossed his arms and scowled, refusing to talk, but Smoky responded to Mr. Oxinos' questions and seemed to relax slightly, though she still trembled. They still terrified her, so Mr. Oxinos spoke to her with a calming tone.

She tried to guess at their conversation, but understood none of the strange words. Noting her curiosity, Mr. Oxinos said, "Understanding their language—or any language—is another talent you will eventually master. But for now, I'll translate."

He continued, "Her name is Rigashun, but she liked the nickname Smoky. She and her brother," he said, gesturing toward Zapfoot, "accompanied their father, who we called Blue, here to the Primal Realm. She wasn't sure why they came."

"Once here, she became curious about the elemental creatures. It was her first time here as well. Blue told them the elementals were toys to be played with and disposed of. She followed her father's commands, namely to keep the elementals captured. Unfortunately, Blue had a mean streak and devoured several of the elementals, as did her brother. Blue turned the central plaza into something of an audience chamber. According to her, several other titans came here yesterday."

Aliki thought for a moment, then asked, "So is she immortal like us? You mentioned that only immortals can shift into these hodgepodge elemental forms."

Mr. Oxinos translated the question for Smoky, who responded. He translated her response. "She and her brother were the only two of Blue's fifteen living children who inherited their father's immortality and abilities. While the titans don't have a source of immortality, there are a few who either remain from the era when they did, or who inherited it. Immortality can be passed to children, though it is rare."

"So why is she so afraid of us?" Aliki asked.

Paul again translated, and the two of them talked for several minutes. "According to her, the titans tell tales of small evil creatures that torment them, steal trinkets and treasures, and occasionally wield fierce magics against them. Just as we have monstrous giants and ogres in our myths and fairy tales, they have small, nasty, powerful, magical beings. In short, we have become their bogeymen. It doesn't help that they blame us for stealing the Fountain of Souls."

"Does Smoky know about the Fountain of Souls?"

"No. I already asked her. She isn't sure why her father hated us. Now she just wants to go home."

Kyle sat quietly, watching the others. His emotions churned, and he felt confused. Pride for helping save others, frustration that he couldn't do more, and sadness over Tarskax's death all whirled around his mind.

Edward Swing

"All I can do is sense things. No great abilities, and I can't even transform into the bear here," he muttered in frustration. He watched Coach Brown and Dr. Fathy search Blue's corpse for clues. He wondered if the one talent he'd mastered could be useful here. So he tried to relax and extend his senses into the ground.

He sensed Dornum clearly and felt everyone's feet on the ground. He could feel the Blue's body lying prone, and the earthen rubble that he'd used for a throne. He could feel metal lying against the stone and water rushing through channels underground.

In the rubble, he felt something odd, something moving.

"Coach Brown? Dr. Fathy? I felt something through the earth. It was moving around underneath that pile of rubble," he said, pointing to a large pile of stone.

The two of them pulled the rubble aside. Underneath, they found a giant-sized satchel, obviously some sort of carrying pack. It was large enough that Kyle could have fit in it. Some of the contents had spilled—a bit of dried food, a pouch containing some coins, a few rags.

The teachers carefully opened the satchel flap and peered inside. Dr. Fathy gasped and dropped the flap.

"Paul? I think you need to see this," Coach Brown said.

Both Mr. Oxinos and Miss Olsen came over to see what Dr. Fathy had discovered. The students gathered around as well, though Jason and Mike kept an eye on Zapfoot and Smoky.

"What is it?" Kyle asked. He saw something dark on the ground, but it seemed to be hard yet amorphous at the same time. His mind struggled to comprehend it—the thing looked

191

like nothing he had ever seen. It moved in an alien way, flowing and jerking. The world seemed to warp around the strange object.

Beside him, Mike gasped. "What is THAT?"

Mr. Oxinos replied, "Do you remember when I said that the titan's world shared some realms with ours, but not all of them? That we both share the Animal Realm and the Primal Realm, but we have realms they do not, and vice versa? Well, that is something from one of the realms we don't share. Since you have no frame of reference to comprehend it, your mind refuses to identify it."

Miss Olsen continued. "Once you visit those realms, you will learn about the states of matter and life in each realm. Paul, Greg, Tom, and I see this for what it truly is. But I'd guess each of you perceives it differently from each other."

Mr. Oxinos paused to ask Smoky and Zapfoot whether they knew about the strange creature. Zapfoot still refused to cooperate, but Smoky shook her head.

"So you've visited this thing's realm?" Aliki asked

"Yes, we have," Miss Olsen replied. "To make it worse, it is alive. We call these creatures kuzherits. But that doesn't explain how it came to be here. It shouldn't be able to exist in this realm."

"Why not?" Mike asked.

Mr. Oxinos answered, "Since it is a creature from another realm, it cannot travel here itself. An immortal can learn to summon realm creatures to another realm or world, so that would explain how it might have arrived here. But with Blue dead, the kuzherit should return to its own realm. Since it's still here, Blue didn't summon it. Neither Smoky nor Zapfoot seem experienced enough to summon, and neither of them recognizes it. So another giant must be responsible."

Dr. Fathy stared at the kuzherit. "I will certainly confer with our other investigators to determine if any of them know how the giants might be using kuzherits."

Miss Olsen's face looked grim. "This could be considerably more than a giant father teaching his children about their immortal talents. If multiple giant clans have started cooperating on a significant scale, we may have another war on our hands. We should return and let the others know."

Tiff chatted with Aleara. She knew they would depart shortly, but she didn't want to leave Aleara behind. Tiff enjoyed the company of the curious sylph. Aleara obviously felt the same way.

"So will you come back to our realm?" Aleara asked.

"I'm sure we will. We have a lot more training to do. We all need to master our elemental talents here. How about whenever I return, I'll come back here to the Artisan Exchange? Your family makes artistic winds, right? So I'll ask and find your family's shop."

"Maybe, but they'll think you're a boltling," Aleara replied.

Surprised, Tiff looked at herself. She was still in her elemental lightning form. She said, "Hold on... let me see if I can do this..." She concentrated, thinking of her normal form. She thought of flesh and blood, bone and skin, and hoped it would work.

When Tiff opened her eyes, Aleara looked surprised. She said, "I knew you could transform, but I'd only seen you change into fire or lightning, or your mixed-up form you had when we met. Now you look like Dr. Fathy."

Tiff looked at her arms, now made of flesh. She searched for a piece of reflective metal and saw her normal self in its reflection. "This is my true form."

"I like it, particularly the stuff on your head. Umm... may I touch you?" Aleara said hesitantly.

Tiff replied instantly. "This? This is my hair. Of course you can touch me. You're my friend now. Go ahead."

Aleara carefully touched Tiff's face, then moved her airy hands through Tiff's hair. Finally, she caressed Tiff's arms down to her hands. The entire experience felt like a cool breeze flowing against her face and hair.

Aleara looked like she expected something. So Tiff mimicked her motions, gently touching Aleara's face and arms. Touching Aleara felt like touching a swift breeze. Aleara smiled.

The young sylph rose higher. "Farewell for now, my friend! I hope to see you soon!" She flew upward, back toward her home in the clouds.

Miss Olsen walked over to her and spoke with a gentle voice. "You may not understand the significance of her gesture. Elementals generally do not touch each other. As you noticed, fire still burns wood here, and water extinguishes fire. To avoid hurting each other, elementals are exceedingly polite. Physical touch only happens between family and close friends."

Tiff gazed skyward with a wistful expression. In a low voice, Miss Olsen assured her, "I'll make certain you have time to see her on our next visit."

Coach Brown and MacKenzie gathered the weapons from Tiff, Jason, and Mike. Coach Brown said, "Don't worry. These are yours now. But until you have your own Pocket, I'll take care of them for you." One at a time, he slid them into some sort of nothingness.

"I wondered where you pulled the weapons from," Jason said. "I figured you didn't carry my greataxe in a backpack."

Coach Brown chuckled. "One of the items we usually carry is what we call a Pocket. When we pocket something, we use the device to store it in a miniature private realm—a personal dimension, if you want to think of it that way. You can retrieve those items when you need them. You'll each receive your own Pocket soon enough."

"I can imagine Kyle pocketing a whole library," Jason teased.

Kyle smiled in response. The look on his face suggested he'd thought of the same thing.

Dr. Fathy interrupted. "We need to return to our own world. Let us return to our arrival point in the school. It's already evening, so we should return before your parents worry."

CHAPTER TWENTY-ONE
Suspicions

Mr. Oxinos and Miss Olsen returned Zapfoot and Smoky to their own world. They decided to stay there for a week, both to investigate the kuzherit and to help Smoky adjust.

Miss Olsen also swore she'd ensure that Zapfoot got a proper punishment from his mother or some other authority figure. "He may be a youth, but he did some horrible things to those elementals. I doubt the elementals will welcome him anytime soon."

Kyle wanted to help Dr. Fathy research the kuzherit. But Dr. Fathy had disappeared. Coach Brown told him, "Dr. Fathy is investigating more than the errant titans. He is exploring some esoteric sources of knowledge to help with all of his investigations. He'll return when he finds something."

"Are those sources of knowledge like the book he lent me?" Kyle asked.

"Book?"

Kyle recollected, "Yes, sir. He lent me a book made of a strange material. I couldn't read it at first, but the words themselves changed to English as I watched. It was amazing."

"Those books are part of a personal library that he created himself. For him to loan you one of his books... Let's say it's special," the coach murmured, clearly astonished.

Mike sat in his afternoon art class on Tuesday, wishing Mr. Oxinos would return. The substitute teacher told the class to draw something from memory of a recent experience. Several of the students started goofing off immediately, but most busied themselves with their drawing.

Mike occupied his time with trying to draw the kuzherit. But every time he drew something, his drawing looked different— and *wrong*. He couldn't figure out how to draw what he'd seen. For that matter, he still couldn't figure out what the kuzherit looked like, even though he'd looked right at it.

The bell rang, so Mike tucked his drawings away and wandered toward the band room for his next class. He hoped Mr. Oxinos could help him understand the kuzherit when he returned.

On his way, Aliki joined him. "You look frustrated, Mike. Is something wrong?"

"Art class is totally boring without Mr. O. The sub wanted us to draw something from a recent experience. Talk about no imagination," Mike complained.

"So what did you try to draw?"

"The kuzherit," Mike whispered. "I can't get it on paper right."

"I didn't really get a good look at it," Aliki admitted. "I was watching Smoky, but I did notice the teachers were pretty worried about it."

"But I can't seem to get the image out of my mind and onto the paper," Mike said, frustrated.

"Maybe you're not supposed to. I mean, didn't Miss Olsen say they couldn't exist in our realm? That they didn't have an analogue in the Primal Realm? If that's the case, they're not what we think of as normal matter, right?"

"Good point," Mike admitted. He'd hoped trying to draw it would help him understand the creature, but perhaps it was inherently incomprehensible. "To me, the creature seemed like something I'd seen before, but couldn't remember. Like something strangely familiar, maybe from a dream or something."

The two of them were walking toward the band room when a voice called out from nearby. "Mike Rhee, right?" Mike turned to see an older African-American student. "I'm John Coleman, Kyle's older brother. Got a minute?"

"Sure. Is Kyle okay?" he responded, puzzled. He nodded to Aliki, who continued on to the band room.

"That's what I wanted to ask you. You're his friend and go on these trips with him, right?" Mike nodded. "Well, after the last one this past weekend, something happened. He came back with this odd hunk of glass or quartz or something. And he doesn't know it, but I saw him crying last night. So what happened?"

John's tone was polite, but his eyes locked on Mike's with a challenging gaze. Mike took a deep breath to calm his nerves. John was older, larger, and more physically fit than Kyle. Mike wasn't afraid of John, but he wanted to avoid any unpleasantness.

So he thought quickly.

"Well, something did happen. We were hiking and startled a deer. It jumped out onto a highway and got hit by a truck. The truck wrecked and some of the people were injured. Kyle was right there and saw the deer die. He wasn't responsible, but I think he felt guilty. The glass is a chunk from the truck's window."

"But automobile glass doesn't shatter like that. And his chunk is too thick for even a truck window," John retorted, suspicion creeping into his voice.

Mike realized his mistake and tried to cover it. "It was one of those armored trucks with the bulletproof glass. The impact was pretty severe. Kyle has always seemed like a sensitive type. I'm concerned about him too. If you need anything, please let me know."

John looked like he didn't believe him, but Mike knew the truth was even less believable.

John frowned. "I'm not sure why Mom lets him go on these wild adventures so much. I'm glad he's doing anything to gets his nose out of books, and I'm glad he has friends. But if he gets hurt again, I'm going to make him stop."

As John left, Mike pondered his words. *Why do our parents let us go on these wild excursions?*

The next day, Mike wanted to discuss what had happened with someone. He didn't want to involve Kyle yet, and Tiff and Jason were busy with some school projects. So he chatted with Aliki at lunch. He told her about the confrontation with John.

"It really got me wondering. Why have all five of our parents agreed to let us spend so much of our time with Mr. Oxinos, Coach Brown, and Miss Olsen? We need to understand our abilities, but it seems a little too coincidental to me," Mike said.

"Well, my parents initially opposed my participation. Our family is Greek and my parents immigrated here, so they're overprotective. But Mr. Oxinos talked with them, and they agreed. It helped that he's Greek too. Of course, they don't know he's from Ancient Greece, not modern Greece," Aliki responded, smiling.

"Yes, my mother hesitated a bit. And Mr. Oxinos talked with her too," Mike replied.

"But you're obviously not Greek," Aliki giggled.

"No, half Korean," Mike chuckled with her. "But seriously... do you think Mr. Oxinos did something to make our parents allow our participation?"

Aliki thought for a moment. "Maybe. They have a lot more abilities than we know about. But do you really want to stir up that pot? Confronting him or asking our parents might make our parents forbid us from continuing."

Mike continued, "And if he used some mind trick on them, he could have used it on us too."

Aliki paused, dumbfounded. They both stared at each other, realizing the possible implications.

Aliki and Mike called everyone together over lunch on Thursday to discuss their concerns about their parents. Mike described his encounter with Kyle's brother John, omitting the part about John seeing Kyle crying.

Mike continued, "It made me think. We do some dangerous stuff—traveling to other realms, fighting giants. I don't think our parents would approve if they knew what we were really doing. So why did they all agree to let us participate? Aliki and I discovered Mr. Oxinos visited our parents to convince them to let us participate. Did he do the same with yours?"

He turned first to Jason. Jason finished swallowing his third slice of pizza, then replied, "I've done a lot of adventure camping with the scouts. I'd gotten a little bored with it, so my father was happy when I expressed an interest in this. It wasn't an issue with me. Do you think Mr. Oxinos did some sort of magic on your parents?"

Aliki poked at her salad. "They have abilities we haven't mastered, like traveling between the realms or making trees move. They have special devices, like the Pockets. What if there is a realm of mind control or something? If there's a Demon Realm and a Heaven Realm, they might be able to tap into them. Who knows what else they can do? What about you, Tiff?"

Tiff thought for a moment as she nibbled on some fries. "I guess I never thought about it. My parents pretty much let me do what I want. I've worked hard to keep their trust. They talked to Mr. Oxinos over the phone, but didn't meet him in person until they dropped me off for our first trip to the Animal Realm."

Kyle finally admitted, "I think my mother was so happy I would be doing something other than read books that she agreed. But when I came home injured after the Animal Realm, she got pretty mad. Coach Brown and Mr. Oxinos told her I hurt myself climbing." He turned to Mike. "I'm sorry about John. He can be overprotective."

Aliki continued, "Mike and I are worried that they're affecting our minds, or at least our parents' minds. If not outright control, maybe they have some sort of super-persuasion ability. Are we foot soldiers in a fight against giants? Or new guardians for the Fountain of Souls?"

Mike answered, "They've made it clear that they want us to help protect it. Let's find out more. Aliki, you can read that old scroll in homeroom, right? Perhaps you can find out more by checking out the other stuff in homeroom. Tiff? How about faking an injury to get into Miss Olsen's office?"

Jason waited for a few students to pass by their table. He asked, "What do you want me to do?"

Aliki thought for a moment. "Can you transform to water here? If you can, how about flowing into Mr. Oxinos' house for a quick investigation?"

Jason looked shocked. "That's breaking and entering... or at least entering. I don't feel comfortable doing that. Besides, he might have alarms or something worse."

Mike quickly agreed. "Jason's right. We're trying to figure out what other abilities they have, but let's not find out the hard way."

Tiff added, "Besides, as an immortal, I bet he has a ton of money in all kinds of accounts. So he could afford alarm systems and more. He wouldn't even need special abilities. And if the police show up, what would we do?"

Kyle suggested, "What about simply asking Coach Brown? Or MacKenzie?"

"Not a bad idea," Mike agreed. "I'll talk to MacKenzie.

Jason, how about you talk to the coach? Kyle, talk to your parents about what Mr. Oxinos said when you got back from the Animal Realm. They might reveal something he did."

With football season over, Jason hadn't signed up for any other sports. Originally, he'd planned on trying out for wrestling, but now he didn't see a point. With his immortal gifts, he couldn't lose, and wrestling didn't have as much of a team dynamic as football. So he'd volunteered to be a coach's assistant for the wrestling team, which Coach Brown also coached.

With Mike and Aliki raising doubts about Mr. Oxinos, he wasn't sure what to think about the coach either. So he helped out as usual, but showed little of his normal enthusiasm.

The wrestling practice ended a little early, and the boys headed for the showers. On the way to the locker room, Coach Brown stopped Jason. "Walk with me for a few minutes."

Coach Brown led Jason outside into the cold air where they'd have a little privacy. "You have something on your mind. I can tell. Anything I can help with? Is it about not playing a sport anymore? Or other matters?"

Jason wished he had Mike's ability to concoct a story in an instant. But he could only admit, "We're trying to figure out why we're doing all this. I mean, we're still teens. And we're fighting giants?"

"If you asked the same question to Paul or Ida, they'd say it was fate. Or it could be dumb luck, or coincidence. We knew we'd have five new immortals this year, but not who they'd be."

"How did you know there would be five of us?"

Coach Brown looked away for a few minutes. "We were amazed ourselves. We rarely get new immortals at all, perhaps two or three each decade. Five in a single year is unprecedented. There are those among us who have some ability for predicting the future. Paul has a little of it, but it's a rare talent. We were told—by those with more skill—to prepare things for the five of you."

"Why did there need to be so many new immortals now?"

"Honestly, I don't know. Perhaps something big is coming, or perhaps you are all destined for something important," the coach answered.

"This may sound weird, but how did you convince our parents to let us go on these trips? I know they're necessary, but most parents would yank their kids out of a program if someone got badly hurt like Kyle did."

"Paul is very persuasive. He spoke to Kyle's parents about how his skills and confidence have grown, and he told them how he had his accident because he used new skills to help a friend. So his parents agreed to let Kyle decide whether to continue."

"And Aliki's parents? I heard they're pretty protective."

"Fortunately, Paul is also Greek. I think they were worried their daughter might be exposed to dangers. I wasn't there when Paul met with them, but I imagine he soothed their fears."

"So no magic was involved in convincing them?" Jason asked. "We thought he might have hypnotized them or something."

The coach looked at him with merriment in his eyes once again. "Maybe a little," he grinned.

Mike called MacKenzie on his cellphone and arranged to meet her at a nearby coffee shop after school on Thursday. As he entered the shop, he heard Celtic music playing on the sound system. MacKenzie sat quietly at a table, snacking on some sort of muffin and listening to the music.

Mike had seen MacKenzie happy, enraged, even covered in her own blood. But he never expected to see the ancient Celtic warrior in a somber mood. The contrast with her normal boisterous self was unnerving.

"Afternoon, Mike. What can I get you?" she asked.

"Some hot tea would be nice. Oolong, if they have it," he replied, sitting down to face her.

"Not what ye expected?" she said, reading his expression.

"To be honest, no. But thanks for meeting me here." Mike decided honesty would be the best approach with her.

"It's important to remember those we've left behind. Our history makes us who we are." She perked up. "But ye didn't come all this way just to sit with a melancholy woman, did ye? What's on your mind?"

"Well, I was curious about the range of abilities we have, or that we will eventually have. Coach Brown already talked about pocketing things, and you can move between realms. But what else?" Mike asked.

They paused as the waitress brought Mike's tea and another cup of coffee for MacKenzie. He sipped it and set it aside to steep for a few minutes.

She stirred her coffee. "Well, there are three sources of our abilities beyond the immortality itself. The first ye already know —tapping into the power of the various Realms. The next ye've already glimpsed, and that's the ability to travel to realms, or even other worlds like the giant's world. The last is not innate, but we do have access to more advanced technology than normal folks have."

"Like the Pockets. So where does that tech come from?" Mike asked.

"Well, we make it. Consider someone who can create fire, like Greg Brown. He could use it in a fight, but he can't throw fire like one of your superheroes. Instead, he crafts a weapon that channels the fire. By using materials from the Primal Realm when crafting his weapon, the weapon takes on some properties of the Primal materials. So his sword burns."

"But his sword looks normal." Mike replied.

"Ye haven't seen it up close, boyo. The edge of his blade can get white-hot. That's how he could wound Blue, despite the fomor's metal torso. But we have other tools. Not everything is a weapon."

MacKenzie paused. "Imagine me sayin' that." Mike grinned. "Anyhow, we also create advanced tech gizmos if we choose. It helps that there is a Tech Realm."

"So with all these realm abilities and advanced tech, someone could control someone else's mind?" Mike asked.

"No, that's impossible. We cannot fight free will. Some among us do have a lot of persuasive ability. And harnessing powers drawn from the Realm of Heaven or the Demon Realm— yes, they're real—can help." MacKenzie ate more of her muffin and took another long drink from her coffee cup.

"Heaven? What would that be like?" Mike asked.

"The Heaven Realm isn't fluffy clouds and angels wi' harps. But the Heaven Realm enhances what we traditionally think of as 'good.' Some abilities it grants include affecting positive emotions, like joy or happiness. But like the primal elements or animal forms, each of us can only attune to only a few emotions —if we're able to at all. And it doesn't affect creatures that don't feel emotion," MacKenzie said.

Mike suddenly formed a theory about what Mr. Oxinos had done. "So do you harness the power of the Heaven Realm, MacKenzie?"

"A little, lad. But I draw more from the Demon Realm. Ye've certainly already sensed it. If we attune to an emotion, we always leak a bit if we're not careful. That's one of the reasons I move around so much. In the Demon Realm, I've attuned to the emotions of fear and terror."

The two of them sat quietly for a few minutes, sharing each other's company. Mike remembered MacKenzie's somber face when he entered.

"MacKenzie? Over the years, you've moved around. How hard is it to create new identities? Do you have ways of finding your fellow immortals when you move to a new city?"

"Well, some clans of us get together on a regular basis. I return to Ireland every spring for something like a family reunion, for great craic and passin' stories about. And we have technology to keep in touch with each other now."

She continued after another bite. "As far as new identities, that has gotten a bit harder. Fortunately, we have some talented folks who can create new identities when we need them. New name, new false history, and so forth. We typically move every ten to twenty years."

"So MacKenzie isn't your original name?" he asked.

"No, lad, though I'm rather fond of it. It's close to my original name," she replied, meeting his gaze. "I know that look, lad. Yer curiosity will get the best of you some day. We're not supposed to use our original names around normals, but ye're not normal anymore." She gulped down the last of her coffee. "My original name is Macha."

The next Monday, Aliki arrived in homeroom early, as she had every day the previous week. She gazed around the room at the various clues and remembered the abilities she'd seen Mr. Oxinos use.

First, she reflected on his talent with art. She guessed the ancient Greek scroll she'd discovered on the alcove wall was an award he'd won, not something he'd happened to find. She looked at the laurel wreath on the marble bust and wondered if it were an even more ancient award for something.

She'd heard him playing both guitar and a recorder while on the camping trip with Julisha, so he had musical talent as well. He'd demonstrated considerable skill with a bow and also mentioned a sister who was even more skilled.

As far as his talents with Realm-based magic, or whatever she wanted to call it, she knew he had command over light. According to Mike, he radiated some positive emotion from the Heaven Realm, and that helped influence their parents. From being around him, she knew he sometimes projected an aura of interesting-ness that inspired her to discover artistry in herself and things around her.

She looked again at the name on his prominently displayed teaching certificates. It said "Alexander Paul Oxinos," meaning he went by his middle name. Below the teaching certificates, she found a more modern certificate he'd awarded to one of the seniors. He'd signed it "A. Paul Oxinos."

Carson and Pete wandered into homeroom, chatting about what they'd done over the weekend.

"Hey... do you think Mr. O will be back today?" Carson said.

The truth hit her like a freight train.

Paul Oxinos came in a few minutes later, along with some other students. She knew he'd just spent a week looking for clues in the giant's world and dealing with Smoky and Zapfoot. But now he stood there, casually leaning on his desk, as if he didn't have a care in the world.

Mr. Oxinos talked to the class about his impromptu trip to Paris, eloquently describing visits to art museums and attractions. Aliki listened to his fictitious story, but his smile seemed genuine. The other students peppered him with questions about his trip, and he gave them all an entertaining, plausible story. Mike and Jason even asked a few questions, playing along with his ruse. As usual, Kyle sat with his nose in a book, mostly ignoring everyone.

Tiff scooted into the class right before the bell rang. Mr. Oxinos took attendance, and the other students went about their normal routines.

But Aliki couldn't focus on schoolwork. She stared at Mr.

Oxinos, mentally wrestling with the implications of her discovery. He met her gaze at one point, and she nervously tried to look somewhere else. But her mind and her gaze kept returning to her immortal teacher.

Finally, the bell marking the end of homeroom sounded. The other students filed out, heading toward their classes. Aliki waited for everyone else to leave, then slowly approached Mr. Oxinos.

"I... figured it out. It was right in front of me all this time. I finally figured it out," she mumbled.

"Figured what out, Aliki?" Mr. Oxinos asked, trying to read her thunderstruck expression.

"I finally put the clues together." Her voice changed to one of absolute conviction. "You're Apollo!"

CHAPTER TWENTY-TWO
Gods and Godlings

"You mean he's really a god, Aliki?" Mike asked, incredulous.

The students sat around a table, looking at Mr. Oxinos. He, Coach Brown, MacKenzie, and Miss Olsen sat together at one end of the table. They'd quickly arranged for a meeting during school and called the immortal students together.

"You both owe me five dollars," Coach Brown said with a twinkle in his eye. "I picked Aliki to discover it, remember?"

"My purse is in my office," Miss Olsen said. "I'll get it to you later."

Mr. Oxinos casually pulled out his wallet and tossed a five-dollar bill on the table. Turning to the students, he said, "So you think you've figured things out?"

Aliki spoke with an uncommon assertiveness. "Apollo, god of the sun, light, the arts, music, healing, and lots more. Wields a bow, like his sister Artemis. You match, Mr. Oxinos. Besides, your name... Alexander Paul Oxinos. A. Paul Oxinos. A Paul O."

"I did think that was a clever way to see who could figure it out," Mr. Oxinos said. "Congratulations, Aliki."

"So you admit it?" Tiff asked.

"Am I Apollo, worshipped by the Greeks as a god? Yes, I am Apollo. My sister and I were born mortal, like all of you. Like you, we gained immortality and went through a similar process of training. Back then, we didn't feel the need to hide our abilities like we do now. To the ancient Greeks, we performed miracles, and myths developed around our exploits."

He paused to let his words sink in. "But once the Greek civilization became absorbed by the Romans, then overrun by the Turks, the age of the Greek gods had passed. Rather than fight the rise and fall of civilizations, we became caretakers in the shadows. Our true goals were to guide and protect Earth, protect the Fountain of Souls, and keep the Realms in balance. We met immortals from other cultures and discovered our goals were similar. So we cooperated, ultimately forming the hidden society we have today."

"So are all of you gods?" Jason blurted, trying to understand the new information.

Miss Olsen answered, "You mean, do we have phenomenal cosmic powers, creating worlds, or whatever? No. Are we, as immortals, known in myths as gods? Yes. If you know your Norse mythology, you might know me as Idun, the goddess who tends the tree that bears the apples of youth." She looked at Jason and Tiff. "They taste pretty good, don't they?"

Tiff and Jason nodded their heads, dumbfounded.

"What about you, sir?" Kyle asked Coach Brown. He could barely contain his excitement.

"Most people in the modern world aren't familiar with the gods of the Yoruba, but I am Ogun, god of smithing and war."

212

MacKenzie added, "And I've already told you my real name, Mike—Macha. My sisters and I were collectively known as Morrigan."

"Are we gods too?" Jason asked.

"Define 'god,' Jason." Mr. Oxinos said. "If you believe a god is omnipotent, omnipresent, and omniscient, then no. We aren't gods, and neither are you. If you think of a god as merely a powerful being that is, or could be, worshipped, then we could be considered gods. But then again, so could any of the various superheroes populating the comics, or even famous athletes and celebrities. So let's think of ourselves as immortals with supernatural powers. Whether we are worshiped depends on the culture. Perhaps in a few hundred years, you will have your own flock of worshipers."

"But probably not," Coach Brown warned. "Some immortals have abused their abilities to try to form cults or get away with horrible crimes. When that happens, other immortals will step in to correct the problem. Usually permanently."

MacKenzie added, "And that's another reason why ye're training with us too. Yer teachers have been evaluatin' yer character, and they're pleased with all of you."

Mr. Oxinos stood. "For now, you should all return to class. This is a lot to take in, so take your time. We'll be happy to answer any questions."

Tuesday afternoon, Tiff met her friends Mara, Shelly, and Rachel at the mall. Tiff needed something to distract her from Mr. Oxinos' latest revelation, so she'd hastily arranged a shopping expedition. Tiff looked forward to hanging out and enjoying herself.

They visited their favorite stores, tried on spring clothes, looked at earrings, and chatted about the upcoming Valentine's Dance, school, and whatever else came to mind. After a few hours, they took a break from shopping and ate tacos at the food court.

"So how is your special training going?" Shelly asked. "Still hanging out with Aliki?"

"Yes. Our last trip was pretty eventful," Tiff blurted, then immediately regretted it.

"Really? What happened?" asked Rachel, with an edge of jealousy in her voice.

"Well, there was a... big guy who caused us some problems. But Coach Brown and MacKenzie took care of him," she said, thinking about the fight with the giants. "Oh, and I made a new friend too. Her name is Aleara."

"Aleara? Is she from around here?" Mara asked.

"No. She's from far away. But I'm sure I'll see her again," Tiff answered.

She turned her attention to her tacos. She'd already eaten three and was trying to decide whether to buy more.

"I sure wish I could eat like you. I'd get fat," whined Rachel.

"I burn a lot of energy. That's all," Tiff responded.

They settled on some churros for dessert and went to a movie together. Tiff tried to forget the weighty revelations from Mr. Oxinos and the others and lose herself in a good horror flick. But even though the others enjoyed the show, Tiff's thoughts kept returning to the fight against Zapfoot. The frights on the screen paled in comparison.

Wednesday night, Kyle talked a bit about the next planned outings at dinner with his family. He could barely contain his excitement about learning how the various myths actually happened. But he missed his brother John's concerned glances as he told his family about the next training session. After dinner, he and John helped their parents clean the dishes. Then Kyle grabbed the bag of books he'd checked out from the library and climbed the stairs to his room. He'd found some books about African myths and planned to read any tales he could find about Ogun.

"Hey, Kyle. Got a minute?" John asked.

"Sure. What do you want?"

"Let's talk in your room," John replied.

Kyle shrugged and climbed the stairs to his room. John followed him and closed the door.

"So, what's going on?" Kyle glanced up as he pulled the books out of the book bag.

"More stuff on history? What's that one? Myths?" John asked, watching Kyle.

"Yes. I found a source of information on African myths, so I want to read more about them again."

"Haven't you read all the books on African history in the library?" John asked.

"Well, yeah. But I want to read these again. New facts make me see old knowledge differently."

"Does this have anything to do with these trips you go on

with Mr. O and Coach Brown?" John's tone became more accusatory.

"Sure does. Coach Brown is a wonderful source of information," Kyle answered.

"Look... Kyle... I don't think you should go on those trips anymore," John said hesitantly.

"Why not?" Kyle asked.

"You got hurt on one. And on the last one, something else happened, didn't it? Something that still bugs you." John walked over to the chunk of glass and picked it up carefully.

"LEAVE THAT ALONE!" Kyle yelled.

John, surprised at Kyle's reaction, carefully set the glass back in its place. "Calm down, bro. That's what I mean. You're not thinking straight."

But Kyle was upset. John wanted him to stop going on the trips. John was messing with the remnant of Tarskax. John always told him what to do.

"You want me to stop because I finally found a group of friends! And they're not you! And I'm doing things you can't do!" Kyle argued.

"No! It's not like that! I'm worried about you! Mom and Dad are busy with their jobs, so I try to look out for you. And I don't want you to get hurt!" John said.

"You don't need to look out for me! I can take care of myself!" Kyle yelled back.

John finally got angry. "With what? Your books? What if something happens on one of these trips and you get hurt again? What if it's more serious? The teachers don't seem to care about what happens to you. But I DO!"

Kyle yelled back, "I said I can take care of myself! I'm not a child anymore!"

"But I'm older, and you should listen to me!"

"Stop babying me!"

But instead of continuing the argument, John looked terrified. "Kyle?" he said, in a very small voice.

Kyle paused, looking at his arms. They were bear paws. He'd turned into the bear in front of his brother. He reverted back to human form as quickly as he could.

"What have they done to you?" John stammered, still plainly terrified.

Now human again, Kyle quickly wrapped himself in his blanket. "It's okay. I'm still me. It's something special. Mr. Oxinos and Coach Brown are helping me learn about it."

Confusion and fear mixed on John's face. He opened his mouth as if to speak, but no words emerged. Finally, John sat on the bed beside Kyle. He took a deep, shuddering breath. "Are you some sort of monster? Some sort of were-bear?"

Kyle could see John shaking. "John! It's still me. They haven't turned me into a monster. I have some new abilities. Mr. Oxinos and Coach Brown are helping us learn to control them." He looked John in the eyes. "I'm sorry I scared you."

"Does Mom or Dad know?" John asked, trying to comprehend. "Are the others like that too? Do they change into bears or whatever?"

"Mom and Dad don't know, and they can't. Please don't tell them. If they knew, they'd freak out," Kyle said quickly.

"Kyle, *I'm* freaking out. My brother turns into a bear. That's not normal at all. So I have every reason to freak out!"

"Look, we're trying to learn about all this. There's a lot going on. But I'm going to be careful. Please believe me." Kyle pleaded. "I also heal faster, and I'm stronger too."

John's skepticism was obvious in his reaction. So Kyle stepped over to his desk and placed his elbow on the desk in an obvious arm-wrestling position.

"You're kidding, right? You've never been able to beat me. But you'll turn into the bear and win, right?" John said, walking to face Kyle.

"Come on... let me show you. No bear," Kyle answered.

With a shrug, John knelt, placed his elbow on the desk, and took Kyle's hand, ready to arm-wrestle. "Ready whenever you are," he said.

Kyle nodded, and the arm-wrestling contest started. John began using his greater size to his advantage. But to his surprise, he couldn't turn Kyle's wrist. Kyle exerted more strength and pushed John's arm back. After several minutes of quiet struggle between the brothers, John's hand hit the desk.

Kyle crowed, "See? I told you!"

John was still struggling to understand it all. After several minutes, he spoke with an odd tremor in his voice. "So where does this leave me? I guess you really don't need me anymore. If you're going to continue this strange stuff, I can't help you. I can't look out for you." With a dejected look, he stood, and turned toward the door.

"Wait, John. You can help me," Kyle pleaded. "I'm not sure how to make this work, but I could use your help. You can help me explore my abilities, and help cover for me. There's so much I'm still trying to figure out."

The two brothers locked gazes again. John spoke, "If this is what you want, I suppose I could help. But you have to tell me everything. If I'm going to help cover your activities, I want to know what to expect." He paused to take a deep breath. "How weird is this going to get?"

Kyle smiled. "Pretty weird, bro."

Dr. Fathy returned on Thursday and met Paul Oxinos at his house for dinner. The Egyptian paced nervously as Paul set the table.

"Did you discover anything more about the disappearances?" Paul asked.

"Yes, unfortunately. I went to Marseille to look for clues about Michel Durand. Do you know him?"

"Yes. He's a talented artist and an avid tennis player. He became immortal in 1719 and fought in European wars of the 18th century. As an immortal, he's talented with wind and glass, and has both a demonic form and a rat form," Mr. Oxinos replied.

"He has some talents with the Ghost Realm as well. Anyhow, I checked his house. His most recent paintings looked like spirits, so I stepped into the Spirit Realm near his residence. What I discovered there..." Dr. Fathy paused, worry etched on his face.

"Go ahead, Tom," Paul prodded.

"The area near his home in the Spirit Realm looked like a war zone. He lives in a small house overlooking the sea, but in the Spirit Realm, it had collapsed into the sea. Shards of glass were embedded in the rock, and fresh furrows from giant-sized hands scarred the ground nearby."

Dr. Fathy sipped some wine, then continued. "The spirits had scattered, but I talked with a few of them. From what they told me, a pair of giants ambushed him. Though he fought back, they captured him. They disappeared with him, probably taking him back to Yothrun," Dr. Fathy finished with an ominous tone.

"So the disappearances and the titans are connected. I was afraid of that." Paul sighed.

On Friday, Mr. Oxinos sat in his room, looking at the students' latest art projects. The school would be having an art show in conjunction with the upcoming Valentine's Dance, so he needed to pick the best art for the school's display cases and walls. He was examining several students' still-life drawings when he heard a knock on the door. Turning, he saw an older African-American student standing in the doorway.

"Mr. Oxinos? I'm John Coleman, Kyle's older brother. Do you have a minute?"

He knew about John Coleman and had seen him a few times, but never had a chance to talk to the young man. "Certainly. Is Kyle all right?"

"Yes, he's fine... I guess." John entered the room, closing the door behind him. "I didn't want to talk to you about this, but something upset him on your last training trip. And now things are weird."

"There were some problems on the previous trip." Mr. Oxinos said. "What did he tell you about it?"

"He didn't talk about it, so I asked that Mike kid. Mike gave me some story about a deer being hit by an armored truck. I could tell it wasn't the truth," John replied. The last sentence sounded more like an accusation.

"I see," Mr. Oxinos said.

"I told Kyle I didn't think he should keep going on those trips. We had a short argument," John continued, his voice becoming more agitated. He shifted his weight nervously and clenched his hands at his side.

"Family always brings out the best in people, but family also can get under your skin far easier than anyone else. Siblings quarrel. But are you getting along now?"

"You don't understand. The argument got cut short when Kyle turned into a bear!" John exclaimed.

Mr. Oxinos sat down at his desk and gestured for John to sit. "That was unfortunate. I assume he didn't hurt you. Have you told anyone else about this?"

"No. They'd think I was crazy. But I know what I saw. I don't know how you did it, but you turned my brother into something else." John paced for a moment, waving his hands in frustration. After a deep breath, he gathered himself and sat across from Mr. Oxinos. "Now, he's different. A monster, maybe. He seems okay, and he said he doesn't need me to look out for him anymore. But I still worry about him."

"As you should," Mr. Oxinos agreed. He'd already deduced that John considered himself Kyle's protector. "Kyle is going through some challenging times. While he doesn't need you to look out for him physically, he will need your compassion and support."

"But what exactly did you do to him?" John asked.

"What has Kyle told you? It might be easier to discuss this if you tell me what you already know," Mr. Oxinos suggested.

"Kyle told me about changing into a bear, and that he can sense things in the ground. He also talked about these magical places—one with talking animals, and one with people made of glass or rock or plastic. He said you guys had a big fight and a glass person he knew got shattered. And that chunk of glass he has came from that fight." John's words came tumbling out in a rush.

"Go on," Mr. Oxinos urged.

"Well, he said you and Coach Brown were helping him learn how to use his abilities, and the trips you're making are to those magical realms."

"That's all correct. The training can be a little dangerous, so we train him somewhere hidden. We wouldn't want him accidentally changing into a bear and hurting someone," Mr. Oxinos confided. "And because we don't want people treating him as a freak, we need to keep these activities a secret."

"When he turned into a bear, he terrified *me*," John admitted. "So where did these abilities come from? Was it an experimental drug? Or a magical potion?"

"Something like an experimental magical potion," Mr. Oxinos admitted. "Kyle was chosen by fate to gain these abilities —or you might say he accidentally drank it. The change is permanent, so we need to help him quickly understand and control his new abilities. That's really why we've been working with him so much."

"So you're really trying to help him? And not using him as

some sort of guinea pig?" John asked.

"You have my word." Mr. Oxinos reassured him. "Please let me know if you have any more concerns in the future. But please keep it between us for Kyle's sake."

"Okay, I guess." John looked calmer. "But are the other kids —Mike, Jason, and the rest—also affected? Are they turning into bears too?"

"That's not for me to discuss. They will have their own tales to tell."

CHAPTER TWENTY-THREE
Back to the Realms

The next weekend, the students gathered in the elemental version of their gymnasium in the Primal Realm, dressed again in the fireproof clothing provided by the teachers. But rather than train individually as they had on their previous excursion, they all remained in the gym-arena. Coach Brown had brought along several freestanding full-length mirrors, which he set in various places. Neither MacKenzie nor Dr. Fathy had joined them on this particular training.

Mr. Oxinos stood before them. "One of the things you'll need to master is maintaining your normal form while within a realm. It means you must maintain a clear image of your own identity and not allow the realm to overcome you. We'll have you work on this here during the morning and do some individual training in the afternoon. This shouldn't be too difficult to master, since each of you has managed at least one transformation either in this realm or the Animal Realm."

Miss Olsen added, "The mirrors are so each of you can focus on your own progress. Remember you are flesh and blood, not fire, earth, or water."

The students each stood in front of a mirror and tried to focus on becoming flesh and blood. The three teachers moved from student to student, giving suggestions and observing their progress.

Tiff had already mastered her transformation during her previous visit to the Primal Realm, so Coach Brown stood near her, watching her demonstrate. "Excellent, Tiffany. You should experiment with transforming between forms faster. You can also try to work your transformation to eagle form as well. See how quickly you can transform from human girl to firebird."

Jason succeeded in transforming his arms to flesh after about fifteen minutes. His legs followed after another ten minutes. Finally, he returned to human form as Mr. Oxinos watched.

"Good work, Jason. Keep practicing. Transform from human to water and back again. See how fast you can manage it," Mr. Oxinos suggested.

Mike and Kyle both managed to transform into their normal human forms after about an hour and a half. But Aliki couldn't manage it by the time they paused for lunch.

At lunchtime, Mr. Oxinos stepped back to Earth to order pizzas from his favorite pizza place. He brought a stack of them back with him, and everyone sat down to devour the delicious food in the elemental version of the school courtyard.

Miss Olsen sat beside Aliki. "Don't worry. You'll get the hang of it."

Dejected, Aliki gazed at the floor. "Everyone else has managed some sort of transformation. I haven't yet. Kyle, Mike, and Tiff have animal forms, and Tiff and Jason have elemental forms. I can make it darker here and turn into a half-formed rhino or dolphin. But I can't transform completely in either realm."

Mr. Oxinos said, "Let's focus on your darkness abilities after lunch, Aliki. Kyle? I'd like you to work on exploring your connection with earth. I want to see what else you can manage. Mike, I know we haven't identified an element for you yet, so I'll try to help out." He turned to look at Tiff. "I think you have a promise to keep, Tiffany. You've already mastered elemental transformation, so you could visit your friend. Jason can go with you, since he's got water pretty well mastered too."

Coach Brown spoke. "I'll volunteer to chaperone them. If there's any problem, I'll send Tiffany here for help."

Tiff brightened at the thought of seeing Aleara again. She ate another slice of pizza and asked, "Miss Olsen? I have a question for you."

"Go ahead, Tiffany," Miss Olsen replied.

"I noticed in the fight with Zapfoot, you made the wooden trees twist and grab him, rather than turning to wood or something like that. How do we manipulate the elements like that? Could I make lightning or fire shape into something?"

"Good question, but that particular talent uses abilities from the Spirit Realm. When I shape the trees, what I'm actually doing is convincing tree spirits to help."

"So what's the difference between tree spirits and wood elementals?" Mike asked.

"A spirit is the essence of what it means to be a tree, but isn't necessarily made of wood. A wood elemental is made of the wood itself, but isn't a tree. If you chop down a tree and turn it into a chair, it ceases to be a tree, but is still made of wood. A different spirit might inhabit a chair. Or think about fire. A fire elemental is formed of the element of fire. In our world, an elemental would burn continuously but still retain its shape. But have you ever felt mesmerized when gazing into a campfire? That feeling comes from the spirit of fire."

"Okay... I'm even more confused," Jason said, grinning. "I'll have to have another slice or two of pizza while I think about all of that."

In the afternoon, Mr. Oxinos split his time between Kyle and Mike. Both boys were trying to attune in the courtyard, so he could easily move from one to the other, offering encouragement.

They even encouraged each other. "C'mon, Mike!" Kyle urged. "Try lightning again. Imagine having control over the electricity flowing through your game controller."

"No luck," Mike admitted. "How are you coming?"

"I think I can tell when I'm using my earth sense," Kyle replied. "It's a bit weird though."

"So what does it feel like when you sense something through the earth?" Mike asked.

Kyle struggled to explain. "Well, it's kind of like walking when your foot's asleep. You feel something with your leg, but it's your foot feeling the ground."

"So maybe I can sense with one of the other elements," Mike said hopefully.

Mike had finally had a breakthrough after another hour. He

discovered he could generate swirling winds around his arms, though he couldn't manage any of the rest of his body.

"So what good will windy hands do me?" he asked to no one in particular, staring at the miniature cyclones around each arm.

Mr. Oxinos overheard him though. He picked up a stone from the ground and told Mike, "Catch this, then throw it."

Mike caught the stone, then let the winds lift it. He marveled at how the winds around his hands buffeted the stone strongly enough to keep it from falling. "Cool," he muttered. He tried to throw the stone. To his surprise, the stone rocketed out of his hand.

"Whoa..." Both he and Kyle gasped in surprise.

"Control over air can be useful," Mr. Oxinos advised. "You may be able to find other uses for it too. But you should also focus on transforming the rest of your body."

He turned to Kyle. "Let's do a bit more experimenting with your talents. See how far down you can sense. Close your eyes and reach downward."

"I could sense about thirty feet before, when Dornum helped me. I thought I might be sensing things further away, but I wasn't sure."

"Let's see if we can work on extending and strengthening your sense. Hold on a minute," Mr. Oxinos wandered into the building. A few minutes later, he returned carrying several wooden sticks. He picked up one of the mirrors, paced out twenty feet, and planted the mirror firmly so its support legs sank into the ground. He paced another ten feet and stuck a wooden stick into the ground. He continued until all of the sticks were firmly planted.

"Now, stand here and see how many of the sticks you can sense," he directed.

"I can sense six of the sticks." Kyle said after several minutes of concentration.

"Good. Now see if you can sense the difference between the mirror and the first stick. Can you tell one is metal and the other wood?"

"Not really. But I can tell the mirror legs are larger, and shaped differently," Kyle replied.

Miss Olsen carried a mirror into one of the smaller buildings near the transformed gymnasium. Aliki followed her into the building and gazed around. It held a few large objects composed of different elemental materials. A few resembled soccer nets, so Aliki guessed they were some sort of sports equipment. Shelves held several glowing objects that seemed to be made of light.

Miss Olsen turned to face Aliki. "I hope this room will make you more comfortable, so you can reach your potential. You've struggled with both elemental and animal forms, and I think I know why."

Aliki felt both a sense of relief and a sense of dread at the same time. "So why can't I master it?" she asked in a small voice.

"Who are you, Aliki? How do you identify yourself?" Miss Olsen demanded, her ice-blue eyes locking onto Aliki's.

"Wha... What do you mean?" she stammered, confused. "I'm just a girl. My family is from Greece. I attend the school like all the rest."

"But you're not like all the rest. You aren't your family. What makes you *you*? Who do you want to be in five or ten years? Mike has a quick wit, a quiet self-assurance that could turn into leadership, and plays jazz. Jason enjoys playing the athlete, but is also active in the Boy Scouts. Kyle loves history so much that he's devoted much of his life to it. Tiffany is a cheerleader, and physically gifted, but also smart and a hard worker. But how do you define yourself? How do you distinguish yourself?"

"I don't know. I've never been anything special," Aliki said, her voice cracking. She felt like running, but knew that wouldn't accomplish anything.

Miss Olsen pressed her point. "Will you open your eyes? You do have gifts that the others don't. Who figured out that Paul is Apollo? Who scored the only hit on MacKenzie? Who noticed Julisha taking an unusual interest in our activities?"

"Me," Aliki whispered, trying to sort out Miss Olsen's words.

"You have talent for figuring things out, for observing things. Do you think it's any coincidence you seem to learn riflery so easily? That takes good observational skill, which you excel at. What you lack is confidence in yourself," Miss Olsen said pointedly.

"But—" Aliki interrupted.

"No buts, Aliki. Remember when you charged the first giant, even though you hadn't mastered the rhinoceros form you were trying for? You reacted, not to flee, but to help your friends. Draw that confidence out again. You have more mettle than you realize. Get that fire in your belly!"

Aliki remembered the first fight and how she'd tried to help. She thought back to her willingness to challenge the team's faith in their teachers, not because she didn't trust them, but she wanted to discover more. And she thought of all the successes Miss Olsen had mentioned—successes she had dismissed as unimportant.

Miss Olsen nodded. "Now you're beginning to know who you are, and who you could be. Fire up that bit of determination, focus yourself, and call the darkness around you."

Aliki generated darkness again. As before, it took the form of a hazy black cloud around her.

"Now pull it in yourself. You are the darkness. Own it! Control it! It is part of who you are!" Miss Olsen commanded.

Aliki followed Miss Olsen's words and focused on the darkness for several minutes. But she didn't feel any different. "I guess it isn't going to work," she lamented.

"Do you really think that?" Miss Olsen pivoted the mirror towards Aliki.

In the mirror, a perfectly black shape, a silhouette within a hazy cloud of darkness, stared back at her.

Tiff, Jason, and Coach Brown walked the few miles to the Artisan Exchange. As they approached, Tiff could see the elementals had already started repairs on the structure. As she approached, she observed small crowds of different elementals entering or leaving the Exchange. She noticed that many of the groups consisted of all the same type of elemental, but a decent proportion of them were mixed.

Coach Brown suggested, "Let's assume elemental form for now. We don't want to attract attention. Many of these folk may still be afraid of outsiders. And I wouldn't blame them."

Tiff assumed a lightning form, and Jason assumed his watery form. Coach Brown became a being of solid metal. After a moment, he asked, "Tiff? If you please, don't get too close to me. Physical contact could hurt. The same goes for you and Jason."

"Right. Don't shock the water or the metal. Got it," Tiff quipped.

They entered the Exchange and watched the elementals wander through shops. Tiff felt like she was in the mall again. And in a sense, she was.

The elementals had cordoned off the central area of the Exchange, preventing anyone from entering the work area. Fire, metal, and earth elementals all pitched in to rebuild the infrastructure of the collapsed section, while other elementals helped out in other ways. The stores in both the north and south ends of the Exchange had reopened for business, and a mix of elementals browsed through the stores.

Hoping to find Aleara, Tiff looked around for a store directory, but couldn't find one.

Coach Brown noticed her confusion. "Excuse me, friend," he said to a passing fire elemental. "Can you tell me where I might find the makers of artistic winds? My friend is searching for something special."

"Past the next ramp, on the upper tier. It's on the left, I think," the fire elemental replied.

"Thank you," Tiff said, relieved.

They climbed the ramp and spotted the shop. Several sylphs floated inside the small store, talking with other elementals. As they entered the shop, Tiff grew fascinated by the different wind-sculptures inside the shop. There was one with three balls of fire suspended within it, and another wind-sculpture incorporated small bits of metal within a twisting vortex. Occasionally, the tiny metal slivers would collide with a pleasing sound, which reminded Tiff of a wind chime.

"TIFF!" came a voice from a corner in the back of the store where a wooden screen divided a work area from the main shop. Aleara darted from behind the screen and glided toward Tiff, a huge smile on her face.

The two of them chatted for a few minutes, and Aleara introduced Tiff, Jason, and Coach Brown to her family.

"I'm so glad you came back. We've helped occasionally with rebuilding, but sylphs aren't particularly good at building with earth or metal. They're too heavy."

"We came back for more training. I'm working on switching between my normal form and elemental ones," Tiff replied, shifting back to her normal form to demonstrate.

The other sylphs gasped in surprise, and Tiff thought they looked afraid. Aleara announced, "Tiff's a friend. She helped fight the big ones when they wrecked the place."

Fortunately, the other sylphs seemed to accept Aleara's assurance. A few of the customers looked a little uneasy, but they didn't panic.

"I like you better this way," Aleara said. "Oh wait! I made something for you." She darted back into the work area.

After a moment, she returned, holding a small wind-sculpture. "I made this for you. It is my first real piece I made on my own. Do you like it?"

Tiff looked at the small wind-sculpture. It looked like a puzzle-knot made of cycling cloud-stuff, weaving in and out in a complex whirling nexus of winds. As Tiff examined the intricate design, she noticed small sparkles within it. The entire sculpture was less than two inches tall.

"It's beautiful. I love the sparkles in it. Did you really make it for me?" Tiff asked in wonder.

Aleara nodded. "I put a bit of glass in it to make the sparkles."

"Glass? Is that..." Tiff asked.

"I thought the sparkles made it more beautiful." Aleara beamed. She added, "I'm sure Tarskax wouldn't mind if I used part of his corpus for something artistic. He'd like that."

Coach Brown inspected the sculpture. "It's beautiful, Aleara. You have some real talent."

Aleara smiled and thanked the coach. Tiff wondered if sylphs could blush.

Then Tiff sighed and said, "I didn't bring anything for... Wait... Do you have a larger piece of glass handy? Or a sharp piece of metal?"

"There's a small blade in the back. We use it for etchings. Will that do?" Aleara answered.

"If it has an edge," Tiff replied.

Aleara retrieved a small metal blade from the work area. Tiff had remembered how Aleara enjoyed feeling her hair. She gathered a lock of hair into a small ponytail and looped a hair tie around the end. She cut off about three inches and gave the small bundle of hair to Aleara.

Aleara looked surprised. "Didn't that hurt?"

"No. Hair doesn't have nerves, so it's fine." She noticed Aleara's confusion. "It really didn't hurt. But don't take off the hair tie, or it could get everywhere." She smiled. "It's a part of me, and I want you to have it."

Aleara tried to contain her happiness, with little success. She took the small bundle of hair back into the work area, then returned. "Let me show you around the Exchange," she said with a smile.

"Sure! That sounds like fun!" Tiff replied. She always enjoyed shopping, even if she couldn't figure out how to bring anything home. "Um... do you guys want to come too?"

Jason and Coach Brown looked at each other. "No, you two go ahead. We'll explore on our own," Jason answered.

The coach grinned. Neither of them wanted to get between Tiff and a shopping spree.

Later in the day, the students gathered once again. Tiff cradled the small wind-sculpture in her hands.

"How can I take it home?" she asked, obviously concerned. "And how will I explain it to my family?"

"If you don't mind, let me hold on to it for a few days," Coach Brown answered. "I think I can solve the problem for you." He pulled a small metal box from his extra-dimensional pocket and opened it. "It should be safe in here."

Tiff carefully placed the wind-sculpture into the box, and the coach returned it to the extra-dimensional pocket.

Miss Olsen congratulated them. "Everyone has succeeded in transforming back into their human form. Even Aliki. I think we can call today a success. Next weekend, we'll do the same exercise in the Animal Realm."

CHAPTER TWENTY-FOUR
A Glimpse of Other Realms

The students sat around the campfire in the Animal Realm, staying warm and eating bowls of chili from Coach Brown's large cooking pot. Mr. Oxinos praised all of them. "Excellent work, everyone. You've all maintained your normal form here in the Animal Realm—even Jason."

Aliki shivered in the wintry air, wondering if all of the realms shared Earth's seasons. Beside her, Jason was relaxing in his human form while inhaling his third bowl of chili. She watched the teachers as they discussed their training. All five teachers accompanied them, though Dr. Fathy seemed distracted.

As Coach Brown extinguished the fire, Miss Olsen announced their next task. "We'll extend this exercise. Your next goal is to maintain your form when arriving in a new realm. So each of us will pair with one of you and take you back to Earth. We'll shift you to either the Animal Realm or Primal Realm. Your goal is to maintain your normal human form upon your arrival."

Dr. Fathy added, "You will need to maintain your self-image as you transfer to the new realm. Part of learning realm transference is learning to shift forms at the same time as you shift realms. You should also recognize the feeling of transferring to a new realm. Each realm has its own feel—its own particular set of sensations you perceive as you arrive."

The students helped to clean up after lunch. They all returned to Earth, and each paired off with a teacher. They soaked their tunics and sweatpants with warm water so if they assumed a fiery form in the Primal Realm, they wouldn't catch the clothes on fire.

Throughout the afternoon, the teachers would move each student to one of the two realms, testing if they could maintain their human form. Toward the end of the afternoon, each of the students managed to succeed in keeping their human forms upon arriving in either the Primal or Animal Realm.

Mr. Oxinos gathered the students in the school courtyard again, obviously proud of them. He quickly conferred with the other teachers, then addressed the students, "Once again, you've all succeeded in this training. Now it's time for a real test. Remember what you've learned and focus on your self-image." The teachers paired with the students again, and each shifted realms.

Mike gazed at the strange realm Coach Brown brought him to. While the area resembled the school courtyard in its general shape and layout, an open plaza of some type replaced the athletic wing of the school. The wing containing the classrooms seemed to be made of some sort of translucent material, and Mike could see some human-shaped figures moving inside. The cafeteria and administrative wings looked like something from a science fiction story, with gleaming high-tech spires rising above them. Lights glowed in different patterns across all of the buildings.

Overhead, streams of multicolored lights pulsed in the air. Some flowed from one tower to another, while others simply moved through the air. Hovering in the sky were several things that looked like floating buildings, slowly moving along some predetermined path.

Mike gazed around the courtyard. It was too clean; there was no dirt at all. The courtyard's benches and tables seemed to be made of some high-tech plastic rather than the weathered wood and concrete of Earth. The ground looked like grass, but when Mike ran his hand over it, it felt more like artificial turf than natural grass.

"Welcome to the Tech Realm, Mike," Coach Brown said. "You seem to have passed the test and retained your human form."

"So is this realm like cyberspace or something?" Mike asked. "It all looks so shiny and clean."

Coach Brown answered, "In part. In many ways, the Tech Realm provides a view into what is possible with technological progress. When I first became immortal long ago, it looked more like a medieval village, which at the time was still a thousand years in the future. From what we can tell, it evolves technology, some of which manifests on Earth. I'm not sure if the realm helps define the laws of physics, or simply bends them sometimes."

Mike gazed around. He spotted a strange bird with a shiny

metallic body and multiple tiny rotor blades embedded in its wings. It perched on a nearby rooftop and looked back at them, chirping with a droning sound. "It seems so fabulous," Mike marveled.

"Perhaps, but the realms each have their downsides too. You might miss the natural animals or the spontaneity of nature. Here, technology controls everything, even the weather," Coach Brown replied.

Mike looked upward toward the few clouds in the sky, perfectly ovoid instead of the random puffy clouds of Earth. The wind didn't rise and fall, but blew with a constant, even force.

"So there are no storms here?" Mike asked.

"Only when the inhabitants decide they need one," Coach Brown answered.

Mike thought for a few minutes. "You're right. I guess I would miss those things. But it still seems nice."

"Oh, it's one of my favorite realms too. And far better than the Demon Realm or the Ghost Realm."

"Don't be afraid, boyo. Keep yer focus!"

Kyle glanced around and tried vainly to suppress a shudder. A field of twisted spiky metal structures replaced the peaceful school courtyard and gymnasium. Bones, mostly broken and unidentifiable, littered the corners of the area. Bloodstains decorated the walls, and vile-smelling liquids dripped from the rooftops. Overhead, the blood-red sky contained only a few black clouds.

The school building itself still retained its basic shape,

though a horrific jumble of stonework vaguely shaped like enormous bones had replaced the classroom wing, and a pool of some unidentifiable liquid, bubbling and churning, occupied the space where the administrative wing should be. The gymnasium resembled a nightmarish arena, and the odor wafting from the cafeteria made Kyle gag. The buildings incorporated prominent spikes on the outer walls, and the windowpanes resembled fields of jagged glass rather than smooth sheets. The doors Kyle could see looked more like heavy dungeon doors than the simple wooden doors of his own school.

Kyle turned toward MacKenzie. Though the fierce woman didn't look any different, Kyle could sense the menace radiating from her. Despite his best intentions, he felt the bear part of him fighting to reach the surface. He struggled to restrain the instincts to fight or flee.

"Keep calm, lad. I'll not let anythin' happen to you," MacKenzie tried to reassure him.

Kyle forced himself to take five deep breaths before asking, "MacKenzie? Where are we?"

"The Demon Realm, lad. We wanted to throw each of you into an unfamiliar realm to see if ye could keep your focus. This is possibly the most challenging of the five realms we chose, but ye're doing well. It's not easy to keep focus in the Demon Realm," MacKenzie answered.

"So what kind of place is this, MacKenzie?" Kyle asked aloud. He tried to maintain his courage, but found even MacKenzie terrifying.

"Believe it or not, this is something like a school for young demons. I scouted it before bringing you here." she grinned. "Of

241

course, it's not a particularly pleasant school. I don't think you'd like it here. Young demons are thrown into this place, and they learn to inflict nasty tortures on each other and dominate their fellows. The instructors aren't particularly caring as to which students survive, an' they hate their roles, so there's a lot of attrition."

"I thought this area looked like a bloody arena," Kyle said. He felt a weird sense of relief that he'd guessed right, but he also felt horrified at the implications. "So does this realm influence Earth?"

"Have ye never been bullied at school?" MacKenzie asked.

Kyle nodded. His older brothers could only protect him so much. "Why would anyone want to come to this realm?" Kyle wondered aloud.

"Power. Freedom to inflict one's will on another. A belief that the strongest should survive by crushing those weaker than themselves," MacKenzie responded. "But aggression is not always a bad thing. It fuels the desire to conquer, to grow, to strive for better things."

"So I guess there's no room here for being smart instead of strong." Kyle said. He already hated the Demon Realm.

MacKenzie shook her head. "Wrong. More intelligent demons're much more dangerous. They plan their malicious activities with all the precision of a surgeon. An' many are fiercely talented at manipulation. Fortunately, the smart ones are much fewer here; many fall prey to their fellows before finishin' their schemes."

Suddenly, a demonic creature emerged from the bony stonework structures and ran into the courtyard. It stood about five feet tall, with broad shoulders and a horned head. It was mostly blue, but had streaks of red running through the fur covering its lower body. Its feet and hands sported vicious-looking claws. But the creature looked scared.

Glancing around, it noticed MacKenzie and Kyle, and then looked back the way it came. A group of four other demons in various shapes sauntered into the courtyard. They were flexing their claws and baring their teeth, grinning in wicked anticipation.

The blue demon looked at them, with a pleading look in its three eyes. "Should we help it, MacKenzie?" Kyle whispered.

MacKenzie shook her head. "We try not to interfere with the order of things on the realms we visit." MacKenzie pulled a nasty-looking battle-axe from her personal pocket dimension, and Kyle began to tremble as she drew power from the Demon Realm. MacKenzie's hair turned black, but she stood passively, her axe held defensively between them and the demons.

The four demons, reassured MacKenzie would not interfere, closed in on the first demon, slavering with a savage bloodlust.

"We best head on, lad. Ye're not wantin' to see this."

Jason gazed around in wonder at the beautiful vista. The school structures seemed perfect, gleaming, and welcoming. The sun shone brightly.

Mr. Oxinos watched him carefully. "Keep concentrating on your own form, Jason," he said.

Jason looked at his arms. They looked normal enough. So he looked around the transformed school buildings in the new realm.

Part of the athletic wing had been replaced by a large number of floating hoops, each at least four feet in diameter. They formed a maze-like pattern, though Jason couldn't figure it out from the ground. The other wings of the school resembled their counterparts on Earth, but Jason noticed none of them had any doors. He could freely enter or leave any of the buildings.

"So what realm is this, Mr. O?"

"This is the Heaven Realm," he answered. As if to underscore his statement, a group of winged humanoid figures flew overhead, glowing with a soft light. They saw Jason and Mr. Oxinos and glided down into the courtyard. He guessed they were angels, though their wings resembled flowing gossamer instead of feathers.

"Welcome, Lord Apollo," one hailed.

Surprised, Jason turned to his teacher. "They know who you are?"

"Of course." Mr. Oxinos addressed the angels, "This is one of my students, Jason King. It's his first time in your realm."

"Then welcome, Jason King, to heaven," another angel called.

"Um... so you're angels? Do you live in the clouds?" Jason inquired, bewildered.

The angels chuckled or smiled. One answered, "No. We live in our homes, in that direction."

"You could call us angels, or devas, or any of several different terms," another added.

"Not all of the inhabitants here look like the traditional angel, Jason," Mr. Oxinos explained. "I think we can give you a passing mark on this challenge too. I thought I saw feathers in your hair. But it was only for a split second, if at all."

Jason stood, his mouth agape.

One of the angels asked, "Is something bothering Jason?"

"No. He's a little overwhelmed. Perhaps some privacy would do him some good," Mr. Oxinos replied.

"Then privacy he shall have. We therefore take our leave of you. Farewell!" one angel declared. They flew off, leaving Jason and Mr. Oxinos behind.

Jason slowly regained his wits. "Angels. In heaven. Have I died? Were the other realms some form of Purgatory?"

"Not that I'm aware of, Jason. While the Heaven Realm is idyllic, it has its own problems too," Mr. Oxinos answered.

Jason gave him a skeptical look. "Really? This seems like paradise."

"It would be to some. But think for a moment. What do you really enjoy?"

"Sports and athletic competition. Leading a team to be the best. Exploring," Jason replied automatically.

"That competitive edge? That aggressive drive? The Heaven Realm doesn't align with that, particularly when it comes to physical sports," Mr. Oxinos replied. "To prove yourself the best, you have to conquer your opponent. You have to defeat them, crush them, make them inferior to you. A need to dominate is antithetical to the Heaven Realm. The beings here thrive on cooperation and collaboration, not competition."

Jason nodded slowly, but he still struggled to reconcile his preconception of heaven with the Heaven Realm.

"Perhaps we should return. We've been here long enough,"

Mr. Oxinos said.

Aliki glanced around nervously, trying to maintain her self-image. A gloomy vista dominated her vision. The school buildings were bathed in twilight. No sun hung in the sky, though the moon shone through the clouds. Oddly enough, she could not see any stars either. The school itself looked run-down, and only weeds grew in the courtyard. Part of the athletic wing had collapsed, as if it had worn out. A cold breeze blew through the courtyard, chilling her to the bone.

Aliki hugged herself for warmth and looked over at Dr. Fathy. He responded, "Focus on yourself, not me."

She nodded quickly and went over a mental checklist. Hair, skin, eyes... *ow!* She'd bitten her tongue. *No, wait...* She ran her tongue over her teeth. One of them, one of her upper canines, had become longer and sharper. She focused on her teeth and felt them transform into their normal shape. She finished her mental checklist and looked expectantly at Dr. Fathy.

"Excellent. You briefly showed signs of transformation, but quickly reverted to human form. I believe a three-second gap is acceptable for your first time in a new realm."

"So where are we?" Aliki asked.

"This is the Ghost Realm, or the Realm of the Undead. It has been called Duat, Hades, Niflheim, and many other names," Dr. Fathy replied. Aliki looked at the erudite Egyptian and wondered which ancient god or gods he had inspired.

"So there are like zombies and stuff here?" Aliki asked, remembering the latest horror film she'd seen.

He replied, "No zombies. Zombies are mindless animated corpses. There are ghouls, which fit some depictions of zombies —partially intelligent, but hungering for flesh. But they don't turn you into one of them if they bite you. There are also ghosts, vampires, and a few other beings commonly considered undead."

Aliki shuddered. "Why would anyone want to reincarnate here?" She kept looking toward the open areas of the courtyard, expecting ghosts or ghouls to spring out.

"The Ghost Realm is inhabited by those who died with a strong want or need. For instance, those who died of starvation have become ghouls, eternally hungry. A person dying without a meaning to their life would become a ghost, seeking something of substance that would give them meaning. A vampire arises from someone who dies alone without the ties of family; they instinctively hunger for blood and the ties of family bonds. And so forth..." Dr. Fathy explained. He still sounded like a college professor.

"Sir? Can we be done here? I'd like to go home."

"Yes, Aliki. We'll return now."

The courtyard seemed alive.

Tiff looked around at the school buildings. Both the athletic wing and the wing containing the cafeteria and auditorium looked magnificent. An open patio filled with proud statues of athletes and other students replaced the upper floor of the administrative wing. Although the classroom wing itself was missing, she did see several of the classrooms appearing as a glowing aura; some appeared inviting, while a few seemed repellent. Tiff noticed a manifestation of her homeroom—Mr. Oxinos' classroom—floating in the air, glowing in a welcoming kaleidoscope of color.

Beyond the classrooms, everything seemed more vivid. Colors seemed stronger, the air felt excited, and birds glowed brightly as they chirped in perfect harmony. Even the clouds in the sky glowed as if they had an actual silver lining.

"Miss Olsen? Is this like a Life Realm or something?" she asked.

Miss Olsen smiled and replied, "This is the Spirit Realm. Spirits can be distracting, so keep your focus."

Tiff thought it would be easy at first. But she kept seeing something out of the corner of her eye. No matter where she looked, there was always something moving just outside of her vision.

"I didn't see any signs of transformation, so you've passed the test. You can look around. This realm should be safe," Miss Olsen suggested.

Tiff wandered toward the cafeteria. She passed by where the vending machines would have been and paused. A single vending machine—one that dispensed chips and other snacks—stood in the alcove. But she noticed something odd about it.

She peered closer into the vending machine. A strange voice startled her. "And I'm not gonna give you any, even if you do give me quarters!" It sounded brattish and came from the vending machine itself. A face resembling something a child would draw on foggy glass appeared on the main panel.

Miss Olsen laughed. The corresponding machine in the real world was notorious for taking money and failing to provide snacks. Tiff gasped, "Is that you, Mr. Vending Machine?"

"I'm not gonna give you any! They're all mine!" the vending machine responded.

Miss Olsen wiped the tears of laughter from her eyes. "Whenever we imagine a particular thing in the real world has a personality, a spirit may be the cause. Or if something provides a strong feeling, a spirit likely is responsible. Look back to the courtyard."

Tiff did and gasped. Wandering through the courtyard was the Jefferson Hill Javelineer. It matched the school mascot perfectly, resembling an ancient warrior of some type that carried a javelin in one hand and a round shield in the other. The being stood over eight feet tall.

"That's the spirit of the school itself," Miss Olsen said. "He patrols the grounds. During sporting events, he stands on or near the field, urging our school to victory. The only time he leaves the school grounds is for special events, like graduation."

Miss Olsen led Tiff back into the courtyard. The Javelineer turned to gaze at them. He smiled. "Hello, Idun and Miss Gardner," he said in a strong but gentle voice.

"You know us?" Tiff asked.

The Javelineer replied, "I do. You and your squad promote the school spirit. So I'm grateful to you, Miss Gardner."

"It's a pleasure to meet you, sir. I mean..." Tiff stammered.

"You've known me since you came to this school, Tiffany," he replied fondly. "Do you need anything, Idun?"

Miss Olsen replied, "No, thank you. I'm introducing Tiffany to the Spirit Realm. She is one of us now. So you'll see more of her."

"Very well. I look forward to it. Until next time." The Javelineer moved on, continuing his patrol of the school grounds.

"So how does the Spirit Realm help us?" Tiff asked.

"Spirits also can animate objects. Think of all the children's stories about cars that can talk or household objects that animate. The source of those tales is the Spirit Realm."

"So that's how you make the trees move!" Tiff said excitedly.

"Right. By summoning a spirit into a tree, I can coax it to move or change its shape as I need. You'll learn more about that in time. But for now..."

The world around them changed, and they were back on Earth.

CHAPTER TWENTY-FIVE
Gifts

On Monday morning, Coach Brown dropped by Mr. Oxinos' room during homeroom period. He knocked politely, and Mr. Oxinos nodded.

"Tiffany?" the coach asked. He held the metal box.

She stood and went out into the hall to talk to him.

He presented her the box. "Does this meet your style?"

She opened the box and gasped. A delicate pendant made of gold filigree sat within the box. It formed a small lacy cage with her precious wind-sculpture inside. Glass panes filled the spaces between the delicate metalwork. The gold design echoed the pattern of the wind-sculpture, and the whole effect took her breath away.

"It's beautiful..." she said, awestruck.

"I also fashioned a small display case, so you could put it on a shelf if you wish," he said proudly. He held a slightly larger case with a similar design. "You can open the pendant so you can move the sculpture from one to the other. Don't worry about the glass. It's a special high-impact material and won't shatter under normal circumstances. It would take a strong blow with a hammer or a fall from over twenty feet to break it."

She looked at him in amazement.

"Did you think I could only make weapons or only work in steel, Tiffany?" he asked, smirking.

"This is wonderful. Thank you so much!" Tiff exclaimed.

"My pleasure. There is something else you need to know, but I'll have to tell you later. The bell is about to ring." Coach Brown waved and headed towards the gym.

She rejoined her friends before the bell rang. On the way to their next class, Tiff couldn't resist showing the pendant to her friends Shelly and Mara. Fortunately, the two of them believed some optical trick caused the wind effect.

"Wow! Where did you get it, Tiff?" Mara asked.

Shelly couldn't contain her enthusiasm. "I definitely need to find that shop!"

"Do you remember me telling you about Aleara? She made it."

"So she makes jewelry? When can you introduce me?" Shelly implored, still excited.

Tiff hesitated, realizing she had already said too much. "That might be hard. She's not from around here."

"You met her on one of your trips, right? So was she camping with you?" Mara asked.

"Yeah. That's where we met." Tiff realized keeping her secrets would be harder than she thought.

Kyle looked forlornly at the books Dr. Fathy had lent him. He had read each book at least twice, the special one more than that. The books answered so many questions, but even more filled his mind.

Dr. Fathy himself had written the special book with the transforming text to record his cultural observations in different parts of the world over the millennia. Dr. Fathy had spent time not only in ancient Egypt, but also ancient Greece, Rome, India, and many of the kingdoms of Africa. He had also traveled through Asia and Europe. He'd even traveled across the Atlantic to visit the Mayans.

Each chapter of the book included information about the various cultures, with descriptions of topics ranging from technological innovations to societal customs. The enigmatic book offered a treasure trove of knowledge. The man had a passion for writing, and Kyle found his prose both eloquent and descriptive.

Kyle reluctantly placed the books in the return envelope Dr. Fathy had provided. He hoped he would get another chance to read Dr. Fathy's personal books. He drafted a quick thank-you note, added it to the envelope, and sealed it.

He wasn't surprised when the envelope collapsed, as if the books inside had disappeared. He left the envelope on his desk, unsure of what to do with it, then went downstairs for his Sunday dinner.

He was surprised when he came back to his room afterwards. The envelope looked full again. He cautiously opened it and discovered two more books inside.

"Thank you, Dr. Fathy!" he exclaimed. He opened the next of the Egyptian's treasured tomes.

On the following weekend, the students gathered again in the side room of the gym for training. Mike noticed the weapons rack standing near the center of the room, but they had added a small table. Mr. Oxinos, MacKenzie, Miss Olsen, and Coach Brown stood near the door.

Dr. Fathy entered, carrying five boxes, each about the size of a shoebox. He set them on the table and handed a box to each student. "You can open them," he said after he finished distributing them.

Mike opened his box. Inside he found a strange strip of material, about an inch wide and two feet long. It felt a little like cloth and plastic, but seemed to have some metal and even glass woven into it.

"What is it?" Mike asked. He tried to gently stretch it and use it as a belt. But the material didn't stretch.

"A gift, and what we'll be training with today. These are your own Pockets." Dr. Fathy said proudly.

"So how do we use them?" Jason asked. He held the strip up to the light and ran his fingers up and down the length of the strip.

"First, join the ends together, forming a loop," Dr. Fathy instructed.

Each of the students did so. The ends snapped together as if magnetized. A few lights glowed softly near the seam. Mike noticed that the color and pattern of each student's lights differed.

"Now, twist the end half-way, forming a Möbius strip. Then

reach through the loop, and feel around," Dr. Fathy continued.

As the students reached into the loop, their arms disappeared from view. "We're reaching into a different dimension?" Tiff asked.

"Exactly. The Pocket is a hyperspace manifold which synchronizes with a randomly selected dimensional resonance to —" Dr. Fathy began.

"Perhaps ye should tell 'em how ta use them first," MacKenzie interrupted.

Dr. Fathy looked abashed. "Of course. Anyhow, you should feel a thin membrane. Once you find it, pull it through the loop. Don't worry. It won't tear."

Again, Mike followed his instructions. As he pulled his hands back through the loop, the loop itself disappeared from view. Only the glowing lights remained visible. He could see neither the original loop nor the membrane.

"What happened? Did we break them?" Jason asked.

Dr. Fathy answered with an amused look. "No. The strip itself is now in the pocket dimension. That keeps it protected and hidden from view. The lights let you see the Pocket's location. At first, you'll practice using them with the lights on. But your Pocket bonded to you when you closed the loop, so you can manipulate it by thought. It will remain within a few inches of you unless you consciously command it otherwise. You can turn the lights off or on with a mental command as well."

Coach Brown stepped forward. "Allow me to demonstrate. I'll pull things out of my Pocket, but slow it down so you can see how it works. But first, you'll need to see where my Pocket is."

At his silent command, a set of glowing lights, similar to

theirs, appeared beside the coach. He held up his hand, as if he were reaching for something. At the same time, the lights moved up to his wrist, then paused in his open palm. After a pause, they slowly moved away, but as they did, a hunga-munga gradually appeared in his hand. It was if he were drawing the weapon slowly from a sheath.

The coach repeated the technique in reverse, sliding the hunga-munga back into its pocket dimension. He repeated the process several times, speeding up slightly each time.

The coach elaborated, "The Pocket will retrieve whichever object you want from what you have stored. When you store an object, you have to maintain a clear mental picture of it. You use that image to retrieve it. So you can only pocket things you're familiar with."

Miss Olsen warned, "One more important thing. Never pocket a living creature. The pocket dimension is lethal to most life."

MacKenzie joined in. "Now, lads and lasses, you'll try pocketing your practice weapons. You've used the same ones for months now, so you should have a good mental image of them. First, put the object in the Pocket. Then try to retrieve it."

The students picked up their practice weapons and tried to pocket them. Mike, Tiff and Kyle seemed to grasp the technique fairly easily. Jason looked at his padded greataxe with dismay. "I don't think it will fit, sir," he said to the coach. Aliki likewise looked confused, holding her paint-gun rifle.

Mr. Oxinos spoke up. "The opening is as large or small as you need it to be, within reason. You can't pocket a car, but anything you could wear or carry could be pocketed. Don't think about the physical size—the physics of the pocket dimension are different."

Puzzled, Jason guided his Pocket to the head of his greataxe. Then he carefully lowered it, hesitating until the axe head began to disappear. Jason's bewildered expression didn't vanish, but finally his greataxe did. "Wow... this is cool."

Similarly, Aliki managed to pocket her rifle, and pull it out again. She dropped it on the ground the first time she pulled it out of the Pocket, but caught it the next time.

"So can we get each other's stuff from the Pocket?" Mike asked.

Dr. Fathy responded, "No. When you connected the strip to form the loop, it attuned itself to your aura and brain pattern. So you can only command your own Pocket. Furthermore, when you twisted the loop, the Pocket selected a dimensional resonance based upon your aura. Since no two people have the same aura, each person's personal dimension is different."

Mike nodded, though Dr. Fathy's explanation did little to dispel his confusion.

For the rest of the morning, the students practiced storing and retrieving their weapons. By lunchtime, they had all managed to pocket the items quickly enough that it appeared instantaneous.

After lunch, the teachers separated themselves and the students by gender. Tiff and Aliki followed MacKenzie and Miss Olsen to a separate secluded room, while the boys stayed with Coach Brown, Mr. Oxinos, and Dr. Fathy.

"The next challenge," Mr. Oxinos began, "is to pocket your clothes during a transformation. You'll want to transform without wearing the special clothes we've provided for your first realm visits. So we've separated you so you'll be able to transform without risking your dignity."

To demonstrate, the coach slowly transformed into his leopard form. As he gradually shifted shape, the boys could see the lights of his Pocket floating near his waist. It moved upward, and his shirt disappeared. As his body became feline, the Pocket returned near his waist, moving downwards to pocket his pants. Finally, after about a minute of transformation, the leopard's face turned to the boys. "Your turn," he said.

Mr. Oxinos elaborated, "You'll move your Pocket around your body, willing it to remove your clothes as you transform. Moving items in and out of a Pocket requires both mental control and manual dexterity."

"Won't we get sucked into the pocket dimension?" Mike asked.

"No. Once you activated your Pocket, you anchored yourself in this dimension. Even if you wanted to, you physically cannot enter your pocket dimension," Dr. Fathy replied. "The exact reason for this is that the pocket aperture creates a dimensional polarity which..."

Playing with the Pocket fascinated Mike, so Dr. Fathy's explanation fell on deaf ears.

For the rest of the afternoon, the boys manipulated their Pockets, trying to get their clothes to disappear as they transformed. By the end of the afternoon, Jason's clothes were soaked, and Kyle had ripped his t-shirt. They'd endured a lot of embarrassment during their shared challenge. But they eventually succeeded. Their transformation and pocketing weren't as fluid as the coach's, but the boys all had high spirits.

As the girls rejoined them, they seemed to be having a giggling fit, but MacKenzie and Miss Olsen nodded. They also had conquered the challenge.

The teachers let the students keep their practice weapons. On Sunday, Mike paced around his room, pulling his tonfas from the Pocket as he performed his taekwondo exercises. He kept practicing until he could retrieve them as he executed a strike.

He experimented by pocketing his shirt and retrieving it. But that didn't provide a challenge. So he tried pocketing things around his room.

First, he pocketed his pillow and retrieved it. He grinned as he imagined using the Pocket in a pillow fight. He experimented with one of his trophies, pocketing it in one hand and retrieving it in the other. He tried pocketing his desk chair, but failed. He guessed it was too big.

He experimented a bit more, throwing a ball into the Pocket, and trying to retrieve it while it was in motion. To his surprise, the ball didn't fly out of the pocket, no matter how quickly he tried to retrieve it. The physics inside the pocket dimension obviously differed from the real world. He resolved to try more experiments, but decided to grab some lunch first.

On Tuesday, MacKenzie and Coach Brown asked Aliki and Kyle to meet them in the shop room after school. Aliki phoned her mother to tell her she had a short meeting, then wandered toward the shop room and got lost.

She wandered around for ten minutes until she stumbled into MacKenzie, who had come to find her. By the time they reached the shop room, Coach Brown had already started talking with Kyle.

He stood before a small security cabinet. Inside, she glimpsed Jason's greataxe—the real one, with the ornate blades. She noticed what Kyle held in his hands. It was a morningstar—a club-like weapon with a heavy spiked head. The morningstar had etchings along the haft and the head of the weapon, and it looked as ornate as the greataxe or Tiff's katana.

The coach pointed to a long leather loop at the bottom. "The lanyard will keep you from accidentally flinging it, and I made it long enough to loop around your paws in your bear form. You may not be able to wield it accurately in bear form, but if you need extra power, you could use it."

"Thank you, sir," Kyle said. He took a few gentle swings with the weapon, trying to get the feel of its weight.

MacKenzie called out to them, "I found our explorer."

"Glad you could make it, Aliki. I have something for you as well." Coach Brown turned to retrieve something from the cabinet. When he turned back to her, he held a long case in his hands. Inside was an ornate rifle.

"It's a custom piece with a few extra features beyond what you'd find in a normal rifle." He offered the gun to her. "Don't worry. It isn't loaded."

She gingerly picked up the weapon. It was beautiful, with elaborate designs on the stock and delicate etchings over the entire length of the weapon. She didn't see a safety though.

"Are you sure it's safe?" Aliki asked.

Coach Brown answered, "Positive. Even if it were loaded, it can't fire yet. Now hold it in firing position, then say your name."

Aliki raised the rifle to her shoulder and peered through the scope. Despite the rifle's perfect fit, she still felt uncomfortable holding it. She took a deep breath, then said "Aliki Papadaki".

The coach gave her a satisfied smile. "Now only you can fire it. It has a voice-activation chip embedded in it. To enable firing, you have to say 'rifle ready'. To disable it, you would say 'rifle shutdown'. Only MacKenzie, myself, and you can activate it."

Aliki exclaimed, "Rifle shutdown!" and gently put the rifle back in its case. "It's beautiful, sir, but I can't shoot a real gun."

"Like it or not, girl, ye'll be running into danger at some point. Ye've already dealt with giants twice, and that can't be a coincidence." MacKenzie gently put her hand on Aliki's shoulder. "Children much younger than you have had to fight with guns, swords, knives, and clubs in countless battles. It ain't fair, but neither is life."

Coach Brown gently placed the rifle case back in the security cabinet. Kyle handed him the morningstar, and he placed it beside the other weapons. He turned back to Aliki. "Better to have it and not need it than to need it and not have it."

MacKenzie added, "I'll be teaching you how to use it too. I've already found a good shooting range."

Coach Brown locked the cabinet. "I'll also move the storage cabinet and weapons to my workshop at my home. The weapons will be safe there. Eventually, you will all keep them in your Pockets. Now let's get you to your parents. I'm sure they're ready to pick you up."

CHAPTER TWENTY-SIX
Visitor at the Dance

On the following Thursday night, the school held its Valentine's Dance. Many students came even without dates, since it was a welcome break from the winter doldrums. All of the students were looking forward to the long weekend break, which included Friday and the President's Day holiday on Monday.

Kyle recalled how he had been persuaded to come to the dance. Tiff and Mike had suggested they go as a group. Tiff had admitted she needed a break from training and wanted to have fun as a group. Aliki and Jason had agreed, so Kyle knew he'd have to come too. When he asked his parents whether he could go, they'd looked surprised and pleased. So he was trying to make the best of it, despite the loud music and dizzying lights.

Kyle fidgeted as he gazed around the transformed gymnasium. Pink, red, and white helium-filled balloons littered the ceiling, and streamers dangled between the light fixtures. Heart-shaped decorations and cupids covered the walls. The DJ played popular songs, and students danced, snacked on pizza and wings, and goofed off.

He looked around the dance floor. Tiff and Mike had paired up for the current dance. Tiff wore an elegant purple dress with a scooped neckline and ruffles at the bottom to add a flirty touch. He noticed she also wore the pendant containing the wind-sculpture that Aleara made for her. Mike sported a goofy bow tie with LED lights and some silly suspenders. Kyle spotted his brother John dancing with his girlfriend on the far side of the room. He glanced over toward Jason, who looked a little uncomfortable in a formal suit.

Standing beside Kyle, Aliki wore a cream-colored dress, but she looked almost as uncomfortable as he felt. She must have noticed his nervousness; she took his hand and gently led him out onto the dance floor. "It's okay. We're friends, right?" she said.

The music and dancing bewildered Kyle. He tried imitating some of the other boys' motions during the upbeat song. He felt like everyone was watching him—was he doing it wrong? Aliki didn't seem to mind though.

"I really don't know how to dance," he tried to say over the music.

Aliki nodded and replied, "I'm making this up too. Don't worry!"

The song ended, and they danced to a second song. Afterwards, they returned to the side of the dance floor. Jason and Mike smirked at him.

"Atta boy, Kyle! You've got moves!" Mike teased.

Jason played along. "I guess we'll have to enter him in the dance competition!"

Kyle's grin was genuine. He felt a little more confident with his friends around him.

He fetched some water bottles for them from the snack table. By the time he rejoined Mike and Jason, Tiff had wandered off to hang out with some of her fellow cheerleaders. Aliki chatted with Julisha nearby. Every so often, he thought he saw the two of them glance his way.

It's just nerves, he tried to reassure himself.

Mike gave him a friendly backslap and nodded toward the girls. "You should ask Julisha to dance," he said with a grin.

"What? No... I can't," Kyle stammered. He felt butterflies in his stomach.

"Sure you can. Why not? She wants to dance. We're all friends, remember?" Mike added. "You can fight giants, but you can't ask a girl to dance?"

Jason came to his rescue—sort of. "Hey, it's okay. I'll ask Aliki, and you ask Julisha."

Kyle nodded, and the two of them walked over to the girls. As planned, Jason asked Aliki, and she brightened. The two of them headed out onto the dance floor, leaving him with Julisha.

"Umm... Julisha?" Kyle hesitated. He summoned all of his courage and plunged in. "Would you like to dance?"

To his surprise, she gave him a smile and said, "Sure!"

Jason and Aliki joined in the current peppy dance. They enjoyed moving to the upbeat music, but Jason was starting to sweat under his suit coat.

"My dad suggested I wear this," he admitted, "but I'm getting too hot."

"I'm glad you wore it. You look nice," Aliki said, smiling at him. "But you could take the jacket off."

"Good idea." Jason led Aliki toward the edge of the dance floor. When the song changed, he quickly took off the jacket and tossed it onto a nearby chair. "Much better," he sighed in relief.

The next song started, and they resumed dancing. Jason glanced over at Kyle and Julisha. They seemed to be having a good time too.

Jason let himself enjoy the moment. He didn't want to think about giants or angels in heaven. He wanted to have a good time with his friends.

The song ended, and a slow song started. And as luck would have it, the tune was the same slow ballad they'd danced to together at Homecoming.

"I guess this is our song," Jason said, trying to remember how to lead Aliki.

She flashed a charming smile at him and answered, "I guess it is."

Tiff had been dancing with several boys, including Mike, Jason, and even Carson, who joked that she owed him a dance after the thumping she gave him at the sparring exhibition. The dancing finally tired her, so she took a break and chatted with her fellow cheerleaders Rachel and Kennedy. Kennedy's boyfriend wanted to hang out with his friends, so the three of them spent time gossiping and appraising the other girls' dresses. Rachel also gazed at Jason, but tried to hide it, glancing away every so often.

"Check out Sarah and Jen. Is that a spiderweb dress? It's Valentines, not Halloween," Kennedy joked about the two goth girls.

"So what do you think of Julisha's dress?" Tiff asked.

"Classy," Rachel admitted. "She doesn't look like a sports girl in that."

"Hey, look. Jason's dancing with Aliki." Kennedy pointed them out. The two of them seemed to be handling the slow song well. Neither Kennedy nor Tiff noticed the scowl on Rachel's face though.

Tiff nodded. "I'm glad she's coming out of her shell. Even Kyle is here."

"Kyle?" Rachel and Kennedy gasped in unison.

"Uh huh. He was standing next to Mike," Tiff replied, trying to locate him. Mike was easy to find with his glowing bow tie, and she could spot his mischievous smile across the room. She spotted Kyle on the dance floor with Julisha. Surprised, she pointed Kyle out to her friends.

"Now I've seen everything!" Kennedy laughed. "He looks cute."

Not everything, Tiff thought. She idly fingered her pendant. *I wish Aleara could be here.*

A few moments later, a breeze seemed to waft through her hair. "Wow. This place is neat," said a soft voice in her ear.

Turning to look, Tiff glimpsed Aleara floating beside her, and dropped her snack plate in shock.

Mike gloated with smug satisfaction as he watched the

results of his cajoling. Kyle had actually asked Julisha to dance, and the two of them were on their third song. Then he saw Tiff making a beeline toward him. After a moment, he noticed why. Aleara was here, floating above Tiff. Fortunately, her translucent body was barely visible in the dim light.

Mike whipped out his cell phone and sent a quick text message to Mr. Oxinos. *Help. Aleara is here at dance.*

Mike found it challenging to read Aleara's expression, but the sylph girl seemed as bewildered as they were. Tiff's face was a near-panic.

"What do we do?" she gasped as she reached Mike. "Somehow she appeared here!"

"Is this a dance? It isn't like anything I know," Aleara wondered, gazing at the students gyrating on the floor. "Is everything okay?"

"How did you get here, Aleara?" Mike asked.

"Oh, I heard Tiff wanting me here, so I came. I don't know how I did it," Aleara responded, sounding as puzzled as they were.

"It's a miracle no one's freaked out!" Tiff exclaimed. "Can you go back home, Aleara?"

Aleara looked a little hurt. "You don't want me here?"

Mike tried to calm both of them. "No one has seen a sylph here, so they might get weirded out. But it's dark, and the lights are changing quickly. No one has seen you yet, right?" Internally, he grasped for ideas. "As long as we're careful, she could stay here until Mr. O arrives."

"But how?" Tiff asked.

Mike pointed toward the ceiling. "There's enough room up

267

there for her to fly around and watch. The balloons and streamers should be enough to hide her. And if anyone spots her, we could claim it's a special light trick."

Tiff nodded. It could work.

Aleara gazed at the balloons. "What are those?" she asked.

Mike explained. "They're called balloons. They're like thin plastic bags filled with concentrated air. But that type of air rises, because it's lighter than normal air." He remembered she didn't have any conception of chemical elements like helium.

"You can float near the balloons and mess with them a bit, if you want," Tiff suggested. Seeing Kennedy and Rachel heading toward her, she added, "but you should stay high until I wave at you."

"Okay." Aleara grinned and darted upwards toward the ceiling.

"Tiff? Is everything okay?" Kennedy asked.

"You look like you saw a ghost." Rachel added.

Close enough, Mike thought. He glanced toward Aleara, who had started to push the balloons around on the ceiling.

By the time Miss Olsen and Coach Brown arrived, Tiff and Mike had spread the word about Aleara to Jason, Kyle, and Aliki. All of them tried to avoid frequent glances at the ceiling. Aleara had explored the balloons and streamers and tried imitating the movements of the dancers below. Fortunately, between the darkness and the flashing lights, no one else seemed to notice her floating above their heads.

Miss Olsen chastened Coach Brown. "I thought you told her

about it!"

"I thought *you* were going to tell her," Coach Brown confessed.

Miss Olsen rolled her eyes. "Let's get Aleara to safety first. Then we can teach Tiff how to return her home." She gestured for Mike and Tiff to join her outside in the courtyard. "Bring her too," she said, glancing upward. "Greg, keep the others here. If all five of them disappeared at the same time, it could look suspicious."

Tiff waved at Aleara, who floated down. They followed Miss Olsen outside to the courtyard.

Miss Olsen said, "Paul couldn't come, but he forwarded the message to us. Mike, keep an eye out for peepers. So what happened, Tiffany?"

Tiff answered, "Well, I was thinking about how I wished Aleara could be here. Then, all of a sudden, she was."

"I see. Tell me... were you holding your pendant at the time?" Miss Olsen asked.

Tiff thought back. "I think I was."

Miss Olsen sighed. "You two have formed a special bond with the exchange of heartfelt gifts. Your friendship, coupled with the wind-sculpture, allows you to summon her to you. I thought Greg would tell you about this when he gave you the pendant."

Tiff had been ecstatic when Coach Brown gave her the pendant, but she only vaguely remembered their conversation. "He said he had to tell me something about it, but never got around to it. I guess he forgot."

Aleara, hovering above, asked, "Did I do something

wrong?" She sounded upset.

Miss Olsen smiled reassuringly at the sylph. "No. Tiffany tapped into a talent she didn't know she had, and we forgot to warn her. As long as no one else saw you, there's no harm done. In fact, since you're here, there's no reason you can't stay for a few days. I'll let your family know once we decide how to keep you safe."

Aleara brightened. "Oh, thank you!"

"But how do we keep her hidden?" Tiff asked.

Miss Olsen had an odd look on her face. "When creatures from the realms arrive on Earth, either by summoning or accident, we immortals must conceal their presence. So we'll turn this into a training exercise for all of you. Show her around for a day or two. As long as you're careful, and keep her out of sight, we shouldn't have a problem. Otherwise, you'll need to figure out how to explain her to anyone who sees her. Are you ready for the challenge?"

Mike grinned, "This could even be fun."

CHAPTER TWENTY-SEVEN
Hosting Duties

At the end of the dance, Tiff soared through the air in her eagle form, leading Aleara to her home. Once inside, she opened her bedroom window for Aleara. It was still cool outside, so Aleara stayed in Tiff's bedroom throughout the evening. As she tried to settle down after the excitement of the dance, Aleara inspected different things in the room.

Eventually, exhaustion overtook the sylph. She murmured something in her soft breezy voice and retreated into one corner of the ceiling to sleep, floating in mid-air. Tiff snuggled under her covers, closed her eyes, and let the dreams come.

On Friday morning, Tiff went through her morning routine, occasionally explaining various things to Aleara. The shower baffled the sylph. As Tiff waited for the water to warm up, Aleara stuck her hand under the shower stream. Tiff noticed that the water dripped around her hand as if she were solid, rather than gaseous. Tiff guessed she had enough internal air pressure to keep the drops from penetrating her body.

"We use this for cleaning ourselves. Does the water bother you, Aleara?" Tiff asked.

Aleara watched the water dripping from her arm. "No. It's an unusual sensation, but not unpleasant. It's nothing like touching one of the water folk."

Aleara watched with interest as Tiff chose an outfit and tried to help Tiff arrange her hair. Tiff went downstairs to discuss her plans with her mother over breakfast, then returned to her room to finish getting ready.

"So where are we going?" Aleara asked.

"Give me a few minutes to get my phone and check my messages," Tiff replied. She scrolled through the messages from the others. Kyle and his brother John had volunteered to take Aleara to the zoo after lunch. Aliki suggested a movie that evening for everyone to enjoy, though she would have to bring her little brother along. Jason would take her on a tour around the park tomorrow morning as he went for a morning jog and offered his house for a movie night. Mike said he'd come up with something for Saturday afternoon. Tiff had already decided to take Aleara to the mall.

Tiff quickly described everything the students suggested. "But I'm not sure how we can keep you from being noticed in the daytime."

Aleara looked outside. The morning was cool and foggy, blanketing much of the neighborhood. "Look! The clouds are on the ground!" she gasped.

"We call it fog. It happens when the air is wet and cool. It usually disappears in a few hours."

"We have it too, but it happens when the windlords want to show off. I have an idea," Aleara said. "Let me show you."

Tiff nodded. She opened the window for Aleara to fly out,

then ran downstairs.

"Mom? I'm going to catch the bus to the mall," she called to her mother. Once her mother acknowledged her, Tiff went outside. She found Aleara in a secluded spot in her yard.

"Now how do we keep you hidden?" Tiff mused.

"Wait here a moment." Aleara darted into a dense cloud of fog. After a few minutes, a piece of the fog cloud drifted towards her.

"What do you think?" came Aleara's voice from inside the small cloud.

"I can't see you, but we'll have to be careful. Clouds don't normally float this low, and fog rolls around slowly. So we'll take our time," Tiff replied. "Now follow me. I want to show you our mall. It's like the Artisan Exchange."

Tiff transformed into an eagle, and the two of them flew to the mall. Along the way, Tiff pointed out their school and the park. Aleara paused to peer inside a few buildings and would stop to examine everything from stoplights to gas stations. Tiff worried that someone would notice them, but fortunately Aleara's fog cloud disguise only attracted a few distracted looks. Finally, they arrived at the town mall.

On Friday morning, the mall was not particularly busy. Early morning mall-walkers mixed with dedicated shoppers hunting for bargains in the President's Day sales. Tiff perched on one of the roof windows and transformed back into her human form so she could talk clearly. Aleara left the shelter of her miniature cloud, and the two of them watched the shoppers from above.

"I wish I could figure a way to bring you inside."

Aleara gazed down through the window. "But it's fun

273

watching. So many strange things down there. I never imagined what the Exchange would look like with humans."

Tiff smiled. For the next hour, the two of them moved around the roof of the mall, peering in through the skylights. Tiff pointed out some of her favorite stores. Aleara didn't understand clothing, so Tiff tried to explain the different functions of coats, blouses, dresses, and pants.

Tiff occasionally shifted into eagle form to move around the roof and to peer at the various sales with her sharp vision. She spotted Rachel and Kennedy trying on scarves at one of the vendor carts.

"See those two at that cart? They're two of my friends."

Aleara peered through the skylight. "Do you want to see them?" she asked.

"No. I'm with them almost every day at school, and I can't let them see you. They don't know about our abilities or the realms. Besides, I'm happy to spend time with you."

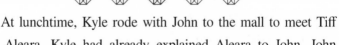

At lunchtime, Kyle rode with John to the mall to meet Tiff and Aleara. Kyle had already explained Aleara to John. John could barely contain his curiosity about the sylph, but Kyle didn't have many answers.

They pulled into the parking area near the mall food court. While John purchased lunch for them, Kyle called Tiff on his cell phone. "Tiff? We're here at the Food Court entrance. I'll stand outside the car."

He stood outside in the cool air, but left the car door open. A few minutes later, an eagle glided down and landed on the seat of the car. Tiff transformed into her normal shape and stood beside Kyle. The two of them waited for the parking lot to be free of others, then waved to Aleara. The sylph drifted down, settling into the back seat. Tiff sat beside her.

As they waited, Aleara explored the car. She wandered into the front seat, and examined the steering console. Kyle tried to describe the different functions of all the buttons, dials, and other controls, but soon confused himself.

John returned a few minutes later, carrying take-out Chinese food. He sat in the driver's seat and let Tiff choose her meal, then turned to Aleara. John tried to figure what to say, then just blurted, "Nice to meet you. Do you eat?"

Kyle smiled inwardly. He'd never seen his brother embarrassed before.

Aleara smiled. "I don't eat your food, but it has an interesting aroma. Thank you."

John started the car. Aleara jumped as the engine churned to life. She returned to the back seat next to Tiff.

"Okay, everyone. Buckle your seatbelts." John paused, looking at Aleara. "Does that work for her?"

Tiff explained the seat belt. Aleara tried to manipulate it, but found wearing the seatbelt uncomfortable.

As they drove from the mall, John couldn't contain his curiosity. "So, Aleara, what's it like where you're from? Do you have a big family?"

Aleara didn't answer. "Aleara?" Tiff asked.

"Dizzy..." Aleara finally responded.

Kyle glanced back at her. "Hold on. You're not used to the car's motion. We'll be at the zoo soon."

Twenty minutes later, they arrived at the zoo. Once the car stopped, Aleara peppered John with questions of her own. "How did the car make the hot wind? What makes it move? Where did the music come from?"

John tried to explain. "The car engine burns fuel to get the power to move. It also heats the air flowing in from the front of the car, and we use that to keep warm. The music came from the radio."

Aleara's baffled expression showed she didn't understand.

Hoping to distract them from delving into automotive mechanics, Tiff suggested, "Let's go see the animals. Aleara? Why don't you fly to the top of those trees? We have to go through the gate, but we'll wave you down once we're through."

John, Tiff and Kyle entered and looked for a secluded place. By the time Aleara rejoined them, she already had many questions about the animals she could see. The rest of them took turns answering her questions and keeping watch. Whenever other visitors came close, Aleara hid among the treetops again.

They had a few close calls though. As they watched the hippos, a group of kids came running around the corner. Aleara darted inside the animal pen, hiding below their line of sight.

In the lions' exhibit, they had another close call. Despite the cool temperatures, the lions relaxed in a secluded spot. To get a better look, Aleara drifted into the enclosure from above. Unfortunately, a family arrived at the exhibit when the lions grooming each other distracted her.

"Is that a ghost?" a little girl asked, pointing at Aleara.

Her father replied, "There's no such thing as ghosts. Maybe they're making a movie, and it's a special effect."

Fortunately, Tiff was already using her cell phone to record Aleara with the lions, so Kyle played along with the father's guess. "That's right. We're making a student film for our school."

The father nodded. "We can come back when they're finished, Chrissy. We don't want to bother their filming."

As they wandered through the zoo, Tiff snapped selfies and videos aplenty, sharing the best with Kyle and the other immortal students. For Kyle, the zoo offered an additional challenge. He remembered his encounter with the dog in the park, and how she had seemed to understand him, so he spent time trying to communicate with different animals. Some of the various birds and reptiles reacted, but Kyle seemed to have a better rapport with mammals.

At the bear exhibit, he had his best success. One of the brown bears perked up when he growled at it and meandered over to the quartet. He asked it to show off a bit, so it obliged by splashing in the cold water. Kyle had it pose for a picture behind them.

As they left the bears, John said, "So it seemed like you and that bear got along well."

"Yes. She was lonely and bored. I think we made her feel better," Kyle replied.

At the end of the afternoon, they returned to John's car. Aleara couldn't contain her excitement and talked about the different animals all the way to Jason's house for their movie night.

It drizzled the next morning, but the rain tapered off by

lunchtime. With the break in the weather, the late winter winds picked up. The sun broke through the morning clouds, so the temperatures were mild for late February. Mike suggested a picnic at the park near the town reservoir, and Tiff agreed. Unfortunately, Mike's mother thought a picnic was good for his brother and sister too, so he had to bring them along.

After they ate lunch, the twins scampered off to the playground. Aleara drifted down, joining Tiff and Mike.

"So that big wall holds the water?" Aleara asked, looking at the dam.

Mike answered, "Right. It's called a dam. By holding the water, we can use it for drinking, irrigation, or other needs. The land that would have been underwater on this side can be used for other things, like this park."

Aleara looked uncertain. "That seems mean to the creatures in the water though. I don't know if the undines would like that or not."

"I don't think the fish mind though. Part of this reservoir project has safe places for them to swim, and nesting areas," Tiff replied, remembering a news article she'd read about it.

As the day dried out, a few other people arrived at the park, and Aleara had to hide above the trees once again. With the windy weather, some diehard picnickers flew kites, which delighted Aleara. Mike and Tiff climbed a tree so they could continue talking with the sylph.

"What are those flying things?" Aleara asked, gazing at the kites.

"They're called kites. We fly them in the winds for fun. It's a peaceful activity," Tiff answered.

Mike saw her forlorn expression. "Would you like to fly with them?"

"I'd love to. But all the people would see me," Aleara sighed. Her sighs sounded like the breeze itself, Mike thought.

"C'mon, Mike. Don't tease her. She'll be seen in a heartbeat!" Tiff sounded worried.

"I thought of that already. She can hide in plain sight," Mike grinned, pulling a ball of twine out of his jacket pocket.

Moments later, Aleara soared merrily among the other kites. At the other end of the line, Mike pretended to fly a unique kite. As long as Aleara didn't tangle the line she held, no one would be the wiser. Even Mike's brother and sister came to watch.

An hour later, Aleara swooped and sailed among the kites. Several other people gathered to watch, and asked Mike about his unusual kite. "It's a special balloon kite. She bought it on the internet," Mike smiled, pointing to Tiff.

Suddenly, Mike heard the squeal of brakes. He spun around and saw a car moving way too fast, careening down from the road that crossed the top of the dam. Mike guessed it had missed a turn on the wet road, perhaps hitting a patch of ice. He saw it roll down the embankment on the dry side of the dam and slam into a tree.

Mike handed the twine to Tiff. "Call 911, then get her down. You can calm her and explain better than I can. I'll see if I can help."

He dashed toward the car. As he ran, he manifested his fox ears long enough to hear the cries from the car.

Once he got to the wreck, he spotted the two screaming children in the back seat. A boy about four or five years old sat in a child safety seat, and a baby girl screamed in an infant seat beside him. Their father slumped in the remains of the driver's seat, not moving.

Mike gulped and tried to quell his own fear. He leaned into the car to put his fingers on the man's neck and felt a pulse.

The trembling little boy stared at him with wide eyes. Mike remembered back to that fateful day, months ago, when he had clung to life after being struck by a van. His own pain and fear returned to him like a fresh wound, but he knew this boy needed him. Mike tried to put on a friendly face. "Don't worry about your daddy. I promise he will be fine." His words resonated with a dim memory, but he couldn't place it. Somehow they seemed right and bolstered his resolve.

Mike tried to unbuckle the straps of the safety seat, but they wouldn't release. In his haste, he couldn't identify the cause of the problem. He frantically yanked on the straps, but they held firm. Finally, he decided on a desperate gamble.

He glanced over his shoulder. Though a few other people were approaching, none were close enough to see him clearly. He turned back to the boy. "Want to see a magic trick?" he asked. The boy stared at him with a baffled expression.

Mike transformed his head into a fox's head, bit through the straps, tore the restraints, and pulled the boy out. He bit through the straps holding the baby seat secure and pulled the girl free too.

He transformed his head back to normal, winking at the boy. "Now don't tell anyone about that trick! It's a special one!"

By the time he pulled both children to safety, Tiff had reached the wreckage. A few other townsfolk followed her. "I left your brother flying our kite. I also called Miss Olsen, just in case," she gasped.

One of the picnickers was a doctor, so Mike followed his instructions and helped him with the father. By the time the ambulance arrived, the doctor had already diagnosed a mild concussion, cracked ribs, and a broken arm. But the father would live.

Miss Olsen arrived about an hour after the accident. The ambulance had left with the victims, and a tow truck driver was wrestling with the car to remove it from the park. The accident upset Mike's siblings, so they curtailed their afternoon at the park. His mother had already picked them up. Tiff and Aleara had stayed in the park.

As she led Tiff and Aleara to the warmth and privacy of her car, Miss Olsen asked Tiff, "Are you okay? That looked like a severe accident."

Tiff recalled, "Mike got the kids out of the car and waited for help. We were lucky a doctor was in the park."

Miss Olsen nodded and turned to Aleara. "That's enough excitement for today. So did you enjoy your visit?"

The sylph babbled, "It was wonderful! Tiff took me to your Exchange and showed me her favorite places. Then we went to see your animals. Did you know there are some that look like shock hounds and charcats? Kyle made friends with a bear, and there were birds and..." Aleara paused, trying vainly to remember the names of all of the animals. "There were so many. And then we went to see some picture shows with Jason. We saw humans on the water, and they fought big monsters like you did."

Miss Olsen looked inquisitively at Tiff. "Movie night. We watched a fantasy adventure," Tiff explained.

"And then we came here, and I got to fly with those kites. That was fun. But then that car broke, and Mike and Tiff went to help."

"I'm glad you enjoyed yourself, Aleara. But it's time for you to return home," Miss Olsen said gently. Aleara's expression showed she wished she could stay longer.

Miss Olsen smiled at the sylph. "Now that Tiffany knows how to call you, I'm sure she'll find excuses for you to visit again. But let's get you back home, shall we? Do you have your pendant, Tiffany? To return her, all you need to do is touch your pendant again, and thank her—for her service, for visiting, for anything. But thanking her for being here provides the closure needed to return her home."

Tiff pulled the pendant out of her Pocket and put it around her neck. She raised her hands toward Aleara, and the sylph responded. The two touched each other again. "I'll see you soon, my friend. Thank you for visiting. It's been wonderful."

With that, Aleara faded from view, a smile on her face.

CHAPTER TWENTY-EIGHT
Locker Problems

Spring break was coming soon. On the way to the science class they shared, Jason chatted with Kyle and Aliki about his upcoming vacation. "After Easter, we're going to a resort for a few days. It has a large indoor water park with huge water slides and water sports! Last time we went, we had a blast! My dad played some golf, and Mom got the spa treatment. Helen and I played in the water the whole time."

Aliki laughed. "It sounds like fun. I wish my family could go to some place like that."

"Yeah. You guys would love it." Jason lowered his voice. "I'll try exploring some other water tricks too."

Kyle and Aliki both immediately knew what Jason meant. Kyle whispered, "That could be handy."

The trio crossed paths with Tiff and her friends Rachel and Shelly. "Hiya, Tiff!" Jason called.

"Hey, Jason!" Tiff replied. "Where are you going on your vacation? You mentioned a resort, right?"

Jason couldn't contain his exuberance. "It's gonna be pretty wild! I was telling Kyle and Aliki about it. There were—"

Aliki interrupted. "Jason, we're going to be late to class. Catch you later, Tiff!"

The trio hurried toward their science class. Kyle, silent until now, suddenly spoke up. "Did either of you notice Rachel giving us some weird looks back there?"

Jason shrugged his shoulders. "Maybe she's not going anywhere for spring break and felt jealous."

As she walked through the school to her next class, Tiff's mind wandered to the upcoming weekend. She knew Mr. Oxinos had more training planned, but he hadn't elaborated, so she thought about the different realms they'd visited. While the Spirit Realm and Mike's description of the Tech Realm intrigued her, Kyle's horrific portrayal of the Demon Realm frightened her. From what Aliki said, the Ghost Realm wasn't much better. Her mind raced.

Rachel walked beside her. "Hey, Tiff! Are you in there?"

Tiff jolted herself out of her musings. "Huh? Oh, yeah. What's up?"

"I was hoping we might hit the mall this weekend. It's been a while, and I have Saturday free. We can get Mara and Kennedy, and—"

Tiff mumbled, "I have more training this weekend. This one is something I can't miss."

Rachel looked hurt. "You spend all your time with this all-skills team! You don't hang out with us anymore!"

Tiff looked down at the floor, unable to meet her friend's gaze. "I'm sorry. It's something I have to do." She forced a happier expression to her face. "Hey—I'm free Friday night, and Sunday may be open too. What about then?"

"I'm busy Friday night, and I have to check my schedule for Sunday," Rachel replied. "But try to make some time for your real friends. We miss you."

Stunned, Tiff stopped walking. Rachel's words had struck a nerve. *Real friends? But what are Jason, Mike, Aliki, and Kyle to me?*

The next morning, Mr. Oxinos received a phone call just as homeroom ended and withdrew into his storage area. Aliki glanced at the other immortal students as they rose from their desks. Mike gave a quick nod and pointed at the storeroom with his thumb. As the others left, Aliki paused to eavesdrop on the conversation.

She overheard Mr. Oxinos, though he spoke quietly. "... and we need to teach them realm transference. I understand. But languages too? That's pretty aggressive."

He paused to listen, then replied again. "I'm concerned we may burn them out. Realm transference isn't simple to grasp, nor is... Yes, I understand. Can't you tell me more?"

Another pause. "We'll get started on it. I'll talk to you soon."

As Aliki started toward the door, she heard Mr. Oxinos' voice again. "Did you hear enough, Aliki?" He stepped out of his storeroom with a knowing smile on his face.

She started to apologize, "I'm sorry, sir. It's just that..."

"It's okay—this time. We're going to speed up your training a bit." He turned toward the students entering for his classroom.

"You don't want to be late for your next class."

"Yes, sir. So who was that on the phone? Anyone I know?"

He locked eyes with her. "Lachesis."

After her second period gym class, Aliki stopped by her locker to gather her books. She knew Lachesis as one of the three Fates of Greek myth. So she was real too?

Aliki was lost in her reverie. But as she opened her locker door, the mess inside shocked her. Bits of banana and crumbs of some type of muffin covered the top of her backpack, and some had gotten on her books. She quickly examined the door and discovered that someone had shoved bananas and muffins through the slots in the door. Amongst the mess, Aliki found an index card with two words written on it: DROP OUT.

Then Jason arrived beside her. "What the...?!" he exclaimed, looking at the mess.

Aliki tried to hold back the tears. "Why.... Who would do this?" she sobbed.

"Not cool." Jason had a few guesses about possible suspects. "Not one of us, but someone close? Julisha maybe?"

Too numb to think, Aliki grabbed the science book she needed and closed the locker door.

Kyle ate his lunch slowly, trying to read a library book about naval powers of the colonial age at the same time. But he couldn't focus on the book. Mike and Jason had spread the news about the locker vandalism throughout the school. By lunch, the school gossip chain had gone to work, and most students had heard about the incident. One of the teachers had helped her clean the mess, but the emotional wounds wouldn't heal so easily.

Kyle looked across the table at Aliki. She nibbled her fish sticks with a detached expression, but she hadn't spoken much at all during lunch.

Bullying was far too familiar to him. Kyle didn't always have his brothers around, and he'd never developed Mike's quick wit or the imposing physique of Jason.

So he tried changing the subject. "Jason mentioned you overheard someone giving Mr. Oxinos some orders?"

Aliki looked up from her lunch tray. "Mr. Oxinos said it was Lachesis." Seeing the blank looks on the others' faces, she elaborated. "In Greek myth, she is one of the Moirai, or Fates. She measures a person's life and determines his or her destiny."

Jason finished his lunch. "So you think she's calling the shots? Is she Mr. O's real boss?"

Aliki shrugged her shoulders. "It would fit the myths."

Jason, still thinking about the locker incident, turned to Mike. "Hey, Mike! Do you think you could figure out who messed with her locker by sniffing it? Don't dogs do that all the time?"

"Not yet," Mike replied. "I'm still figuring out my senses, so I can't track by scent. And I'd have to know what each student smelled like. But I could take a whiff."

Kyle piped up. "Bears have a strong sense of smell too, even better than dogs. Let me try."

Mike and Jason nodded.

During his algebra class after lunch, Kyle asked to be

excused to go to the nurse's office, complaining of a headache. He took a route that passed by Aliki's locker. Before transforming into a bear, he glanced up and down the hall to make sure no one could see him.

He could smell the strong scent from the banana, as well as the odor from cleaning supplies. Aliki's scent lingered on the locker door, but after a moment, he thought he could smell two other people. He transformed back into his normal form and went to see Miss Olsen in the nurse's office.

He tried to describe the smells to her, but couldn't find the right words. However, he noticed a scowl on Miss Olsen's face.

Kyle pleaded, "I was careful, Miss Olsen. I kept listening for anything, and I kept looking too."

"Well, let's be glad you weren't seen. But the only way you'll be able to identify the culprit is if you smell them as a bear. I don't think having a bear wandering through school sniffing at each of the students is such a good idea."

Kyle's voice fell. "I hadn't thought of that. I'm sorry."

Miss Olsen's frown gave way to a gentle smile. "No harm done. Remember to think things through. At your age, rushing into things is natural. But what would you have done if you were spotted?"

"I don't know," Kyle admitted.

"Think about what a bear would do. In this case, you could plausibly have been attracted to the smell of food. Had you been spotted, you should have run outside as quickly as possible and hid. Change back into a human when no one is anywhere close."

Kyle nodded.

"One more thing. Did you try using your earth sense while

you were a bear? It could provide an additional warning."

Kyle brightened. "That's a good idea! Thanks!"

After the sparring exhibition, the principal had bowed to the collective student demand and invited MacKenzie to teach more students as an after-school activity. MacKenzie had agreed and had since become a school celebrity. Now, every Wednesday afternoon, she and Coach Brown taught twenty students in the unusual art of weapons combat.

As Jason walked into the sparring session, he glanced around. Julisha sat near Coach Brown as she listened to MacKenzie discuss pole weapon combat styles. Carson stood on the mat, wearing padded armor and helping demonstrate some of the moves. They both saw him enter, and Carson waved his weapon awkwardly at Jason.

His distraction earned him a leg sweep from MacKenzie. "An' that's why ye never let yerself get distracted while in a fight!" The other students chuckled.

Jason stood watching the other students spar with MacKenzie and each other. He waited until Julisha finished her turn, then casually sat beside her after she stepped off the mat.

"Hi, Jason!" she whispered. "What brings you here?"

"I wanted to see how you and the others were doing with this," he whispered in return. "I need to talk to you afterwards."

After the sparring, as the students left the gym to meet their waiting parents, Jason stepped to the side and gestured for Julisha to join him.

She peered toward the parking lot and waved to her waiting

mother. "So what's going on? Is there a problem?"

"How's the sparring going?" he asked, trying to figure out how to bring up Aliki's locker.

"It's great. I'm getting a good workout, and it's a lot of fun, despite the bruises." She paused to look at him. "But that's not what you really wanted to talk about, is it?"

Jason couldn't read her expression, so he decided to plow ahead. "Do you know anything about Aliki's locker?"

"I heard someone slipped something messy into it and got her upset." She stopped and looked Jason in the eyes. "Wait. You don't think I had anything to do with it?"

"Well, you were interested in joining the all-skills team," he recalled. "I'm not saying it was you, but we want..." He paused, trying to find the right words.

"I didn't do it. I swear, Jason. I wanted to join the all-skills team, but that was mainly for the sparring—and I already have that. Mr. Oxinos said I could help in other ways. I even helped Dr. Fathy with some of his weird research too."

Jason became curious. "Really? What did he want you to do?"

"He wanted to learn about some old of the folktales of the area. He also wanted to know about the Native American tribe that used to live here. I couldn't help him with that, but he seemed interested when I told him about the haunted house on Fourth Street."

"So you're happy with the way things turned out?"

"Absolutely. I like Aliki." Julisha dropped her voice further. "She held off that cougar, remember? If it had attacked me, I'd be dead!"

Jason nodded, relieved that Julisha wasn't the culprit. "Thanks for being honest. I'm glad you're happy."

She added, "If I hear anything, I'll let you know, or maybe Aliki. She's tougher than she looks, so I pity whoever did it."

Thursday, Tiff joined her fellow cheerleaders at lunch. Kennedy chatted with her about classes, while Danielle gossiped with some other juniors and seniors. Rachel seemed distracted though, not looking up from her lunch tray.

Tiff tried to draw her out. "Rachel? Are we still on for hitting the mall on Sunday? I talked to my mom, and I can be there around noon."

"That'll be okay," Rachel responded quietly.

Tiff lowered her voice so the other cheerleaders wouldn't overhear. "C'mon, Rachel! What's bothering you? I'm trying to fix things and make it up to you. I don't have too much to do this weekend. Our training is going to be light activity on Saturday only. No camping."

Rachel suddenly stood and mumbled, "I gotta go." She hurried away from the table.

Baffled, Tiff followed her. "Rachel! Wait up!"

Once out of the lunchroom, Rachel paused, and Tiff caught up with her. "What's bothering you? I told you I'm trying to fix things. Give me a chance!" she pleaded.

Rachel seemed more upset. "You don't understand. Everything is easy for you. You have the squad, your honors classes, and your all-skills team. You don't really need me anymore. I wanted things to go back to the way they were."

"We're growing up, Rachel. I'm going through changes, and I'm sure you are too. But we'll always be friends, right?"

By now, Rachel had broken into tears. "I thought that if the all-skills team broke up, maybe you'd spend more time with me. But you stick together more tightly than the squad does." Rachel paused, looking at Tiff for the first time in their conversation. "Don't you see? I put the stuff in Aliki's locker. I thought if Aliki dropped out, maybe you'd spend more time with me and drop that stupid team. And Jason wouldn't have eyes for her either. I hate her! It's all her fault!"

Tiff stood, stunned. She had always believed she could make her different friends like each other. But now, her hidden immortal life and her previous normal life were colliding violently. She turned away from Rachel, trying to hold back the tears. She couldn't accept it.

Tiff ran away from Rachel, sobbing. She dashed toward the nearest school exit and ran outside.

"Tiff! Wait!" Rachel called after her, trying vainly to follow her. By the time Rachel arrived at the front of the school, she couldn't see Tiff anywhere. But a lone eagle flew away from the school.

That night, Tiff ignored every call and message on her cell phone. For the first time in her life, she didn't want anyone around her. Unable to reconcile her feelings of guilt, she cried herself to sleep.

The next day, Rachel was not at school. After she confessed to Tiff, Rachel had summoned her courage and confessed to the teachers. They had suspended her for one day and gave her probation until spring break. Tiff received a reprimand for leaving school without permission, but Mr. Oxinos interceded to prevent a more serious punishment.

Aliki didn't talk at all about Rachel and ignored the school rumor mill. For that, Tiff was grateful.

After dinner, Tiff retreated to her bedroom and called Rachel on her cell phone, opening a video chat. When Rachel's image appeared on the phone, Tiff put on her best smile. "Rachel? It's me, Tiff. Do you want to talk?"

"I thought you didn't want to see me any more," Rachel sobbed.

"No! It's not like that!" Tiff pleaded. "I still want to be friends. I want to hang out at the mall with you, and cheerlead, and everything like we used to."

"But you're always busy with the all-skills team."

"I have to spend time with them. I really can't explain it easily, but I promise I'll make time for you. Let's plan our mall outing on Sunday, okay?"

Tiff and Rachel continued talking for another hour that evening, trying to mend things between them.

CHAPTER TWENTY-NINE
Language Lessons

Saturday finally came, and with it, more training. Mr. Oxinos, Dr. Fathy, and Miss Olsen gathered the students together. The days had grown warm, and the students all felt a bit of spring fever. Anticipating that, Miss Olsen had suggested they gather outside in a park instead of at the school.

Looking around at the gathering, Kyle asked, "Where are MacKenzie and Coach Brown?"

Mr. Oxinos replied, "They both had some business to attend to. If we want to keep MacKenzie's role as a combat trainer plausible, she needs to establish a private gym. So they're checking out possible sites."

Dr. Fathy added, "Fortunately, our lesson for today isn't a physical one. We plan to teach you how to understand and speak other languages."

Aliki looked puzzled. "I already speak Greek and know a bit of Spanish. What other languages are we going to learn?"

"All of them," Dr. Fathy replied. "Language is the vehicle for communication between individuals. Each language incorporates and reflects both the speaker's culture and their intended message. However, one of our gifts enables us to perceive the actual intended message as well as the cultural 'seasoning,' if you will."

Kyle looked at the other students. They all seemed as bewildered as he felt, so Mr. Oxinos tried to paraphrase. "What Dr. Fathy means is that we can intuit the speaker's meaning automatically. Some of you already have some natural talent, so we'll try to encourage that."

Kyle tried to maintain his focus as Dr. Fathy resumed his lecture. "You can train your mind to perceive the subconscious clues a speaker gives off, and by adapting to the—"

Miss Olsen interrupted. "Tom, let's try to give them concrete instruction first." She turned to the students and said something in a language none of them understood. Switching back to English, she challenged them, "Now what did I say? Any hints or clues?"

Mike raised his hand. "Your posture suggested you were talking about yourself?" he guessed.

Miss Olsen nodded. "Correct. Any other hints?"

"Your eyes darted around the park for an instant," Aliki added. "Does that have any meaning?"

Miss Olsen smiled at the two of them. "It does, Aliki. What I said was 'I am the guardian of the Tree of Life' in Old Norse. What you were able to intuit is about the limit of a normal person's ability, but now we'll introduce you to the subconscious perceptions only we immortals possess. They will allow you to understand the entire meaning and communicate in the same language."

Mr. Oxinos jumped in. "But first, we need to move to a new

realm, which will help you tap into this particular talent. Gather in a circle, and maintain your focus on your physical forms. This realm is a bit dangerous if you let your focus wander."

The students followed his instructions, and the world shifted once again.

When Kyle opened his eyes, absolutely nothing surrounded him—or it seemed like nothing. Though he could see the sun, the sky was black as night, and he could also see other stars. Occasionally, swirls of gauzy color resembling glowing ribbons or clouds would flow through the dark sky. Unlike the other realms they had visited, they saw no sign of the school.

Kyle looked down. He saw no ground under his feet—he could see stars below him as well. He tried pushing down into the non-existent ground. He felt nothing, but couldn't push his foot below ground level. They seemed to be standing on nothing at all.

"What the..." Jason blurted.

Mr. Oxinos explained, "This is the Astral Realm. Here, normal matter doesn't exist. If you want to think of this as sort of a psychic plane, you can. Your normal senses are sharper here, and you can learn to tap into some secondary senses. There are other talents you can tap into while in the Astral Realm. But this realm is dangerous. If you fail to maintain your form, you'll manifest as astral energy here, and controlling an astral form is challenging."

Miss Olsen added, "The Astral Realm will also enhance your intuition, and may even let you sense auras. For a few, tapping into the Astral Realm gives them glimpses into possible futures. Others learn to project their senses using their astral form. But we're here to teach you to intuit spoken languages. Now, let's begin."

For the next several hours, the students listened to each of the teachers speak different languages and try to understand them. The students, with varying degrees of success, managed to pick up bits of the language and meaning.

Kyle glanced at Mike and Aliki, who seemed to grasp the techniques naturally. By the end of the day, Mike could answer back in any of the languages the teachers used. Aliki stumbled a few times and made some mistakes, but learned to communicate with basic sentences. Kyle himself had grasped some of the different languages and could speak at a child's level. Jason understood many of the languages spoken, but couldn't figure out how to reply.

Tiff, on the other hand, seemed to be struggling. She still couldn't comprehend anything the teachers said. Worse yet, she seemed to be getting upset.

Miss Olsen noticed Tiff's emotional state and pulled her aside to talk privately. The two of them vanished, returning to Earth. *Good,* Kyle thought. *Miss Olsen is really good at helping people with their problems.* He remembered how she'd managed to draw him back out from the bear when he first changed.

Kyle turned his attention back to Dr. Fathy, who had finished reciting a story in ancient Egyptian. Kyle could follow most of it, but lost some of the nuances of the tale.

He remembered Dr. Fathy's books and raised his hand. "Dr. Fathy? Does this talent have anything to do with those books you lent me? Particularly the ones that changed their language?"

"Indeed it does, Kyle. Those books utilize the same basic

297

principles as the talents we are teaching. I devised them when I discovered I could employ elements within the Tech Realm to create a cerebro-adaptive membrane that..." And just like that, Dr. Fathy lost himself in another impromptu discourse.

Mr. Oxinos let Dr. Fathy ramble for a bit before interrupting. "So do you have any further questions? We're about done for today."

Kyle raised his hand again. "We learned to listen and speak in other languages. Does it work for reading too?"

Mr. Oxinos replied quickly, "There is a similar principle for reading and writing. But that's more complex. So we focused today on verbal communications."

Jason raised his hand. "Why do we need to learn languages? I'm glad we can learn them, but why now?"

"Honestly, I don't know," Mr. Oxinos admitted. "We received instructions to accelerate your training, and that you'll need to learn languages. I'm not sure why, although I've had a few premonitions recently. I'm still trying to make sense of them. Something is going to happen soon."

Back on Earth, Miss Olsen beckoned Tiff to join her. Tiff followed her to a nearby table in the school courtyard and sat across from her.

"So what's wrong, Tiffany?" Miss Olsen asked. "You're usually the one that's on top of the world. I've never seen you so distraught. Is this about the locker incident with Rachel?"

Tiff nodded. She described Rachel's conversations with her and how Rachel had become jealous of the time she'd spent in training. She recalled Rachel's confession, and how she'd blurted out that she blamed Aliki for everything.

"Do you have any idea why she'd blame Aliki and not Paul or myself?" Miss Olsen asked pointedly. "Is there anything more she said in her confession?"

Tiff remembered, "Well, she mentioned Jason for some reason. Wait—do you think she..."

"... has a crush on Jason? Of course. You didn't notice that?"

"I may have noticed, but I guess I never thought much about it," Tiff admitted.

"Mmm hmm. Let's put Rachel's issues aside for now and focus on you. Why do you think you're having problems with languages?"

"Maybe because I'm still mixed up about Rachel?" Tiff pondered.

"That's part of it. But the fact you didn't even notice her crush is another reason."

"It is? How?"

"Let's back up. How do you feel about your problems with languages?"

"Frustrated," Tiff admitted. "I've always been able to figure things out and succeed. But this... I can't do it! I don't understand!" She dabbed tears from her eyes.

"You can and will, but it may take time. You've always been successful, but have you ever challenged yourself with something where you weren't confident? Like playing a musical instrument, for instance?"

"Not really," Tiff replied. "My mom always let me pick what

activities I wanted to do. She never tried to force me into something else. I wanted to dance and do gymnastics, and that led to cheerleading. I did some ice skating for a year or two, but lost interest—not because I wasn't any good though."

"But other girls were better?"

"Some were."

"My guess is that you've triumphed at things you know you can do, but you're not comfortable when you have to develop skills where you may not be among the best. Rather than pushing your limits in new directions, you've stayed in comfortable roles."

Ida paused to let her words sink in before continuing. "Now, with all of these new abilities, you have to step outside your comfort zone and challenge yourself to develop new talents. You can do it, but it will take work—real work. Are you ready for the challenge?"

Tiff sniffled, "Yes, ma'am."

"Now, on to your problems with this particular challenge. Do you have any idea why languages are so hard for you?"

Tiff shook her head.

"Why do you think Mike is so adept at learning this?" Miss Olsen prodded. "What skills does he have that you don't?"

"He's musical and funny. Is that it?"

"In part. Mike relies on his quick wit to get him out of situations or to devise an outlandish tale. When he doesn't have that kind of challenge, he goofs off. But humor and wit also rely upon knowing your audience. That same skill applies to learning the languages. Unfortunately, you've always been successful, so many of the people who surround you have told you what you want or expect to hear. But things like Rachel's crush: you didn't perceive it because you haven't learned to read people like Mike, or even Aliki. That's the skill you need to develop."

Tiff wiped her eyes. She still felt the frustration of failure, but Miss Olsen was right. She could conquer this challenge, and she would pay more attention to all of her friends. She would start at the mall with Rachel tomorrow.

That Sunday was Palm Sunday, and Jason joined his family at church. He sat patiently, as he had for years, listening to the priest talk about Jesus, heaven, hell, and salvation. His little sister fidgeted beside him, but Jason tried to focus on the sermon. His father sat with rapt attention.

Jason tried to use his new talent with language to understand the few passages in Latin. But his mind kept wandering back to his visit to the Heaven Realm with Mr. Oxinos—with *Apollo*. The angels were real, but Heaven was one of several realms where souls migrated after death. Would he become an angel when he died? Or a water elemental? Or something else? He struggled to reconcile his faith with the fantastic revelations he'd seen himself.

The sermon concluded, and he rode home with his family. His parents chatted about their friends at church and their plans for the upcoming spring break week. Helen looked forward to a week of playing at the resort and chatted to him about her plans.

But Jason felt confused. He stared at the miniature cross made of palm leaves he'd been given at the service. From what he understood, Mr. Oxinos had lived for over two thousand years. He'd lived through the birth of Christianity, not to mention so much else. The ancient Greeks worshipped him as divine.

Now Jason himself had gained powers that some might call miraculous. Could Jesus have been someone who had received similar powers?

Troubled, he gazed back toward the church as the car drove home.

During lunch on Tuesday, Mike noticed Dr. Fathy and MacKenzie visiting the school. They chatted with Coach Brown in the courtyard, and the expressions on their faces seemed grim. Normally, Mike wouldn't intrude into a teacher's conversation, but he knew their conversation involved him and the rest of the immortal students. He noticed MacKenzie clenching her fists and shifting her weight, clearly worried about something. He sauntered towards the gathered teachers, listening as he approached.

"...and you're sure you found signs of them in the Demon Realm?" Coach Brown asked MacKenzie.

"I had ta knock a few heads, but they told me of a group of six fomori makin' a real stink there." MacKenzie nodded at Mike. "Good morning, Mike."

"More giants?" Mike asked.

Dr. Fathy replied, "Yes, it looks like they are planning something, which is unusual enough itself. Normally, they do not work together, except for family groups. From what MacKenzie discovered, they are likely planning an assault on Earth." He turned toward MacKenzie. "I'll send word to other warriors among us. I'm sure they can root out the giants from the Demon Realm. We don't have the strength between the five of us, particularly with the students to protect."

Mike knew better than to suggest that they could fight, or even defend themselves, against a determined bunch of giants. Blue and his two children had been scary enough. "So what should we do?"

Coach Brown replied, "Continue your training for now. Let us worry about the giants."

Dr. Fathy looked thoughtfully at Mike. "Perhaps we should inform them about more of the details. I believe they are old enough. Fresh perspectives could help us."

The students gathered at an impromptu meeting arranged by Mr. Oxinos the next day during their lunchtime. The students ate their lunches in his classroom while the immortal teachers spoke.

As usual, Mr. Oxinos opened the discussion. "You should be aware of Dr. Fathy's frequent trips elsewhere, as he's pursuing several different investigations. One of those investigations relates to a few immortals who have disappeared."

Dr. Fathy stepped in. "During a recent investigation in Marseille, I discovered that one of the immortals, Michel Durand, had been visiting the Spirit Realm. When I stepped into the Spirit Realm myself, I discovered signs of giants and signs of a struggle, so we can only assume giants captured or killed him."

MacKenzie jumped into the discussion. "An' ta make matters worse, I entered the Demon Realm, and found that six fomorians had tried to appoint themselves as local warlords. The demons fought back. They made a complete haymes of the area."

"So there are signs that the titans are planning something," Mr. Oxinos continued.

Jason raised his hand. "But why did they show up here? Are they drawn to us immortals?"

Miss Olsen murmured, "We believe they are, but we aren't sure why."

Tiff wondered aloud, "So if they don't have the Fountain of Souls anymore, how are more giants born?"

Dr. Fathy replied, "Not all souls on Earth migrate to one of the realms. A few remain and reincarnate here. So I assume the same happens to the giants. They also have long lifespans."

Kyle wanted to learn more about the giants. "They gather into family groups, right? So do they have a society? What kind of culture do they have?"

Miss Olsen paused for a minute. "They have a tribal society, formed around their immortals. The giants do not hide their immortality like we do, but use it to dominate their fellows. The immortal giants also try to have large families to increase the chances of an immortal heir."

Mr. Oxinos added, "Titan society is generally primitive by our standards, and each clan has different customs, varying according to the immortal's taste. Many clans are semi-nomadic, and violence between clans is common."

Miss Olsen continued, "When we returned Smoky and Zapfoot, their clan fell into a bit of a quandary. Some of them wanted to follow Smoky, particularly the young men who wanted to court her. Others wanted to promote Zapfoot to Blue's position as chieftain. Still others left the clan, seeking their fortunes elsewhere. Smoky and Zapfoot may fight for the leadership position if both want it."

"But they're brother and sister!" Jason exclaimed. "Why would they fight each other?"

"Power. Just like here." Coach Brown scowled.

"Different clans are workin' together," MacKenzie added. "The six in the Demon Realm came from at least four different clans. So somethin' is gettin' them to cooperate. If a leader can unite them and lead them to Earth..." She let her words trail off, but everyone could imagine the consequences.

"Is that where the kuzherits come in?" Mike pondered.

Dr. Fathy answered, "Perhaps. We know little about the realms beyond the giant's world. The physical properties of the kuzherits' realm don't follow our conventional ideas of physics. We do know that the kuzherits play havoc with reality, warping it in unusual ways. I theorize their realm is a non-Euclidean space that—"

Mr. Oxinos cut off Dr. Fathy's impromptu lecture. "Dr. Fathy and I have discussed venturing to the kuzherit's realm to uncover more information about them. But it would be a longer visit, and quite dangerous."

Coach Brown glanced at the clock and stood. "If the giants could use the gates to send armies to Earth, you could imagine the catastrophe."

The bell rang to signal the end of lunch. The students filed out, fear and uncertainty on their faces.

Spring break came none too soon for the immortal students.

All of them needed a respite from training and worries about a potential giant invasion of Earth.

Aliki's family had no real plans, so she spent the week puttering around the house, visiting the mall, and relaxing. She kept in touch with the others through frequent text messages and video chats.

Tiff and her mother left on Saturday to visit her uncle, who lived a few hours away. According to Tiff, her mother had wanted to visit for some time, and spring break provided a good opportunity to get away. Tiff had admitted that she looked forward to visiting his place in the country. She wasn't particularly fond of her uncle, but he did live near a lake with plenty of open sky for flying.

Aliki smiled and glanced through Jason's messages. He'd included a few pictures of him helping Helen find the eggs left by the Easter Bunny, as well as pictures of their elaborate Easter dinner. Jason had mentioned attending church services in one of his chats. Aliki sensed something bothered him about it, but he clearly didn't want to talk about it.

Jason's next message came on Easter Monday in the evening, once they arrived at the resort. He included more pictures, and the rest of his messages showed him on water slides and in the pools having fun with his sister.

Kyle traveled with his family to visit his oldest brother David at college. Kyle mentioned that John would attend the same university in the fall, so they needed to find a place for him to live. Kyle also divulged that he'd brought some books on Greek, Norse, Hindu, and Celtic mythology, hoping to get some insights into both the realms and the giants.

Like Aliki, Mike didn't travel over spring break. His divorced mother couldn't afford a nice vacation. Mike planned to spend as much time as he could playing video games. Evidently, he had to look after his two siblings too.

Aliki chatted with Mike frequently and also found time to meet once or twice at the mall. They speculated on the giants' activities, wishing they could do more. Aliki confessed to Mike she felt apprehensive—she had a hunch they would all be tested soon. After all, Lachesis needed them trained for something.

CHAPTER THIRTY
Crash Course in Transference

Once school resumed, Mike spent time trying to hone his ability with languages by using the internet to watch foreign movies and videos. He found he could understand some of them, at least in part. He also tried to hold conversations with Aliki in Greek in the few moments they had alone.

He arrived at the school on Saturday morning, eagerly anticipating the next lesson. The teachers planned to teach them how to transfer to different realms, and the opportunity to explore excited him. Each of the students had visited one new realm before, and Mike had become fascinated with the Tech Realm and Tiff's description of the Spirit Realm.

An hour later, he was bored. The students sat around the school's courtyard, listening to Dr. Fathy. MacKenzie had other obligations again, so she missed their training today. Mike missed her talent for interrupting long-winded explanations.

Dr. Fathy tried to describe the metaphysical arrangement of realms and worlds—whatever that meant. Miss Olsen stood beside him, interjecting occasionally. Mr. Oxinos and Coach Brown had already stepped into the Primal Realm and Animal

Realm respectively.

Finally, Dr. Fathy finished his cosmological descriptions and Miss Olsen took over. "So what I want each of you to do is focus on either the Primal Realm or the Animal Realm. Remember the feelings and sensations of that realm. Now, stand and close your eyes."

Each of the students stood.

"Keep your mental picture sharp and remember your particular affinities. Now, if you are focused on the Primal Realm, imagine becoming part of the Primal Realm. Your world becomes pure simple materials, and so forth. If you focus on the Animal Realm, imagine the abundant animal life surrounding you. Lessen your higher thoughts and try to tap into your instincts."

Miss Olsen walked over to Aliki. "Aliki? Which realm are you focusing on?"

"The Primal," Aliki answered.

"Imagine slipping though shadows to your destination. Jason?"

"Um... the Primal Realm, ma'am," Jason answered. He sounded a little confused though, like something worried him.

"Imagine either crashing onto the realm like a wave or flowing through the boundaries as water. Mike?"

"Animal," Mike answered. He'd already started thinking of wriggling through a dimensional boundary like a fox.

"Don't change into a fox, Mike!" she warned. "I see those ears! Focus on getting through the boundary, not becoming a fox!"

Mike quickly changed his ears back to their normal human

shape.

Miss Olsen continued to encourage the students and help them visualize their destinations. After about ten minutes, she said, "Okay, take a break."

Mike opened his eyes. Kyle had vanished, but the rest of the students stretched or sat down.

"Where's Kyle?" Tiff asked.

"I assume he's in the Animal Realm by now," Dr. Fathy answered.

They relaxed for a few minutes, then resumed their focus. After a short time, Mike felt something give way, then felt a familiar rush of sensations—images of fur, feathers, and trees, the sound of howls and hisses, and musky smells. For a moment, he thought he'd imagined it, but then heard Coach Brown's voice. "Congratulations, Mike." He opened his eyes and soaked in the sights of the Animal Realm.

Aliki arrived in the Primal Realm shortly after Tiff succeeded. Mr. Oxinos sat on a stone nearby, pleased that they'd both arrived.

After a few more minutes, Miss Olsen arrived in the Primal Realm. "They've all successfully transferred realms. Mike and Kyle transferred to the Animal Realm; Tom went to check on them. Jason and the girls came here." She paused. "Wait! Where's Jason?"

Mr. Oxinos' face grew anxious. "Ida, take the girls back to Earth. I'll check with Tom and Greg in the Animal Realm. He probably didn't go there, but let's make sure. We may have to comb the other realms."

Five minutes later, the students and teachers had returned to Earth, except for the missing Jason.

"So where did he go?" Aliki asked. She tried not to worry, but it seemed each new talent they learned opened new dangers.

Mr. Oxinos replied, "I have my suspicions, but let's eliminate the most dangerous ones first. Greg, can you check the Demon Realm and the Tech Realm? Ida, you check the Astral Realm and the Spirit Realm. I'll check the Ghost Realm and the Heaven Realm. Tom? Is there anything you can think of to track him?"

Dr. Fathy considered for a few seconds. "No, Paul. We don't have that ability yet. But perhaps I could investigate it after this crisis?"

"Sounds like a good idea," Coach Brown said. "Now let's move."

Seconds later, the other teachers disappeared, leaving the students with Dr. Fathy. Tiff whispered, "You don't think the giants grabbed him or something, do you?"

"Unlikely. The chances that the giants could intercept a realm-transit are... Well, let's say infinitesimal," Dr. Fathy answered. "I'm sure we'll find him."

Jason opened his eyes and looked around at his surroundings. He wasn't in the Primal Realm. But he knew where he was. He'd returned to the Heaven Realm.

A cluster of angelic beings floating overhead began to descend toward him. A male angel, apparently the leader of this particular group, landed in front of him. "Greetings. You are a stranger to our realm. I am Kamuviel. Are you one of the exalted ones?" The other angels landed on top of the buildings nearby.

Jason sat on the ground and looked up at him. The angel was exquisitely beautiful, perfect in both his voice and appearance, and his gossamer wings vaguely resembled a scroll unfurling around him. Jason stammered, "I'm Jason. Jason King. Exalted ones? Do you mean like Mr. O? I mean, Paul Oxinos. Or Apollo. I guess I'm trying to be like him and Coach Brown and Miss Olsen and...."

"You are confused? Uncertain in yourself? Lost?" Kamuviel probed. He had an unusual tone to his voice, and Jason couldn't decide if the angel was guessing, or if he could read him well. Jason felt like he could trust Kamuviel—the angel seemed earnest.

"I'm not sure," Jason admitted. "I mean, yeah, I'm confused. My reverend taught that if you're good, God lets you into heaven when you die. But I'm here, and I'm not dead, am I?"

The angel touched his shoulder. "You seem alive to me. If you are one of the exalted ones like Lord Apollo, you can visit here whenever you wish."

As he focused on the angel, feelings of helpfulness and companionship washed over him. The angel's touch seemed comfortable and sincere; Kamuviel truly wanted to help someone he'd just met. Jason gulped, trying to ask the question plaguing on his mind. "But with us exalted ones and the Heaven Realm..." He gulped down his apprehension. "Is there a God?"

Kamuviel looked puzzled by the question. "Humans worshipped Lord Apollo as a god a few thousand years ago. Is that what you mean?"

Jason grasped at an explanation. "No. I mean, is there a God above everything, one that makes everything happen?"

But Kamuviel wasn't focused on him anymore. He looked over Jason's shoulder. Jason turned his head and saw Mr. Oxinos standing behind him.

"Lord Apollo," the angel smiled. "You have returned. Are you staying long?"

"No, Kamuviel. Jason got lost during our training. I'm here to retrieve him," Mr. Oxinos replied. He crouched down beside Jason. "How are you, Jason?"

"I'm okay, sir." Jason answered. But his voice cracked.

"I heard part of what you were asking Kamuviel. He can't give you an answer, Jason. Neither can I."

"Sir?"

Mr. Oxinos placed a comforting hand on Jason's shoulder and spoke with a gentle voice. "You were hoping there would be a real God that you could reach out and touch? Some positive affirmation of your faith? Some proof?"

Jason nodded. He couldn't get the right words out.

Mr. Oxinos stood. "I can't give you an answer, Jason. That's not the way faith works. In my centuries of life, I have not seen any definitive sign of a power higher than us. But neither do I have all the answers. Even we haven't solved the mysteries of existence." He looked away, gazing first at the angels, then at the horizon. "There could be a God who created the Earth and the realms. Or there might not be." He turned back to Jason. "Ultimately, your faith is something personal to you. I can't tell you what to believe."

Jason still felt confused. But he had to find his own answers.

"Thank you, sir." He stood and started to brush off dirt from his jeans, but his jeans weren't dirty at all.

"Now, are you ready to go back to Earth, Jason? You can always come back anytime."

"Sure, but wait a moment." Jason turned to Kamuviel. "I appreciate your kindness. I'd like to talk, or even maybe hang out some time. Maybe you and your friends could show me around this realm?" Jason asked hopefully. Perhaps a tour of the Heaven Realm would set his mind at ease.

"Of course, Lord Jason. You are always welcome. My flight regularly visits here." Kamuviel clasped his shoulders. Jason guessed the gesture was a friendly gesture, so he clasped Kamuviel's shoulders in return.

Jason looked around at the Heavenly version of the school courtyard. He could see where the flagpole rose over the school offices. Here, the flagpole took the form of a thin column of light rising to the clouds. "I'll use the light column to signal you when I'm back."

Ten minutes later, Jason had returned to Earth. He still had a lot to think about. But the companionship shown by Kamuviel and his fellow angels did make Jason feel better.

The students took a break for lunch. As the students devoured the subs Coach Brown provided, Kyle dwelled on an earlier lesson. The horrific sights of the Demon Realm still disgusted him, and Jason's misadventure had spooked him.

He decided to admit his concerns. "What prevents us from wandering to the wrong realm? Could we accidentally arrive in the Demon Realm?"

Mr. Oxinos answered, "Normally, you'll arrive at your destination if you have a clear mind. Jason's mind wandered, so he naturally wandered into a different realm."

Miss Olsen continued, "This afternoon, we'll teach you how to return to Earth from the different realms. It's the same basic principle."

After lunch, the students helped clean up. Kyle found himself beside Jason as they took out the trash. "Is everything okay, Jason?" he asked.

"Yeah. I've got some things I'm trying to figure out. Nothing for you to worry about."

"My brother John helps me sometimes, especially when I'm confused," Kyle admitted.

"It must be good to have someone like that. I'm the oldest, and I don't think my little sister could handle this."

"Probably not," Kyle agreed.

Later that afternoon, the students practiced returning to Earth from both the Animal and Primal Realms. They had no further mishaps, and the students learned the technique fairly swiftly.

By mid-afternoon, the teachers were satisfied with their progress. Miss Olsen cautioned them, "You can now venture to either the Animal or Primal Realm on your own, but we want you to follow several rules. First, when you venture into another realm, please call or text us to let us know where you're going. Second, if you see any signs of giants at all, immediately shift back to Earth and tell us what you saw. Finally, no trying to venture to a realm you're not familiar with. No Tech Realm, no

Ghost Realm, no Demon Realm, and certainly no Astral Realm."

Mr. Oxinos added, "Jason? You can venture to the Heaven Realm if you want. You're familiar with it now, and it's safe. One of us can help you explore abilities you can derive from it later. We'll take the rest of you to the Heaven Realm soon enough."

CHAPTER THIRTY-ONE
Kuzherit Gates

Three weeks had passed since Mike and the others had learned to transfer between realms. The teachers had let the students explore their new abilities, and Mike had become proud of his growth. For the past few weeks, the Saturday training sessions had become demonstrations of the students' newly discovered abilities.

With the warmer weather and the end of the school year approaching, other sports teams didn't need the gym for practices, so the immortals could use the space without fear of discovery. Coach Brown, Miss Olsen, and MacKenzie arranged for private gym time and reviewed the students' progress.

Mike sat with the others on the mat, watching Aliki. Last week, she'd showed them a full transformation into a dolphin, and today she stood before them as a rhino.

Coach Brown was particularly pleased. "Very good, Aliki. You've managed multiple transformations, and both of them give you new capabilities."

Mike asked, "So do you or MacKenzie have multiple animal transformations?"

Coach Brown replied, "I'm not sure about MacKenzie, but I certainly do." To demonstrate, the coach transformed first into his familiar leopard form, then a hunting dog of some sort. Finally, he transformed into a large black cobra, which made Kyle jump.

The coach reverted to his human form. "My dog form was my first form, but it's not as showy."

MacKenzie joined in, "I've used many animal forms. But the raven and horse are my favorites. Anyhow... Mike? Your turn. Have ye anything to show?"

Mike stepped into the center and winds swirled around his arms. Then he showed the ability he'd learned in the Primal Realm and the air around his legs churned. "I can't cover my body yet. But watch this."

The swirling cyclones around Mike's legs intensified, and he rose off the gym floor, hovering about ten feet above the ground. He hovered in place for a few minutes, then drifted slowly across the basketball court. He'd figured how to move as fast as a brisk walk while in the air. Seeing a basketball, he floated down to pick it up, then glided over to one of the hoops. He dropped the ball through the hoop. "Two points!" he cried.

Coach Brown smiled. "Mike, I don't think the basketball team can use that particular play. Anything else?"

Mike shook his head and said, "Only more practice with languages, sir." He sat back down, and Jason stood.

"So how is your cooperative aura developing, Jason?" Miss Olsen asked.

"I've been experimenting with it, ma'am. Whenever I focus, people around me work together toward a single goal. I guess I really like being part of a team. And my little sister Helen is much more helpful around the house."

Mike glanced around. The other students were baffled too.

Seeing their expressions, Miss Olsen explained. "Jason has been visiting the Heaven Realm. Under Paul's guidance, he's explored abilities from that realm. Anything else, Jason?"

"Well, I wanted to have an angel form, but I can't do it yet," Jason replied. "I can sort of grow wings, and some of my hair turns feathery, but I can't fly or anything."

Tiff blurted, "Show us!"

Jason took off his shirt and focused. The hair on the sides and back of his head faded to white and transformed into a soft down. From his back, two large wings emerged, covered in white feathers. Jason flapped his wings a few times but didn't rise from the ground.

Aliki suggested, "Don't some angels have more than two wings? Maybe you need more wings to help your lift."

Miss Olsen nodded. "Good idea, Aliki. In case you are wondering, we fashion our own angelic form rather than following a standard design. The same applies to the Demon Realm. Some immortals' angelic or demonic forms will resemble mythical creatures. Of course, older immortals inspired their culture's angel or demon myths."

"Tiff? Your turn," Coach Brown called. "Show them what you've learned this week."

Tiff stood and transformed into an eagle. She spoke in English, "Coach Brown taught me how to talk while in eagle form." Her voice had a bit of the eagle's screech, but was unmistakably her own. "It's not showy, but I can talk while flying now."

MacKenzie's cell phone sounded. She stood up and looked at the screen. "Paul is out front, so I'll be leaving now. I'll be back in two weeks."

"Are you really going back to Ireland, MacKenzie?" Mike knew she had planned a vacation, but he already missed her.

"I am. 'Tis our annual Beltaine gathering, an' I'll not miss it. I'll be returning soon enough. Paul offered to take me. You have my cell number if I'm needed."

The students followed her to the front of the school. There, Mr. Oxinos stood beside a familiar golden car. "Ready, MacKenzie?" he asked, opening the door for her.

"Thank you, Paul. Traveling by chariot will be much easier than fightin' through the airports." MacKenzie turned to the students and waved. "May your neighbors respect you, an' trouble neglect you!"

She ducked into the car and closed the door. Mr. Oxinos entered the driver's side and started the car. Both waved to the students as the car drove off.

Mike noticed the car was almost silent and didn't sound like a normal engine. It had no identifiable manufacturer's symbols or logos, and the license tag read CHARIOT2.

"Did she say she's traveling by chariot?" Kyle asked. "Is that...?"

"He calls it his sun chariot." Miss Olsen said. "Yes, it flies. Elliot, or Helios if you prefer, builds them, and gave one to Paul. Paul doesn't use it much, but as MacKenzie said, it beats traveling by airplane."

"And with that, I think our session for today is done," Coach

Brown said.

After school on Tuesday, Jason joined Tiff in the Animal Realm, hoping she could help him learn to fly in his angelic form. They had gone to the park and crossed into the Animal Realm.

Tiff watched as Jason pocketed his shirt, shoes, and socks. Wearing only a pair of sweatpants, he transformed into his angelic form. In addition to the large wings on his back, she noticed he had smaller wings growing from his ankles.

Jason saw her glancing down. "I got the idea from a Greek picture of Hermes. He had these winged shoes, so I thought maybe I could get more lift that way."

Tiff nodded and transformed into an eagle. "Okay, now try lifting with your wings." Tiff demonstrated slowly, flying to a nearby tree.

Jason awkwardly rose about a foot, but didn't keep his balance. His hips wobbled, and he dropped again. Sprawling on the ground, he laughed. "It's a start!"

"Maybe more lift?" Tiff suggested. "You lost it when you bent at the waist."

Jason nodded and spent a few minutes focusing. As she watched, he grew a third pair of wings, smaller than the ones on his back but larger than his ankle wings, from his hips.

Tiff couldn't contain her curiosity. "How does it feel?"

"Odd, but good." He looked over his newest pair of wings. "This feels right."

"Ready to try again?" Tiff asked.

Smiling, Jason tried lifting with his wings again.

Minutes later, they both flew over the treetops. Jason's six-winged angelic form wasn't as aerodynamic as Tiff's eagle form, but he quickly adapted.

They had spent about fifteen minutes flying around when Tiff's eagle eyes spotted something.

"Jason! I see something weird over that way." She tried to gesture with her wing, but caused herself to flutter instead. "Follow me."

The two of them flew toward an obviously artificial structure toward the northeast. Two tall trees had their leaves and branches stripped, and several long branches spanned the gap across the top between them. Where the branches met the trees were two structures resembling enclosed nests. A variety of animal skins bound the entire structure together and wrapped around both the tree trunks and the branches across the top. The ground near the base of each tree had been disturbed, as if something violently uprooted each tree, then replanted in the ground. The assembly looked like a gigantic doorframe, over thirty feet high.

Tiff wished she had her real katana in her Pocket, but she approached the structure anyway.

Jason tried to keep up. "Tiff! Be careful!"

Tiff landed on the span near one of the nest-like structures. She grimaced when she landed on some sort of sticky residue that glued the branches and animal skins together. She'd guessed that the nests held something important, so she decided to peek inside.

"I can't believe I'm going to do this again," Tiff muttered to herself, and transformed her wings back into human arms. She gripped the crossing span tightly with her talons and tried to pull open one of the nest structures with her hands. After several minutes, she pried it apart.

The inside of the nest looked distorted, as if she were gazing through funhouse mirrors. Inside the nest, she found a kuzherit. The bizarre creature undulated or skittered—Tiff couldn't tell which—away from her, seeking refuge within the nest.

Surprised, Tiff screamed with a half-eagle, half-girl voice. She jerked back from the kuzherit nest, but her motion made the branches shift. She held on tightly with her talons as she teetered over, but ended up dangling from the crossing span, like she was awkwardly trying to impersonate a bat.

"Jason! A little help!"

Jason flew under her and called out, "Drop!"

Tiff did so, transforming back into her human form as she fell. Jason caught her in midair, but couldn't maintain his flight with the extra weight. They settled to the ground and gazed up at the structure.

"Giant work?" Jason guessed.

"There's a kuzherit in that nest, and I'll bet another is in the other one. What do you think it means?"

"Let's get Mr. O and maybe Dr. Fathy." Jason glanced around. "Do you think it's safe to transfer back here?"

"I don't know, but I don't want to face giants here. Let's risk it. But you need to lose the wings."

"Oh, right."

Moments later, Jason and Tiff stood on Earth, at the

outskirts of town. Jason glanced over at Tiff, who frantically tapped at her cell phone. Once he heard Mr. O's voice from her phone, Jason surveyed his surroundings.

They had arrived in someone's back yard in a small housing development on the outskirts of town. Fortunately, they saw no one in the large yard. Jason tugged on Tiff's sleeve, and the two of them walked toward the street.

"Hey! What are you kids doing in our yard?" a voice rang out from the house. An older woman stood on the deck, glaring at them.

"Sorry, ma'am. We got lost while hiking," Jason answered.

"Lost your shirt too?" the woman eyed the two of them.

Jason remembered his shirt and shoes were still in his Pocket. "It tore on some branches."

"Uh huh." The woman's eyes stayed on them until they passed the corner of the house.

Jason heard the sliding glass door open, then shut. "C'mon. Let's get to the street before she calls the cops on us. I don't want to get into trouble."

The two of them stepped onto the cul-de-sac that the house faced. Half an hour later, Mr. Oxinos arrived, driving his normal car. "Greg, Ida, and Tom are looking at the gate, but I should get you two back to your homes. I've already called your parents. Get in."

Jason had been hoping for a chance to ride in the golden sun chariot, but he squeezed into Mr. O's small mundane car. Tiff climbed into the back seat, gently pushing aside a crate of art supplies and Mr. O's guitar. Once inside, Jason unpocketed his shoes and shirt. "That's better. No more half-dressed crazy guy," he said.

From the back seat, he heard Tiff say, "Aww, darn," in mock disappointment.

The next day, Mr. Oxinos called the students together during lunchtime. Aliki entered Mr. Oxinos' classroom with her lunch from the cafeteria and sat down. Jason had already told her about the gate earlier that morning, but Aliki wasn't sure what it meant. The teachers' faces were as grim as she'd ever seen, and she could feel the tension in the air. Even Dr. Fathy, who normally enjoyed intellectual challenges, seemed worried.

Once all of the students arrived, Coach Brown barricaded the door and locked it. He stood a silent sentry as Miss Olsen stood to describe what she'd seen.

"The giants definitely constructed the gate. The presence of the kuzherits proves that, not to mention the size of the gates and giant footprints nearby. We discovered three kuzherits—one in each of the nests, and a third underground. The giant or giants used the root ball of the tree as part of a nest."

With none of his usual mirth, Coach Brown announced grimly, "We destroyed the gate and captured the kuzherits."

Miss Olsen continued, "We did find a few animals from the realm who saw the giants building the gate, but they had no idea why. Most were too busy trying to stay alive."

Dr. Fathy finally spoke. "We decided to check the other realms as well. Last night, we found a similar gate in the Spirit Realm. It wasn't as complete as the gate in the Animal Realm, but it followed the same design. No kuzherits though. But this one was to the northwest, not the northeast."

Mr. Oxinos joined the discussion. "We're going to investigate the Demon Realm and Primal Realm next, after school this afternoon. We don't want you getting involved. Stay out of the Primal and Animal Realms for now."

Dr. Fathy pointed to three metal cases stacked in the corner of the schoolroom. On top and sides of each, a high-tech interface glowed, and a shimmering effect surrounded each case. "I'm taking the three kuzherits we found back to one of our research labs. Perhaps I can discover what they were planning."

Kyle raised his hand. "Do you want help, Dr. Fathy? I'd love to see your research office."

"No, but thank you, Kyle." Dr. Fathy seemed relieved for some reason. "I'll be in touch. We also told MacKenzie what's going on. She's ready to come back if needed."

"Hopefully it will be a quick strike," Coach Brown said.

The next morning, Mr. Oxinos wasn't in homeroom. One of the office staff sat in his place, her face shifting between nervousness and annoyance. She periodically checked her cell phone for messages, but many students were ignoring her inexperienced attempts to maintain control.

Mike tried to suppress his growing apprehension. Most of the students kept goofing off, even after the first bell sounded. But he looked at Jason, Kyle, and Aliki. Their faces showed concern and worry, as his probably did.

Mike gestured to them, and they gathered around his desk. "I texted Tiff. She's running late, so I told her to check on Miss

Olsen and Coach Brown before coming to class."

Julisha inserted herself into their conversation. "What's going on? Did something happen to Mr. O?"

Mike took it in stride. "We're not sure. He may have been in an accident."

Suddenly Tiff burst in. "Coach Brown and Miss Olsen are gone too!"

Some of the class turned to look at her. Only slightly embarrassed, Tiff joined the others gathered at Mike's desk. "So what do we do?" she asked.

"Give me a moment." Mike thought quickly. "Tiff? Do you have Aleara's pendant on you?"

Tiff nodded, pointing at the pocket of her jeans. He knew she meant her Pocket.

"Get in touch with her and ask her to look around her place for anything odd. That covers the Primal Realm. Unfortunately, the other realm..." Mike recalled Kyle's description of the Demon Realm. "We might need some extra things. Aliki? Do you have Coach Brown's home address? Or Mr. O's?"

Aliki quickly checked her cell phone and nodded. "I have both of them, and Miss Olsen's too. I'll forward them to all of you." She looked speculatively at Julisha. "What about her?"

Julisha looked nervous as the group turned to her. "I'm cool, guys. I want to help."

Mike thought for a few more minutes. "We may need her. Let me think about it. But we need to get the real gear Coach Brown fashioned for us." The others nodded, knowing Mike was referring to their real weapons. Thoroughly confused, Julisha sat quietly.

"When and how, Mike?" Aliki asked.

Mike felt the growing pressure of leadership. He ran his fingers through his hair. Suddenly a strong arm clasped his shoulder.

"No worries, Mike. You can pull out another one of your wild ideas and we'll make it work. We're a team, remember?"

Mike felt the subtle pull of Jason's cooperative aura. He appreciated Jason's eagerness. Taking a deep breath, Mike pulled out his cell phone and looked at the locations of the teachers' houses. "Do any of you know how to drive?"

Kyle replied, "No, but my brother does. But we don't have a car here."

Mike doodled on some paper for a minute, drawing stick figures and houses. "If Aleara finds them where she is, we can try to reach them. But if not, we'll head out at lunchtime."

"You're gonna skip school?" Julisha asked.

Jason sighed. "It's serious, Julisha. Life or death serious."

"So call the cops!" Julisha exclaimed.

"The police can't help them. We have to. We're the only ones who can now," Kyle growled.

Julisha turned to look at him with a stunned expression. Kyle's assertiveness surprised even Mike.

The bell rang, and Mike snapped out, "Aliki, call MacKenzie. Kyle? Dr. Fathy. Tiff? Find a place to talk to Aleara. Julisha, come with Jason and me. We have something to show you."

CHAPTER THIRTY-TWO
Rescue

As the rest of the students meandered through the school, heading to their first period class, Jason and Julisha followed Mike to Coach Brown's locked office. Mike glanced around, gestured to Jason, then to the door.

Jason gripped the doorknob and exerted his strength. He felt the metal give way, and the door to the office opened.

The three students entered Coach Brown's office. Piles of sports equipment littered the floor. Trophies sat on shelves, and teaching certificates covered other sections of the wall. Jason looked up and noticed the ornate hunga-munga in a display case. It reminded him of the beginning of the school year, when Kyle had asked him about the coach.

"So what's this really about, Mike?" Julisha insisted. "All that fighting with padded weapons, that camping trip with the cougar, now the teachers are all missing. Tell me what's going on —for real this time!"

Jason leaned against the door, keeping it closed. He guessed Mike's plan, but wondered how Julisha would respond.

Mike glanced at Jason, with a smirk on his face. "We could

lock her in here so she wouldn't blab," he joked.

Julisha's eyes went wide. She glanced toward the door, then around the room looking for a place to hide.

"Not funny, Mike. You pulled her here. How's she going to help?"

Mike dropped his smirk. "If we need to get MacKenzie, we'll need someone to go with Kyle's brother to fetch her. And if something goes wrong, we'll need someone to tell our folks."

"Isn't MacKenzie in Ireland? How are we going to pick her up?" Julisha asked.

Mike ignored her question. "We also may need someone to cover for us if we need to go to Coach Brown's house for the weapons."

Julisha tried to follow Mike's plans. "Weapons? You mean the padded weapons? MacKenzie left them in the storeroom down the hall."

"Not padded weapons, Julisha," Jason answered.

Her eyes widened again. "Are you gonna kill someone? No, wait. I'm calling the cops."

Mike snapped, "No cops. Jason? Angel."

Jason quickly pocketed his shirt and shoes. He realized that his jeans would confine his hip-wings, so he had to pocket them too. He stood before Julisha in his boxers, then transformed into his angelic form.

"Where'd your clothes... Oh my God!" Julisha fell back into the coach's desk chair, staring at Jason. "Mike? Did you know Jason is an angel?" She turned towards Mike and gave a little scream before Mike's hand covered her mouth.

Julisha's eyes darted over his face, trying to make sense of what she saw. He had transformed his head into a fox's and twitched one of his ears. "So what do you think?" Mike asked mischievously, slowly pulling his hand away from her mouth.

"I think I'm going crazy," Julisha admitted.

Suddenly a knock on the door startled them. Both Jason and Mike reverted to their normal forms and opened the door. Kyle and Aliki stood on the other side.

"How'd you find us?" Jason wondered aloud.

Kyle pointed to his nose. "Bears can smell food miles away. I could follow you easily. Uh… Jason, you forgot to unpocket your clothes."

Aliki squeezed past Jason into the office as he retrieved his clothes from his Pocket. "Tiff is contacting Aleara in the girls' bathroom and filling her in. She'll summon her again at lunchtime. Oh hi, Julisha."

Julisha tried vainly to understand. "All of you? What are you, space aliens or something?"

"Not space aliens, Julisha. More like..." Jason paused, trying to think of a good way to explain quickly.

"Gods in training," Kyle suggested. "You know about the Greek Pantheon of gods—Zeus, Apollo, Poseidon? And the Norse pantheon?" Julisha nodded. "Well, we're sort of like a new pantheon."

Mike looked thoughtful. "New pantheon. I like that."

Jason frowned. He wasn't sure how he felt about claiming to be gods. But it explained things simply enough for now.

Before lunchtime, Kyle called his brother John and quickly

updated him on the situation. The immortal teens, along with Julisha and John, all gathered at lunch to plan. Tiff wolfed down a burger and went toward a bathroom to summon Aleara.

With a twinkle in his eye, Mike suggested, "Take Julisha with you. She can provide lookout, and I'm sure she'd love to meet Aleara."

"So what's the plan?" Kyle asked.

"If they're in the Primal Realm, we go and get them. Simple enough. But if not, we have to check the Demon Realm. And that's where we'll need you, Kyle."

"Me?" Kyle had been dreading a return to the Demon Realm.

Mike nodded. "You're the only one of us that's been there. So you'll have to try to pull us along. But I don't want to go into the Demon Realm without weapons."

"Coach Brown moved our weapons locker to his personal workshop," Aliki said. "His house is about two miles from here."

They finished their lunch, awaiting word from Tiff. She and Julisha rejoined them after about ten minutes. Tiff looked worried, and Julisha had a shell-shocked expression. "Aleara said there's a partial gate structure to the southwest of town, about a mile from the Exchange. She saw a giant working on it, but no signs of a struggle," Tiff reported.

Kyle whispered, "That means the Demon Realm."

"Jason and Aliki, get the weapons. Pocket both of yours, then carry ours. We also need to get MacKenzie. Mr. O's sun chariot can get there, but none of us can drive a car. John, you may need to drive to Ireland to get MacKenzie," Mike said.

John sputtered, "Ireland? That's across the ocean! You can't drive to Ireland."

"The car flies," Mike deadpanned. "I already called MacKenzie; she's trying to find another way to get back here in a hurry. You and I will get to Mr. O's house, try to find a way in, and see if we can figure out how to use the flying car. If we need to, you take Julisha with you to pick up MacKenzie. Until then, Julisha is our switchboard. She'll keep Dr. Fathy and MacKenzie up to date."

"This is crazy," John muttered.

"I told you it would get weird, bro." Kyle tried to force a grin, but failed. "So what do you want me to do?"

Mike answered, "Try to reach the Demon Realm on your own at first. If you can get across, pop back immediately. Tiff will stay with you, and on your second trip, you try to take her along. Or tell her how to get to there herself."

"How do I do that?" Kyle asked.

"I don't know," Mike admitted. "Guess. Use mental imagery, like we did before. Now, how do we get away from school?"

John suggested, "I can help with that—it's easy. A fire alarm will give you enough cover to slip away."

Twenty minutes and one false fire alarm later, all of the students stood outside the school. During the confusing exodus from the school, Jason, John, Mike, and Aliki slipped away. Mike followed John to his house to borrow one of the family cars. Coach Brown's house was close enough for Aliki and Jason to walk. Kyle watched them go, envying them and dreading his own role in their plan.

He turned to Tiff and Julisha. Reluctantly, he asked, "Where do we want to do this?"

Tiff looked around. The other students were still milling about, waiting for the fire department to finish checking the building. "It'll be maybe ten to twenty minutes until they're done. How about we slip into the apartments across the street?" Kyle and Julisha followed her across the street and found a place to hide among the maze of apartments. "Okay, Kyle. Do your thing."

Kyle shuddered, but closed his eyes and thought dark angry thoughts. He imagined fighting savagely to tear down the walls between Earth and the Demon Realm. He thought about being a bully instead of being bullied. He kept imagining different ways to dominate others, to be cruel and selfish. It felt horrible to him, and he loathed it.

Fifteen minutes later, he sensed a change. Visions of torture filled his mind, and foul smells made him gag. No longer could he feel a cool breeze wafting its way through the apartment complex. He couldn't hear birds. But he could hear echoing screams and smelled something rank. He opened his eyes.

He arrived in some sort of horrific labyrinthine maze within the Demon Realm. Several demons had been impaled on nearby spikes growing from the ground or walls. The floor oozed with unidentifiable liquids. Here and there, rifts in the floor opened onto what looked like an underground lava flow. Hastily, he returned to Earth. He welcomed the sight of the girls' faces, which showed a mixture of surprise and relief.

"You made it?" Tiff asked him.

"Yeah. You have to think mean thoughts about ripping down the barrier and such. I hate it."

Tiff pulled her boken from her Pocket. "I'm not looking forward to this, but do you want to try to pull me across?"

They spent another half hour, with Kyle trying to pull Tiff with him. But he hadn't figured out how to do it yet. So he tried to coach Tiff. Eventually, Tiff succeeded in transferring herself to the Demon Realm.

Standing in the gruesome labyrinth, Tiff remarked, "I see why you don't like this place." She hugged herself, turning away from the demonic corpses. "Let's get back to Earth."

Aliki followed Jason to Coach Brown's house. It was a modest house with a large fenced yard. Jason quickly looked around for any observers, then climbed over the fence. Aliki waited nervously until Jason opened the gate for her.

A small building stood about twenty feet from the house. A stone patio with a fire pit in the center spanned the space between the house and the building. Nearby, an anvil sat near a fireplace with a chimney and bellows; metalworking tools hung from hooks on a metal pegboard. She imagined the coach using it to forge their weapons.

"Check the house. I'll check the workshop," Jason suggested. He strode over to the building and looked for a way in. When he couldn't enter the building, he peered through a small window, looking for the weapons or a storage cabinet that might hold them.

Meanwhile, Aliki peeked through the sliding glass door on the back of his house into the room beyond. It held some of Coach Brown's personal memorabilia: elegant weapons mounted on the walls, sports and hunting trophies, two oak barrels on their sides, and a plethora of other knick-knacks. Through an open doorway into an adjacent room, she could see a large flat-screen television and comfortable couch. In one corner, she spotted the storage cabinet.

"Jason! I found it! But the door's locked. What do we do?"

"We could break the glass," Jason suggested in a hesitant voice.

"What about an upper-story window? You could fly up and see if one is open."

Jason assumed his angelic form, rose to the upper story, and checked windows. About ten minutes later, Jason opened the sliding glass door from the inside.

"Coach Brown left a clue on the roof. I saw a set of off-color shingles pointing to an unlocked window," Jason explained. "I guess he figured only immortals would look at the roof."

The two of them dashed to the weapons cabinet. Jason grabbed his greataxe, looked over it, and pocketed it. He gathered Mike's tonfas, Tiff's katana, and Kyle's morningstar. He stepped aside, letting Aliki reach her rifle.

Aliki stood, staring at the rifle case. Several ammunition boxes, which wouldn't fit in the case, sat beside it at the bottom of the cabinet.

"C'mon! The others will be waiting for us," Jason urged.

But Aliki felt uncomfortable taking the gun. She'd spent many afternoons with MacKenzie at the rifle range, but she'd always used the rifle under supervision. MacKenzie had claimed she had natural talent, but Aliki had only shot at targets. Now she might need to shoot a live being.

"What's wrong, Aliki? Grab the gun and let's get out of here."

"I… can't." Aliki felt close to tears. "I don't want to hurt anyone. I wish I'd never picked up the paint-rifle."

Jason's voice was sympathetic. "I didn't know if I could hurt anyone either. But when I had to protect the elementals at the Artisan Exchange, I acted." He took her hand and looked into her eyes. "Hopefully you won't need the gun. But our teachers need us, and we may need these."

Aliki thought about Miss Olsen, Coach Brown, and Mr. Oxinos. They'd been teachers, mentors, and friends. She recalled the savagery of the first giant they'd fought in the Animal Realm, and remembered how the three of them had fought to protect the students. She tried to imagine their positions being reversed, but found it difficult. Could she really shoot someone to protect their teachers?

Finally, she remembered Miss Olsen, chiding her about her self-confidence. Aliki had grown stronger over the past year, and Miss Olsen helped her realize it. Now she faced yet another test of her strength and resolve.

Aliki grabbed the rifle case and opened it. The rifle was still in perfect condition. She snapped the case shut and pocketed the entire rifle case, along with the boxes of ammunition.

"I'm ready," she declared.

By the time everyone returned to the school grounds, the school day was ending. Buses lined the parking lot, and both students and teachers streamed out of the school. Mike glanced around at the others, hoping no one noticed the weapons Aliki and Jason carried.

"So where's the chariot?" Tiff wondered.

"We couldn't get into it. It had a thumb-print key lock," Mike lamented. "But we called MacKenzie, and she said she was borrowing transport from some of Miss Olsen's kinsmen. She'll be here late tomorrow evening."

"Are you okay, Julisha?" Aliki asked.

Julisha still had a bewildered look on her face. "In one day, I learned one of you can be an angel, met a girl made of winds, and now I'm watching you go off to face demons. Let me know tomorrow this isn't all a dream. I thought things couldn't get any crazier after you got attacked by that cougar."

"The leopard was Coach Brown," Mike said with a smirk.

"What?" Julisha's mouth gaped.

"Anyhow, we have to get to the Demon Realm. Julisha, once you get home, keep in touch with Dr. Fathy and MacKenzie, and tell them what's going on. We'll contact you when we're back," Mike urged. "Kyle? How do we do this?"

Mike watched Julisha step away as Jason handed out the weapons and Kyle described how to travel to the Demon Realm. They pocketed their weapons and waved goodbye to her.

As they wove through the students leaving the school, Mike asked, "So why aren't we going to Mr. Oxinos' room?"

"It doesn't have a good landing point. The classroom wing doesn't exactly exist in the Demon Realm. It's this weird stonework that looks like a pile of enormous bones." Kyle answered.

They reached Coach Brown's office and tried to cross into

the Demon Realm. Mike focused on nasty feelings like Kyle suggested, but he'd always preferred humor to brutality. He forced himself to imagine being a nasty villain in one of his computer games.

Eventually, he joined the rest in the Demon Realm. Looking around at the chamber of horrors where they arrived, he wished he were anywhere else. Parts of demons littered the walls, arranged in macabre patterns. Blood and other fluids oozed on the floor and leaked down walls. Vents from below spat bits of lava into the room.

Tiff opened the heavy door leading from the room. "Aleara said the Primal gate was to the southwest of town. The others were to the northeast and northwest. So that leaves the southeast. But the others were miles off. So how do we get there?"

"I'll fly as an avenging angel," Jason replied, transforming as he spoke. He also retrieved his greataxe from his Pocket. "Tiff can fly as a firebird or a thunderbird. But Mike can only hover and fly slowly with his wind-limbs, and Aliki and Kyle don't have a flying form. I can't carry anyone while flying yet."

"Kyle? Do you think you can build a flying demonic form?" Aliki suggested.

"I don't want to try without one of the teachers. I almost lost myself to the bear. I will not risk losing myself to a demon," Kyle replied with unusual ferocity.

"So be the bear, and I'll run as a rhino," Aliki suggested.

Kyle assumed his bear form. But the bear seemed larger and more horrific. Savagery replaced the gentleness in his eyes, and his jaws twisted into a ferocious snarl.

"Kyle? Are you in there?" Aliki asked.

The bear's head nodded in response, and he growled in a barely recognizable voice, "Run!"

Aliki nodded and shifted into her rhinoceros form. Like Kyle, her form seemed larger and more ferocious. Mike hoped the two of them could keep any bestial urges in check.

"Okay, let's go," Jason said, and took to the skies, followed by Tiff in firebird form. Mike hovered, staying above Kyle and Aliki. They set off at a brisk pace, but soon accelerated to a full running speed.

Mike watched the others, feeling the burden of taking charge. He hoped they could save their teachers without getting anyone else hurt.

After half an hour, Tiff cried out, "I see it. The gate—it's complete!" She could see farther than the others with her eagle eyes.

Jason, flying below her, called back. "Any sign of the teachers?"

"Not yet. The area around it looks pretty wrecked. But that could be the giants, or just the realm." She swooped back, not wanting to get too far ahead. Already, they'd encountered several roving groups of demons. Most gave them no trouble, fearing the huge bear, rhino, and greataxe-wielding angel. However, one group had threatened to fight until Kyle savagely barreled through them.

Tiff didn't want to remember the carnage. Clearly, Kyle struggled with the Demon Realm. She felt strong predatory urges, desires to swoop down and burn her foes, or claw out

340

demons' eyes with her flaming talons. She tried to rationalize it away, remembering the demons were reincarnations of truly wicked people.

After another ten minutes, the group slowed as they approached the gate. Littering the ground around the gate were the bodies of five huge giants with demonic features. As they neared the giants' corpses, demonic scavenger beasts scurried away from the group. Tiff observed that two of the giants had suffered sword wounds, while two others had fallen from headshots courtesy of Mr. Oxinos' light arrows. A thorny tree had crushed one, thanks to Miss Olsen. Tiff felt nauseous, so she stared at the gate itself.

The giants built the towering gate from demon bones and viscera. Two nests—one fashioned from an oversized demon's skull, the other from a huge ribcage—sat at the upper corners. As she flew around the gate, Tiff spotted a kuzherit within one of the nests. But the gate itself troubled her most of all.

Through the gate's framework, Tiff could see another world. Its sky was as blue as their own, but she spotted strange scrub trees and semi-amorphous creatures with her eagle-sharp vision.

"Any sign of the teachers?" Jason called out.

"Only dead giants," Kyle replied. He and Aliki had reverted to their normal forms once they arrived at the gate. "Wait... What's this? Over here!"

The other students quickly gathered around what Kyle had discovered. It looked like a huge cocoon made of thick wood, branches weaving together, about eight feet long. "Something's in there. I feel it through the ground," Kyle said.

Jason started to cut it with his axe, but the tenacious wood resisted his efforts. Tiff reverted to her human form and drew her katana from her Pocket. "Careful with that axe, Jason," she warned. "We don't want to hurt whoever's inside."

Tiff and Jason slowly broke open the cocoon. At times, Tiff used her fiery form to burn away or weaken particularly stubborn branches. Finally, they could see blonde hair peeking through.

All of the students pulled at the wood to free Miss Olsen. Blood covered her and still flowed from several wounds. Her wooden buckler-shield had been shattered, and the torn remnants of her thick leather armor clung to her body. Tiff noticed the branches protecting Miss Olsen had grown long thorns that pierced her body. Tiff was horrified. *Did she grow the thorns for some reason, or did the demonic tree do it by itself?*

Mike checked her pulse. "She's alive. Let's get her home."

"Mike? None of us know how to bring someone with us when we cross realms," Jason said. "How do we get her back to Earth?"

"We try to wake her," Mike replied. His voice belied his uncertainly and fear. "Hopefully she can bring herself back. C'mon, Miss Olsen. Wake up!"

Jason pulled a first aid kit from his Pocket. He carefully removed the remnants of her armor, and started cleaning and bandaging the wounds, but ran out of bandages. He lifted her head slightly and waved some antiseptic under her nose, hoping the smell would awaken her. "Wake up, please," he pleaded.

Tiff took one of her hands in hers. "Miss Olsen? We need you! Miss Olsen? Ida?" Desperation crept into her voice. "Idun?"

After what seemed like an eternity, Miss Olsen's eyes

opened. "Where...?"

Tiff answered, "Demon Realm. We have to get you home. But we can't transport you to Earth. Can you get back?"

Miss Olsen groaned. A moment later, her purse appeared in her lap. She withdrew the cylindrical device, passed it over her body a few times, and glanced at the symbols. "Not good," she whispered.

"Can we do anything?" Mike asked.

Miss Olsen focused on the device and touched several symbols. Needles sprang from one end, and she injected herself with them.

A few moments later, she seemed more alert, but in intense pain. "Need... to be awake... to cross. Please... home." She disappeared.

Wasting no time, the teens followed her back to Earth.

CHAPTER THIRTY-THREE
Into the Giant's World

The teens, with John's help, returned Miss Olsen home. She passed out from pain during the car ride, but her breathing was even and strong. Mike guessed that she'd given herself a stimulant to cross, followed by some painkillers.

The next day was Friday. The school administrators chastised the students who had left school during the fire drill. Fortunately for them, the immortal students weren't the only ones to sneak away on the beautiful spring day, so they didn't receive as harsh a punishment.

At lunchtime, each of them received a text from Dr. Fathy, instructing them to meet in the park after dinner. Mike called his mother to tell her he was going to a friend's house to play video games that evening. On the way home after school, he stopped by Miss Olsen's house to check on her.

Trees and gardens surrounded her small, cozy house. When he tested the front door, it was unlocked. He knocked and called out to her, then let himself inside. Inside, the rooms held simple furniture and only a few decorations.

Mike tiptoed toward Miss Olsen's bedroom and peered

through the open doorway. She was lying in her bed, apparently asleep. He started to turn away, but spotted the strange cylindrical object she had used on herself on a side table near her bed.

Mike's curiosity got the better of him, so he crept in to look at the device. It was about two inches in diameter and eight inches long. Rows of symbols, which he now recognized as Norse runes, covered the object.

"It's a healing wand." Miss Olsen's weak voice came from behind him, startling him.

He turned and smiled. "How are you feeling?"

"Better, but still not great." She reached for the wand, activated it, and passed it over her torso a few times. Mike noticed some of the runes glowing and changing. Mike thought it resembled a cylindrical touch-screen. Miss Olsen looked at the runes, took a deep, shuddering breath, coughed twice, and returned the wand to the side table. "The others? Paul? Greg?"

"We don't know. We saw the signs of your fight and the giant's bodies. But Mr. O and Coach weren't there."

"What were you... You shouldn't have gone to the Demon Realm. Too dangerous."

"We all went together. We're all fine, though we didn't see any giants." For that, Mike was grateful. "How does that work?" Mike asked, pointing to the wand.

Miss Olsen grimaced through the pain. "Analyzes our vitals. Injects super-medicines. Or immortality nutrients. It saved you and Kyle."

Mike looked at the device. She had used it to grant him immortality, and again to preserve her own life. "Can you teach me to use this?"

"You're going back to get the others," she chided him. "Giants... Even more dangerous."

"MacKenzie's on her way back. She'll lead the charge."

Miss Olsen lay back, defeated. They wouldn't stay out of danger, and she knew it. She pointed to a cabinet on the other side of the room. "Top drawer. Take six."

He opened the drawer. Inside were smaller cylinders, each about four inches long and a little thicker than his thumb. He gathered six of them.

"Emergency healing. Push silver end and inject," she instructed. "Don't push before then."

Mike examined one of the smaller cylinders. One end had a silver cap, similar to a pen. "Thanks. Hopefully, we won't need them." He put them into his pockets. "Can I get you anything?"

"Juice in fridge, please. Bread and cheese."

Mike went into her small kitchen and returned with a glass of apple juice and slices of bread and cheese on a small plate. He put the plate on the table and helped her sit to sip the juice.

"When?" she asked.

He knew exactly what she meant. "MacKenzie's arriving tonight, somehow. I don't think she'll wait around too long."

"Careful. Macha's not good at protecting. Particularly in heat of battle." Her words were becoming more forced. Weary, she fell back into her pillows, and her eyelids drooped.

"You rest. Please. I promise we'll be careful. I don't want to waste this immortal life you've gifted me with."

She looked at him, but he couldn't read her expression. He prepared to leave, but glanced at the healing wand again. He stopped, feeling that he needed to say something more.

"When I first woke after you healed me, I was confused. I wondered why you had given me such a great gift after a dumb accident. But when the car went off the road near the reservoir a few months back, I helped save a family. Now I'm going to help save Mr. O and Coach Brown. You've all given us so much. It's the least I can do."

"Often times it is not numbers that win the victory, but those who fare forward with the most vigor," she replied. "Be brave, and I'll expect to hear a skald's tale from your lips upon your return."

"It's a promise, Miss Olsen."

Kyle had John drop him off at the park and help cover for him. Tiff and Jason were already there, along with Dr. Fathy. As he left, John called out, "Have fun at your movie!"

Jason looked at him curiously. "Movie?"

"I told my parents we were meeting to watch a movie at the mall," Kyle explained.

Tiff chimed in, "That sort of fits with my story about meeting my friends at the mall."

"I said I was going out for an evening jog," Jason said. He wore a sweat suit and had obviously jogged to the park.

A few minutes later, Mike arrived. "I'm here. Sorry I'm late."

Kyle looked around. "We're still missing Aliki."

"No, she's already here, practicing," Dr. Fathy replied. He called out, "You did well. No one noticed you."

Aliki appeared from a stand of trees. The others hadn't noticed her in the shadows, using her darkness talent.

Dr. Fathy checked his cell phone. "MacKenzie should arrive in about fifteen minutes. We'll need a secluded spot for her to arrive."

"I know a good place. I know the park like the back of my hand," Jason said. He led the group to a small field surrounded by woods.

Dr. Fathy pulled some glow-sticks from his Pocket. "This will do nicely. Tiffany? Could you fly up and place these in the tops of the nearby trees? It will help MacKenzie find us."

As Tiff flew to the tops of the trees with the glowing sticks, Kyle asked, "So she's flying in?"

"Yes. She couldn't fly across the ocean in her raven form, so she borrowed a ride."

Tiff called down, "I see something big in the air."

"Come back down. Give her plenty of room," Dr. Fathy replied.

Tiff rejoined the group while the others strained to see MacKenzie.

"Oh my gosh! Is that a pegasus?" Aliki blurted in amazement.

Indeed, MacKenzie rode on the back of a white horse with large, feathered wings. She landed in the midst of the group and immediately hopped off. She took a few minutes to stretch her legs. The pegasus nibbled on the grass, ignoring the students.

Kyle watched the pegasus warily. He had never been around horses, much less mythical ones. "I thought the Animal Realm only had natural animals."

"It does. Pegasi are from the Heaven Realm," Dr. Fathy explained.

MacKenzie returned to the pegasus and rubbed its shoulders. "I borrowed him from Skogul. They can fly faster than I could, and they're intelligent too." Seeing the puzzled expression on the students' faces, MacKenzie elaborated, "Skogul? Oh, she's one of the valkyries."

MacKenzie opened her phone and punched in a number. A video link opened, with a blonde woman on the other end. MacKenzie told the woman, "We've arrived. He did well. I stopped in Iceland and Newfoundland to let him rest, but he's tired. Thank you so much for lending him to me." MacKenzie held the phone to face the pegasus.

Over the video link, Skogul spoke in Norwegian, "Both Macha and I thank you for your great service. Your task is done, and you may return to the heavens."

The pegasus gazed at the video and took one last nibble of clover. It vanished in a nimbus of soft light, returning to the Heaven Realm.

The students stood, speechless for a few minutes. Aliki and Tiff hugged MacKenzie, while Mike tried to brief her on events. Kyle stared at where the pegasus had stood. *And I thought things couldn't get weirder,* he thought.

The quintet returned to the Demon Realm with MacKenzie and Dr. Fathy. Jason and Tiff, in their flying forms, led the others toward the giants' gate. MacKenzie's face was unusually grim. She had already pulled a nasty-looking axe from her Pocket.

Dark, horrifying thoughts of suffering, bloodshed, and violence blossomed in Mike's mind when he glanced her way. MacKenzie's terrifying aura was radiating from her, more intense than on Earth, and it took all his will not to hide or flee.

She had also manifested armor and a cloak of dark feathers. Like Coach Brown's armor, it mixed leather and metal, but unlike the coach's armor, the steel and leather were both black. Skulls and spikes decorated the armor, adding to her fearsome presence. She confidently strode through the Demon Realm, looking every inch like an evil commander of a dark fantasy army.

Dr. Fathy explained his discovery about the kuzherits while they walked. "They emit a distortion aura affecting the fabric of reality in a small radius. Normally, this effect dissipates beyond about a meter. However, with the ones I have at the lab, I discovered two of them can create a field between them, causing a larger area of instability. They seem to function like two poles of a magnet. Adding the third didn't seem to have any effect, which I assume is because it created a third, unbalanced pole. But with a fourth..."

"You mean like the four corners of the gate?" Aliki asked.

"Exactly. If four of them are present, they could set up a stable planar field that warps reality. How this creates a portal to another world—"

"Tom? Beggin' yer pardon, but we have company," MacKenzie interrupted. "Weapons out and ready, but I'll handle it."

A gang of about twenty demons, led by a huge twelve-foot monstrosity with four thick arms ending in talons, had gathered in front of them. They reminded Mike of a street gang surrounding a bully of a leader.

As MacKenzie approached the large demon, her hair and eyes both turned pitch black. On the ground around her feet, a field of severed heads appeared—some skeletal, others with flesh clinging to their skulls—which shifted with her as she walked. The other demons in the gang took a step back.

MacKenzie looked their leader straight in the eyes. "I'll be sayin' this once. We are traveling through on personal business, and we'll have none of yours. Now, I'll be thankin' you to stand aside as we pass."

Mike watched the demon, who either didn't know the danger he faced, or couldn't back down without losing status. The demon leader looked surprised at MacKenzie's assertiveness, but stood his ground.

"I am Kruntha. This area is mine. I'm not letting you pass without payment," he growled. He glanced at Aliki. "She'll do."

"I said stand aside, ye gobdaw. Do ye not know me? I am Macha of the Morrigan!"

The demon's expression showed he didn't. MacKenzie uttered an Irish curse that made Mike blush. In a single instant, she sprang, her axe whirled, and the demon's head rolled on the ground.

She turned to the other demons. "Now do ye remember who I am?"

The gang of demons tried to melt away, but MacKenzie pointed two of them out. "You, and you. Come here. You dare not make me give chase."

The two demons glanced at the head of their fallen leader,

still staring stupidly. They stepped forward slowly, plainly terrified.

"Good. Now, ye both look like more reasonable fellas. So you," she said, pointing to one with a vertical fanged mouth, hooves for legs and tentacle arms, "go to any and all nearby, and warn them against sticking their noses or whatever into our business. And you," she said as she turned to the other one, who looked like a fanged frog with the small wings and faceted eyes of a fly, "you'll be coming with us, and telling us about anything that happened at the big gate." She turned back to the first demon. "G'wan! Off with ye!"

As they walked, their demon escort, whose name was Mebaloth, told them what he'd heard about the gate. "The giants started building it about two weeks ago. They squished two of the gangs nearby and strung up their guts as part of it. So we stayed away. But two days ago, three humans came through our territory." He paused, looking over the group. "Kruntha tried to challenge them, but one made a thorn tree squeeze him. We laughed at that for a while until he got free."

Walking beside him, Mike snickered.

"So a few of us with wings followed them. They went to the gate and fought the giants. They killed five giants, but one escaped through that weird gate. Then a bunch more giants came."

"Mebaloth? What happened to the humans?" Dr. Fathy probed.

The demon admitted, "Dunno. I saw the giants take the glowing one back through the gate. The giants all left, but one comes back every so often." He glanced at MacKenzie. "Please don't let her kill me. That's all I know."

Once the group arrived at the gate, MacKenzie turned to Mebaloth, who cowered before her. "Mebaloth, you've served me well. Go without fear. Ye have not earned a death today."

Mebaloth didn't hesitate. With a backward glance, he half-hopped, half-flew as fast as he could away from them.

Dr. Fathy examined the gate, pulling several pieces of arcane technology from his Pocket. He tapped several of the devices, pointed each at the gate in turn, then studied the device again. Eventually, he finished, and stowed his gear.

MacKenzie surveyed the situation and snapped out commands. "Mike and Jason, weapons out and come with me. Tiff? Go airborne to make sure no demons get any stupid ideas. Kyle and Aliki? Guard and assist Tom. Come on, boys." She stepped through the gate.

Mike looked at Jason, who shrugged his shoulders. They followed MacKenzie through the gate, stepping onto another world.

Jason surveyed the new world. It resembled Earth at first glance—there were clouds in the sky, and the sun had recently set over nearby mountains. He saw no signs of civilization, and the native life seemed sparse. He spotted several animals—birds flew in the sky, and one or two creatures that looked like oversized cattle grazed in a field nearby. In addition to horns on their head, the creatures also had horns protruding from their shoulders and hips.

He glanced at the trees nearby. Something seemed odd

about them, so he took a closer look. Growing around some of the nearby trees were odd tendrils. They didn't appear to be a type of vine, but squirmed as though alive. Large round nodules grew on the tendrils, creating a shaking noise as the tendrils writhed. The trees themselves didn't resemble anything on Earth either—some trees had unusually straight branches, while others curled in on themselves like a corkscrew. Asymmetric leaves sprouted from the trees.

"Welcome to Yothrun. Remember, we're not here for sightseein'," MacKenzie admonished. She had returned to her normal form once in the giants' world.

"Sorry, ma'am. Do we want to follow the giant's path? It should be easy enough," Jason suggested. He crouched down to examine the obvious footprints.

"Too hard to see the tracks without our own light, and we don't want to give ourselves away yet," MacKenzie replied.

Mike wrinkled his nose. "It smells odd here."

"This world only shares half of its realms with Earth. The others are different," she reminded him. She peered around. "There," she said, pointing. They all noticed the twinkling of campfires in the distance.

Aliki stepped through the gate from the Demon Realm. "Dr. Fathy says he's finished and ready to head back. He'll call our parents and cover for us too." Kyle, on the other side of the gate, waved upward. Jason assumed he was signaling Tiff.

MacKenzie glanced at her and the others. "Good. Now all of you head back. I'll be travelin' from here on my own. It's too dangerous."

"Not gonna happen, MacKenzie." The force of Jason's

response surprised himself as much as MacKenzie. But he continued, "You're in hostile territory, and things can go wrong. If there's anything I know, it's that once a play starts, you never know where the ball is going. We're blitzing into an enemy camp, but don't know where Mr. O and Coach Brown are. And if something happens to you, we have even less of a chance to rescue the three of you."

Mike stood beside Jason and added, "I don't think even you can take on a whole world." Aliki quietly stepped up beside them.

MacKenzie looked like she wanted to argue. As she stood there, Tiff and Kyle came through the gate. "Dr. Fathy's returned to Earth. He's spreading the word about what we found," Kyle said. "What's going on?"

"MacKenzie wants us to return to Earth too," Jason said.

"Without Mr. Oxinos or Coach Brown? Uh uh. We're helping," Tiff asserted, shaking her head. Kyle nodded his agreement.

Defeated by their collective resolve, MacKenzie sighed. "Ye're all mad as a box of frogs, the lot of you. I'll take your help. If things get too messy, you escape to the Animal or Primal Realm. But for now, let's move."

CHAPTER THIRTY-FOUR
The Clan of Kundomal

Tiff flew above the others in her eagle form as they moved toward the flickering firelight. Though the daylight was dimming, she could still see giants milling around the campfires ahead. Several giant-sized ramshackle huts stood around the fire pits. The few giants she could see appeared to be on guard, cautiously peering into the night. A few tall poles with cross-beams, each draped with a pelt, ringed the settlement. Each pelt displayed a runic symbol vaguely resembling a bunch of snakes with multiple heads coming out of the ground. Since each of the banners showed the same design, Tiff guessed the design was some sort of clan emblem.

Tiff flew a little higher, directly over the camp to spot as much as she could. Her eagle eyes, though superior for hunting in the daytime, didn't see as well at night. She resolved to land as soon as possible.

A larger cabin displaying one of the banner-poles beside its entryway dominated the settlement. It also was completely made of wood, rather than the wood-and-hide combination of the other huts. From the assortment of hides and bones decorating it, Tiff guessed it was the chief's cabin.

She landed on one of the other huts and watched the entrance, occasionally glancing back with the hope of spotting the others. She saw a glow-stick, and recognized Jason's face in its light. He shielded the light with his hand, but her sharp eyes noticed it immediately.

Relieved that she knew where the others were, she focused on the leader's hut and the giants themselves. They had a basic human form, but many were misshapen. Some had one arm larger than the other, and some had tusks or fangs. One giant had only one eye in the center of his head—an actual cyclops—and most of their faces were hideous. She noticed about half of them were female, and at least one child giant, taller than Jason, played around the fire.

Each of the adults wore a sash or mantle with the clan symbol branded onto it. Each of them also carried a spear, club, or similar primitive weapon. A large crude metal hammer leaned on the side of the chief's hut beside the doorway. The giants were prepared to fight.

As Tiff watched, an older giant emerged from the chief's cabin. He wore a sash made from animal hides, emblazoned with a symbol that didn't match the one on the banner poles. The older giant talked to someone still inside the chief's cabin.

Tiff wished she'd learned how to understand languages. She guessed the older giant came from a different clan, but she couldn't guess anything about their conversation. As the elder walked to a different hut and ducked inside, a younger giant emerged. She guessed his age in human years would be about twelve, but the other giants seemed to defer to him. She spotted a tattoo of the clan symbol on his chest. Was this boy-giant the chief?

The elder emerged from his hut and spoke a few words in a commanding tone. But the boy-chief responded angrily and picked up the hammer. A few other giants stood beside the boy-chief, obviously supporting him.

The elder spoke a few more harsh words, and the boy-chief responded in kind. His tone was somewhere between a spoiled child and an imperious warlord. Then the boy-chief transformed. His arms shone in the firelight, with his hands ending in sharp glass talons. His torso transformed into plastic, his legs changed into lightning, and his head became shining metal. He hefted his huge hammer with one hand, and commanded the elder giant, who retreated into the hut.

Now she recognized the boy-giant. "Zapfoot!"

Aliki listened as Tiff described Zapfoot's clan and their camp. After her report, the students waited for MacKenzie to provide a battle plan. MacKenzie stood apart from them, peering through night-vision binoculars from a small rise.

"So how many did you see, Tiff?" Mike asked.

"At least a dozen warriors or guards, and more other villagers. But they were all bigger than any of us," Tiff replied.

MacKenzie finally spoke in a slow, deliberate tone. "We could fight them, but we're not even sure Paul and Greg are there. The elder comes from a different clan, so something's afoot. Zapfoot's clan seems to be having a time of it, though. Those huts aren't permanent and haven't been here for too long.

The giants haven't worn down the vegetation around the huts, so this camp may be temporary. Any sign of Smoky?"

Tiff shook her head.

"Their clan must have split, and Zapfoot got the smaller share. Could we use that, MacKenzie?" Kyle asked.

"Good thinkin', lad. We'll sneak in for an audience with the chief," MacKenzie said with a wicked gleam in her eye. "Aliki? How far can you extend your shadows?"

Aliki jumped. "Um... I don't know. Maybe three or four feet?"

MacKenzie thought for a moment and glanced around at the students. "Not enough to cover all of us. Aliki, Mike and I will enter his hut from shadows. Kyle? You go with us to the back of the cabin and rip a hole big enough for us to sneak in. Keep your earth sense working too—it may help. Tiff? If things go bajanxed, you provide a distraction by lighting whatever you can on fire. Jason will stand by to help anyone escape with an airlift or assault, whichever strikes your fancy at the time. Questions?"

"Why did you pick me?" Mike asked.

"You're the best at talking and understanding. I'll be the threat, while you talk him up a bit," MacKenzie replied.

Aliki raised her hand. "What should I do once we're inside?"

"You listen to what Zapfoot says and help Mike understand him. I also want you to use your rifle once or twice," MacKenzie answered.

Aliki blanched, and MacKenzie continued, "You don't have to use the rifle on Zapfoot. Shoot something in his cabin, something showy. We want to scare him. But if he attacks, he's a target. Any other questions?"

"Hold on, MacKenzie," Mike said. He pulled out several small cylinders and handed one to each person. "Miss Olsen gave these to me. I think they're emergency first aid injectors."

"If you can, save them for Paul and Greg. They'll need them," MacKenzie replied.

The group crept toward the giants' camp. Mike followed Aliki and MacKenzie; Aliki spread her darkness as far as she could, hoping to conceal them from any giant sentries. Fortunately, the giants didn't spot them, and they arrived at the back of Zapfoot's cabin without incident.

Once there, Kyle transformed into a bear and used his strength to pull apart some of the wood planks that made up the back wall. Meanwhile, Mike used his wind-limbs to hover up to peer inside the cabin through a window. He would signal if Zapfoot noticed Kyle's damage to the walls.

Fortunately, Kyle's efforts went unnoticed. As he floated down, Aliki extended her shadows and crept through the hole, followed by MacKenzie.

Kyle reverted to his human form, but looked worried. Mike clasped him on the shoulder, whispering, "Not a mouse-hole, but a bear-hole." He smiled, and Kyle smiled nervously back. Then Mike ducked inside.

Zapfoot sat on a huge pile of furs, eating from a large platter. A noxious odor permeated the cabin, particularly near the fur pile. Mike guessed the fur pile served as his bed, but the giants didn't bother cleaning the animal pelts. He tried not to gag and noticed Aliki holding her nose. Even in her darkness form, he could sense her distress.

MacKenzie pointed to a low table and whispered something to Aliki. She gestured to Mike and leaped onto the table. Mike took the hint and followed. As he landed, the crack of Aliki's rifle sounded, and a drinking horn in Zapfoot's hand shattered from the gunshot.

Zapfoot jumped at the sound. Startled, he looked around the room and noticed Mike and MacKenzie standing on the table. MacKenzie held her axe in her hands, and Mike tensed and trembled as waves of panic washed over him, but he gulped back his own fear. Her terror aura seemed to be in overdrive.

"What are you doing here?" the young giant chief demanded. "I'll crush you!"

"I doubt it. And you'll waste a good opportunity," Mike began, speaking the giant's language. "We could have killed you when we entered... like this." He picked up one of Zapfoot's wooden plates from the table and casually raised it over his head with one hand. Another rifle shot cracked, and the plate broke.

"We want to talk, not fight. We've already beaten you once, remember?" Mike prompted. "She killed your father, and would have no problem killing you," he said, pointing to MacKenzie.

Zapfoot looked at MacKenzie, then peered at him, and recognition dawned on his face. "You were in the elemental place!" he exclaimed. He looked nervous. "What do you want?"

Secretly, Mike was glad Zapfoot was neither fully grown nor savvy enough to bargain from a position of strength. His childhood fears, standing in front of him, gave them extra leverage. Mike decided to be direct. "Two things. First, we want to know all about the gates, and why you're trying to invade.

Second, at least two of our folk were captured and brought here. We want them back alive."

"Why should I help you?" Zapfoot countered. "What do I get?"

Mike thought quickly. "Your camp here looks poor. You haven't been here too long. Where's your sister who was with you in the Primal Realm? Is she here?"

"Rigashun won over more of the clan after you killed father. She kept our old clan hold. These giants follow me as clan chief, and we settled here. Her clan is trying to make demands of us, but we resist."

When he mentioned Smoky's real name, Mike realized he still thought of the giant lad as Zapfoot. "So what is your name? My name is Mike Rhee."

"Kundomal."

Mike continued. "Anyhow, you mentioned her clan making demands? Is the old giant we saw from her clan?"

Zapfoot—no, Kundomal—nodded. He seemed more relaxed, though he still glanced at MacKenzie frequently. "They want this territory. Something about the gate. They built it, but they want to do more. We're close to the gate, so they want our camp."

"Did you help build the gates?" Mike prodded.

"No. Rigashun has an advisor named Veltornen who serves another like us named Chulgaroth. The gates are Chulgaroth's idea," Kundomal replied. "He's smart."

"Where are our companions?" Mike asked, struggling with the language. The giants didn't seem to have a term for "friend."

"Rigashun or Chulgaroth probably have them."

"Okay. I get the picture now. Where is this Chulgaroth?" Mike asked.

"He moves around, talking with different clans, and leaving advisors with his allies. He's powerful too. His clan is across the big sea on a small island. Father told me about it."

"So this advisor... If he disappears, then Smoky... I mean, Rigashun won't be messing with the gate anymore? Maybe that's where we can help you."

Kundomal shrugged his shoulders. "Maybe. I can take you to Rigashun's clan-hold. You can see if your friends are there. I'll point out the advisor, and Chulgaroth too if he's there. But I want something else too."

"What?" Mike asked.

"A teacher. Rigashun has both Chulgaroth and his advisor teaching her. Without Father, I can't learn anything new, so I can't defend my clan." Kundomal pointed to MacKenzie. "I want her to teach me."

"What?" sputtered MacKenzie.

"You heard me. I want to learn the other realms and how to use them. But I have no teacher. She teaches me, or you can find Rigashun's clan-hold yourself." Kundomal crossed his arms. He was a quick learner at negotiations.

Mike smiled ruefully. "I can't speak for her, but perhaps we can work something out." He turned to MacKenzie and spoke in English. "Can he understand us?"

"I doubt it. The Astral Realm doesn't touch here."

"What do you think?" Mike asked her.

"Me teachin' a fomorian? I'll not be such a fool."

"He seems insistent. And he's lost his home and clan, so he's

363

feeling alone. It might be an opportunity to gain an ally here."

MacKenzie looked at the boy giant. "All right, ye great lug. If we recover our friends alive and well, I'll be teachin' you, once a week for a year. But if they're dead, you'd better hide yourself well, for I'll lead the warriors of four clans here and paint the ground red with blood."

Her threat clearly terrified Kundomal, but the young giant said, "Okay. But I need to sleep. We'll find them in the morning."

Mike smiled. "Agreed. Aliki? Tell the others." He paused, then said mischievously, "Kundomal, I have an idea that could give you even greater status. Want to hear it?"

MacKenzie and the teens camped some distance away from the giants' camp. Before they settled down, MacKenzie pronounced the campsite safe and told the students she'd know if the giants or anything else hostile came near them.

Kyle was grateful. He had maintained his earth sense during the negotiation with Kundomal and felt uneasy. In addition to the strain of keeping his focus for such a long time, he'd also sensed something underground. It felt like something large wriggling and pulsing deeper within the earth. This world looked similar to Earth on the surface, but it wasn't their world. He wasn't sure how MacKenzie could know they were safe even while asleep, but he trusted the fierce woman. So he curled up and slept.

When he woke in the morning, Jason and Mike handed out granola bars and water bottles for breakfast. It took the edge off his hunger, but he realized they hadn't packed for a long expedition. He wondered if the cattle-like creatures they had seen were edible.

Once they were ready, the six of them set off toward the giants' settlement. As they approached, he noticed that Kundomal had assembled most of his warriors on the far side of their camp. The six of them crept into the boy-chief's cabin.

Kyle glanced around the primitive dwelling. He remembered how the boy giant had killed Tarskax with his mallet, and felt a rage growing inside him. This immature boy-chief had caused the deaths of several elementals, and Kyle wanted to tear into him.

Kundomal drummed his hand on one of the support beams in the hut as he watched MacKenzie lead the teens onto the table. A giant-sized drinking horn, carved sticks, and animal pelts spread across the tabletop next to a basket the size of a car. The others climbed into the basket, but Kyle hesitated.

A soft hand touched his shoulder. He whirled and saw Aliki gazing at him. *Is that sympathy in her eyes?* "It's okay, Kyle. I know you're angry at Zapfoot. But rescuing Mr. Oxinos and Coach Brown is more important than vengeance. Right?"

He stared at her, at the rifle she still carried in one hand. He remembered how she hated the idea of using the rifle on a living creature. But she seemed ready to confront her reluctance. He had to control his anger for the good of everyone.

Kyle drew a slow breath. "I'm sorry. Zapfoot... I can't forgive him for Tarskax. But I've been getting angry a lot. Maybe it's because of the Demon Realm."

"Maybe. But if you need to talk, let me know."

"Thanks, Aliki." He joined the others in the basket and

waited. Aliki fired her rifle as a signal, then crowded into the basket with the rest of them. Shortly, Kundomal entered his cabin and looked over the six of them. "Good. Are you ready?"

Mike nodded, and Kundomal threw one of the pelts over the basket to conceal them. Kundomal then picked up the basket and carried them somewhere. Kyle glanced over at Mike, who didn't seem nervous at all. Jason fidgeted, tracing the etchings along his axe blade. Tiff tried to peer through the holes in the basket. MacKenzie looked anxious, but she always seemed ready for action.

Kyle agonized over how Zapfoot might betray them. But the giant boy placed the basket on something wooden and started talking to the gathered giants.

"Rigashun's clan has taken too much from us!" Kundomal shouted to his followers. "Today, we strike a blow against her clan! Bring Yugnareb before me!"

There were sounds of a scuffle. Kundomal continued, "Yugnareb! You say I have no power compared to Rigashun, that I should bow before her and accept her rule and the domination of Chulgaroth. But I have discovered new power! Behold!"

Kundomal yanked the pelt off the basket, and the six of them leaped out, landing on the giant-sized table. But MacKenzie didn't stop moving. She vaulted, changed into a raven, and flew toward the elder advisor. When she approached close enough, she transformed back, her axe in full swing. The elder's head hit the ground amidst stunned silence. Then the giants cheered, "Kundomal! Kundomal!"

Kundomal smiled grimly and lifted the severed head. The giants cheered even louder for their young leader. He raised his mallet. As his clan quieted, he continued his speech. "I have bound these magical ones to my will! They shall strike at Rigashun's camp with me. I need only two warriors to join me, for my power has grown!"

Kyle watched five eager giants step forward, their misshapen faces eager for glory. "Ponwex and Ongrez," Kundomal said, pointing out two of the warriors. "Grab your weapons and gear. We leave now."

CHAPTER THIRTY-FIVE
Rigashun's Clan-Hold

The journey to Rigashun's clan-hold took most of the day. During that time, they encountered a few groups of giants. They avoided some, and Kundomal talked to others amicably.

As they traveled, Jason also had a chance to see more of the terrain and native life. At one point, he noticed a large semi-amorphous creature stalking the bovines. When the giants saw it, Ongrez speared it and brought it back to the group.

Ongrez sliced the strange creature with a bone knife and offered a portion to the teens and MacKenzie. Kundomal and Ponwex each swallowed part of the creature, slurping it down contentedly. MacKenzie cut a small piece with her knife and tried a bite.

Jason's stomach heaved, and he noticed Tiff looked a little queasy. Mike followed MacKenzie's lead and tried a small bite. Aliki also tried it, but spat it out.

"You don't eat *zensek?*" Ongrez asked.

"We've never tried it," Jason admitted, trying to be polite.

"This much *zensek* will keep our belly full for days. What do you eat?"

"Burgers and pizza," Jason answered, then regretted it. The other teens looked toward him with hungry eyes.

MacKenzie stood. "I'll hunt down one of those huge cattle beasts for us." She transformed into a raven and flew off.

An hour later, she returned with cuts of meat. With Tiff's help, Jason started a fire and cooked the strange meat. The tough meat had an unusual taste, but it filled their stomachs.

Later that afternoon, Tiff spotted a band of warriors from Rigashun's clan while scouting in eagle form. After a hasty discussion with Kundomal, MacKenzie ambushed them.

As the sun set, the group reached the clan-hold of Rigashun. Jason surveyed the well-defended settlement, which sprawled near a lake. He thought it resembled a frontier town, or perhaps an American Indian village. The houses were more permanent than Kundomal's camp, formed from what looked like mud or clay plastered over logs and sticks. The roofs were made of thatched wood. Like Kundomal's camp, banner poles with Rigashun's clan insignia ringed the settlement. Her insignia reminded Jason of a river crashing over rapids.

Beside him, Kyle studied the houses with interest. "They're wattle and daub. People in Europe built houses that way in the late Stone Age."

"If you say so," Jason muttered without understanding. He spotted several specialized buildings for craft-workers—one was for a tanner, another for a toolmaker, and there were some other work areas he couldn't identify. Near one large house, a few giants gathered in an odd clearing where a number of logs, carved into primitive shapes resembling totem poles, enclosed a rectangular area.

As clan-chief, Rigashun's house dominated the other dwellings in the village, easily twice the size of the next largest house. The central part of her sprawling building had two stories and stone walls, while the rest resembled the other huts in the village. Outside the main entrance, Rigashun's clan banners stood on display with her insignia proudly branded onto them.

"What's the totem area for?" Kyle asked.

"Ceremonies," the giant boy-chief replied. "The captives will be in Rigashun's house or with the shaman," Kundomal said, pointing to the house beside the odd totem logs.

"So we scout," Jason replied.

Mike hovered toward the shaman's house and wove through the buildings carefully. Even with Aliki clinging to his back, extending shadows as far as she could, he moved cautiously. Aliki's darkness clouded his vision, so he relied on her to guide him.

"A little higher and to your left, Mike," Aliki whispered. She didn't seem to be affected by the darkness at all.

Mike altered his path. "I still can't believe your shadow form is so light," he whispered back to her.

"Me neither. Hold on. Movement to your right."

Mike froze in place. A pair of giant women, each carrying a primitive broom, wandered into the totem-field area. They swept the grounds in some type of ritual pattern. While the giantesses could easily step over the totem-logs, Mike noticed they avoided crossing over them. After about fifteen minutes, the giantesses entered the shaman's house.

Relieved, Mike hovered toward one of the windows. They were simple openings in the wall. There were no glass panes, but a heavy pelt covered each of them. Mike settled quietly on the window ledge, and Aliki slowly moved the pelt to peer inside.

"No sign of them here. Kyle would have a field day with all the primitive trinkets, though," Aliki whispered. They moved on to the next window of the shaman's house and repeated the same procedure.

Eventually, they checked each window, but found no sign of either Mr. Oxinos or Coach Brown. Mike guessed it was about midnight by the time they finished searching, but he floated over to Rigashun's sprawling house.

After another hour, as they peeked into one of the upper windows, Aliki whispered excitedly, "I think that's them! But they're in some sort of cage on a table, and they're not moving."

"Can you tell if they're still alive?" Mike asked, though he dreaded the answer.

"Not from here. Do you want me to check?"

"Let's both go," Mike replied. Aliki hopped onto his back once more and guided him through the dark room. Eventually, they landed on the table.

Both Mr. Oxinos and Coach Brown lay on the table under a giant wooden cage. One of the giants had stacked a pile of bones and broken pottery on top of the cage.

Aliki was slender enough to squeeze through the bars, but as she did so, the pile of bones shook and rattled. Mike hovered up to the pile and held it in place. He called down, "The bones are a primitive alarm. We can't move the cage without making a lot of noise!"

Aliki checked both of the teachers, then carefully wormed her way out. "Both are alive, but not responding to anything. They both had some of this bluish goo in their mouth." She held something in her hand.

Mike couldn't see the goo, much less discern its color. "Let's get back to the others and tell them what we found."

"It's *gesvek*," Ponwex said when Aliki showed them the bluish goo. "We chew it when we hurt. It makes the pain go away. *Gesvek* are smaller than *zensek*, but they're sneakier."

"So this is from another of those amorphous creatures?" Tiff asked, still yawning. Like the others, she'd been sleeping when Mike and Aliki returned, and she still felt drowsy.

"Are you okay, Tiff?" Kyle asked.

"Need coffee," she grumped with a false surly attitude. She glanced over to where MacKenzie, Jason, Mike, and Kundomal were holding a strategy session. Then she paced for a few minutes to clear her head.

"Aliki? We may need some of that *gesvek* if Miss Olsen needs to make an antidote," Tiff suggested.

"Why would they give them this goo?" Kyle pondered.

Tiff thought for a moment. "Two possibilities. They were badly hurt, so the giants let them have some of it to kill the pain. Or they're using it as a tranquilizer to keep Mr. Oxinos and Coach Brown asleep. Either way, it's good news. The giants want them alive for something. I hope."

Ongrez looked on at their conversation, puzzled. He couldn't understand their language. So Kyle translated for him.

372

"*Gorvands* like Kundomal and Rigashun prize *dilinkas*, if they can be tamed," Ongrez said. "They can even make more *gorvands* with them." Kyle translated that too, clearly baffled by the giant's terms.

Tiff guessed that *gorvand* was their term for the immortal giants. "What's a *dilinka*?" she asked.

When Kyle translated the question for Ongrez, he pointed at the two of them.

The war council ended, and Jason strolled over to the rest of them. He looked both tired and excited, like he was in a football game. "Okay. We have a plan. Listen up."

Jason outlined the plan and the part each of them would play. Once Jason finished, they all tried to get a few more hours of sleep.

But as Tiff lay on the ground, her mind raced back and forth. She replayed the tumultuous events of the past year. In a few hours, they would be jumping into a life-or-death fight to save their teachers. Sleep refused to comfort her.

"Arright. Up and at 'em!" MacKenzie's call sounded in the pre-dawn light.

Jason sat up and stretched. He felt stiff, so he did a short workout to ease his muscles and settle his mind.

The previous night, to his surprise, MacKenzie had pulled him and Mike into a strategy session with Kundomal. She had maintained control of the discussion, but listened to suggestions from both him and Mike. He felt once again like he was part of a team effort. He'd missed the camaraderie, but now he felt fulfilled.

Aliki stood beside him, clutching herself despite the warm weather. She looked tired.

"How are you feeling?" he asked.

"Terrified," she admitted.

Jason put his arm around her, trying to comfort her. "Whatever you do, don't freeze. Acting—even if it's the wrong thing—is better than standing still. You can do this."

'Thanks, Jason."

"Is everyone ready? Let's move out!" MacKenzie called. Then she shifted into her raven form and flew straight toward Rigashun's house.

Following her lead, Jason assumed his angelic form and picked up Aliki, holding her at arm's length so her shadowy aura wouldn't cloud his vision. Mike followed Tiff, flying in her firebird form, towards the shaman's house. Kyle galloped as a bear. Ongrez had offered to carry him, but Kyle refused. Having to work with Kundomal angered Kyle, but Jason hoped Kyle would keep a clear head.

A few of the giants in the village were awake, but most still slept. Tiff landed on one thatched roof after another, igniting them. Mike followed behind her, using his winds to fan the flames. Soon, most of the buildings in the village were on fire.

Waking to smoke and fire, many of the giants panicked. A few grabbed huge buckets and ran toward the lake, calling for others to fight the fires. Jason saw one point toward Tiff and Mike spreading the flames. The giant threw a spear towards Mike, but it fell far short.

Below him, Kyle, Kundomal, and Ponwex blitzed into

Rigashun's house through its front door. Ongrez turned and stood waiting outside. Kundomal had assumed his elemental form, which Jason still called Zapfoot. Kyle led the way, using his keen bear nose to smell the teachers.

Jason turned his attention back to his own mission. He followed MacKenzie towards the upper window where Aliki found Mr. O and Coach Brown. As she landed on the window ledge, MacKenzie shifted to the form she'd assumed in the Demon Realm—black hair, nasty-looking black armor, raven-feathered cloak, wicked axe, skulls at her feet. He could feel her terror aura though he was still twenty feet from the window.

At the window ledge, MacKenzie's axe flashed, and the fur covering the window fell. The dawn light entering the room from the window revealed Rigashun and another giant in the room. Jason dropped Aliki on the window ledge and pulled his greataxe from his Pocket. Aliki pulled the darkness around her, and Jason could see the silhouette of her rifle appear in her hands. Below them, Ongrez waited below the window, basket in hand, ready to carry the teachers to safety. Everything was going according to their plan. He flew upward and waited.

As MacKenzie launched her attack on the pair of giants, Rigashun assumed her own elemental form. She also carried a spear, which ignited in her fiery grip. The other giant—Veltornen, he remembered—assumed some sort of quasi-demonic form. Veltornen's immense body grew a wreath of barbed tentacles from his torso. His face, already misshapen, became little more than a giant fanged mouth, while his eyes relocated to his shoulders. His arms and legs ended in sharp claws. A second mouth opened in his abdomen, and a pair of huge, bat-like wings erupted from his shoulders. A snake-like tail ending in a huge bony knob waved menacingly. The demonic giant exuded a stinging, acrid odor, and bile dripped from his abdominal mouth. In one of his clawed hands, he held a sharp bone blade.

Jason felt a strong sensation of revulsion from Veltornen, but guessed the giant's demonic aura caused the intense feeling. He relied on MacKenzie to attack, while he freed his teachers. Already, he heard MacKenzie's war cry as she joined the battle, leaping to strike at Veltornen.

Jason waited for his reinforcements and hovered near the thatched roof, out of reach of Rigashun's spear. He hoped she would be reluctant to set her own house on fire. After a few minutes, Kyle and Kundomal barreled into the room. Kundomal swung his massive hammer at his sister, and Kyle plowed into the back of Veltornen's knees with his sharp bear claws.

Once Rigashun and Veltornen engaged in battle, Jason landed on the table and swung his axe at the wooden cage, splintering it. The bones stacked on the cage crashed down with a loud clatter. Jason inspected the teachers and determined that Coach Brown had suffered more—it looked like one of his legs was broken, and he had a deep stab wound in his abdomen. The shattered remains of his metal armor cut into his chest and one of his arms. His immortal body had already healed a lot of the damage, but Jason wondered if the blue gunk in his system might slow the healing down.

Jason injected Coach Brown with the healing capsule they'd received from Miss Olsen. He decided to move Mr. Oxinos, then come back for the coach. Jason grabbed Mr. Oxinos and tried to fly with him, but couldn't get airborne with the added weight. He dropped back to the table and glanced toward the melee.

Kundomal and Rigashun seemed evenly matched. Despite Rigashun's superior size and age, Kundomal seemed to relish the fight more. Jason noted a shimmering effect that distorted the space around Rigashun, deflecting some of Kundomal's blows. MacKenzie's axe had already severed some of Veltornen's tentacles, but they slowly regrew. MacKenzie had already suffered several wounds from Veltornen's tentacles and clawed hands, but fortunately she had avoided his more dangerous blade, deflecting or dodging the horrible force of his blows. Kyle had retreated to catch his breath after a nasty kick. Veltornen bled from numerous axe wounds, but MacKenzie couldn't end the fight as quickly as she hoped. Clearly Veltornen was an experienced warrior.

While Kundomal and Rigashun fought, and MacKenzie attacked Veltornen, Ponwex could assist him. "Ponwex!" Jason called. "I need you to push the table to the window!"

Ponwex lumbered over to the table, but kept his eyes on the fight and his spear in front of him. He heaved himself into the table, shoving it to the window. More bones and broken crockery clattered to the floor, and Jason fell over when the table hit the wall.

Jason grabbed Mr. Oxinos again and carried him to Aliki. She injected him with her healing capsule and lowered him to Ongrez. Meanwhile, Jason turned back to fetch Coach Brown.

At that moment, Rigashun noticed what they were doing and called out to Veltornen. "The *dilinkas!* They're taking them!"

Seeing their activity, Veltornen launched a savage assault on

MacKenzie with his blade and free hand. Once again, MacKenzie dodged the blade, but Veltornen's clawed hand slammed into her, knocking her across the room and into a giant-sized stool. Ponwex tried to strike the demonic giant with his spear, but Veltornen dodged to the side and seized the spear with his tentacles. Then Veltornen's massive jaws snapped shut on Ponwex's neck, spraying the table with blood.

As Ponwex's body slumped to the floor and MacKenzie regained her footing, Veltornen turned to Jason and Coach Brown. At first, he tried to grab the coach's prone body, but Jason chopped into his forearm with his axe. As the giant withdrew his arm, Jason stood over the coach to protect him.

Frustrated, Veltornen swung his bone blade toward Jason, but Jason brought his axe up to block the massive weapon. The tremendous blow staggered him, and his arms went numb, but he stood his ground. The giant grabbed at him with his free hand, and Jason turned, slamming his axe into Veltornen's hand with all his might. Veltornen cried out in pain, and swung his blade again.

Jason felt the blow in his arm and his side as the blade bit deep. As his axe fell to the ground, his right arm still holding it, Jason tumbled across the tabletop. He looked dumbly at the stump of his arm and heard Aliki cry out. Then the world went dark as he fainted.

"JASON!" Aliki cried as she saw the horrific giant's blade cut through Jason's right arm and into his side. She watched him crumple to the tabletop, his face a pasty white. The giant raised his blade for another strike.

She remembered Jason's words to her, only days ago, an eternity ago. *"But when I had to protect the elementals at the Artisan Exchange, I acted."*

Her mind cleared, and the rifle in her hands felt like an extension of herself. It spoke once, twice, three times, more. She emptied the clip into Veltornen and snapped another into place.

Multiple bullets pierced the giant's chest and face. Bewildered, Veltornen glanced around, trying to find the source of the attacks. Hidden in darkness, Aliki fired again. The bone blade shattered.

MacKenzie's war cry echoed through the room again. Rather than fight both MacKenzie and an unknown threat, Veltornen grabbed Coach Brown's prone body and spread his great wings. He threw the remnants of his bone blade toward MacKenzie as Aliki fired more shots. Then he rose, tearing a hole through the thatched roof, and fled into the air.

Mike and Tiff arrived at the window. "The fires are keeping the other giants busy, but that giant demon has coach! What do we do?" Mike asked.

MacKenzie had recovered her footing and slammed her axe into Rigashun's wooden back, cutting through the distortion effect. The giantess cried out in pain. "Mike, get in here. Tiff? Slow that monster down, but don't let him hit you. Aliki? Keep peppering him once Tiff gives you a target. Bring him down!"

As Tiff flew towards Veltornen, Mike stepped onto the table. Aliki heard him gasp.

MacKenzie hopped onto the table and turned to Mike. "I'll take you, Jason, and Paul to the Animal Realm, then return here.

Put a tourniquet on Jason and hold his severed arm in place. Wait there for me to return and do what you can to help him." MacKenzie strode over the window and called out, "Ongrez? Change of plans. We need Paul back here. Hurry!"

As Ongrez ran inside, Aliki tried to hold back tears of fright and rage. She focused on the flying giant, now slowed by Tiff whirling around him in firebird form. She raised her rifle.

CHAPTER THIRTY-SIX
Chasing Veltornen

Mike crouched beside Jason and Mr. Oxinos in the Animal Realm. MacKenzie had transferred the three of them and injected Jason with a healing capsule.

"Inject his arm with your healing capsule. It might help it to survive. I'm not sure how they work," MacKenzie urged. "I'll be back soon, hopefully with Greg. Keep him safe and warm." She disappeared, back to Yothrun and the battle.

Following her instructions, he injected his own healing capsule into Jason's severed arm. Then he started shaking. He wished he knew more about first aid. Jason did, but he had fallen unconscious.

Mike turned his attention to Mr. Oxinos. Like Jason, Mr. Oxinos was out cold.

Mike felt alone. He had always thrived on the company of others. Whether he was goofing off or performing music, he loved an audience. But now, the only ones who might hear him were the denizens of the Animal Realm.

Mike shuddered, worrying that a predator might decide they were an easy snack. However, even the herbivores avoided them.

He whistled a merry tune, hoping the simple act would lift his spirits.

Kyle watched MacKenzie vanish with Mr. Oxinos, Mike, and Jason. He turned toward Kundomal and Rigashun. The boy-chief stood over his sister, who clutched at the wound in her back. Ongrez stood beside his chief, his spear pointing at Rigashun. But the giantess still held her flaming spear, and the distorting effect around her persisted. Rigashun still had strength and will to fight.

"Kundomal! We need to get the coach back and stop the other one. Leave her!" Kyle yelled in frustration.

"I can kill her and reunite my clan!" Kundomal protested.

"If the coach gets away, our deal's off! And I'll kill you myself!" Kyle growled. He struggled to keep his temper. The last thing he wanted was for them to lose the coach while these idiot siblings squabbled over clan politics.

Kundomal considered Kyle's words. "Fine. Come with me. Ongrez, you too. We leave her here."

The three of them ran down the stairs and out into the village. Most of the other giants were still trying to extinguish the fires, but a few noticed them. One of the village guards brandished a club, but stood baffled by what he saw.

"Follow Veltornen!" Kyle urged, running as fast as he could toward the flying giant.

Veltornen had already left the area of the village, but had to pause as Tiff whirled around him as a firebird. He batted at her with his uninjured hand, but Tiff evaded his swings.

Kyle heard Aliki's rifle fire again, and the giant flinched. But Veltornen was still too high.

Behind him, Kundomal shouted. "Ongrez! Can you reach him?"

Ongrez hurled his spear, but it fell short.

Kundomal looked at the flying Veltornen. "*Dilinka*. Do you trust me?"

"Not on your life," Kyle growled.

"Do you want to save your friend?" Kundomal countered. "If you do, curl into a tight ball. And don't hurt me."

Out of options, Kyle followed Kundomal's instructions and curled into a ball. He felt Kundomal's sharp glass hands on him, picking him up. The giant did something with his electric legs and leaped high into the sky. At the peak of his jump, Kundomal threw Kyle directly at Veltornen's back.

"His wings!" Kundomal called as he dropped back to the ground.

Just before Kyle slammed into Veltornen's back, he uncurled himself. He landed squarely and dug his claws into Veltornen. The giant yelled in surprise and flailed at him with his barbed tentacles.

Kyle ignored the pain in his ribs. He ignored the stinging tentacles ripping into his body. He pulled himself upward on the flailing giant, pausing only when he heard another rifle shot from Aliki. He reached Veltornen's wings.

Kyle yielded to his anger and frustration, and his world turned red.

Tiff shuddered as Kyle tore into Veltornen with a savage fury. Biting and shredding the giant's back, Kyle resembled a wild wolverine in his ferocity. Veltornen tried in vain to reach him, but Kyle shrugged off the giant's barbed tentacles, and Veltornen's knobby tail couldn't reach him.

Finally, Veltornen dropped Coach Brown and tried to pull Kyle off with his good hand. Tiff dove for the coach, reverting to her normal eagle form, and snatched him with her claws. But Coach Brown was far too heavy for her to lift, so they both continued falling.

She estimated the distance to the ground and tried to time her transformation into her human form. She held the coach in her arms and used her years of gymnastics training to tuck before she hit, softening the blow. She still felt a sharp pain in one of her ankles, but she rolled on the ground, still holding Coach Brown.

Tiff winced in pain from a twisted, possibly broken ankle. She gritted her teeth and forced herself to her feet. At least she and the coach were alive and free of Veltornen.

She turned her attention back to the fracas in the sky. More shots from Aliki struck the giant, and Kyle's savage attack continued. He bled from multiple wounds, but Kyle finished maiming the giant's wing. The giant dropped.

The two of them crashed into the ground thirty feet from Tiff. Fortunately, Kyle clung to the giant and landed on top when the two of them hit. He rolled off and lay still. Veltornen still lived, but the fall left him groggy. He tried to rise, but failed.

Tiff limped over to the two of them. Kyle breathed heavily, still stunned from the fall. If Veltornen gained his footing, both she and Kyle were easy targets. She summoned her katana from her Pocket.

She took a deep breath to steady herself, then slashed through Veltornen's throat with her blade.

When the demon giant crashed to the ground, Aliki leaped down into the house and started to run toward the steps. But Rigashun blocked her way with her flaming spear.

"Veltornen is down! Don't make me use this on you, Smoky!" she yelled, brandishing her rifle.

Surprised, Rigashun lifted herself into a standing position with her spear and leaned on the table. She peered out the window for a moment. Aliki saw a strange look on her face, then she reverted to her normal form.

Rigashun pulled at a pelt she wore, ripping it off. Aliki noticed it had a different clan-rune than hers, one matching the one tattooed on Veltornen's chest.

"Now what? Will you kill me too?" the giantess asked.

A raven appeared. It glanced out the window at Veltornen's prone body. Then it flew down to land on Aliki's shoulder "MacKenzie?" Aliki asked.

"I just got back. It looks like you took care of the beastie already. Good job. Now let's get Greg and get home."

"Wait, MacKenzie." Aliki turned back to Rigashun. "We don't need to kill you. We have our friends back, and we will destroy the gates. That's what we came for."

"Chulgaroth will kill me now, with his son dead," Rigashun replied, a tremor in her deep voice. "The gates are his. He offered me strength if I followed him. Now he will think I betrayed him."

"But if you and your brother stand together, you'll be stronger," Aliki suggested. "You can bring your clan back together, or keep separate but work together."

MacKenzie suddenly hopped off Aliki's shoulder and assumed her normal form, though her axe appeared in her hand. "It sounds like this Chulgaroth is our true foe on Yothrun." She paused, thinking something over. "I must be off my own rocker for thinking this." She addressed Rigashun. "All right. I'll offer you the same I offered Kundomal. One day of training each week for a year. You become strong that way. In return, you and your brother stop feuding and work together. You give us information and aid against Chulgaroth. You tell us about other immortal giants—as much as you can."

MacKenzie started to leave the room. "Oh, and you have until we take our fellows back to decide."

Aliki followed MacKenzie out of Rigashun's house. Rigashun followed slowly, still nursing the wound in her back. Several of the village guards followed her, hefting their spears. But Rigashun commanded, "No attack unless I order it!" Her guards lowered their weapons, but still stayed by her side.

As they approached, Aliki saw Tiff injecting Kyle, now in human form, with a healing capsule. Tiff stood when she saw them, but favored her left leg. Coach Brown also lay nearby, dwarfed by Veltornen's bloody corpse.

"Is the monster dead?" Aliki asked.

Tiff nodded her head, but sniffled. MacKenzie walked around the giant's corpse slowly. She stared at his face for a moment.

Then she returned to Tiff and put a sympathetic hand on her shoulder. Tiff turned to MacKenzie and started crying. MacKenzie looked a little uncomfortable at first, but put her arms around the distraught girl.

Aliki saw Rigashun striding slowly toward them. The giantess' eyes darted between Veltornen and Kundomal. Aliki held her rifle ready, hoping she wouldn't have to use it. Kundomal and Ongrez raised their weapons, ready to attack.

"Wait!" Aliki shouted to them. "I think she wants to talk."

Rigashun stepped forward. "You have bargained with them?" she asked, pointing to MacKenzie. Kundomal nodded. "They do not trick you?" she asked.

Kundomal replied, "Not so far. They speak what they mean. Their trickster helped me already."

Aliki realized he was referring to Mike's idea to let Kundomal use them as a show of power. She called to Rigashun. "His position as clan chief is stronger because of us."

"She will train you?" Rigashun asked again, pointing to MacKenzie.

"She will make me stronger," Kundomal replied. "I can take back the clan-hold!"

"That's not the way to negotiate, Kundomal!" Aliki yelled again. "Agree to stop attacking her clan-hold. In return, she will send supplies to help you build your own clan-hold. Welcome each other in your domains without fighting. Once you do, you can trade goods with each other and both become strong."

The giants' culture clearly didn't include working together. But they both had tired of the fighting.

"I agree to the shadow-girl's terms," Kundomal said.

"I also agree," Rigashun replied. She turned to MacKenzie. "I also agree to your offer, dark warrior."

"Wonderful," MacKenzie replied. "But we need to get our friends to a healer in our own world. I'll be returning in three days. We can discuss things then. Swear neither of you nor your clans will harm the other while I am gone."

Both giants nodded.

A groan came from Kyle's lips. He pushed himself into a sitting position, looked around blearily, and stared at Veltornen's corpse. He gazed at the gashes and tears in the giant's back and wings. In a dazed voice, he asked, "Is it over? Did we win?"

CHAPTER THIRTY-SEVEN
Summer Break

Despite the crowd of people inside Ida Olsen's house that evening, it was quiet. Jason lay on her bed, while Coach Brown rested in her guest room. Mr. Oxinos lay on her couch, weak but conscious. Dr. Fathy had commandeered the dining room table as a small biochemical analysis station to investigate the bluish *gesvek*.

Kyle sat in a recliner, trying to get comfortable. His anger had evaporated, but he felt uneasy. He remembered landing on Veltornen's back, and then nothing until he woke on the ground in a daze.

Miss Olsen, still weak on her feet, checked Kyle's wounds. "They're healing nicely, Kyle. You'll be sore for a few days, but the healing capsule accelerated your recovery."

"It still hurts. How are Mr. Oxinos and Coach Brown?"

"Weak but recovering. They'll need another day or two."

"Miss Olsen? Jason's awake!" Aliki's voice came from the back room.

Miss Olsen led the others into her room. Aliki yielded her chair to Tiff, who still limped from her twisted ankle. Mike helped Kyle stand, and they crowded the doorway.

"How are you feeling, Jason?" Miss Olsen asked.

"Tingly and weird," Jason replied, looking at his right arm, wiggling his fingers. Not all of them moved naturally. "It feels funny, like it's asleep."

"In a way, it is. We were able to reattach it, thanks to quick thinking and our advanced treatments," Miss Olsen explained. "The nerves still need time to regrow, so it will feel numb for the next few days."

"How about coach and Mr. O? Are they okay?" Jason asked. "Do I smell pizza?"

"MacKenzie brought it. I'll get you a few slices," Mike called from the doorway.

"Everyone is fine. Everyone except Veltornen," Tiff said. Her voice had an odd timbre to it.

They chatted about the events of the past few days for another hour, though Tiff spoke little. Jason got out of the bed, still wiggling his fingers occasionally. Miss Olsen gave him a sling to protect his arm as it healed. She had already given Tiff an orthopedic boot for her ankle.

Finally, MacKenzie called to all of the students. "If we're all ready and have our stories straight, I'm sure your parents will be glad to see you. I'll be taking you all home now."

"Paul and Greg will be fine after another day or two," Miss Olsen added. "I'll see you at school tomorrow."

The next day, the students returned to school. Tiff still nursed her sprained ankle, and Jason kept his arm in the sling.

Their parents had been worried about them, but MacKenzie had given each of them a fabricated story, and Miss Olsen gave the same story to the school officials.

Jason chatted with Carson and Pete in homeroom. Already their cover story had spread through the school.

"What did I miss yesterday?" Jason asked his friends.

"Not much. So you and the others really helped rescue Mr. O?" Carson asked.

"Yeah. They were preparing us for a survival challenge in the wilderness. It took a while for us to find them because of the bridge collapse," Jason replied. He found it much easier to follow a planned lie than concoct some wild story.

He glanced over at Mike, who was narrating his own version of the story to his fellow band members. As usual, Mike enjoyed being the center of attention, and loved to embellish. Jason hoped Mike didn't exaggerate too much.

He turned to the others. Kyle had his nose in a book about Vikings, apparently untroubled by the wounds he suffered. Aliki chatted with a few other girls. She seemed bolder, more confident of herself. Tiff listened to Mara and Shelly talk about their plans for summer vacation, but she spoke only a little.

"Do you know when Coach and Mr. O are coming back?" Pete asked.

"Miss Olsen says Mr. O should be back tomorrow, and Coach on Thursday or Friday," Jason replied. "They got pretty banged up."

At lunch, Mike and Tiff told Julisha about the giant's world, what they saw, and their fight with Veltornen. When Tiff told her about the end of the fight, she simply mentioned that the demonic giant had dropped from a great height and died on the ground. Jason could tell that delivering Veltornen's death blow still haunted her.

"Did you really have your arm cut off, Jason?" Julisha asked, her eyes wide.

"Yup." He gently took his arm out of the sling and showed her. New skin, not yet tanned and still tender, ringed his arm and revealed where the arm had been severed. "It still tingles. Miss Olsen says it should be fine in a few days, but I need to drop by her office for another shot of stuff." Jason returned his arm to the sling and finished wolfing down his burger.

Two weeks after their return, Mr. Oxinos gathered the immortal students in his classroom after school. Coach Brown and Miss Olsen also joined him. The teachers sat in a circle with the students.

Aliki had lost count of the number of times they had gathered like this. She hoped there wouldn't be more giant troubles.

"First, I'd like to thank all of you for rescuing us," Mr. Oxinos said to the students. Coach Brown and Miss Olsen murmured their agreement. "Though foolish and crazy, it shows how capable you are, how well you work as a team, and how much you've developed. We couldn't ask for better students."

Coach Brown stepped in. "But if you're going to keep throwing yourselves into danger, I'm going to make armor for each of you."

Mr. Oxinos continued, "Dr. Fathy passed on his information

about the gates to the other immortals. Already, we've found three similar efforts by the giants near Marseille, Oslo, and York. Larger teams of immortals have already dealt with them. Unfortunately, we haven't located Chulgaroth, who we think is the mastermind. Nor do we know how he would coordinate such an effort."

"MacKenzie has already started training Kundomal and Rigashun. The two of them formed an uneasy peace, but we hope we can show them the power of cooperation," Coach Brown said. "She'll be around to continue your combat training too. But you've all earned a long break."

"Now I'm sure you all have questions. So please ask," Miss Olsen urged.

Mike began, "Umm... We didn't want to tell you this, but we kinda told Julisha about the five of us when we needed her help."

"We thought that might happen. She'll have her own path to follow, and we'll watch over her too," Mr. Oxinos said. Aliki had worried the teachers might do something to Julisha, but Mr. Oxinos' words reassured her

"So what was that blue gunk?" Kyle asked.

Miss Olsen answered. "Dr. Fathy analyzed both the *gesvek* and the *zensek* samples you brought back. They apparently are a form of life we don't have on Earth. They are similar to viruses, but on a much larger scale. Apparently the giants have found uses for them. From what he told us, the *zensek* they use as a food supplement slows their metabolism and provides concentrated nutrients. It also resists digestion, so it takes a while for it to digest. Therefore, the giants don't get hungry so often. The *gesvek* is similar, but it gives off powerful soporific and

393

analgesic enzymes—numbing pain and making you drowsy."

"From what Ida said, they gave us a huge amount of it," Coach Brown added.

Tiff finally raised her hand. "Why did the giants try to build a gate here of all places? And in those other cities? What makes this town so special?"

Mr. Oxinos replied, "Another good question, Tiff. Do you remember when I discussed the Fountain of Souls? For whatever reason, this town is one of the focal points of the Fountain, as are the other gate sites. Only a few immortals know how to perceive the flow of the Fountain."

"We suspect Chulgaroth may also be able to perceive it," Coach Brown added. "The Fountain is why the three of us originally came to this town—to keep an eye on its activity, and guard against giant threats."

Miss Olsen added, "Or even activity from the other worlds."

"There are other worlds?" Mike blurted.

Aliki felt the same way. She wasn't ready for another giant fight. *What's next? Dragons?*

"Including Earth, there are a total of eight worlds and sixteen realms. But you don't need to worry about them right now," Coach Brown added. "You have all earned a well-deserved break. Enjoy your summer. We'll be around if you need us."

The school year was almost over, with one week of dreaded finals remaining. The five immortal students decided to have one last get-together before summer vacation. They gathered at Jason's house for a movie night on Saturday.

Mike helped Jason and his father grill the burgers and chicken. Aliki entertained Jason's younger sister Helen, who insisted on showing off her doll collection. Tiff helped Jason's mother in the kitchen. Kyle assisted where he could, but spent most of his time keeping the family dog away from the grill.

Later that evening, after Helen had gone to bed, the five teens finished watching a fantasy adventure movie and argued about what movie to watch next.

"Maybe a buddy-cop drama? Hopefully the next movie will have more realistic action. Those fantasy fight scenes were totally fake!" Jason joked.

"And the dragon wasn't scary at all," Tiff added. The gathering had boosted her spirits, and Mike hoped she would overcome her guilt soon.

"Nothing like the real thing," Aliki added. "At least they used real animals in the movie. Right, Kyle?"

Kyle gave her one of his sheepish grins.

Mike stood in front of his friends. "I'd like to say something, if you don't mind. Something's been on my mind."

"Go ahead, Mike," Jason prompted.

"The five of us started this year as strangers. It's been one heck of a year, one that none of us could have anticipated. We've fought giants and learned from gods, befriended animals and elementals, and ventured to another world. But we're all still here, stronger than before, because we worked together and formed a team. So I'd like to toast our team."

Tiff poured sodas for a toast. "Here! Here! But if we're a team, don't we need a team name?"

Jason said excitedly, "Like one of those superhero teams!

395

Yeah!"

Aliki teased him, "You can be the Winged Wave, right Jason? And Mike's the Floating Fox?"

Kyle joined in on the teasing. "How about Wonder Wings?"

Jason threw a pillow at him. "Be quiet, Bear Boy!" They all laughed.

But Mike remembered Kyle's words when they revealed themselves to Julisha. "We don't need any superhero names. We're not superheroes. But we've learned from Apollo, Idun, Ogun, Macha, and..." Mike paused. He didn't know Dr. Fathy's real identity.

Kyle read his expression. "Thoth. Dr. Tom Fathy is Thoth. I figured it out a while ago."

Mike continued. "Right. That makes sense. Anyway, we'll follow in their footsteps—the footsteps of the gods. But we're not part of the Greek Pantheon or the Norse Pantheon, or any of the others. We're our own group. So let's toast to all of us, the New Pantheon."

About the Author

Edward Swing is a writer of stories, software developer, avid gamer, and otaku. He has been a member of the Society for Creative Anachronism, learned taekwondo, traveled both within the United States and internationally, and studied diverse topics including astronomy, mythology, and mathematics. He lives with his wife, three children, and several pampered cats.

Made in the USA
Columbia, SC
06 March 2020